ABS   Absolute magnitude.

$23.95

DATE			

ABSOLUTE
MAGNITUDE

ABSOLUTE MAGNITUDE

Edited by
Warren Lapine
& Stephen Pagel

TOR®

A Tom Doherty Associates Book
New York

ABSOLUTE MAGNITUDE

Copyright © 1997 by DNA Publications, Inc.

This book is printed on acid-free paper.

Edited by David G. Hartwell

A Tor Book
Published by Tom Doherty Associates, Inc.
175 Fifth Avenue
New York, NY 10010

Tor Books on the World Wide Web:
http://www.tor.com

Tor® is a registered trademark of Tom Doherty Associates, Inc.

Library of Congress Cataloging-in-Publication Data

Absolute magnitude / edited by Warren Lapine & Stephen Pagel.—1st ed.
    p. cm.
  "A Tom Doherty Associates book."
  ISBN 0-312-86335-7
  1. Science fiction, American. 2. Adventure stories, American. I. Lapine, Warren. II. Pagel, Stephen.
PS648.S3A27   1997
813'.0876208—dc21   96-52645
                           CIP

First Edition: May 1997

Printed in the United States of America

0 9 8 7 6 5 4 3 2 1

The editors would like to thank Ellen Datlow.
For without her introducing us, *Absolute Magnitude*,
let alone this book, would not exist.

We would also like to thank Hal Clement,
Allen Steele, Barry B. Longyear, and C. J. Cherryh
for being the first established authors to
take a chance on us.

This is for Angela, who helps me keep the magic alive.
—WARREN LAPINE

For Steve & Marcia, Mike & Marcia, Karen,
Elliot, Beth, and Teddi. Thanks for all the nights of
soda and chips, and for putting up with me.
—STEPHEN PAGEL

Contents

Introduction

Hard science fiction with an adventure slant has always been the lifeblood of science fiction. In recent years the short fiction market has been drifting away from this classic form; phrases such as "cutting edge" and "pushing the envelope" have begun dominating the field, as if novelty were the only measure of artistic merit. Science fiction has almost begun to apologize for the Golden Age.

To everyone here at *Absolute Magnitude*, that attitude is unacceptable. The Golden Age was glorious, and the sense of wonder is everything. We will not apologize for publishing traditional science fiction. We don't care what the mainstream critics think about us. Science fiction fans have made us the fastest-growing science fiction magazine in America, and that is the only criticism that matters.

When we decided to begin publishing an adventure science fiction magazine, we were told that no one read adventure science fiction anymore, that the sense of wonder was dead. We ignored the conventional wisdom and printed the first issue without so much as a single distributor. To the surprise of many, our first issue sold out and dozens of distributors began knocking on our door. The sense of wonder was not dead!

Our first two issues were published under the moniker of

Harsh Mistress after the Robert A. Heinlein novel. While science fiction fans understood the allusion, many magazine distributors didn't, and we decided that it would be better to change the name than to try and educate our distributors.

It is now clear that we are on the threshold of a second Golden Age. At no time since the first Golden Age has the field supported so many science fiction magazines. There are a number of reasons for this. One is the ailing health of the major magazines: circulation is down at *Asimov's, Analog,* and *F&SF; Omni* has become an "on-line magazine," and for the first time in the history of science fiction *Amazing Stories* has ceased regular publication.

This is not usually the kind of news that ushers in a new Golden Age, but most of the major magazines' circulation troubles can be traced to large corporations' questionable fiscal policies; and to the fact that these corporations care nothing for science fiction. The major magazines simply have not received the support from their parent corporations that they deserve. Beyond this, these magazines seem to have become complacent. Consequently, there is room for a number of independent magazines to flourish.

One has but to look at the newsstand to see just how well the independent magazines have flourished. *Absolute Magnitude, Pirate Writings, Aboriginal, Worlds of Fantasy and Horror, Adventures in Swords and Sorcery!* and a host of others sit side by side. And these magazines are published by people who care about science fiction.

In the past the major magazines have also been complacent, but the financial realities of publishing kept new blood from challenging the established magazines. Until desktop publishing, professional-level layout was prohibitively expensive; now it is at anyone's fingertips. A new magazine then had to deliver hundreds of thousands of copies in order for the magazine distributors to be willing to distribute them. Once the distributors took the magazines, they often failed to get them into stores, kept bad records, or deliberately misrepresented sales figures, causing most new magazines to go out of business after only a few issues. Distribution can now be obtained from book distributors, and this change in distribution has been a great boon to the magazine industry. It allows new magazines to get national distribution without going out of business, as the book distributors are willing to deal with numbers in the thousands rather than the tens of thousands; thus a new magazine has time to build up a strong base before taking on the newsstands of America.

Absolute Magnitude was created to explore the human spirit and test its mettle. In doing this we have gone on many grand adventures. I'm sure that those of you who have been along for the ride have already fastened your seatbelts; and for those of you who have just discovered *Absolute Magnitude* for the first time, buckle up, it's going to be one hell of a ride as we blast off to adventure!

WARREN LAPINE

Greenfield, Massachusetts
October 1996

A one-year subscription to *Absolute Magnitude* is $14.00. Send checks to:
DNA Publications
P.O. Box 13
Greenfield, MA 01302-0013

DNA Publications is
Brian Murphy
Kevin Murphy
Stephen Pagel
Warren Lapine

ALLEN STEELE BECAME A FULL-TIME SCIENCE FICTION WRITER IN 1988 FOL-
LOWING PUBLICATION OF HIS FIRST SHORT STORY, "LIVE FROM THE MARS
HOTEL" (*ASIMOV'S,* MID-DECEMBER 1988). SINCE THEN HIS WORK HAS AP-
PEARED IN ENGLAND, FRANCE, GERMANY, SPAIN, ITALY, POLAND, BRAZIL,
AND JAPAN. HIS NOVEL *ORBITAL DECAY* RECEIVED THE 1990 LOCUS AWARD
FOR BEST FIRST NOVEL, AND *CLARKE COUNTY, SPACE* WAS NOMINATED FOR
THE 1990 PHILIP K. DICK AWARD. STEELE WAS A RUNNER-UP FOR THE 1991
JOHN W. CAMPBELL AWARD, AND HE RECEIVED THE DONALD A. WOLLHEIM
AWARD IN 1993 AND A HUGO IN 1995 FOR HIS SHORT STORY "THE DEATH
OF CAPTAIN FUTURE."

Working for Mister Chicago

Allen Steele

One hundred and two years after he choked on a McDonald's
cheeseburger and died at his office desk, Paul McLafferty found
himself on his hands and knees, polishing the floor of the Great
Hall in Mister Chicago's palace.

The Great Hall was a large rotunda whose walls were
draped with priceless tapestries and whose dome ceiling, supported by tall Doric columns, was painted with a reproduction
of Michelangelo's Sistine Chapel mural. The floor was a mosaic
composed of thousands of tiny pieces of multicolored ceramic
and quartz, with long threads of hammered gold outlining its
elaborate patterns. When he sat up on his haunches to rest his
aching back, McLafferty was able to see that the mosaic formed
a heliocentric map of the solar system, the orbits of the planets
and major asteroids forming spirals around the Sun, the constellations of the Zodiac forming a starry background.

McLafferty scrubbed the floor of the Great Hall once a
week, down on all fours with a horsehair brush and a pail of
soapy water, working at the dust that found its way into the tiny
cracks between the tilework, polishing every inch of the mosaic until he could see the reflection of his rejuvenated face.
Although he always came away from this chore with chafed

fingers and sore muscles, he had never ceased marveling at the craftsmanship that had gone into the making of this beauty.

"Must have taken years," he murmured.

"I'm telling you, it only took four hours," Yeats answered. He was arranging flowers in the Grecian urns that stood beneath the columns. "One of the chambermaids told me. It was nano . . . nano . . . it was little bitty robots. They spilled a bottle of 'em on the floor, threw in the raw materials, stood back . . . " He raised an arm. "Fwoosh! Off they went! Four hours later . . . "

"Instant masterpiece," McLafferty finished, unconsciously reiterating the same line Yeats always used. They had discussed this many times before, although neither man had more than the barest recollection of having done so. He shook his head. "I understand what you're saying, but I still don't accept it. How can you program something smaller than a dust mote to make . . . something like this?"

Yeats didn't look up from his work. "Hey, you're the rocket scientist," he murmured. "You tell me. I just . . . "

"Do stocks and bonds," McLafferty finished. He shook his head again, this time in faint bewilderment. Déjà vu. Had he heard this before? "Where did you say you used to work?"

"Umm . . . " Yeats had to concentrate for a moment. "New York Stock Exchange. Munici . . . municipals? Does that sound right? And you . . . "

"I used to work at NASA. Right?" McLafferty frowned. Sometimes it was so hard to think. "Some place in California." He snapped his fingers. "Pasadena. JPL. That's it."

"Like I said . . . a rocket scientist." Yeats gave him a sharp look. "Hey, have we talked about this before?"

"Probably." McLafferty picked up his brush and bent over again to hide his embarrassment. "Maybe last week."

"Yeah. I think so, too. Are you . . . ?"

The faint sound of approaching footsteps, coming from the upstairs corridor leading to the master's private chambers. Both men fell silent as they pretended to concentrate on their work, neither of them daring to glance up. The footsteps grew louder until they entered the circular balcony overlooking the Great

Hall. There they paused for a few moments, and McLafferty could feel contemplative eyes at his back.

Then the footsteps turned and receded, going back down the corridor. Mister Chicago had come to check on them; satisfied, he had left them alone once again.

Neither of them spoke after that. The message was clear. The master was having his party tonight, and wouldn't tolerate anything that interfered with its preparations.

McLafferty was almost grateful for the interruption. It saved him the further embarrassment of having to admit that he couldn't even remember Yeats' first name.

The only reason McLafferty knew his own name was that someone had told it to him, during the long days of reeducation that had followed reanimation.

This much he knew for certain: his name was Paul Joseph McLafferty, and he had been born at Worcester City Hospital in Worcester, Massachusetts, on July 21, 1946. His father's name was Bruce, his mother's name was Emma, and he had an older brother named Richard and a younger sister named Catherine. He had earned his B.S. in engineering from Worcester Polytech, then gone on to earn his M.S. and Ph.D. at Stanford. He had married a woman named Elizabeth . . . he faintly recalled knowing her as Liz, and that she was a blonde and very pretty . . . and they had a son named Bruce, whom he had last seen playing with some toy figures called Mighty-something-Power Rangers on the kitchen floor.

And then he had died on February 21, 1995. Cause of death was accidental choking, or so he had been told. He had the vaguest memory of the taste of a cheeseburger, of helplessly fighting for breath, of a dull roar in his ears and darkness closing in around him . . .

Everything else was a mystery, his only clues a few barely glimpsed forms and shadows swathed in thick black smoke that parted only for a moment at a time. Sometimes, when the long workday was done and he lay awake in his bed in the servant quarters—the lights dimmed, the silence undisturbed except for someone snoring in his sleep—he would stare at the ceiling, struggling to remember his former life.

A dog he had once loved. He didn't know its name, but he cried one night when he recalled how it used to bound on his bed every morning and lick his face to wake him up. A best friend—another teenager, the features of his face only barely remembered—who had his own car and was the coolest guy in town. An associative remembrance of the scent of marijuana, smoked on a warm summer night. A girl—not Elizabeth, although she had blond hair, too—who also liked some TV show called *Star Trek;* they used to screw on the couch of her parents' house while Mr. Spock watched. He thought her name was Shelly, but he could be wrong; it might be Sally or even Shelby. Another TV image: cheering along with a roomful of college kids as they watched a spacecraft rise from a distant launch pad, wishing more than anything else that he could be aboard . . . *Columbia?* was that what it was called? . . . right now.

Like shards of broken seashells, he collected scenes and voices from his past during those midnight strolls down the alien beach that was his mind. A long corridor of office doors *(third floor, five doors down, one o'clock sharp, Mr. McLafferty);* a classroom chalkboard filled with equations *(a Hohmann trajectory, simply stated, is . . .).* Taking a dump while studying a textbook *(goddammit, Paul, are you dying in there?).* Cool autumn wind in a graveyard *(he would have been proud of you, son . . .).* Someone shaking his hand *(welcome to the team, Dr. McLafferty, we're glad to have you . . .).* A gold ring slipped on his finger *(you may kiss the bride . . .).* A first glimpse of palm trees *(dammit, Liz, where's the map, I can't . . .).* A baby crying *(he's beautiful, what do you want to . . . ?).* A long row of tall, cold metal tanks *(we call it cryonic biostasis, Dr. McLafferty, not . . .).* Liz, pissed off, shouting at him about something that he had signed *(what are you wasting money on this for, we can't . . .).*

The taste of a fast-food cheeseburger.

Choking. Grasping at his throat. Fumbling across a desk for the telephone. Chair tipping over. Collapsing on a carpeted floor. Limbs growing numb, head pounding, ears roaring, vision becoming gray. The long, slow plummet into darkness . . .

Then, quite suddenly, the harsh white glare of resurrection.

* * *

And now here he was, on a space colony constructed above an asteroid called 4442 Garcia, working for Mister Chicago.

Evening came, not as a sunset upon a western horizon, but as the gradual brownout of the elongated filaments that ran down the colony's cylindrical ceiling. In forest groves below the biosphere's upward-curving walls, crickets and night birds struck up their nocturnal symphony, while lights glowed from the windows of the Byzantine stone palace at the center of the sausage-shaped artificial world.

Mister Chicago was holding a dinner tonight, and it wasn't long before his guests began to arrive, walking up the lighted paths from the dachas surrounding the palace to the open doors leading into the Great Hall. Most lived in other colonized asteroids of the Main Belt, but a few had traveled from as far away as Mars, Callisto, and Europa. If one visited the colony's central control room, located in a subbasement deep beneath the mansion, and peered at flatscreens arranged in long rows above banks of luminescent consoles, their vessels could be seen in orbit around the massive rock.

No one McLafferty had spoken with seemed to know exactly what Mister Chicago did or exactly how he had amassed his fabulous wealth. Most of the servants believed that he was an entrepreneur of some sort; others claimed that he was an exiled prince, although no one knew from which country. There were also whispered rumors that he was a gangster, a hermaphrodite, even an android. Whatever he was, he had enough money to buy an asteroid and have it turned into a private estate, and sufficient power that when he threw a party, rich people traveled millions of kilometers to accept his invitation.

After he had finished preparing the Great Hall for the festivities, McLafferty had been allowed a few hours to himself. He had used them wisely; after showering and catching a nap, he ate a quick meal in the kitchen along with the rest of the servants. Then, as his master required, he went back to the servants' quarters to put on his attire for the evening.

Twentieth-century white-tie formal: tails, bow tie, vest, striped trousers, faux-pearl studs and cufflinks, patent-leather shoes. Examining himself in a mirror, he decided that he looked as if he were ready to conduct a symphony orchestra. Liz should see him like this; he hadn't looked this good since . . .

Liz, in her wedding gown, in his arms as they waltz across a parquet floor. "Ow," she whispers, trying to maintain her poise. "Paul, you're stepping on my feet . . . "

The moment shimmered at the edge of memory, then was gone.

He winced, then hurriedly walked away from the mirror.

The kitchen, calm earlier, was now in a state of chaos: cooks preparing salads, stirring kettles of lentil soup and grilling skewers of lamb more precious than gold. Waiters hastened back and forth, carrying out trays filled with drinks and indescribable appetizers. The air was filled with smoke and succulent, untouchable aroma.

The majordomo handed him a pewter tray of champagne glasses. "Remember," he murmured, "don't offer any to the googles. They don't drink anything alcoholic, and take offense if you even offer it to them. Okay?"

Okay. A word from his century. He felt a momentary feeling of reassurance. "Okay. Got it."

The majordomo—whose face was familiar, but whose name escaped his memory for the instant—favored him with a quick nod and a pat on the shoulder. McLafferty backed through the swinging doors leading out of the kitchen.

The Great Hall was filled nearly to capacity. All the guests had finally arrived, and they mingled on the mosaic floor, the balcony, and the outside terrace overlooking the colony's sweeping vista. They wore loose, brightly colored robes that changed hue with each movement, elegant strapless gowns that briefly turned translucent before becoming opaque again, military uniforms decked with insignia and medals, capes and codpieces and vests and kneeboots and brassieres. Clothing that would have been considered outrageous, hideous, or downright bizarre in his time. In comparison, his white-tie tux was as drab and archaic as sackcloth.

Keeping a fixed smile on his face as he tried not to stare at the guests, balancing his tray on one hand at shoulder height, McLafferty maneuvered through the crowd, speaking as seldom as possible when he stopped to give someone a drink. It wasn't hard to pick out the googles and avoid them; the bioengineered Superiors—as they preferred to be called, and as they were in polite company—generally stood a head taller than baseline humans. With thin, almost avian bodies, whose double-jointed legs ended in long, hand-shaped feet that wore glovelike shoes, they looked a little more like prehistoric raptors than homo sapiens. Proud and somewhat remote, their faces tattooed with intricate designs, they regarded McLafferty with oversized dark-blue eyes as he passed them by, their disdain for the barbarian in their midst evident from the pinched expressions on their narrow faces.

He caught a brief glimpse of the master of the house when he walked out onto the terrace. Pasquale Chicago was holding court by the wrought-iron balustrade, surrounded by a small cluster of friends, business associates, lovers, and those who wished to be one or more of the above. As he chatted easily with a beautiful woman whose outfit was gradually fading into invisibility, Mister Chicago's right hand rose to casually toss back his braided, waist-length white hair from his albino face.

When he did so, his cool pink eyes happened to glance in McLafferty's direction. The look he gave him was enough to make the waiter retreat back into the hall. In the six months he had been working here, McLafferty had talked with Mister Chicago no more than a couple of times, and then only briefly. Although he frequently observed them from afar, Mister Chicago seldom spoke directly to his servants, preferring instead to issue directives through message screens in their quarters.

The guests were thirsty tonight. His tray was empty in no time at all, and McLafferty returned to the kitchen in hopes of getting a moment of rest, only to be handed a platter of hors d'oeuvres that faintly resembled raw squid wrapped in blue spinach leaves and smelled much the same. He nearly collided with Yeats on the way out.

"Having fun yet?" Yeats whispered.

"Please kill me."

"Hey, check out the babe with the . . . "

The rest was lost behind the swinging doors. McLafferty grinned as he carried the tray into the Great Hall. When this

was all over and done, at least they would have something to discuss besides the floor.

Circulating through the party goers, he found three people
standing alone near the entrance to the dining hall, carrying on
an animated conversation. Two men and a woman, each of them
young and beautiful. He would have liked to have known what
they were talking about, but they shut up as he approached
them.

"May I offer you an hors d'oeuvre?"

One of the men gazed at the tray with arch disdain. "I'm not
sure," he said. "What is it?"

McLafferty smiled. "I'm not sure, m'lord, but I'm certain
it's quite good."

"I'm not sure, m'lord, but I'm certain it's quite good." The
other man mimicked McLafferty's voice as an effete whine,
causing the woman to titter behind her gloved hand. "Oh, my
word . . ."

"Then what are you doing offering one to me?" The first
man's haughty gaze traveled from the platter to the servant carrying it. "If you don't know for yourself, then how can you be
so certain?" He regarded the appetizers as if they were dog
turds. "Have you sampled any yourself?"

McLafferty felt his face grow warm. "No, m'lord, I haven't,"
he confessed. "These are for the master's guests, and I've eaten
already, and . . ."

"Give up, Ronald." The second man sipped his champagne
glass. "This is one of Pasquale's deadheads. He wouldn't know
the difference between macédoine and *pomme de terre* if you
shoved it in his mouth."

"A 'bot might," the woman mused, "but they're not as much
fun, are they?"

"Pasquale doesn't like 'bots, Clarity," Ronald replied.
"That's why he has deadheads instead."

If this was a joke, it must have been funny, because all three
laughed out loud. Feeling uncomfortable, McLafferty put a
plastic smile on his face and started to turn away, only to have
his right arm snagged by the second man.

"Oh, so you're one of Mister Chicago's pets!" This was pro-
claimed with false astonishment, as if he had just learned some

new and unique fact. "I don't think I've ever met one of your kind before," he went on as he forcibly dragged McLafferty back into the circle. "A man from the twentieth century!"

"Well, I . . . " McLafferty looked away, trying to find a reason to escape this unwanted attention. "Yes, well, that was when I was born, but . . . "

"But you must have witnessed so much history!" The second man circled his arm around McLafferty's shoulders. "Please, tell us all! Did you . . . ?"

"Did you ever meet the Beatles?" Clarity asked, as she cast a sly wink at Ronald. "I've been studying classic music recently. They were so adorable."

"What about William Faulkner, or Hemingway? Vonnegut?" The second man snapped his fingers. "I know! Stephen King! He was around then! Did you ever meet him?"

"John F. Kennedy . . . "

"Jeffrey Draper . . . no, I mean Jeffrey Dahmer. Was he someone you . . . ?"

"Charles Manson!" Clarity had a smoldering look in her eyes. "were you a member of his group? They were so deliciously evil . . . "

"L. Ron Hubbard, perhaps? Now there was a maniac . . . "

"Who?"

"I'm sorry, but I didn't know any of those people." McLafferty felt suffocated. "I never met them. They were all . . . they were famous people. I heard of them, sure, but you never . . . "

"Certainly. We understand, don't we?" Ronald cast a broad look at his companions. "It's been so many years, and our friend here spent the last century with his poor, decapitated noggin floating in liquid nitrogen. No wonder he doesn't remember anything."

Clarity *tsk*ed with false sympathy. "Poor, dear deadhead." She stepped forward to run the back of her hand across McLafferty's face. Her breath was redolent of liquor. "I wonder if you even remember your name."

"McLafferty . . . " he began.

"McLafferty," she whispered, looking into his eyes. "That's such a nice name." Her fingertips trailed down from his face, across his throat and chest, down toward his stomach. "And

such a fine new body Mister Chicago has cloned for you," she
sighed. "Tell me, do your only duties for him include simply
serving canapés to his dinner guests? Or do you also . . . ?"

Startled by the touch of her fingers at his groin, McLafferty
instinctively jumped back. The platter toppled from his hand;
he lurched forward to catch it, but it crashed to the floor, the
appetizers spilling as an oily mess across the orbit of Neptune.

"Oh, now, look what you've made him do!" Ronald cried
out.

As the trio shrieked with laughter, McLafferty fell to his
knees, trying to scoop up the slippery food with his hands. Only
this morning he had slaved for hours to make this floor spotless, yet this wasn't what made him hiss between his teeth.

He was the manacled primitive, the captured savage in loin-
cloth, the barbarian put on parade. His humiliation was complete; as the first man had said, he was a pet. . . .

With this, unbidden, another memory: a young boy, bigger
than he was, pushing him down in a muddy playground, and
pushing him down again when he tried to get up.

(c'mon, four-eyes, put down your stupid books and . . . !)

"Come now," the second man said from behind him. "I'm
sure he means no harm."

(get up, you sissy . . . !)

Then he felt fingertips lightly caress his raised buttocks. "If
we speak to Pasquale, perhaps he'll lend him to us for a little
sport . . . "

Without thinking, balancing himself on his hands, McLafferty blindly lashed back with his right foot. His sole connected
with something soft and fleshy, and he heard a high-pitched
shriek.

"Oh, my!" Clarity screamed. "He attacked Willie!"

Suddenly, conversation around the Great Hall fell away as
all eyes turned toward him. Embarrassed, McLafferty started to
rise. "I'm sorry," he murmured. "I didn't mean it, but he . . . "

"Animal!"

Ronald's left hand sailed about, catching McLafferty in a
savage backhand that knocked him off his feet. The other guests
cried out in fear and outrage, and the rest was lost in pande-
monium.

Clarity's face, captured in a moment of absolute terror as she backed away.

The second man curled up on the floor, moaning as his hands cupped his injured testicles.

Ronald standing above him, kicking McLafferty in the ribs.

Then another guest joined him, and another, until there was a solid mob of Mister Chicago's friends surrounding him, beating him with their shoes and fists, until he sank into a dark, jagged womb of pain.

His last conscious thought was the hope that he was finally dead, for once and for all.

But he didn't die again.

When he awoke, he found himself in the infirmary.

He knew this place, located in another part of the palace, from an earlier visit for a sprained wrist.

The lights had been turned down low, but sunlight filtered through an open window; the fresh air carried with it the scent of Garcia's perpetual summer. The sheets around his naked body were cool and crisp. The autodoc hovering near his bed— one of the very few 'bots in the colony—was withdrawing a syringe-gun from his bare right arm.

"Good morning," a voice said from behind him. "I trust you're feeling better."

As McLafferty raised his head and looked around, Mister Chicago stepped from the shadows.

He was dressed differently from the last time McLafferty had seen him. Now he wore the white cotton robe he usually donned in the morning, when he was being served breakfast in the garden. In his thin, long-fingered hands he held a china coffee cup and saucer.

Although he felt exhausted, McLafferty started to sit up, but Mister Chicago shook his head. "Please, lie down," he said, raising a hand. "You've suffered some severe injuries, I'm afraid. The nanites have healed most of the internal damage, but the nasty concussion you took will take a little longer to get over."

"I'm . . . " His throat was parched; McLafferty swallowed

what felt like a ball of lint and tried again. "I'm sorry, sir. I . . . I didn't mean to cause a . . . "

"A scene?" The master shook his head again. "Think nothing of it. I witnessed the entire incident. Petersen is a rude chap, one I should not have invited in the first place. He had what was coming to him, nothing more or less. I'm just sorry his companions got to you before I did."

Stepping closer, Mister Chicago reached up to touch the keypad on the medscanner above the bed. "Good," he murmured absently, peering at the screen with his strange pink eyes. "The left kidney's recovering quite nicely. You took a nasty kick there from Ronny duBois . . . I doubt you recall it, but he's hardly a gentleman in a fight . . . and I was worried that we might have to replace it."

McLafferty remembered, but that was beside the point. "I thought . . . you would be angry," he rasped.

"Throat dry?" He glanced at the autodoc. "A little water, please." The 'bot floated away, and Mister Chicago laughed out loud. "Angry? I'm actually rather thankful. The party was becoming such a bore. If anything, it gave everyone something to talk about."

Stepping away again, he located a carved wood stool beneath a counter. "Of course," he said as he pulled it out and settled down on it, "we'll have to keep you out of sight for the next couple of days. I informed my guests that you have been taken down here to be lobotomized."

Noting the expression on McLafferty's face, he favored him with a droll wink. "If you want to play the part, of course, I could have you make a reappearance just before they leave. Just shamble around and drool a bit . . . I'm sure they'd enjoy it. But I have no intention of doing so, believe me."

McLafferty managed a wan smile. The autodoc returned with a paper cup of water, and the bed flowed into a reclining position. McLafferty accepted the cup gratefully; the water was cool, and tasted vaguely of lemon.

"But we do have a few things to discuss, you and I," Mister Chicago went on, turning more serious now. "Because this occurrence wasn't your fault, I'm not going to discipline you . . .

but you do need to be reminded of where you stand in the grand scheme of things."

Mister Chicago paused to sip his coffee. "Please understand, though," he said as he put the cup and saucer aside, "that whatever you were in your time, you are no longer now. I understand from your biographical records that you were once an astronautical engineer, employed by the . . . "

He frowned, trying to conjure a name. "NASA," McLafferty whispered.

"That's it." Mister Chicago snapped his fingers. "National Aeronautics and Space Administration, correct?" McLafferty nodded, and the master shook his head. "Long since vanished. Decommissioned more than eighty years ago, if I recall my history tutelage."

Surprised, McLafferty opened his mouth, but Mister Chicago waved him off. "It's a long story. At any rate, your former position in life is null and void, yet before you deanimated . . . or died, if you prefer to call it that . . . you spent a considerable amount of money to have your brain preserved in neural biostasis."

He paused. "In short, your head was decapitated and placed in a tank of liquid nitrogen by a private company that didn't last very much longer than NASA. The Immortality Partnership, I believe it was called."

McLafferty blinked hard. Shards of memory, recovered piecemeal over the last several months, were beginning to come together, as if they were parts of a broken seashell that were being painstakingly glued back in place. Cold steel tanks . . . his wife shouting at him . . . the taste of a fast-food cheeseburger . . .

Mister Chicago intently searched his face. "You're beginning to remember some of it now, aren't you?" he said softly, less a question than a statement. "Your memory is incomplete, isn't it?"

"Yes . . . "

The master nodded with great sympathy. "Cryonic biostasis was something that went in and out of vogue during the late twentieth century. About a hundred or so people signed up for it before the idea fell out of fashion."

Obviously enjoying his role as lecturer, Mister Chicago leaned forward, resting his elbows on his knees. "You see, the long-term problem with cryonic biostasis wasn't reanimation. That was solved many years ago, by the same biotechnology that allowed tailoring the human genome, which in turn gave us humankind capable of living in null-gravity environments . . . the Superiors, of whom you met a few last night." He sighed. "Of course, the practice isn't completely widespread, so there's a few random mutations still lurking about. If my parents had only chosen to . . . "

As if something had reminded him not to reveal too much about himself, Mister Chicago stopped short. "Never mind," he said, quickly shaking his head. "The point is that nanotech repair of frozen brain tissue isn't faultless to the point that someone can be revived with their mental facilities completely intact. Certainly, we're capable of producing clones of their bodies . . . you, for instance, are a near-perfect duplicate of the man you were at age twenty-one . . . but the mind is a far more delicate thing than a heart, a lung, or even a thyroid gland."

He hesitated. "Are you following me so far?"

McLafferty slowly nodded.

"The Immortality Partnership possessed a little more than a hundred sleepers from the twentieth century," Mister Chicago continued. "Their heads had been transferred from California to a space colony in Earth orbit before the company went bankrupt. Some of these sleepers had established trust funds in their names, and that's what had kept the company marginally solvent until it finally went bust in the middle of the century. Now, what do you think happened to all those heads?"

"You . . . bought them?" McLafferty said hesitantly.

"Excellent." Mister Chicago smiled with satisfaction. "I knew I made a wise decision when I purchased you, Mr. McLafferty."

Standing up from the stool, Mister Chicago began to pace the infirmary, his hands clasped behind his back. "Have you met Kirkland?" he asked. "A tall gentleman who works in the kitchen?"

He didn't wait for a reply. "A recipient of the Pulitzer Prize for poetry. I have a couple of his books in my collection. Now he does well if he can follow the recipe for potage Rossini without help . . . and he doesn't recognize his own verse even when I recite it to him."

Almost self-consciously, Mister Chicago walked back to the stool he had vacated. "Cerebral damage was a risk I accepted when I purchased you," he went, "but don't fool yourself by thinking for a moment that I did this out of charity. To me, you're an investment. You, Kirkland, your friend Yeats, all the others . . . you're damaged goods. Even then you're lucky, because most of the sleepers suffered neural damage so severe that, had I bothered to revive them, they would have been little more than vegetables. Even with you, one of the fortunate survivors, your talents and skills have been erased. Even if they weren't, nothing that you once possessed, even if you remembered it, could possibly be of any practical use to me now."

"Then why . . . " McLafferty stopped, then went on. "Why have you . . . ?"

"Why did I purchase a collection of decapitated heads from a bankrupt company and have them reanimated in cloned bodies?" Mister Chicago shrugged. "Because I can afford to do so, just like I can buy a minor asteroid with a peculiar name . . . I don't suppose you know what it means, do you? no? . . . and have it transformed into my private domain. Because it amuses me to have a space engineer mopping my floors, a poet stirring my soup, a once-wealthy financier tending my garden. Robots could do the same thing . . . "

He nodded toward the autodoc. "But everyone has 'bots. They're cheap, inexpensive, always do as they're told . . . but they have no history behind them. But you, on the other hand . . . you're history in itself."

"We make great pets," McLafferty murmured.

"You . . ." Mister Chicago's voice took a strident edge; he took a breath, calming himself down. "A century ago," he said with great patience, "the people of your time did their best to ruin the only planet they lived on. You damned near succeeded, too. A few of you tried to find a way out through biostasis, in the conceit that the people of the future would receive you with open arms. Perhaps you thought you would be treated as ancient scholars, that we would even worship you as immortals."

McLafferty wished he could deny this, but he couldn't. He didn't know what he had been thinking a hundred and two years ago. Perhaps he had been frightened of death and all that it represented. Perhaps he had only been disappointed with life.

"I don't know," he said.

"If you don't," his master said, "then neither do I, yet the fact remains. Only out of my grace do you live again . . . and only out of my grace are you still alive, after what you did to one of my guests last night."

Pushing back the stool, Mister Chicago stood up once more. "And, yes," he finished, "your assessment is correct. You make great pets."

Picking up his cup and saucer, he walked toward the door, disappearing back into the shadows from which he had emerged. "And if I were you, I'd . . ."

"Keep on trucking," McLafferty said.

Mister Chicago stopped. "Pardon me?"

"Sometimes the light's all shining on me," McLafferty continued.

Hesitation. Mister Chicago glanced at sunlight streaming through the window. "Sorry? I don't . . ."

"Other times, I can barely see." McLafferty sat up in bed. "Goddamn, well I declare, have you seen the light?"

"What are you talking about?" Mister Chicago demanded.

"You asked me a question. Now I'm asking you one." McLafferty shrugged, then glanced over his shoulder at his master. "You know the answer, don't you, Cosmic Charlie? Strutting in style along the avenue?"

Long silence.

Then Mister Chicago melted further in the shadows, his footsteps hinting at dark puzzlement. "Get well soon, Mr. McLafferty," his voice said, no longer as warm as it had been before. "You need to help the others clean up from my party."

Then he was gone. Footsteps receding down a short corridor, finally disappearing.

"Go on home," McLafferty whispered to the shadow. "Your mother's calling you."

He sank back beneath the cool sheets, his hands clasped behind his head.

Now the broken seashell was intact again. Before, he only had a few scattered pieces. Mister Chicago, in an unguarded moment of arrogance, had supplied the glue.

He would scrub floors. He would clean tapestries. He would water the flowers in the garden and rinse the dishes in the kitchen and rake the compost bins, and all the while he would smile and play the part of the barbarian imbecile.

Meanwhile, he would bide his time, and learn everything he could, starting with the map of the populated solar system in the Great Hall.

One way or another, there had to be a way off this goddamn rock: Asteroid 1985RB1, discovered in 1985 and formally re-named 4442 Garcia during a conference of the International Astronomical Union in 1995 in honor of a deceased rock musician. Because if Mister Chicago didn't know the origins of the name of his own world, then this was evidence that he wasn't as omniscient as he pretended to be.

Where there is knowledge, there's hope. Sometimes all it took was a simple, long-forgotten song.

"God bless you, Jerry," he whispered, and then he went back to sleep.

F. GWYNPLAINE MacINTYRE WAS BORN IN SCOTLAND AND RAISED IN THE AUSTRALIAN OUTBACK. HIS MOST RECENT SCIENCE FICTION NOVEL, *THE LESBIAN MAN,* GARNERED QUITE A BIT OF CRITICAL ACCLAIM.

The Minds Who Jumped

F. Gwynplaine MacIntyre

The barmaid had changed sex three times that year, traded bodies bimonthly, and she'd hocked her memories and bartered her thoughts so often that she couldn't remember her own birth-shape anymore. She believed that her name was Jen, and that she was originally female, human, and Earthborn, but of course there was no way she could know. The memories inside Jen's head might be hers, or they might be someone else's bootleg memories that Jen had picked up cheap on some back-alley planet. It was also possible that they were nobody's memories: the counterfeit memories could have been scripped in a computer, on any of three hundred planets, and then downloaded into Jen's head. Of course, it wasn't Jen's real head.

Jen had lost track of her original body. She vaguely remembered being blue-eyed, red-haired, and freckled at some yesterpoint in her life, but that was all. When she'd sold or bartered her original head, she had sold all its contents . . . including her memories. Her mental image of her original self—blue-eyed and freckled—might not be one of Jen's own rememberings. It could have been a remnant bit of a rememory that had been left inside Jen's latest brain by the brain's previous occupant.

Jen was wearing a hyde, like everybody else in the bar. The Jumpjoint was crowded with visitors from a dozen different worlds, but there wasn't a single real body in the whole room. There wasn't a cubic centimeter of flesh nor a smear's worth of body fluids anywhere between the jukebox and the airlock. They all wore hydes. Jen's hyde was encased in bright pink syntheskin, molded into the contours of an adult female humanoid with tendersex genderspex. Most of the Jumpjoint customers were wearing neuter hydes without gender options. Either they couldn't afford anything better, or they were just passing through on a Jump to some other planet and didn't feel like paying extra for gonads. Jen was here on Venator to work, so her hyde didn't come with eat-options or sleep-options. Her plastic body stayed awake twenty-seven hours a day, nine days a week, without meal breaks or downtime.

There were four conflicting memory tracks elbowing each other inside of Jen's head—inside her hyde-head, that is—and so she remembered four different explanations for why the cyberbodies worn in interstellar space were known as "hydes." Reason One: the hydes were invented by someone named Hyde. Reason Two: "hyde" was short for hydraulics, because the cybernetic bodies had hydraulic servolimbs. Reason Three: after you Jump out of your original skin, you trade your hide for a hyde. Reason Four: when you've lost your own body you still need somewhere to hide, so you hide in a hyde. Maybe all four versions were true. Jen didn't know.

The Jumpjoint relied on the nearby Jumpshack for its customers. Most of the hydes in the joint lacked eat-options or pleasure modems, so the bar wasn't selling much food or drink or smoke. The hydes were loitering between Jumps, flipping spare jingle into the jukebox and tasting various rememories. One selection in the jukebox—B-17, a memory of committing murder—was very popular; several customers had played the rememory four or five times and were reliving it in greater detail every time. Kill-memories were popular fare hereabouts.

The Jumpjoint was on Venator, the fifth planet of Beta Delphini, a white star 109 light-years (and change) away from Earth. Most of the hydes in the bar looked like Delfs: their cyberbodies were built to resemble the Beta Delphini system's native humanoids. The minds inside the Delf-shaped hydes probably weren't real Delfs, because if they'd been born in this neck of the galaxy they would probably be wearing their own bodies.

Just a 5.769-light-year Jump away from Venator's white sun is Gamma Delphini, the most beautiful double star in known space. Gazing out the window of the Jumpjoint at the sky overhead, with her enhanced optics, Jen had a fine view of the binary star: two suns within a single gravity well, orbiting each other in eternal cosmic foreplay. Gamma Delphini A is a yellow-white spheroid, and Gamma Delphini B is a golden egg-shaped sun, balanced precisely between yellow and orange. Two stars like joined lovers, forever. Gamma Delphini A has no planets, but the golden sun Gamma Delf B was encircled by a dozen Biodomes. Someday, if Jen could save up enough jingle to leave Venator, she hoped to visit the crystal Biodomes of Gamma Delphini.

A man made out of metal flesh was drinking graphite juice. The customer at the end of Jen's bar was inhabiting a male-shaped hyde, which meant that the mind inside his cyberskull was either male-born or a female spending a genderstint in male shape. He was called Doctor Johnny, and his hyde was more detailed than most of the other synthetic bodies on Venator because Doctor Johnny worked for the Sector Council and his body was paid for with taxpayers' jingle. Jen was sweet on Doctor Johnny. He'd visited every planet in the Delphinus sector, and he always came back to Jen's bar with tales of the places he'd been and the memories he'd tasted. The syntheskin that encased his artificial arms felt almost flesh-real whenever Jen touched it with her hydraulic fingertips. Doctor Johnny's plastic throat contained a liquid larynx that made his voice sound almost human. Most hydes on Venator had metal voices, cybersquawks, but Doctor Johnny's electric baritone sounded like it almost had flesh in it. Sometimes, when Jen closed her plastic eyelids and just listened to his voice, she could convince herself that Doctor Johnny was really standing there beside her, in a body made of flesh.

Doctor Johnny's torso was government property. It was rigged with eat-options so he could keep his internal servos lubricated, and now Jen watched as Doctor Johnny drank the carbon cola that kept his innards moist. Then he flashed his sweet silicon smile. "Gotta get back to work, Jen," he said in that almost-flesh voice. "Expecting that new cargo down at the Jumpshack. Tell you all about it tomorrow." Then he winked, which was something to see because most of the hydes on Venator were built with unwinkable eyes. A second later, Doctor Johnny was gone.

The door opened and in came a man made of meat. Human flesh. His body was alive, flesh and blood, so Jen knew he had to be someone damn-sure important, and he was probably jingle-rich. Most travelers couldn't afford to bring their bodies along on interstellar trips; it wasn't cost-effective or energy-efficient. Much cheaper and easier to travel by Jump: leave your own body behind, and have a new body waiting for you at the far end of the journey. Some of the more expensive hydes came with counterfeit flesh, but Jen could always tell the fakes from the genuine fleshers. The people wearing artificial flesh didn't sweat, for one thing.

The meat-faced man swaggered up to the bar, and now Jen knew that his body was genuine flesh, in all its sweating, stinking glory. Her hyde contained olfactory sensors, so she could get a whiff of the stranger. He wore a neon-colored suit. The man who was flesh had a spreadchuckle smirk on his face. He parked his butt on a bar stool and flipped Jen a wink: "My name's Starbuck. Got anything to eat here?"

From underneath the bar came limping Quarrel. Quarrel's body limped because his portside leg had a hydraulic leak. Quarrel was the Jumpjoint's manager. He was big and ugly, with brutal servolimbs in case any customers got nasty. Jen didn't know whose mind was actually encased inside Quarrel's cyberskull; it was possible that the person who called himself "Quarrel" might really be several different minds taking turns in the same body, because Jen had noticed that her boss's moods kept in synch with Venator's nine-day cycle. Quarrel was friendly on Mondays and Thursdays but he was gruff on Tuesdays and Pluterdays. Today was Wednesday, so Quarrel was just plain *mad*.

Quarrel grunted at the flesher who called himself Starbuck. "You want food? Pay in advance."

The stranger reached into a Moebius pocket in his tesseract vest, and he flipped a gold ingot onto the counter. Quarrel sneered. "You must think I'm a skeeve, mister. We got matter replicators on this world. Gold is cheap as dirt. We use diamonds for doorknobs."

Starbuck's cocky grin disenchuckled itself. "But I thought that Venator uses a matter-based currency."

"Yeah, we do. Give me something with a complex atomic structure that can't be replicated. A seashell, maybe, or a freeze-dried human fetus."

Starbuck's grin broadened. "So your currency is based on artifacts?" He reached down and picked up his suitcase: a Mandelbrot satchel that was bigger on the inside than it was on the outside. He took something out of the satchel and set it down on the bar. "Ever see one of these?"

It was a little model car. To Jen it looked like a cheap plastic mass-produced toy, with no intrinsic worth. Still, the plaything had a slight value here on Venator, because of the tremendous amount of energy that must have been expended to transport those few grams of plastic across the interstellar void at faster-than-light speed. But now that the toy car was *here*, on Venator, Quarrel could key its specs into any replicator, dump in a kilo of raw carbon molecules, and churn out a hundred little toy cars just like it.

Quarrel's artificial face remained impassive as he examined the toy. Then suddenly his hyde-eyes widened, and his hyde-lips let out a whistle of astonishment. "Take a look at *this*, Jen."

The barmaid looked. The toy car was unique. It had started as a mass-produced plastic kit, but the pieces had been hand-assembled, and there were glue-smeared fingerprints on the plastic where somebody—some child of flesh—had carefully and lovingly built this model, piece by piece. The imperfections enhanced the value of the artifact, because the flaws complicated the toy's molecular structure; they *uniqued* it. Hand-made artifacts couldn't be copied cheaply; a matter replicator would churn out quasi-copies with all the flaws smoothed out, or else the replicator would use up an unholy amount of energy making duplicates that weren't cost-effective.

Quarrel put the toy car down carefully, almost in awe. "Okay, mister. Trade you one meal, even up, for this car."

Starbuck shook his flesh-born head. "Guess you don't know what I'm selling, friend." He took a small crystal out of his pocket. Jen the barmaid recognized it as a biochip, like the biochips that powered the jukebox at the far end of the room.

The flesher named Starbuck plunked the crystal onto the bar. With a high and distant thrum, the crystal began to vibrate. Jen reached out with both her hyde-hands, and one of her synthetic fingers touched the trembling crystal. Instantly, she *remembered*. There was a rememory stored within the crystal biochip, and now it slipped gently into Jen's mind.

As Jen glanced at the plastic toy car, suddenly *she remembered building it*. She savored the pleasure of fitting the pieces together, the sheer sweet joy of creation recalled as she lovingly painted the model and affixed the decals. She remembered the smell of the glue, the click of polyplastic pieces snapping into place. It was a cheap toy, but she had crafted it, and . . .

The crystal stopped vibrating. Quarrel had touched it too, with his own thick hyde-fingers, and he had shared the rememory. Again he whistled. "A genuine artifact, *plus* the original craft-memory that goes with it? That's a rare commodity here on Venator, mister."

Starbuck's head smirked a wraparound grin. "Tell you how I got it. Knew a lady on Earth with a son nine years old. I taped some electrodes to his scalp, and I recorded all his sensory input and his emotional feedback while he built this model car. How'd I bring it here, you ask, a hundred light-years from Earth to Venator?" Starbuck flipped another wink to Jen the barmaid. "Hell, I've got enough jingle to ship an elephant from here to Prox' Centauri, if I want." He winked at Jen again. The barmaid had never seen a real flesh-and-blood wink before—at least, her cyberskull contained no memories of winks. Starbuck's eyelid seemed to dance across his eye. He had a real wink, a flesh-wink; more alive than the stuttering hydraulic flickerwink that Doctor Johnny's artificial eyes always made. But Jen still liked Doctor Johnny better than this cocky flesher-man named Starbuck.

Quarrel grabbed the toy car and the rememory-crystal before Starbuck could change his mind. "How long you staying on Venator?"

"Only two days this trip." There was a ruckus at the far end of the bar as Starbuck spoke; the jukebox was playing a particularly violent rememory, and several customers were crowding in to get a taste of it. "I'll be moving on next Scatterday."

"Fine. We'll give you room and board till then, and finance your next Jump . . . long as it's anywhere in the Delphinus system." Quarrel opened a compartment in his torso, stowed the precious toy and crystal within, and lurched away, clicking his metal fingers along the bar's menu-monitor. "Treat him right, Jen. I'll be belowdecks."

Starbuck scrolled through the menu and ordered a double glopping of Altairean prognosh, extra spicy. "And keep the beers coming, honey," he said. Jen had trouble keying the sequence for *beer* in the food replicator; it had been a while since any actual bodyflesh capable of drinking alcohol had walked into this bar. While she served the flesher, she asked: "Where you headed, mister?"

Starbuck hoisted his beer, faced the window, and drank a toast to the golden egg-shaped star Gamma Delphini B, that he knew was floating in the sky 5.769 light-years above Venator. "I'm on my way to Gam' Delf B, honey. Gotta get there by Scatterday."

"What for, mister?"

"Tell you, honey. You see how them two Gamma Delfers are so close they're practically kissin'?" As Starbuck spoke, Jen looked out the window. The two components of the binary star Gamma Delphini were indeed much closer together than Jen had ever seen them before. "Happens only once every 7.3 years," Starbuck went on. "I heard it from a tutordisk, scripped by some glitchwipe who didn't have sense enough to cash in on what he knew." Starbuck swigged beer and swiped his hand across his beery mouth; it was a strange sensation for Jen to see actual droplets of moisture on a pair of genuine fleshed lips. The native humanoids on Venator got drunk on methane gas.

"At 1530 hours, come Scatterday," said Starbuck, staring into his beer while he recited the wisdom he'd snatched from a tutordisk, "the two suns Gamma Delphini A and B will attain periastron. That's the binary star's interchange phase. A stellar flare will shoot up from the yellow-white star and kiss the golden sun. The energy transfer means that Gamma Delphini B will gain luminosity, while it sheds stellar mass into Gamma Delf A. Damnedest thing you ever saw. Crystal tides of plasma gas will ripple across Gamma Delphini B. Sunspots and corona and flares, yes, and liquid jasmine flame. Most beautiful sight in the galaxy." Starbuck quaffed the rest of his beer, and then he belched. "So I came here to make some money off it."

This was news to Jen. "You're going to *sell* a stellar flare?"

"Pack it and bottle it for sale to the highest bidder, hon." Starbuck tapped his beer mug, gesturing for Jen to key a refill. "Ain't every day that two halves of a binary star share an orgasm. Gamma Delphini does it only once every 7.3 years. I'll be in a ringside seat above Gamma Dee B when it comes, aboard Biodome Seven; that's the one that achieves periapsis when . . ."

"Periapsis?"

"Closest orbital approach, hon. There's twelve Biodomes orbiting Gamma B, but Number Seven will have the best view when those two orbs of stellar plasma get all hot and bothered." Starbuck smirked. "I'll be front row center with a row of stim-spigots taped to my scalp, recording every precious drop of awe and bliss and beauty that I experience when it happens. You have any idea how much a copy of *that* memory can be sold for at the Prox' Centauri memory-auctions?"

So now Jen knew why this man had come all the way to the Delphinus sector in his own flesh-and-blood body or in someone else's Rent-a-Flesh. Starbuck's body was well fed; he weighed at least a hundred kilos. He must have paid plenty of jingle for the tremendous quantity of energy needed to accelerate his physical mass through 100-plus light-years from Earth to Venator at hyperlight-speed. Most people who couldn't afford to pay starfare would have come here the easy way, by leaving their bodies back on Earth and traveling in Jumps from one star-system to the next, with a different hyde greased up and ready for them at each Jumpshack way-station. But Jen knew that a hyde's cybersensors were incapable of recording a memory in great detail. You needed the sophisticated wetware of a *brain*—dendrites and neurons and ganglia—in order to get a

good recording for a memory crystal. To fully experience the
majestic spectacle of Gamma Delphini's stellar kiss, and in order
to *record* the experience and his emotional reactions to it, Starbuck's mind would have to inhabit a flesh-and-blood brain.

The half-life of a dream is sixteen seconds, or the half-
remembered savor of a whisper or a kiss. Any short-term sensory pattern on the human brain's cortex—such as a visual
image—will diminish by 50 percent in the first sixteen seconds.
Half of the remainder fades in the next sixteen seconds, and so
on. Like radioactive decay, it never quite reaches zero. What remains are the dregs; long-term memory. You recall that the
wine tasted sweet, but your mind can never reconstruct the precise flavor. Memories die. That's why Starbuck was rich: he put
his dreams into bottles and his memories into cages, and he sold
them all to the remember-addicts.

Most of the crowd in the Jumpjoint had run out of jingle by
now, and were leaving. Starbuck poured himself another beer,
and swaggered over to the jukebox while Jen the barmaid collected the customers' empty bottles and the dregs of methane
juleps, to feed into the recycler. Venator's sun, Beta Delphini,
had set nine hours ago, but high in the night sky the two stars
of Gamma Delphini strained toward each other, yearning to
touch. For the rest of that night, the man named Starbuck leaned
against the rememory-jukebox, sipping beer and playing B-17,
the murder-memory, over and over.

While Jen the barmaid was tending bar in a Jumpjoint on Beta
Delphini's fifth planet, another woman named Jen was on duty
aboard the science station on Biodome Nine, orbiting Gamma
Delphini B. Or maybe the two Jens were both the same woman.
Their synthetic bodies differed, of course: barmaid Jen was em-
bodied in a barmaid-shaped hyde that was designed to look sexy,
to please the customers, while the mind of Jen the scientist was
encased in a prosthetic body that was custom designed for her
lab duties in the Biodome. Yet it was possible that both Jens were
the same woman, or two overlapping women. Because the mind
of Jen and the mind of Jen contained mutual memories. The
half-remembered self-image of blue eyes and freckles, details of

childhood, specific nightmares and joys: these were all encoded within the memory-tracks of one Jen's cybernetic brain. Likewise in the brain of Jen the other.

It's expensive to Jump a whole person—the caboodle of memories and choices that compose an *individual* across the gulf of interstellar space. Much easier and cheaper to transmit just *part* of a mind from one Jumpshack to the next. And then, when the mind comes out the other end with Swiss cheese holes, you plug the holes with bootleg memories or second-hand thoughts that were scavenged or scrounged from the skulls of unoccupied hydes. Every Jumpshack crew does this. Nobody likes to talk about it. The memories shared by Jen the barmaid and Jen the scientist didn't belong to either one of them. Those memories had originated in the brain of Jen some-other.

While barmaid Jen was working on Venator, Jen the scientist was doing *her* job on Biodome Nine, assisted by a smith.

The smith was named Smith, like all the smiths. His name had once been Brock, and he'd signed on as a grunt on a cargo ship, chugging through the galaxy at sub-light speed. He stayed sober at his first few ports of call, but at his fourth planet-port he jumped ship and got into a crap game with a psychokinetic Centaurian who made the dice dance just by wiggling his eyestalks. Brock gambled away all his possessions, except one: his physical body.

Bankrupt and desperate for jingle, Brock pawned his body at the nearest hockshop, knowing they'd have the legal right to sell his body to the Rent-a-Flesh traders if he didn't redeem the pledge in ten days. He left the hockshop in a badly-dented hyde, and went looking for work. When the hyde broke down, and Brock couldn't afford the repairs, he traded it in for an older hyde with fewer body-options. Then that one broke, and nobody would repair it on credit. Stuck in a malfunctioning hyde, and hard up for jingle, Brock sold his memories to the thought-leggers, one at a time, and of course the mindsuckers wiped each memory from his cybercortex as they bought them.

That's a drawback of hydes. If you live inside that meat-knob called a *brain*, you can make copies of your memories just by sticking a stim-spigot to your scalp and duping off what you want. The original memory stays in your brain. If you leave your birth-body and climb into a Rent-a-Flesh, with all your memories downloaded into somebody else's skull, it's still possible to lift copies of your memories from the second-hand brain, even though most memory-collectors won't pay top price for memory reprints. But once your mind steps out of flesh and enters a hyde, you can't make copies of your memories and still keep the originals. The only way to download an imprint from a hyde's cybercortex is to wipe that part of the memory-tracks.

That's what bollixed Brock. With his body hocked—and his mind in a busted hyde—he needed jingle, but the only marketable assets that Brock still possessed were his memories. He sold them all, one by one, for whatever they fetched in the memory-markets, and each time he sold a fragment of his mind it was gone. Wiped. Forever. The Brain Police found a rusted hyde stumbling around, leaking hydraulic fluid, and when they did a skullscan on the mind inside the metal brain it registered only three points on a mindscale of 100. Practically mindless.

So they made him a smith. It's illegal for a body to walk around with nobody inside it, but the government isn't going to cough up the jingle to buy new memories for every skeeve who gambles away his own brain pattern. Sector Control had a prefabricated brainwave template that had been copied and recopied, and the worn-out personality in the template was named Smith. They took the rustbucket skull containing the last few crumbling remnants of the mind of Brock, and they topped it off with Smith. Afterward, of course, he had no memory or knowledge of his own: he was just Smith. Interchangeable with several thousand other Skid Row cyberskells on a hundred-some planets. Each of them had once been a unique individual. Now they were all a bunch of smiths, with the same personality and memories.

This particular smith had wangled a few days' gruntage on Biodome Nine, where manual labor was still needed because Sector Supply hadn't shipped out the robots yet. The Biodomes orbiting Gamma Delphini B have a twelve-day week, so the Biodome crew hired the smith to haul fusion rods from Thursday till Lackaday.

Come Scatterday morning, the accident came.

The rusted-out smith was hauling cargo up a ramp when,

suddenly, one of his legs snapped. Fifty kilos of hardware went clatterjangling down the ramp, and hit Jen the scientist. She got knocked across the deckplates, and she cracked her cybernoggin.

Skull fractures don't mean diddley to anyone inside a hyde, because usually the hyde can be repaired or replaced. But when Jen the scientist hit the deck, her skull's inner casing split open and her cybercortex shattered. The magnetic bytes on her memory tapes became exposed, and they started to scramble. Only a cyberneticist with steady hands and twenty years' experience could transfer the damaged cortex into a new hyde without erasing the tracks and killing the person encoded on them.

Doctor Johnny was on Venator when the SOS arrived. Sector Control had rigged his multitronic brain with a receiver tuned to the distress band, so he knew he was needed.

But Venator is 5.769 light-years away from Biodome Nine. In order to get there pronto, Doctor Johnny would have to Jump.

What's the fastest thing in the universe?

Light waves? Phooey! Light waves are slowpokes. Tachyons? Double phooey on tachyons! Give up?

The fastest thing in the universe is *thought.*

Thoughts exist as a stream of electrons in the brain, and electrons can travel at the speed of light . . . if there's nothing to stop them. But inside a skull, the brain and the bone are like electronic resistors, designed to *slow down* the currents of thought. Unlock the brain, jailbreak the skull, and the thoughts escape free.

Give a thought enough room, and it can travel *faster* than light. Maybe you've heard that tachyons can go beyond the speed of light and travel backward against the flow of time. Well, thought waves are even faster than tachyons, and thought waves can travel backward in time too. Now you know how memory works.

Ever heard of sympathetic vibrations? Take two banjos, perfectly in tune. (There's no such thing as a banjo that's *in tune,* but we'll ignore that part.) Put the two banjos ten meters apart. Twang the G-string on banjo the first, and the G-string of banjo the second will twang the same note all by itself. That's how the Jump works.

The first Jump from Earth to the moon used identical twins. It's been proven umpty-seven times that identical twins are in telepathic contact over long distances. Their brainwaves share the same frequency, just like those two banjos. The first Jump used Japanese twins. (The Jump technology was invented by Americans, but as usual the Japanese were the ones who figured out how to get rich from it.) They put one Japanese twin in Tokyo, and sent the other to the Luna colony in Aristarchus Crater. The twin on the moon was wired to the receiving unit: a catatonic mental patient, who'd been shipped to the moon with no functioning mind inside his brain. Wired up to the twin in Tokyo they had a test subject: a Japanese ax murderer named Sakata who'd been promised a pardon if the stunt worked.

They transferred Sakata's mind into the Tokyo twin, then they Jumped him into the mind of the twin on the moon, and downloaded him into the catatonic brain of the mental patient. They quizzed the body to make sure the guy inside it was Sakata. Then they reversed the polarity, Jumped him home again, and granted him a pardon. Three days later he hopped a freight to Hokkaido, got an ax, and chopped twenty-seven people into teriyaki, but that's not part of this story.

Using the minds of identical twins as transceivers, the Jump engineers stepped up the wattage of the Jump hardware, and amplified the alpha waves emanating from each twin's brain so they could do longer Jumps, from Earth to Venus. Then someone found something that worked better than twins: people with Multiple-Personality Disorder. It's been proven that people who developed multiple personalities in childhood, while their brain tissue was still forming, have abnormal neural pathways in their brains. The Jumpcorp found a woman in Montreal with nineteen different personalities living inside her head, and they teamed her with a teenage boy from Australia with fourteen people in his skull. The two Multees practiced with the Jump interface until they could shunt their extra personalities into each other's brain. The Jumpcorp found a volunteer. They plugged him into the Jump interface and sent his mind through the circuit, from the woman (on Venus) to the boy (on Mars) and then back. Worked just fine.

The techno-geeks kept improving the Jump hardware, while the interplanetary glutcorp that owned the Jump patents started hiring people with Multiple-Personality Disorder. Pretty soon a pair of Multees, wired up to transceivers on the same wavelength—one on Earth, one on Mars—were able to transmit fifty passengers a day. Another glutcorp, named Multiples Unlimited, decided to breed its own transceivers. They adopted children from Third World nations, then they locked the children in boxes and tortured them every night (plus matinees Wednesdays and Saturdays) until the children developed Multiple-Personality Disorder. Then they gave the home-grown Multees big paychecks to work as Jump transceivers. A third glutcorp started building artificial bodies—the first prototype hydes—and shipping them to Mars, so that when the minds came out the other end of the Jump they'd have bodies to Jump into.

Speaking of bodies, what happened to Starbuck? He was the only Terran on Venator wearing his own body, because he'd paid top jingle to travel all the way from Earth on a hyperlight starship.

Well, Starbuck was wearing his body and he intended to use it. On the night before his trip to Gamma Delphini, Br'er Starbuck went prowling in one of the skeevier parts of Venator's red-diode district. The cyberslums. The Beeperbahn. He met a three-breasted cyberslut named Triple-Nipple, who had electromagnetic ferro-moans, and he paid her to give him a . . . well, he never got that far. She stuck a shiv in his sweetbreads and tried to download his credits into her own moolah-modem, but she couldn't crack his access code.

Next morning the Sector Police found Starbuck belly-over, with a cut in his guts from his butt to his nuts. He could walk, but he hurt like bejeezus, and that made Starbuck hopping mad. Today was Scatterday; he had to be on Biodome Seven by 1530 hours, with a set of stim-spigots wired up to his brain . . . so that he could witness the spectacular interphase of the binary star, and record his brain's sensory input and his emotional reactions. If Starbuck felt *pain* during the sensory recording, his pain would be recorded as part of the rememory, which would decrease its value to the memory-merchants. Nobody buys pain-memories, except masochists. And if Starbuck took pain-killers, the drugs in his body would dull the sensory recording. Starbuck needed a functioning body *fast*, before the binary star erupted, or his trip to Gamma Dee B would be a waste of his jingle.

He made some calls. There was a Rent-a-Flesh for hire in the Gamma Delphini system, in a corpse-cooler on Biodome Four. A good body; only three previous owners. Starbuck sent a subspace message to have the empty body shipped to the Jump terminal aboard Biodome One, and he beamed them the credits to pay for it. Then he had his luggage and his memory-recording gear shipped by hyperlight cargo ship to Biodome Seven, with a security prefix keyed in so nobody else could use his rig. Starbuck was about to pay for his own passage on the same cargo ship, when he remembered Quarrel. The manager of the local Jumpjoint had offered to finance Starbuck's next Jump. Why pay starfare if you can Jump for free?

Starbuck took a robo-rickshaw to the main Jumpshack on Venator, and he arranged to have his mind Jumped from Venator to the empty body on Biodome One.

Starbuck's plan was to leave his own body on Venator, come out on Biodome One wearing the Rent-a-Flesh, hop a fast cargo ship to Biodome Seven and have his rented body's borrowed brain wired up to the memory recorder in time for 1530 hours. He paid the mazooma to have his own body kept in cold storage on Venator until he got back, plus he bribed some Venatorian bigwigs to make sure that nothing strange would happen to his body while he wasn't wearing it.

All of this was around the same time that the SOS transmission inside Doctor Johnny's metal skull told him to hustle his hydraulic butt to the Gamma Delphini system, so he could save the life of Jen the scientist. While Doctor Johnny ran to the Jumpshack on Venator, the Jump crew on Biodome One had a body ready to receive him: a custom-built hyde with four sets of hands, and microwelders built into the fingers. Any mind could have occupied that hyde, but Doctor Johnny had the only mind in the Delphinus sector with the experience and know-how to transfer a mental pattern from a damaged cybercortex without wiping it. It was all up to him.

And now this joint is Jumpin'.

Doctor Johnny had Jumped before, so he easily coaxed his brainwaves out of the beta phase (fourteen to thirty cycles per second) and into the more restful alpha state below fourteen cycles. When he mellowed into deep alpha—brainwaves under 9 CPS—the Jumpcrew shunted his mind into the brain of the transmitter, a teenage girl with multiple personalities who could juggle seventeen different ids without glitching. The Multee went into mind-synch with the receiver—another Multee on duty at Biodome One—using a prearranged cycle. When their brainwaves' sine curves matched, peak for peak, the transfer would be made.

Unfortunately, because of the distances involved, it would take nineteen minutes to complete the Jump. Not even a Jump can travel 5.769 light-years instantaneously.

Doctor Johnny cast off his steel body and jaunted. Mind-naked. He was a series of thoughts, a mosaic of memories and experiences. He was the part of a man that remains after all else is removed except the "I." He flew. He galaxied. He Jumped.

And suddenly there was someone in front of him who wasn't supposed to be there, someone blocking his way and slowing him down. And because Doctor Johnny in his Jump-phase had no mouth to speak the words, he had to think to touch the other. One mind tapped another mind on the shoulder, while they cannonballed through interstellar space at two hundred thousand times the speed of light.

"Get out of the way, there," Doctor Johnny told the other. *"I'm on official sector business emergency."*

"You can stick your emergency," guffawed the mind of Starbuck, because he was in the Jump-transmission directly ahead of Doctor Johnny. *"I'm on Starbuck's business, brother."*

Doctor Johnny's mind was in the delta phase now, below five brainwave cycles per second, which is where REM sleep and other strange things live. He had an emergency override signal hypnoed into his mental pattern by Sector Control, for occasions like this. He *thought* the signal. This was supposed to cause frequency gain all the length of the transmission, and enable his mindwaves to bypass any other mental patterns in the Jumpline.

But Starbuck just laughed, and flipped the same signal back extra-jangled. *"Don't skeeve Me, friend. I'm in a hurry, I'm ahead of you, and I plan to stay that way. I gave a guy at the Jumpshack fifty credits to boost that Same overdrive signal into My own transmission pattern."*

Doctor Johnny choked with outrage, if a man without a body can choke with anything. *"Unauthorized use of sector security frequencies is a felony."*

"Blow it out your bazoo, buddy. I've get a date with a hot stellar flare out by Gamma Dee B, and no space-cop can stop me." Even without a body or a brain, Starbuck still retained his nasty chuckle. *"Hell, I've bribed judges who haven't even been born yet."*

Well, Doctor Johnny tried everything. He thought himself this way and that, trying to get past Starbuck. The only weapons Doctor Johnny's Jump-self had were his memories and the facets of his mind, so he hurled those at Starbuck's mind and tried to knock it aside. Starbuck just laughed and kept Jumping. And he notched up the gain on his mental override, so that he could jam Doctor Johnny's brain-wave pattern and fizz it into the background noise of interstellar space.

And at the end of the Jump, Starbuck arrived inside the brain of a multiple-personality case aboard Biodome One. He identified himself to the Multee, and was duly shunted into the Rent-a-Flesh body that they'd thawed out for him. And when Starbuck opened the defrosted eyelids of his bartered face, and turned to see the Biodome's crystal wall and the starscape beyond, the first thing he saw was the binary star Gamma Delphini entering its matter-energy interchange. A tongue of flame from the yellow-white star licked the golden sun, and both stars embraced. The cosmic orgasm was the most spectacular sight ever witnessed by Earthborn eyes, and Starbuck had arrived just in time to see it . . . but too late to record it, too late to stick a price tag on it. And as the cosmos reached its climax, Starbuck reacted in the way he felt was most appropriate:

"Goddamn it to hell," he said. "I could have made *money* off that!"

And on Biodome Nine, a woman in a broken metal body was dying. Doctor Johnny didn't arrive in time to save the mind of Jen the scientist. Doctor Johnny didn't arrive at all. The Jumpcorp checked the pattern logs for any trace of Doctor Johnny's thoughts or memory patterns. There was zilchness. Doctor Johnny was dead.

On Pluterday morning, Jen the barmaid on Venator was visited by two hydes bearing a teleportfolio from Sector Council's legal division. Space-lawyers. Cybershysters. They harrumphed their titanium tonsils and explained. Doctor Johnny had saved up his pay, and he'd bought some insurance. The policy was in Jen's name, and he'd never told her. The loophole-merchants downloaded several kilocredits into Jen's mazooma-module, and then they limboed back to whatever asteroid they'd crawled out from under. Jen was suddenly rich, but she didn't think about that. She'd always wondered if Doctor Johnny had been sweet on her. Now she *knew*, and it was too late forever.

She ditched her job, and then she elsewhered. She asked questions, and learned that Johnny's signal had been lost because someone had jammed him, using an illegal override frequency. She bribed a smith to give her access to the Jump logs, and she saw Starbuck's name. She quizzed a few memory-merchants on Prox' Centauri. Sure, they knew Starbuck. He'd shown up at the memory-auctions with a boodle of brain-bytes for sale, shortly after Doctor Johnny vanished. No, Starbuck had not sold anyone a rememory of the Gamma Delphini stellar interphase. Would have sold one if he'd had one, of course. Starbuck would sell his own grandmother to the bait shop if he'd had a grandmother handy.

So Jen knew who had killed Doctor Johnny. She thought of revenge, and then she thought of forgiveness. Then she thought of revenge again, and then she thought of a plan.

Jen checked a chart. The white sun Beta Delphini is the only star system within twenty light-years of Gamma Delphini. So anybody who heads out to Gamma Delf from Earth or Centauri is sure to stop at Beta Delf first. That's the safest and cheapest way to cross the galaxy: use the stars like stepping-stones.

Now Jen the barmaid disappeared. She invested her money, and she vanished. For nearly 7.3 years. Now it was almost time for the binary star Gamma Delphini to have another interphase. And a man with a spreadchuckle grin and a neon-colored suit showed up on Venator, clutching a Mandelbrot satchel. He was a gimp with a limp and a hopscotch crotch, as if somebody had once tried to subdivide his gonads with a shiv. His name was Starbuck, and he yawped about the awesome stellar flare that would enrapture all humanity if one smart guy could seal it in plastic and make copies of it. He unlatched his satchel, and showed off all the memory recorders and sensory spigots he was carrying. Because these were the gizmos he planned to employ to capture the rapture and shackle the joy.

And in a bar on Venator, he met a woman wearing flesh. She had the only flesh-born female body in the Delphinus sector, and it had cost her plenty of jingle to bring it here by hyperlight starship. She was a class act, far too classy to blink an eyelash at a cybersleaze like Starbuck. Naturally he made a pass at her.

No, she wasn't Jen in disguise. Well, yes she was but no she wasn't. Jen had bought herself a fleshware body, top of the line with designer genes. She'd had a brainwipe, to remove all her least favorite memories, and she plugged the gap in her mind with a custom-designed happy childhood. She had her personality rebooted, and they liposuctioned her soul. Jen had bought herself a new self. She had no memory of Jen the barmaid; it was almost as if her former Jen-self had never existed. In fact, now her name was Neverjen. But there was one part of her soul that she had never let the cybersurgeons touch. Deep down, she was still sweet on Doctor Johnny.

The lady Neverjen went for Starbuck really big . . . or at least she pretended to. She invited him up to a hotel suite that had a zero-gravity waterbed and a holographic mirror on the ceiling. Starbuck was amazed that a classy lassie with a sassy chassis would go for him. So he put the moves on her: "Baby, you and me have got the only flesh bodies on Venator. What say we study biology?"

This was not exactly subtle, but the lady Neverjen seemed

to like it. "I have a better idea," she whispered. "Ever make it with somebody during a Jump?"

"Baby, you're scamming me."

"Don't be so sure." The robutler arrived with a Klein bottle containing an infinite amount of champagne, and Neverjen filled two glasses. "There's a new technology now," she told Starbuck. "They can transmit organic tissue—living flesh—along the Jump frequencies. It's *extremely* arousing, especially when two people Jump together. Only the wealthiest can afford it. Fortunately I can afford two round-trip starfares to Gamma Delphini. How about it? We can Jump . . . *together.*"

She plied him with champagne and coaxed him down to the Jumpshack. The Jumpcrew were all friends of Neverjen, and they assured Starbuck that she had told him the truth. A droid named Floyd told Starbuck that physical mass could now be retained during the Jump transmission, so that two people could Jump simultaneously, and *all physical stimuli* (nudge, nudge, wink, wink) would be heightened nearly to infinity during the Jump. Neverjen disbursed the moolah to pay for two Jumps, plus the cost to transmit Starbuck's memory-recording gear to the Biodome ring orbiting Gamma Delphini B. She promised him, they would get there in plenty of time to record the binary stars' matter-energy transfer.

Starbuck's brain was in his wallet. He was thinking about how much money he would make at the memory-auctions if he could talk Neverjen into wiring herself up to his sensory recorders and then having sex with him while they both witnessed the binary star's contact phase. A stereophonic sex-memory with astrophysical foreplay was worth top jingle to any rememory-collector.

So Starbuck was busy thinking about the two bulges in his pants (one of which was his wallet) when the Jumptechs slipped his head into the brain bucket. And then all at once he

*W*hat the hell is going on here?"

The mind of Starbuck was howling toward Gamma Delphini at two hundred thousand times the speed of light, without physical mass. It was a perfectly normal Jump. But Starbuck had expected to Jump while wearing his body and embracing a blonde named Neverjen. Instead: no body, no blonde, no embrace.

Then a mind came up in front of him and slapped his own mind's face. It was the mind of Jen-and-Neverjen. She'd entered the Jumpline ten seconds before Starbuck, so that she was ahead of him while they Jumped through stellar gulf. *"Does this place seem familiar?"* she asked him.

"You lied to me, lady."

"I may be a liar, but at least I'm not a murderer. Yet," hissed the she-mind of Jen. She had no body in the Jump; all she had now were her mind, her thoughts, her memories. So she showed Starbuck the parts of her memories that contained Doctor Johnny, and then Starbuck knew who she was.

"I've been tricked by a barmaid!" he howled.

But Jen the she-mind just laughed. *"The trick hasn't even started yet, mister."*

Then she told him. She'd bribed the Jumpcrew on Venator to wait until she and Starbuck were halfway to Gamma Delphini, and then to beam a high-frequency shockwave across every wavelength in the Jump range. In the Jump between the stars, Starbuck had Neverjen in front of him and a powerful shockwave barreling up behind him, getting closer every second. It would ripple through space from Venator to Gamma Delphini until it caught up with the sine curves of modulated energy that comprised the mid-Jump mind of Starbuck. The two patterns would mesh amplitudes, and cancel each other out.

"But I'll die!" Starbuck moaned. And just ahead of him, in interstellar void, the voice of Jen-and-Neverjen just whispered: *"Yes."*

Then she told him the rest. *"I went into the jump ahead of you, Starbuck, so that I could see the look on your mind when it dies. I want to see you die trying to get past me in the Jumping, the way Doctor Johnny died trying to get past you. But I won't let you get past me. The shockwave will kill you when it reaches us, Starbuck. There's a chance it might kill me too. But if my mind gets mulled out here, among the stars, at least I'll be wherever Johnny is."*

Starbuck didn't want to get nulled. If he could speed up his thoughts, intensify his brainwaves, his mind could shoulder its

way past Jen's mind in the Jumpline, and get in front of her.
Then, when the shockwave arrived, the first thing it struck
would be Jen. With any luck, her brainwaves and the oncoming
shockwave would fuzz each other out. The barmaid would die,
of course, but Starbuck's mind would arrive in the transceiver
orbiting Gamma Delphini. He'd take whatever body they downloaded him into, and find his own body later.

So Starbuck tried to shove past Jen. One of them had to die
out here, and he sure as hell didn't want it to be *him*. His mind
did everything it could to outrace Jen's. Starbuck magnified his
thoughts, he enhanced his memories. He ensubstanced himself,
or tried to, by recalling the shape and shadow of his flesh.

But Jen kept Jumping right ahead of him. She'd been planning this for more than seven years, and she was ready. She had
gathered her nightmares and hoarded her dreads. She flung an
arsenal of nasty thoughts at Starbuck, trying to repel his mind.

Starbuck was fading fast. His brainwave pattern was beginning to deteriorate. The borders of his "I" were changing
rapidly, dwindling zerowards. He unlocked his thoughts, and
took out all his darkest memories. He flung a fusillade of pho-
bias and fears at Jen's mind, and she cried out in pain. He sucked
the pain-thoughts from her psyche, adding them to his own
stockpile so that his mind became stronger. Then he unleashed
his id. All the unremembered darklings of his mind came leap-
ing out, flapping their bat wings, and they clawed and scrabbled
at the most vulnerable part of Jen's mind: her innocence.

Then Starbuck snatched her, and the two minds fought in
the void, each one trying to claw its way past the other before
the shockwave killed them both. By now Starbuck had peeled
away the crusts of his mind, and he exposed the soft pink un-
derself beneath. Down below here, in the dungeon of his soul,
he kept suppressed the fragments of his weaker selves. The tortured child he'd been once, years ago. The young man with honesty and hope who'd had his teeth kicked in by greedier men
until at last he outgreeded them all. The man he'd been once,
and the man he could have been, and the man he'd wanted to
be. All the others of self, who still lurked in his mind. He un-
buckled the floodgates, and attacked.

And all the Starbucks of his mind overpowered Jen, and engulfed her. Starbuck knew that in order to get in front of Jen in the Jumpline he would have to pass *through* her, have his brainwaves overtake hers and exceed hers without jamming the frequencies. So their minds overlapped, and in that instant every fragment of himself was interlaced with Jen. Soul-naked, they touched.

And Starbuck saw. He saw all the infinite Jens that might have been and were and never would be, and his mind shoved itself across the thresholds of all their infinite doorsteps. And in the corridors of Jen, he saw a million Jens who still loved Doctor Johnny, and a thousand Jens who cried revenge for Johnny's death, and a hundred Jens who wanted revenge so badly that they would go to desperate lengths to scare the hell out of Starbuck. But in all the Jen-minds, Starbuck couldn't find a single Jen who wanted revenge badly enough to actually kill him. That's when he knew she was bluffing. There was no shockwave coming to annihilate him. It was all a trick, just to scare him.

Starbuck guffawed, and his mind reached out to strangle the mind of Jen. *"You little barmaid bitch! You had me going for a while there! But now it's my turn to . . . "*

The galaxy exploded.

In the eyes of his mind, Starbuck saw. He'd calculated the precise moment in its 7.3-year cycle when the binary star Gamma Delphini would attain periastron. But he must have stubbed his toe on a decimal point, because his calculations were off. At that instant—nine hours ahead of schedule—the yellow-white star Gamma Dee A touched the golden sun Gamma Dee B, and the interphase began. And a tidal wave of cosmic energy—X-rays and gravitons and quarks—came flooding into a head-on collision with the two beams of modulated energy that were the minds of Jen and Starbuck.

Jen was in front of Starbuck, so the blast hit her first. And her mind screamed. And in the scream, Starbuck heard another voice:

"Jen! Jen, my darling! Is that you?"

It was the voice of a mind. Starbuck had heard it once before, in a Jump through this same region of space 7.3 years ago. It was the mind of Doctor Johnny, touching Jen. And Starbuck wondered if . . .

Then the blast of energy from the binary star's interphase hit him dead-on, and that was all Starbuck knew.

Aboard the Jump station on Biodome One, they caught an incoming transmission. The receiving unit was a multiple-personality case with twenty-nine different minds inside his head. He felt a stowaway mind coming into his brain, through the Jumpware headset, and immediately he tried to download the pattern into the skull of an empty hyde.

But something was wrong. Cosmic waves were flooding outward from the binary star, so the transmission was garbled. The Jumpcrew had to boost the gain to tune out all the static. Finally the synthetic body of the hyde blinked its metal eyelids, and shook its head, and it spoke: *"Where the hell am I?"*

The mind that made it through the Jump alive was Starbuck.

Well, not exactly. It was Starbuck, but parts of him had been lost in transmission. Some of his traits and memories were lost, and something else had taken their place: the bravery and compassion of a man named Doctor Johnny, and the generosity and innocence of a former barmaid named Jen. The man inside the mind was still named Starbuck, but he'd lost a part of himself . . . the greedy part. And then again, maybe he'd found a part of himself that had been lost.

Starbuck's credit was good, so he booked a Jump back to Venator and scurried into his own body again. Then he went home to Prox' Centauri, and inspected his merchandise. He had ten thousand memories in separate bottles, with little neat labels, that he'd collected all across the galaxy. He had nine thousand different dreams, stuffed and mounted and spread-eagled to show off their wingspans. He thought of setting the memories free, but that was no good because most of them wouldn't survive in the wild without someone to feed them.

So Starbuck built a dream museum, and a memory zoo. Admission was strictly by barter: bring one of your own dreams or memories that you don't want anymore, and trade it in at the braingate. Schoolchildren from ninety-three planets came on field trips to pet the memories (well, only the tamer ones), and scientists came to study and catalogue the contents of Starbuck's dream archive. And twice a year, for members only, the Nightmare Club had a wine and cheese party in Starbuck's soundproofed Nightmare Gallery and Scream Atrium. Stop off at the souvenir stand and buy some thrill pills, or get your personality massaged at the Brainwave Boutique.

What happened to Jen and Doctor Johnny? No one knows. Maybe they died out there in space. Maybe they found a universe next door, and they live there together. But you can bet your bottom quark that sooner or later Old Man Entropy will come and snatch us all, in the heat-death of the universe. Live and enjoy and try to love somebody while you have the chance, because infinity isn't what it used to be. Only death is forever. The rest is just illusions and dreams.

The half-life of a dream is sixteen seconds.

The Prize

Denise Lopes Heald

Stalts landed hard, blasted flat, view plate shattered, flesh compressed, ears shocked deaf. Trying to scream, his lungs seized into stuttering uselessness. He flopped and lay still, fighting—and losing. Heat scorched through the breaks in his armor. Thought disintegrated.

He woke to blinding light—the blast still seared on his retinas—and tried to move. Pain exploded up his thigh, rammed the hollow of his back, and shot through his spine like a tear rocket imploding in his skull. He screamed.

"No." A hand pinned his flailing arm. "Quiet. Gotta be quiet, Cap." Desperation roughened the whispered command.

An armored palm slid over his mouth. A bodyhide pressed his side. But the pain didn't stop, washed up his leg, swarmed his groin and set his entrails writhing. A whimper escaped.

Fingers pressed harder. A plated chest bladder pumped against his. In the distance, thin piping sounded, and unreasoned, instinctual fear froze his heart. The call faded. Pump, pump, pump. The other hide breathed. Then—

"They're past." The hide slumped. The hand lifted from his mouth. "Who?" His whisper escaped thin and tremulous.

"Rorschoxs."

Schoxs. He'd meant, who are you. But the answer cleared his mind. Schoxs ate wounded alive. If this man hadn't quieted him—His leg stabbed pain. He twisted, moaning.

"All right, Cap. All right." Weight lifted from his armored shoulder. "I'll get some damper."

Oh, yes. Maybe he could think then.

"Let me in." Hands tugged at his bandoliers. He keyed the shield tab inside his glove and pressed the t-plate beneath. Such a simple thing. It took forever now. Finally, his armor sighed, exposing access seams. Fingers fumbled at his sleeve and slit the hide's elbow. Chill seeped inward, followed by the sting of a million microscopic tines piercing his skin, spreading relief like a caress. He whimpered. His sleeve snapped shut.

"All right, Cap. Be—"

Weight hit his chest. Something chinked. Something scraped. He stared at blur and white glare, praying. The other man's filter-expelled breath puffed strange and sweet-smelling through his broken view plate, prickled his burns, lifted sweat from his hair and whispered over his ear. So scared, he thought. Even with the armor between them, he sensed the other's heart pounding. Who the hell is it? He still didn't recognize the voice. Where was everybody?

Panic threatened, but the drugs dumped in. His thoughts drifted—

—but startled as the hand lifted from his mouth. Still the damper held. Nothing hurt. His mind sharpened and cleared.

"Who?" he asked the shadow hunched above.

"Fairner."

Sucks. Why Fairner? The nick couldn't be trusted with latrine duty.

"Where're the others?" He shivered. They'd been bunched together. Whatever hit him, hit them all.

"Dead."

Dead. He swallowed hard and closed his eyes, which made little difference to what he saw. It figured Fairner'd survive. But Fairner lied.

"Can you see, Kid?"

"Yeah. Doyle fell on me—took most of the blast." Big

Doyle. "I can't get him off me." Fairner's voice scaled upward, and Stalts knew the kid wasn't lying this time. "If you get free, can you walk?" He kept his own voice low and steady.

"Yeah." He could sense Fairner fighting for control.

"What you see?"

A hard question, make or break. Fairner hesitated a breath, but kept it together. "The fighting's moved on. Isn't much happening."

"We lost, then?"

"Maybe. But the Schoxs act worried for winners."

"Good."

"There's smoke toward Bing-toc. What's the next nearest rally?"

Now Stalts hesitated. If he told Fairner would the kid zip out and leave him to die? Six months ago Command forced the bastard on him, and every time he looked into Fairner's pretty eyes, he saw someone hiding, playing a private game.

Fairner gambled. Fairner joined in anyone's tricks for a laugh—except the man didn't laugh. Fairner made friends with everyone and used the friendship like barter. Broad shouldered, pretty, golden skinned, he might as well be sticky-tar—and women, chew beetles. He attracted them just the same. Only they didn't end up in Fairner's nest. He took their treats and presents, then they found themselves sleeping under someone else. Asked about it, Sarge just said, he's kind to his friends. But which friends?

Damn you, Sarge—can't be dead. And Phil? Stalts shuddered. He and the looey'd been a team for a decade. Can't be dead! Don't leave me alone with Fairner. Fairner lied. He clung to that thought.

"Cap?" The nick waited for an answer.

"Redeye," he said. "Redeye's the nearest rally station." If there was a rally.

Fairner's breath hissed loud in his ear. The tuber knew how to figure the odds too.

"Where you hurt?"

"Bruises. I'm all right." But Fairner always lied—"Got to get Doyle off my foot."

He watched Fairner's silhouette struggle with a darker blob. Having worked this game for twenty years—twenty?—he knew focusing now would be a mistake.

"B-b-blithin' hell—" Fairner's curse broke on a sob. Stalts squeezed his eyes closed. But he couldn't escape the smell—blood, intestinal bacteria—all of it. The kid flopped at his side, curled up knees to chest, and shivered so hard their armor tapped together in a clicky song.

"Kid?"

Fairner hiccuped. Stalts let him be, husbanding his own strength. The Schoxs might come foraging—And it would get damn cold out here after dark with his armor pierced. They needed to move. If Fairner would just do something with his leg.

"Kid?"

"Unnh." Fairner sounded shakier than ever. "I'm fi—" The kid gagged and gulped air.

Stalts gritted his teeth, figuring they were finished. But Fairner struggled up, breath rasping loud against the slaughter field silence surrounding them, strangled a moan, controlled his stomach and pushed onto his feet.

"I can see Corky." The kid sucked a long breath and held it. "I can get the medpak. It's just a few meters." It surprised Stalts that Fairner waited for his order.

"Go."

Panic rising, lying still, eyes closed, he listened to the kid's footsteps move away. Patience. But Fairner didn't return. He opened his eyes and raised his head. A blur of red-splattered hell surrounded him. Nothing moved. He lay back. Panic hovered over his heart and clenched his chest. Call out, he thought, call—A single, short whistle, like a toot on a musical pipe, startled the breath from him.

Gods, they got him. But there should be more piping. The Schoxs were moving warily. And he'd hear the fight if they caught Fairner. The kid must either be gone or grounded too far away to warn him. He lay slack, listening, just listening

A scream froze his gut. Don't let it be Fairner. The scream faded. Dear demon-damned, how could he wish someone else dead rather than the kid? But Fairner stood between him and his own death. Shuffling footsteps sounded—dragging and

rustling—Schoxs. The footsteps stopped. Below, he thought, beneath the lip of the hill where his troop had stood to fight.
Something plopped. Something slurped.

Don't move. Be all right. Lie still—be fine. His stomach
swelled against his diaphragm, and he couldn't find enough oxygen. But better to meet a full Schox than a hungry one.

He held on, struggling to control his breathing, his stomach, his bowels, struggling not to make a sound.

The feeding slowed. Gulping faded to snorts and grunts—
then shuffling that moved away. A whistle sounded, faint and distant. Finally, only the evening breeze rushed over corpses and
shattered armor. Stalts's leg ached. Chill air seeped through his
hide's chinks and cracks, growing cooler. A stray puff found the
burns on his face. He shivered.

Had Fairner been the main course? Had the nick deserted
before the Schoxs arrived? Or decided his captain was filleted,
and why face the remains? He wouldn't blame a man for that,
not even Fairner.

Something rustled—close, not the wind. His gut bunched,
and his bowel threatened. "Cap?"

Breath exploded outward. His eyes flipped open, staring at
a darkening sky and a horrid shadow figure.

"Damn it, Kid."

Blinking, he steadied. His vision cleared. Coated in gore,
one arm of his hide quilled with shrapnel, Fairner looked monstrous. Stalts sucked a deep breath. He could see.

"I got it." Fairner dropped a pack at his side and collapsed
onto it. "You need more damper before I do your leg?" The kid
sounded unreasonably calm.

"Just a graze." He matched Fairner's tone. But opening his
hide again, he wished with all his heart he dared gaze out. A
needler brushed his arm.

"All right?"

"Yeah." He waited. The drift came just right. He hadn't
realized how much he hurt. "Tha—" The sight of Fairner
spreading a puff-splint next to his twisted leg took his breath
again.

"Here goes." The kid's jerky movements betrayed the calm
in his voice.

Fairner lifted. He swallowed a scream and grabbed the kid's arm.

Fairner yanked. Stalts yelped. Pain paralyzed him. Then the splint puffed, and the agony spiraled down. He collapsed beneath Fairner's fussing.

"Close your eyes, Cap."

They were. His broken view plate creaked open. Chill mist hissed over his face, sealing and soothing.

"Look at me."

He obeyed, and before he could focus, liquid slopped into his eyes—superplus saline solution—blessed relief. Blinking, he rolled his head to keep the stuff out of his nose. A cloth blotted the excess. Fairner's armored fingers fumbled a tab behind his ear; an MVB, multi vital bio, to stop infection.

"Gotta move, Cap." Fairner closed the remains of his view plate. "Now."

"What about you? Your arm?"

"Took care of it waiting for the Schoxs to leave." The kid's breath panted against his ear. "Damn. I thought they ate you."

"I thought—you." He gripped the tuber's shoulder. Fairner shuddered. Armored arms slid around his chest and lifted. He'd forgotten how strong the kid was—when the nick felt like exerting himself. In camp, Fairner stood up first for dietary duty and last for anything else. Like a trained scoot, everything the kid did willingly had to do with food. Ought to have Curly check him.

No. Curly's dead. Curly's dead. He shook and trembled. Fairner, in the middle of trying to lift him onto one shoulder while hefting his big firetube over the other, staggered and fell. He fell on the kid, yelping with pain. Fairner clamped an arm around him and hugged.

"Cap?" Fairner held on. "Cap. I know. I know."

If the bastard had said it's all right, he might have killed him. But the "I know" sounded true, as if an old man spoke, who really did know. The shaking stopped. Stalts lay still, face against the kid's shoulder. Then Fairner lost it, went stiff, helmet hissing open, and rolled away to bucket convulsively. That steadied Stalts. This bastard was the last damned bit of his command, the end of his command. But captains took care of their people, and the kid needed help. Squirming awkwardly with his splinted leg, he reached a palm under Fairner's helmet and lifted it out of the muck. The kid shook, and the kid whimpered, then took two big breaths and pulled himself together.

"Gotta move, Kid."

Fairner nodded, hauled himself up, legs quaking like whip-grass, and leaned on his firetube for a long breath. Stalts didn't see how the man could carry him, but Fairner reached for the medpak too.

"Leave it." Fairner let it go. "Leave the tube."

"Against regs, Cap." Fairner's voice rose shrilly, hysteria threatening.

"Whatever you want."

A tuber's launch was a tuber's life. It was no time to upset that balance. And maybe he'd never given the kid enough allowance for being the sort of madman it took to wield such a maniacal weapon. Fairner set the tube down just long enough to heft him onto his back, then gathered it up again, locking it in place down his right side. Through the jarring maneuver, Stalts hung limp and cooperative in spite of a thin spot in his damper buffer. "Hold on, Cap." Fairner swayed, then steadied. Stalts held on.

But every way the kid turned another body, another one of his soldiers, lay torn to shreds. Little Iva stared out of her view plate as beautiful as ever, except she hadn't any body. The sight cut a hole in him too deep to heal. Fairner didn't make a sound. He figured the kid wasn't looking anymore. Or maybe it just didn't mean anything to the nick. Stalts cried. The kid hadn't lied.

Fairner walked, moving them from nightmare to nightmare, trudging off the rise. The last glimmer of light disappeared from the shrouded sky. Fairner kept walking, using enhancers and heat sensors. Stalts's own glowed a halo around his shattered view plate. He hung, a helpless burden on the kid's back, and began to doubt. He'd prayed for Fairner to come back and haul him out of this mess. But alone, the kid could survive—the last of his troop. Why should he kill them every one?

"Better stash me."

"No."

"That's an order."

Fairner walked, only slowing as they came off the rise and into the shadows of a gutted building complex. They could hide in the ruins, but so could Schoxs. "Put me down." The kid walked. "Idiot." Fairner tripped. One knee buckled, and the kid landed on it with a grunt. Stalts rolled off, taking a crack from Fairner's firetube that set his ears ringing. Damn. They'd passed a hundred spots where Fairner could have left him. Tubers were always fritzed.

"Fairner, you're insubordinate."

"And you're delirious." The kid's chest bladder wheezed against him.

"You're stupid. You're not doing any good. Find me a place, get to rally, and send rescue back."

"What if there isn't a rally?"

"Then we're both Schox fodder." Piss on the kid. "At least you'll save yourself some pain in the meantime."

"You're wrong." Fairner grabbed an arm, slid his shoulder beneath it and lifted Stalts onto his feet. "Walk."

He did—sort of—balancing on the splint, gritting his teeth against the pain in his other leg. Their progress was slow and hard on him. But Fairner's breathing steadied. They settled into a haphazard rhythm while his mind wandered.

The nick should leave him. What was he going back to anyway? A captain that got his troop blown the hell away wouldn't find willing recruits to form a new one. No command. Maybe no legs. No Phil. No Iva. No anyone. What would he do?

"Cap?"

He caught himself, realized he'd giggled aloud. Worrying about what he would do, when there wasn't damn gonna be a would. You laughing, Buggs? The odds of them living were the little bookie's kind of bet. Stalts felt himself grin like an idiot.

"More damper?" Fairner's voice shook.

"No." He squashed hysteria. "You take a hit."

"No."

"How deep is that stuff hanging out of your arm?"

"Skin deep."

"Hope you got thick skin."

Fairner laughed. It surprised Stalts all to hell. Well, good; he'd done something right by the kid. But then he slipped, taking them down.

"Get up." Fairner recovered with an effort. "You're wearing me out."

"Leave me."

"No."

Arguing got them nowhere. He stood still while the tuber wrestled him aboard and started off at a better pace than they'd been making. Teeth clenched, he rode it out. Fairner must've taken a shot to the head to put this much effort into anything. It wasn't like the nick, not at all. But the kid's brain would activate eventually.

He woke in darkness, on the ground. Finally. The kid found some sense. But something stirred— Fairner, not gone at all. Stalts lay still, listening, trying to think. Were they hiding? Did he dare make a sound? He decided a Schox could hear Fairner's panting half across the city, so there couldn't be any around.

"Kid?" He groped for Fairner's helmet and found it open. The nick had outrun his internal oxygen production.

"Kid?"

"S'alright." The answer came weak and breathy.

"Damper?"

"Yeah—needler in my belt. My right." Stalts found it by feel, activated it the same way. "Is it set?"

"Yeah."

"Gonna open?"

"Can't open the sleeves."

"What's wrong with the other one?"

"Same thing. I just clipped the shrapnel ends off so I could carry you."

"Damn it, Kid."

"Do it in my neck."

"You'll pass out."

"That's why I crawled in here."

Except for the ragged glow of his sensor lights, Stalts couldn't see what here meant. He reached a hand above his head and encountered a coved ceiling. When he rolled to straighten his leg, the floor seeped and settled, a pile of rubble. If the place didn't cave in on them, it was a good spot. Rorschoxs were claustrophobic.

He ran his fingers down Fairner's sweaty jaw, found the hollow of the kid's throat and pressed the needler to it. The tuber's breathing slowed, muscles relaxing. Stalts slid his fingers to Fairner's pulse. It beat like a force stream. Damn.

Cocking his head, he finally found a small piece of view plate through which he made out the kid's face. The man's heat color wasn't good. He shifted. Fairner startled, startling him. "Cap?"

"Relax. Your heart's beating."

Fairner's breath hissed out. Stalts felt for fever. The kid's face turned into his hand—warm. Too warm? "Cap—hungry." Hungry? What was happening with the kid?

"I'll get it." He reached for the regulation food pocket on the kid's left bandolier.

"Other side."

"You got extras?" He hesitated.

"Yeah." The kid's voice faded.

"This one?" He tapped the corresponding pocket on the right bandolier.

"Yeah."

He dug out two packets, angling his head and closing one eye to focus through his patch of intact view plate. The extras were illegal slosh, subspecies mix that would fill a man if he could stomach it. He cocked his head farther. "Bad stuff, Kid. You'll bucket."

"I'm used to it. Please. I'm starving."

Fairner's voice shook. Stalts sighed. Damn, it was most of the day since they'd eaten, and Fairner'd worked like a q-mule.

"I got regular—"

"No" The kid's voice broke. "Regular won't keep me going."

And finally Stalts understood. Funny smelling breath, always scrounging after food, inhuman strength, accelerated pulse—The kid was hiding, playing an obscene game. "You're a blessed damn breed, aren't you, Fairner?"

"Yeah."

He started to curse. But the kid shuddered so hard it jolted right through him, and he remembered this was his troop, the nick's life his responsibility. And he owed the breed his own. Damn. He rolled onto his back and stared at the fritzing halo of his sensors.

"Cap, please."

His hand still gripped the ration packets. He opened one and held it out to the kid.

"Can't raise my arms anymore."

Lords, hand-feeding a breed. No wonder they forced the kid on him. Give it to Stalts, he's too old to notice. He slit a corner, squirmed to see through his bit of usable view plate and held the rations packet to Fairner's lips. The kid sucked.

"More."

He opened the second packet. The first held enough to make a Homo Sapien S sick already. So Fairner was definitely Homo something-or-other else.

"Army's a piss-poor place to hide."

"No." Fairner swallowed. "Its a good place to hide. Just not damn safe." Bitter amusement tinged the breed's voice, and Stalts relaxed a little.

"How do you get enough of the right food?"

"Don't. I gamble for field rations and save them for maneuvers. In camp, I scrounge."

"I noticed. Did you steal my Holinmas pudding?" He'd wanted to kill for that theft, still had an urge to strangle Fairner.

"No." Fairner rolled his head away from the rations packet. "But I probably ate it."

"So who stole it?"

"Maybe Iva." Fairner's voice shook. Stalts exploded inside.

"She wouldn't." His fists balled. The nick had no right.

"She would. You were getting pudgy—soft. She'd do anything for your own good. But she probably didn't. More like Trixie and Texie. They'd take anything."

"You're lying." His throat tightened another notch.

The part about Iva was true, but not the twins. "I'd know if I had thieves."

"We were all used to it. No one complained. If you needed something, it was safe. If you didn't, and they did, they borrowed it. They'd bring it back when they finished with it or leave something else. They're—" Fairner hesitated, voice breaking. "—they were Normans, but adopted Bhsi culture."

Stalts hadn't known the last. Fairner sighed. "They didn't take that much."

Stalts hung over the breed stunned, mind wandering to better times. Damn.

"Someone left me a cake later," he said.

"Them."

It hurt—hurt bad that this freak knew anything about his own people that he didn't. Damn.

Fairner choked. He grabbed the kid's collar spigot and pushed it against fevered lips. Sucking, Fairner choked again, but finally settled with a moan.

"That damper should be working better."

"Doing as good as ever."

Damn. "What are you?"

"Half s.s., a little Rigl, a little Ush-shangie."

Two subspecies, the last barely sapiens however pretty the things were. Common sense said that a person's non-norm physical requirements should be known by the commanding officer. But regulation, this one time, favored the breeds. If they could pass, nothing said they had to reveal their genetics to anyone, not even the troop medic. Some breeds would rather die of misdiagnosis than take a chance on their fellow soldiers finding them out.

"Did Curly know?"

"Just about everybody knew or guessed."

Stalts felt the rubble running out from under him. He'd thought he knew his troop. Damn them. Damn them for dying on him.

"Why didn't anyone tell me?"

"Maybe the way you treated me, they figured you knew."

He treat the kid that bad?

"You had women flocking from every troop in regiment. Did they all know?"

"No." Fairner's voice dropped "I needed their presents, but it wasn't right to take advantage."

"So you let your friends sleep with them?"

Fairner didn't answer. Stalts slammed a fist against rubble.

Fairner sobbed. Damn it.

Stalts couldn't move. It didn't matter that the man hurt, didn't matter he'd been a fool to forget that Iva and Doyle, Curly and the twins and all the others were Fairner's troop too. He couldn't move, just sat while the kid cried, lost in bad damper.

Eventually Fairner fell asleep. At least he shut up. Stalts wriggled around until he faced the dim, distant circle of glare that marked their egress from this hell pit. He shouldn't have shook the kid up, was sorry he knew about the kid, was even sorrier Fairner'd ever been born.

Shouldn't have been, the triple-scumming abomination. Oh damn, he was sorry everyone was dead.

He drew his Tri-S-10, resting it on a fallen construction block. Those sorries couldn't be helped, but he owed the kid enough to watch over his sleep.

Clank.

He shivered awake.

Clank.

He reached for Fairner, but the kid was already moving, injured arms pinned to his ribplates. Fairner wriggled near. A call echoed through the building rubble. A low hum vibrated the air. Stalts cocked his head. The kid stared back at him.

Rorschoxs.

Fairner grabbed the firetube, his movements desperate and awkward, his breathing short. Stalts clenched the kid's shoulder, stopping— *Baammmmm.*

The blast slammed them flat. Rubble rained on their heads. Stalts wrapped his arms about his weakened helm and prayed.

Baammmm. A second jolt rained more garbage. *Baammmm.* Damn it. The shockwave passed. The big tin gun whined as it recharged. The Schoxs had a firing pad outside. He slapped Fairner's rump, and they scrabbled forward, the noise of their progress masked by the gun's growl. Fairner rose into a crouch, his big tube tucked under one arm, dragging the end of it.

Stalts counted. Twenty seconds. The gun's whine built to a shriek. Ten.

Fairner hit the ground in front of him, armored body shielding his from the forward shockwave. He wondered, as the gun pound-pound-pounded again, if Fairner's positioning was intentional protection. Thirty seconds. They started crawling while the gun's whine spiraled upward again. Twenty. Ten.

They broke into open space next to the outer wall of the building. Light flared. The gun blew. A warm squirt streamed down Stalts's sanitary line and Fairner's body bounced off the ground in front of him.

Ears stunned, he crawled over the tuber and looked out on the Rorschoxs's emplacement. Outside, a mobile launcher supported a double tine unit. Only one arm was operational, which accounted for the thirty-second pause between blast clusters. Schoxs labored over the second arm. When that barrel activated, there would be a constant blam stream. Stalts had lost track of direction, but guessed the guns were trained on Redeye.

He glanced at Fairner. Shadow and light played wildly over the breed as he struggled to get his arms and the big firetube into position.

Lords.

Stalts froze, looking from Fairner to the Schoxs. It was insane. What kind of game was the kid running?

But Fairner dropped limp, unable to lift the tube into position, face twisted with pain. Stalts touched his cheek, and Fairner's pretty eyes opened. They stared at each other. He leaned next to Fairner's half-open view plate.

"If you fire, we're dead."

Fairner nodded. Stalts nodded back. No one lived forever.

Bammmmm!

He rode out the shock. A cave-in sounded behind them.

Thirty. He lifted the firetube.

Twenty. He positioned the kid's hands and got one knee under himself.

Ten.

He knew that even with Fairner's arms half useless, the kid would make a better shot of it than he could. A firetube was an insane weapon. Man, woman, even a mule like Fairner, tubers possessed a special psyche. It took more than training to sense and adjust for the vagaries of an implo-zionate power stream that launched next to your ear. Stalts put his shoulder under the weapon's butt to absorb some of the kick for the kid when it came. *Bammmmm! Bammmmm! Bammmmm!*

Dust billowed around them. Building blocks thudded distantly. He almost dropped the tube.

Thirty. He felt the launcher activate.

Twenty. Fairner tensed.

Ten.

The tube slammed Stalts's shoulder and knocked him backward, Fairner on top. He rolled over the kid—the tuber too stunned to protect himself—and held on as the prime-charged tine gun outside went up with a heart stuttering, lung stunning, mind shattering *whuuummpppfff*.

They stared at each other, face-to-face. The little pocket created by their two helms pressed together had saved them, created a space to breathe with oxygen from both hides feeding into it. Outside of that tiny space, they were buried in debris.

"Kid?"

Fairner's breath caught.

"We did it, Kid."

"Unnh." Fairner's lips moved against his cheek. Damn. This was no fair way to die after what the kid'd just done—taking out a sucking tine unit.

"Come on, Kid. Can you move?"

"Unnh."

Rustling sounded, Fairner trying, but the tuber's breathing weakened. The rustling stopped. Well—

"Hey!" The yell startled Stalts's gut into his mouth.

"You alive in there?"

That wasn't a Schox yelling.

"Kid!"

Fairner didn't answer. Stalts tried to move himself—and screamed, precisely what he needed to do anyway.

"Got a live one!"

Captain?"

"Yes."

"Captain Mi'ing." An attractive woman, she leaned over Stalts. "You two take out this emplacement?"

"Yeah."

"Damn." Mi'ing shook her head. "You got some nukes. One hell of a bang. Can't believe you're still alive."

"Me either. How's my man?"

"Be all right. Where's the rest of your troop?"

"He is my troop."

"Sorry, sir." She didn't sound sorry.

Better, Kid?" Stalts held a water tube to Fairner's lips. The breed sucked thirstily, shaking head to toe.

Mi'ing's meds—damn them—had pulled two blades of shrapnel out of the kid's arm, yanking the shards backward through the armor, taking dangerous risks. The kid squirted blood like a stuck Schoxs, but with sealant pumped into the holes, Fairner had movement in his right arm again.

Stalts wiped sweat from the kid's bare face and checked the fluid push taped to his throat. It was sucked dry.

"Doc." He waved at a med. "Need another push."

"When I get a chance." The man went back to wrapping a smashed thumb.

Stalts gritted his teeth. He'd been afraid the meds would kill the kid out of ignorance. So he'd told them Fairner was breed. After that, they hurt the kid more than necessary. But he didn't dare complain.

Their rescue was tentative at best. Mi'ing's troop, a hundred and fifty strong, had communications with the main army. But it was cut off physically—operating behind enemy lines—and Mi'ing hadn't been looking for survivors. Her people had spotted the smashed end of Fairner's firetube and started digging for its power pak. Every time the troop lieutenant looked Stalts's way, his expression said it was damn bad luck they'd dug out two wounded with the tube. Mi'ing's calculating glances gave Stalts no peace either. She'd set the medics to work on Fairner. So what did she want from the kid?

"What you think, Cap?"

"That we aren't out of this."

"Yeah." Fairner worked onto his side and slowly curled up to lean his head on his knees.

"You ought to rest."

"I am."

The kid's head slid off his knee and against Stalts's shoulder. He wrapped an arm around Fairner. They'd lived through too much since yesterday for him to hold a grudge against the breed. Besides, he needed someone to cling to himself.

"I'll carry you, Cap. Soon's this damper wears off. I'll carry you out." Fairner drooped lower.

"Just rest."

"Yeah—thanks." Fairner went limp. Damn the kid. Thanks for what?

Fairner still slept when the word passed to move out. Expecting to be left, Stalts didn't disturb the breed. But four soldiers showed up, shoveled them onto carriers, and hauled them off. Stalts didn't figure Mi'ing for either kind or generous. So what did she want from them?

They made camp that night in the ruins of a malt-based brewery. The place reeked, but offered solid walls to put their backs against. The troop scattered through the wreckage, finding tunnels and rubble caves for shelter.

Abandoned, Stalts shivered in an exhausted heap until Fairner dragged him to a smelly vat, tucked him inside and sat down, blocking the vat's opening. The accommodations weren't the best to be found—Mi'ing's people had those—but better than nothing. Fairner sucked rations in silence. Stalts did the same, studying the breed. Fairner'd walked most of the afternoon and looked worn and tired, but stronger than this morning.

"Sleep, Cap."

Stalts obeyed without a word, trusting his breed to guard him.

Cap." A hand tapped his armored shoulder.

"Mmmph." He blinked into darkness.

"Mi'ing's coming."

He forced his head up, then his shoulders. Every fiber clamored cell-deep pain, but he wormed against Fairner's back and strained to focus.

"Captain?" Outside the vat, Mi'ing stood alone. Her too casual, too polite tone grated Stalts's nerves.

"Yeah?"

"We need to talk."

Hands on hips, she made no move to kneel to their level. So Stalts pushed Fairner, and they both climbed out, the kid wrestling him onto a pile of building blocks.

"At your command, Captain." Stalts watched her through a haze of exhaustion as Fairner backed off to give them privacy.

"How good is your tuber?"

"Reasonable." He let a note of speculation creep into his voice as if hedging the facts in Fairner's favor. Actually, Fairner was one of the best tubers he'd ever signed—something else for which he'd never given the kid credit.

"He took out the time emplacement with both arms paralyzed?"

"He did." No use trying to deny it. "I placed the tube for him, wrapped his hands around it, held up the back end. He did the rest."

"Could he do it again? Do it alone before dawn?"

Looking for a sacrifice. And why lose one of her own? A captain needed to be popular come recruitment time. The army was business—even more so now than when he'd joined. You had to be a very good soldier to be promoted to captain, and you had to come with your own troop in hand. People meant money. The more people you had, the more security you and they enjoyed. One man did not make a troop. The instant death records were filed for his people, his captain's shield would be retired. He and Farmer were meat in the wind. Except—he was still a captain. That didn't change until the accounts closed. He shook his head.

"He hasn't slept. He's stretched on damper. I wouldn't bet your lives on him. Mine, I've got no choice."

"You're wrong."

Stalts carefully straightened his unsplinted leg.

"I need a second." Mi'ing propped a boot on the block next to Stalts's splint. "Mine dropped in the first fire."

"What about your looey?"

"He's just acting. Isn't a leader."

That was too obvious.

"I don't know, I have favors to call in." He lied. "I'll have a troop before accounts close."

"You can do that anyway, from the safety of a second's slot. Anything's safer than sitting here without legs."

He'd been waiting for the threat. If he didn't surrender Fairner, Mi'ing would abandon them. Maybe she'd leave him anyway. Maybe not. Rescuing an officer earned reward points. Still—Damn. If Mi'ing was serious, he could save his shield.

"Let me talk to him—alone."

Mi'ing hesitated "Whatever. Don't take long."

"No."

She moved away.

"You hear?" Fairner, hovered nearer now than when the conversation had begun.

"Yeah." Fairner knelt beside him. "Trust her?"

"No."

"Its a good deal. Take it, Cap."

"You want to join her?"

"Sure." But the kid took too long—lying.

"They know what you are."

"Most people do."

Still lying. Fairner didn't want any part of this troop. Rubble crunched. Fairner stood.

"I'll take you both in." Mi'ing had been eavesdropping. "I need people. You need a troop. Just do this errand for me."

Stalts strained his neck to get some kind of view of Mi'ing's face. Her voice was wrong.

"Make your life easy." She spoke over his head to Fairner. "Make your Captain's life easy. After what you've survived already, this'll be slidin' easy."

"Could you lay it out, sir?"

Fairner sounded so subservient, it grated Stalts's nerves. The kid was never that proper with him.

"I'll demonstrate every detail," she said, voice suddenly husky, "Come along to my quarters."

Mi'ing beckoned. What Stalts could see of her expression looked hungry, leaving no doubts as to what she offered now. Fairner tensed. "Cap?" Stalts hesitated. Fairner started to go. He grabbed the man's bandolier.

"No. We're too tired for deals tonight."

And through both armored hides, Stalts felt Fairner's relief. The kid took a backward step, planting himself at Stalts's shoulder. "You're making a mistake." Mi'ing spun away. Her retreating footsteps echoed loud in the ruins, and a breeze puffed against Stalts's face like a backlash of rage. Fairner shuddered.

"All right, Kid?"

"Yes, sir."

Respect. It startled him. But Fairner's tone rang true, and it felt good. After all the failures this tour, it felt damn good, even if they had just condemned themselves to slow death.

"C'mon, Cap. The wind is nasty."

Fairner wrestled him hack to the vat and started to shove him inside.

"No." Stalts balked. "I'll sit watch. It's your turn to sleep."

"Doesn't much matter does it?"

"No." He slumped. Mi'ing's people would walk away regardless.

So the kid stuffed salvaged rags beneath his broken leg, providing meager comfort at least, and hugged him near, sheltering the larger holes in his armor.

"You all right, kid?" Doubts gnawed. He'd just robbed Fairner of a night with a toasty female body—a prospect a damn sight better than this.

"I'm fine."

"You sure you wouldn't have liked a little stroking?"

"Not from her."

"You ever sleep with Iva?" The words spilled out, unexpected.

"Yes, sir." Fairner's voice broke. Stalts's jaw clenched. "I'm sorry if that offends you. I loved her."

Stalts forced his teeth apart. "We all loved her, kid." Which was too true. He asked her to marry him once. But she wouldn't give up the rest of the troop, loved them all, family. If she quit fighting, she'd never see them again. He didn't ask twice. He should be outraged to learn she'd knowingly slept with a breed—wasn't. Iva loved people—that's all, and he couldn't imagine a man who loved Iva letting the likes of Mi'ing touch him. It boosted his respect for Fairner.

"Key your helm lamp." He put a hand behind the kid's helmet and tugged it nearer.

Light glowed, illuminating Fairner's face. He stared at the kid's teary eyes and quivering lips. Even coated with days of grime and sweat, the kid was pretty, but worn to the bone, nerves raw, cheek twitching from too much damper.

Mi'ing meant him no good. Rage bubbled up.

"The bitch." He let his head drop. Fairner's arm settled over him. The light went out. "You hurt, Kid?"

"It's all right. Sleep."

He yielded, started to drift, then snapped awake again. "Don't sell me out, Fairner." His heart misbeat. "Don't go sneaking off because you think it's for my own damn good. Mi'ing will leave me now no matter what. And don't do it for duty or honor. Whatever suicide mission Mi'ing's thought up, its only to earn her kill points. Won't make a damn bit of difference to this battle or she'd have sold it that way first. The bitch'll for sure claim the tine kill. She can't do that with either of us alive."

"That's what I figure." Fairner's head sagged. "Thanks for stopping me out there."

"Thanks for offering to go."

Fairner's arm tightened around him. The kid shuddered. Stalts laid his head down and slept deeply.

They woke to the rumble and quake of heavy bombardment in the distance—a big ship sizzling the planet. The question was, whose?

Fairner wriggled outside and crouched at the vat's opening. "We're alone, Cap."

Mi'ing had made good on her threats.

"I—" A groundswell slammed Stalts silent. When things settled, he wriggled toward Fairner. "Better move."

Fairner pulled him out into a murky dawn, picked him up and started walking.

"You can still leave me, Kid."

"No I can't."

The murk grew darker as the day wore on. Airborne debris clogged the sky and weighted the air, making it difficult for Stalts to breathe through his broken filter. By midday—finding no shelter, no safe place to stop—they traversed the flat rubble of preinvasion fire targets. From his perch on Fairner's back, Stalts watched smoke eddy over Fairner's boots and crawl up his thighs. Behind them the bombardment stopped.

Fairner wobbled, failing. Stalts didn't know how the breed had gotten them this far. Pulverized construction stone skittered and crunched. Fairner lurched, legs sprawling, braced his feet and managed to steady, but a sound escaped his chest.

"Stop."

Fairner walked on. Until both his feet skidded and they went down, the kid's arms slamming the ground. Stalts rolled free. Fairner's helm opened, and his body convulsed, strangling on dry heaves.

Stalts lay still. Holes gaped in his damper, but with his extremities numb, his legs hurt less and less. He envisioned the damage progressing up his spine, slowly paralyzing him. Let it go. He choked down despair and squirmed against Fairner's back, slipping his hand inside the kid's faceplate to press chill fingers to the man's forehead.

"Damn you." Burning with fever, Fairner whimpered as he wrestled him over and pulled the water tube from Fairner's collar. The tube was dry. So he tugged his own free and leaned close to reach Fairner's mouth, forced to breathe Fairner's stinking breath. It was worth it to hear the kid swallow and sigh with momentary relief. They were done.

He wrapped himself over the breed—for all the good that

did—and went limp, conserving energy, ordering his thoughts, trying to make his peace.

"Sorry, Cap."

"Don't be an idiot. You did good. You did fine." He hugged the breed's shoulders.

"Not good enough."

"Why? There someone else you'd rather die with?"

Fairner's breath caught. "Yeah. Mi'ing."

Stalts laughed. Fairner giggled.

"Her looey will get her eventually."

Fairner giggled again—fritzed.

"Funny—" Stalts talked to distract the kid. "Funny how you think you know people. I thought I really knew my troop. I loved every one of you. But I never knew the twins were kleptos, you were a breed, or that Curly and Iva would keep that from me. Didn't know them at all."

"You're wrong." Fairner's voice shook. "You knew what they needed. Took care of them. They worshiped you, were good people. You knew that, which is all that counted."

"Worship's a bit strong." Lying there dying, Stalts knew his troop had never been the richest nor most successful. "I never got them as much as they deserved."

"Yeah, you did. You gave them respect."

"They deserved that. Hell, Fairner, I'm sorry I never gave you more."

"I got it secondhand. From Buggs, Curly, and Doyle." His voice broke. He sucked a long breath. "More than I got anywhere else. You took me on, so they respected your decision and gave me respect by default."

"Hell. You were forced on me."

"I know. But I didn't tell them." Fairner swallowed a sob. "Gods, Cap, I should've told them. I should've."

"Let it be." He hugged Fairner, pressing his palms to the kid's burning cheeks. "They'd have resented the forcing more than you."

"Yeah, they hated people to cause you trouble. They worshiped you."

"Don't start that again."

"Why? You think I tried to save your life for myself?"
Fairner laughed, a weak hiccup. "Until last night, I was hauling
you on my back just to keep them from haunting me. They
would if I let you die."

A tear started from Stalts's eye. "Damn you."

"Cap!" The kid shuddered, shivering uncontrollably.

"It's all right." He curled around Fairner and rocked him.
"It's all right." The kid relaxed, then stiffened. "Zammers."
Stalts raised his head and held his breath. Damn. Listening with
aching ears as the craft flew nearer, he recognized the vibrations.
Their own. But the crew would never sensor them in this mess.
Smoke eddied and whirled. The zammers passed overhead. He
clung to Fairner. The kid went limp, past caring.

Captain?"

He woke with an oxygen pad stuck to his face, feeling no
pain at all, just a lightness. It didn't make sense. You don't die
this way.

Someone yelped.

"Fairner!"

They held him down.

"He's all right," the med said. "Just relax." Rescued? By
gods. Rescued!

"How'd you find us?"

"Captain Mi'ing's troop turned in your location."

"Mi'ing?"

"Well, her lieutenant. Mi'ing didn't make it."

Stalts's breath sighed out. "It's happened to nicer people."

Cap?"

Stalts peeked from his bunk, startled. He'd taken transient
quarters while waiting for the army to toss him. His legs were
healing, but he didn't have it in him to try to scrounge a troop
or beg an officer's slot off some old friend. There were favors
he could call in, but none big enough, none he wanted to collect. So who'd be visiting him now?

Fairner.

"Hey, Kid. I thought someone scooped you up." Fairner'd barely stayed in Med two days. The condition they released the kid in was a crime, but Fairner wanted to leave. So Stalts signed his freedom pass. He hadn't expected to see the tuber again.

"How're the legs, Cap?"

"Good, but therapy's a bitch."

"Yeah." Fairner waved the pressure brace on his right arm, evidence of deep muscle reconstruction.

"What's up, Kid?" Fairner had that look, working some game. "You got a berth?"

"Maybe. Been with friends."

Fairner waved behind him, and Stalts noticed the nearest bunks all stood empty. A chill trickled down his spine. His stomach yelled a big unh-unh. But he owed Fairner his life. So he slipped from the bunk and stood his ground as a pack of the ugliest breeds he'd ever seen filled the aisle behind the kid.

"Speak to me fast, Fairner."

"You still have your shield?"

"Not for long."

"You retiring?"

"Something like that."

"Don't."

"You haven't the right—"

But Fairner did, because technically he was still Fairner's captain and responsible for providing him a berth. That's how he'd ended up with the kid to begin with, paying off old debts to another officer stuck with Fairner.

"Cap—"

Sweat popped on the kid's forehead, and his cheeks reddened. The breed pack shifted restlessly. The kid glanced back and wobbled. Stalts's gut wobbled too as he saw the tuber clearly for the first time. Fairner was a ghost—exhausted, bone-thin, hair patchy, not eating right—if he was eating at all. And he hadn't begun to heal. You self-pitying old fool, Stalts cursed himself. He'd abandoned this man with nothing. The breed hadn't escaped the battlefield yet. No troop would take him in this condition. The kid would die.

"Fairner?"

"Cap. You want a troop?" The kid blinked and squinted, his

voice weary, scared, but defiant. "There's fourteen of us. Say yes, and we'll get more."

"Wha—" Stalts took several deep breaths before he understood. "Gods, Kid."

He looked from face to monstrous face as the breeds bunched at Fairner's back. They all wore that look in their eyes—the one Fairner used to wear with him—distrust. They wanted to hope, but didn't dare. How had Fairner coaxed them this far? What scam had the kid pitched? Did they know this captain for sale killed his entire damn troop? He breathed between clenched teeth. These breeds could all be more sapiens than Fairner, but none were passers, all were untouchables, genetic abominations, a captain's nightmare—except he wouldn't be a captain much longer. Fairner staggered. Alien hands reached to steady him. Stalts caught him first.

"Kid—"

Fairner blinked, his expression still hopeful. Stalts started to shake his head. But the kid wouldn't look away—and he owed this man.

"Say the word, sir. And you're still a captain. Give us a shield, and we'll be the loyalest damn troop ever."

Fairner's voice broke.

Stalts tugged the kid's head onto his shoulder, remembering what they'd both lost. Did the memory of his past troop demand that he do better than captain a monstrosity of breeds or demand nothing less? Fairner'd saved him for the love of the troop. The troop loved Fairner too—Iva did anyway. He knew that in his gut, remembering things now that he'd ignored when he'd been smug in possession of the others—Buggs, Rose, Joc, Phil—all of them. Would they haunt him if he let Fairner die? The kid straightened and stood back, aligning himself with the other breeds. His gut danced. "I need officers."

Fairner nodded. "Alta-Lieutenant Osh."

A huge woman stepped forward, all teeth and hard muscle. Stalts stared. Osh stared him back, her eyes intelligent and quick.

"The rest?" He nodded toward the pack.

"All good soldiers," Osh answered. "I keep my eye to the regiment breeds. You got a good one, just young. Phil talked like that—"

Realization exploded over him. He didn't have to retire broke or beg a troop. He could call in debts. Sucks, people would give him breeds. "Fairner," he said. "This game you're playing is dangerous."

"I figure—" The kid shrugged. "—there's a reason we lived, Cap. I've made this mine." Their eyes met.

"They know what happened to my last command?"

"They understand, sir. It wasn't your fault. Most officers try to get them killed." Stalts's lungs seized. His heart stuttered.

Forgiveness. No one else had offered it—not the review board, not himself. He bit down on his lip, tasting blood. Fairner, you damn nick.

"All right." He forced his clenched jaw open. "I'll play."

Fairner blinked, his expression muddled with relief and astonishment. "Yes, sir."

Respect.

It felt good, a prize damned hard to win in Fairner's game.

BARRY B. LONGYEAR HAS BEEN A FAVORITE OF *ABSOLUTE MAGNITUDE* READERS SINCE HIS FIRST APPEARANCE THERE IN ISSUE NO. 1. WE WERE LUCKY ENOUGH TO SERIALIZE HIS NOVEL *KILL ALL THE LAWYERS*. HE IS THE AUTHOR OF MORE THAN A DOZEN BOOKS AND A WINNER OF THE HUGO, NEBULA, AND JOHN W. CAMPBELL AWARDS.

The Dance of the Hunting Sun

Barry B. Longyear

It is Hrokah, Ita hunter of the Green Water clan, here beneath the seven moons, here before this fire, who has a strange story. I tell you now what I see:

There are drums, the calling of the witch child, and the great light. The Hunting Sun glistens, its yellow beams stream through the beards of the ratha trees, warming the land for the chase. Vapor rises where the light touches the moss, filling the air with the scent of wet green. Soon ancient Kibqui will rear on her haunches, lift her forelegs, and raise her withered arms to bless the Ita as the seven of us strike out across the giant grass to slay the swift tikry.

Kibqui's witch child sings the morning sun, the stalk, the chase, and the release of the spirit, the gift of the tikry. The witch child's voice is sharp in the air. I feel my breath quicken with the thrill, then it slows. I feel my back slump. My usual excitement standing before the Hunting Sun fades as I remember there are not seven of us before the sun today, but eight.

I look at the eighth without appearing to look. The edge of my sight takes the image of the visitor in his strange armor. Fadak uses a weave of stone-hard baka quills across his chest for armor, and I string a plate of sun metal over my heart. The visitor, though, is completely covered with ribs of silver and black, his head enclosed in a silver metal gourd with a side of dark glass. Behind the glass must be his face, but I cannot see it. If I cannot see it I cannot read it. I want to ask the witch about him, but Kibqui told us there would be a visitor on the hunt and not to shame her with foolish questions. There is a new amulet hanging from a chain around her neck. It is gray with three black lumps.

Before the hunt Kibqui said that the visitor is not the Lifebringer, even though he comes from beyond the world. "Much less than the Lifebringer," she hissed, sweeping with her claws at the ground before her forelegs. "Much less. He is a *man*." The strange word seemed uncomfortable in her mouth. Kibqui, she who could feel no fear, seemed afraid.

"What is a *man?*" I asked her.

Kibqui rose from her haunches and swept a clawed hand from her front to her tail. The witch's gesture was more than an admission of ignorance. It declared that the answer was beyond her sight—beyond any witch's sight. She looked at the amulet and turned her back on me.

Before the Hunting Sun, she turns her eyes to the sky. "Come, Akienda," calls the witch, bringing my mind back to the hunt. Again she calls the wind spirit, placing it at our faces to hide our scent from the tikry. She warns the spirits of the grass, brush, and stones of our coming and begs them to allow us to pass silently. The witch child cries out and beats again upon the drum that was ancient before her grandmother's grandmother first saw the Hunting Sun.

Before the hunt, Fadak told me that his clan mother, Ivah, had seen the visitor come the evening before, from her hut on the edge of the red cliff far toward the northern stars. She said he descended in a great hollow white log that roared thunder and vomited flame. I listened but said nothing. Too many strange things were happening for me to say them in words and be saying anything. Yet I remember the sound of the thunder in my dream of the night before. In the dream I saw a great plague coming to the land, sweeping the Ita and all of the tribes before it just as so much dust. My dance is troubled and I look to the Hunting Sun and send my prayer to dance once again in step.

At the hunt, in the light of the sun, I feel the hair on my back rise as I feel strange eyes looking upon me. I look again at the visitor, no longer hiding my gaze. The dark glass of his head armor faces me and I am certain he looks at me. It is a soul-stealing look. With my spear in my right hand, I turn and face the visitor. "Why do you look upon me, evil thing?"

The name slips out without thought. Kibqui warned us about asking questions that would shame her and I had asked such a question. It was the question on my heart, though, and my guardian, the Twisted River, would not reproach me for speaking my heart. It is my right as Ita.

Kibqui stares at me, her yellow eyes fierce with anger. Before she can speak, the visitor faces her and speaks, the voice a crackling jumble of sounds. As he speaks, Kibqui's expression hardens. With her magical powers Kibqui understands the visitor's talk. I do not understand the talk, but I do understand Kibqui's face. She is greatly troubled.

The *man* faces me and Kibqui says, "Hrokah, show the *man* your yellow armor."

My claws click against the sun metal as I place my hand on the shield. The visitor takes three steps toward me on his two legs. When he is almost on me, he reaches out his armored hand. I lower mine from the shield and the visitor leans toward me. For a moment I see something behind the dark glass of his head armor. There are tiny red and yellow lights and two blue ones. The lights are smaller than winged daphs. There is a head behind the dark glass yet the face is only a shadow.

The visitor's hand touches my sun metal shield, then he takes his hand away. Reaching up with his other hand, he seems to twist off the first hand, but soon the first hand is bare. It is a fragile, pale thing, with hardly any hair. Instead of claws it has curved plates at the ends of the fingers. The naked hand reaches up and again touches my shield. He moves the fingers across it, then down to the bottom. There he lifts it to judge its weight. When he releases it the visitor faces Kibqui and makes more talking sounds. When he is done Kibqui aims her yellow eyes at me.

"Hrokah," she says, "there is a different hunt for you today.

Take the visitor to the Yellow Valley. Show him the Sun Metal Stream. Help him in his hunt."

All I say, of course, is "Yes, Kibqui." Much in me wants to rebel, though. I lead the hunt for the tikry. Was it not the Twisted River who favored me with my speed, my courage, and my strength? Was it not the wind who selected me from all the Ita to carry the first spear?

Still it is Kibqui who extends the hospitality of the Ita to this visitor, and Kibqui serves the spirit of the fireside, Nanlo, who commands our hospitality to all who come. I serve Kibqui and so I hold out my hands to the *man*, turn, and offer my spear to Yataneh. He takes it from me and, as he holds the weapon across his chest, Yataneh stares at me with brooding eyes.

"The visitor, Hrokah. Why is he here? What is his interest in the sun metal?"

"Am I Kibqui to have such answers?" I demand.

Yataneh is not daunted by my bluster. "Hrokah, before the morning I had a terrible dream."

"I too, Yataneh." I place my hand on his arm and say, "I have fears, but I know nothing. Kibqui commands me to take the visitor to the Yellow Valley to hunt. I will do that. I command you to take the hunt for the tikry. You will do that."

Fadak walks up and holds his arm out, his fingers and forearm pointing straight up, his sign for the visitor's flaming log. Then Fadak lowers his arm and places his fist over his shield of baka quills, signing me to be on my guard.

I turn from Yataneh and take the trail deep into the shadows of the ratha forest. I do not look behind me, but I hear the steps of the *man* following. The witch child stops her singing and the hunt begins.

The shadows are still long as we reach the rocky pass into the Yellow Valley. I look back to see if the *man* has kept up, and he is close behind me. I turn and hold out my hand toward the pass. "The Yellow Valley is beyond."

The visitor rocks his upper body toward and away from me. As I watch he removes both of his armored gloves and attaches them to his waist, where are attached many mysterious things. After that I hold my breath as he grasps his head armor, twists it, and removes it from his head. I almost do not notice him attaching his head armor to his back as I stare at his face. His eyes are deep-set and dark, his skin almost hairless and pale. The skin glistens from moisture and he wipes his hands across his face. He looks very weak; as though the youngest child, born this reason beneath the fourth moon, can overpower the *man*. Still, he does not act weak. Instead he behaves as though all of the gods of land, sky, and water are guiding his footsteps and guarding his back.

He looks at something on his arm. It is a black flap that suddenly erupts in little red and blue lights. Letting his arm fall, he takes a strange tube from his belt, places the wide end of the tube over his mouth and nose, and breathes deeply. Before he takes another breath he cracks open his armor, steps out of it, and gently leans it against one of the few trees that grow near the valley. He takes another breath from the tube, then removes a silver bottle from the armor's belt and attaches it to the pale green skins that now cover his body. The tube is attached to the bottle and the *man* takes another breath from the tube. He takes several more things from the belt and attaches them to his green skins. Finally he takes something and holds it out to me.

The thing dangles from a chain and it is an amulet like the new one Kibqui wears. He gestures toward me to take it. With his other hand he pulls a similar amulet from within his green skins and shows it to me. I do not understand, but I take the amulet. He gestures once more and I place the chain over my head. The human speaks and again the words are just a jumble of sounds. Yet there is meaning to the words. The sense of it is, "Can you understand my words?"

"Yes," I answer, my voice quiet in the face of this magic. He takes a step toward me, plays with the lumps on the amulet, and asks again. "Can you understand my words?"

"Once more, yes."

His head bobs once. "Now I can understand your words." He points at the amulet. "Kibqui told me that I must tell you:

this is not magic. It is a tool of my people, made for under-standing words."

I look down at the thing hanging before my shield. I think a moment about stupid questions and that Kibqui is not here. I look at the *man* and say, "Tell me why you have come."

The skin above his eyes bunches toward the center of his forehead as he adjusts his own amulet. "Say the same thing once more using different words," he says.

"What is your goal, *man*, that brings you to the land of the Ita?"

"Goal?" He thinks for a moment, then he points toward my shield. "I come for to find the sun metal. There are other met-als. And special stones I come for to find them, also."

I hold up my head, my tone suspicious. "This is all?"

The visitor bursts out with odd sounds and shakes his head. The sense I get through the amulet is, "You are amusing." When he stops making the sounds, he says, "This is all. I come for the metals and the stones."

Then it is my turn to make sounds of happiness. I wasn't cer-tain why the visitor had come. I thought he might be here to hunt our souls, to change the Ita life, to hunt and kill the gods, and many other things each one more awful than the next. He asks me, "Why do you find my words amusing?"

"I know you hunt, *man*. I feared what you hunt to be our rare treasures, yet all you hunt are the metals and some stones. We have mountains of metals and stones."

He takes a breath from his tube and points at my shield. "Mountains of this?"

I look at my feet, bend down, and pick up a few pieces of sun metal. I come back up and open my hand, holding it out to-ward the visitor. "Witness this. These are small pieces. In the Sun Metal Stream the pieces are much larger."

He looks into my hand, his eyes wide. He says, "Most sa-cred excrement!" except the *man* words are much shorter. He squats down and picks among the dirt of the trail. After picking up several things, pieces of sun metal, more pieces of night metal, moon stones, blood stones, water stones. "Savior!" he says, and again, "Most sacred excrement!"

It is a gift to me to share in the visitor's spiritual ecstasy and I call to him, "Man, only a few steps from here, in the valley at the stream, there are lumps of those metals and stone that make what you find on the trail look like dust."

He falls over backward, his eyes aiming in different directions. His right hand slaps about until it locates the tube. He places it over his mouth and nose, sucks in deeply three times, and says, "I forgot to breathe." He makes those sounds again, except the sense of them is, "I am so happy."

After a moment he stands and says, "I am ready to see this stream." I turn toward the pass, happy to lead the visitor to something that means so much to him. He follows, but he does not throw away the pieces of metal and stone he picked up from the trail.

Deep within the Yellow Valley, we reach the stream, choked with its lumps of sun metal. The gleam of the Hunting Sun reflecting from the wet metal hurts my eyes and I cross the stream and stand on the opposite side, my back warmed by the sun. The *man* stands before the stream, his mouth open, forgetting once more to breathe. After a breath from the tube, he allows his gaze to move across the sparse brush and flowers to the valley's rocky walls. There great bands of the sun metal reveal why it is called the Yellow Valley. He studies the walls, shakes his head, and squats by the stream. Reaching into the water, he seems to caress one lump of sun metal, then another; he lifts a third, drops it back into the water, then reaches in again and comes back out with a hand full of stones.

I see moon stones and blood stones, a few pieces of warm ice, and greeneye. The visitor takes another look up at the valley walls and shakes his head once more. Another breath and he takes a small thing from his waist and holds it over the stones in his hand. The thing is filled with tiny colored streaks. Quietly I hear him say, again and again, "Most sacred excrement."

I do not understand his spirit communion, nor the part served by the stones and metals. Each of us, though, has different ways. The Ita call upon the Hunting Sun. The Atog follow the matah herds. The Resah burn ratha beards and wash them-

selves in the smoke. It was the Lifegiver who told all our an-
cestors that all ways lead to the spirit, and that no way is higher
than any other. Although it seems strange to me, who am I to
look with scorn upon this appeal to sacred excrement? It is
enough to see the *man* at one with his god.

Later we climb the walls of the valley and he holds the small
thing with the colored streaks over many different parts of the
walls. By then he has lost his words, his eyes wide and lost in
dreams. He fills the pouches in his skins with stones, then emp-
ties them and refills them as he finds a new stone, clearer,
brighter colored, bigger. At last he sees the helplessness of his
efforts to carry the valley and he keeps only one of each kind of
stone and metal. As we walk the ridge above the valley, the *man*
says, "I see no villages, no huts, in the valley. Does no one stay
here?"

"No one makes a village here," I answer. "There are better
places." I push at the trail with my right foreleg and dislodge a
lump of sun metal the size of the visitor's hand. "Little grows
here. In the village there is land that grows food, grains to feed
our animals, thatch for our huts, grasses for our beds and cere-
monial masks and dresses. Such land is very valuable, for most
of the world is like this," I say as I hold out my hand toward the
Yellow Valley below. "It is crowded with metals and stones where
only a flower here, a stem there hangs onto life with the great-
est effort."

"Most of the world," says the *man*. He turns, looks away
from the valley for the first time and faces the Hunting Sun now
touching the mountains far to the west. The sun metal in those
mountains, and in the hills between the mountains and our feet,
fills the eyes with thousands of reflected beams. I took the visitor up here to see this, since the sun metal is so close to that
which he worships. There is no appeal to Most Sacred Excrement, though. Instead he stares silently at the reflections until
the Hunting Sun begins the sleep. We return to the village by
the light of the moons, the dancing sisters of the Hunting Sun.

That night the Ita hunters dance as the others cut the tikry meat,
wrap it in innon bark and layer it in the fire pit above the great

bed of coals. Once the layers are done, atche fronds are placed to cover the pit, allowing Nanlo to mix the steams and juices. The drums and harps begin and are soon joined by the whistlers and singers. Soon the dancers are joined by their mates and by the growers, gatherers, weavers, and builders. As the flames from the corner fires climb into the night, the dancers throb to the drums. In between the corner fires, rising on a pedestal of hammered black metal, now burnished bright silver, is the perfect globe of polished sun metal, the Hunting Sun we carry with us into the night.

I am about to rise and join the dance when the visitor comes out of his silence. He sits on a grass mat, his legs crossed. The look on his face is not the happy look he had in the valley when he was praying to Most Sacred Excrement. "The singing. What are the words?"

"It is thanks," I tell him. "Thanks to the wind for staying in the faces of the hunters, thanks to the trees, branches, and rocks for not warning the tikry of the hunters' approach, thanks to the tikry for allowing us to share its life, and thanks to the Hunting Sun for seeing that we all found today what it was that we hunted."

"All of us?" asked the *man*. "You were taken from the hunt, Hrokah. What were you hunting that you found?"

"I found what pleased you, *man*. I found the sun metal, the dull metal, the black and orange metals, I found the moon stones, and blood stones, warm ice, and greeneye. Mountains of them. Although not challenging, that was my charge today from Kibqui. The Hunting Sun granted me a great success today. What of your hunt, *man?* It too was a success."

"A weak word," he answered.

"I have no other word."

The *man* looks down and shakes his head. "I mean that my hunt succeeded more than I could have possibly imagined."

I study him for a moment, not wanting to be discourteous, but fearing nevertheless that my hunt might not have been as successful as I thought. "When you sit like that, *man*, and your face twisted so, I have learned these are signs of your sadness. What of your hunt are you missing?"

"Nothing." I see his head moving slightly to the beat of the drums. "I think I might have found something I didn't even know I hunted."

"Was this granted you by your spirit, Most Sacred Excrement?"

The visitor holds up a hand. After a moment he waves it back and forth. "No." His teeth bare in a sign of amusement. "No. Most Sacred Excrement is not my guardian spirit." He seems to freeze for a moment. He slowly lowers his hand and stares at the grass mat in front of his knees. "I may be wrong about that." He stays silent and deep in thought. Finally he faces me and says, "None of this has any importance to you. The sun metal, the stones, the other metals."

"They are useful," I answer. "The sun metal is easy to work into cups and shields. The orange metal is very good for cooking pots and needles, but it is very hard to work. We smash the moon stones into dust and use it to wear down and polish wood, metals, and other stones. Moon stone dust is very good for that. The children play with the blood stones and greeneye. I made my mate a rope of greeneye stones to wear down her back. These things have many uses, but they are not important."

The visitor faces the dancers and asks, "What is important?"

I am very troubled by the question, for there are many important things. If the visitor is testing me, Kibqui would want me to do well. "Health is important. Food. And water. Land in which to grow food is important. The hunt. The hunt is very important. Children, our mates, the spirits of the land, water, and sky. Avai is my mate. I am important to her."

"You know this?" he asks.

"Of course. It is part of the dance." I look away because I don't want him to see in my eyes how foolish I judge his question to be.

"What is most important to you, Hrokah?"

I realize how little he knows and I scold myself for thinking the *man* foolish. For one who knows nothing of the Ita, it is a good question.

"Most important to me is the dance."

He nods toward the dancers and asks, "This?"

"Yes. This is part of the dance." I point at him and then to myself. "We too are part of the dance. We hunted for different things, we danced in step with the Hunting Sun, and found what we sought. That is a very important part of the dance. The morning before a hunt, standing silently in the mists, waiting upon the Hunting Sun, is my favorite part of the dance, for then my soul fills with the belonging I have here, with the Ita, with the land, with the Hunting Sun, and with the universe."

He is silent for a long time and I think his questions are at an end. The beat of the drums catches me and I rise to join the circle around the image of the Hunting Sun. Soon my body is filled with the music and my eyes are filled with the light of the fires. The children of the Ita come to the dance ring, staying to the edge as their teachers watch to see how well the children have learned their dances and songs.

My spirit is carried high above the fires, up into the land where the Hunting Sun never sleeps. As I fly among the stars, I smell the scent of my mate. Avai's image comes into my mind, and she sings to me:

> *Hrokah, I see your dance.*
> *It is so strong and clever.*
> *Now has the Hunting Sun honored you today?*
> *What have you brought to the fire?*

I answer her:

> *Avai, you see my dance.*
> *It is more than it has ever been.*
> *The Hunting Sun has granted me all that I wished.*
> *I bring to the fire two full hearts.*

I hold out my hand toward the *man* and see that he is looking back at me, the word amulet in his hands. He looks as though he is being ridden by a ghost. He rises and leaves the fire. Perhaps I am wrong about the fullness of his heart.

That night I am anxious to sleep. Tomorrow there will be another Hunting Sun and I hope to stand before it with my spear.

There is something that needs doing first, and before we sleep Avai and I conceive our first child, named Ka*man* for the visitor.

I dream again about the thunder. I see tribes of strange beings slaughtering other tribes, mighty spirits who once ruled worlds fading into shadows, the Ita facing a bleakness of life and soul bringing a pain that cannot scream. Warriors, hunters, growers, weavers become sick and then become nothing, their souls lost to walk the universe in endless dark while their bodies sit lonely and wishing for death. The dream awakens me long before the rise of the Hunting Sun, the images of lost souls still warring behind my eyes. There is a shadow in the opening to my hut. It is Kibqui.

I rise and go into the night, the corner fires now only coals and sweet smoke. "Can I serve you, Kibqui?"

The witch studies me for a long time. Without moving her gaze she says, "I saw your dream, Hrokah. Did the Dreambringer tell you why she brought you that dream?"

I shook my arms and let my head lean toward my right shoulder. "I did not see the Dreambringer. I thought I might have taken the dream from Avai."

"Not that dream, Hrokah. Avai's dance moves its steps through peace and beauty. The dream came from elsewhere."

I straighten my head. "The *man*. The dream came from the *man*."

Kibqui turns and walks the few steps to one of the corner fires. She lowers herself to the grass mats and looks up at the globe of the Hunting Sun. I lower myself next to her, watching her face. "You like the *man?*" she asks.

"I do. It was great fun finding the things he wanted and pleasing him so. Avai and I have named our first child Ka*man.*"

"A good name. A name of significance." The witch, her troubled face looking up at the stars, says, "I see your thoughts, Hrokah. I see everyone's thoughts. That is the gift bestowed upon me by the Hunting Sun. I see also the thoughts of the *man* but I do not understand them."

"What are the thoughts like, Kibqui?"

"Like your dream."

To have thoughts like my dream makes the visitor a tortured creature. "Where is he?"

"Gone." The witch holds her hand up at the stars and says again, "Gone."

There is the hard feeling of loss in my chest. "Will he return?"

Kibqui looks at my pleading face and her eyes fill with sadness. "He says he will not return, but perhaps he lies. The ghosts that drive him are very dark." She opens one hand and holds it open to me. On her palm are the metals and stones the *man* chose from the valley. I take them and hold them.

I look up at the stars and wonder if he will return. I, too, read something in his thoughts. Once he had the dance but it was taken from him. He wants the dance again. I thought his love for the sun metal would bring him back his dance, but I was wrong. His dance is from another sun. The witch goes to her hut and I look up at the image of the Hunting Sun and pray that, wherever he goes, the *man* will find his dance.

Now that my steps are slow, now that Kibqui dances in the sky and is followed by three more witches, now that my own firstborn is the witch who prays for the Ita each day before the Hunting Sun, I know the visitor keeps his word not to return. I thought he came for the sun metal. I think he thought the same. I do not know why he left. I am not sure he knows. Still I look at the stars and pray for him to find his dance, this visitor, the *man* George Six Eagles.

TERRY BISSON HAS WON THE HUGO AND NEBULA AWARDS AS WELL AS THE STURGEON AWARD FOR SHORT FICTION. WHEN ASKED, AT A PARTY, TO WRITE A STORY FOR *ABSOLUTE MAGNITUDE,* TERRY SMILED AND SAID, "I'M NOT GOING TO SEND YOU A STORY." THIS IS THE STORY HE DIDN'T SEND TO US.

10:07:24

Terry Bisson

Hello?

It's me.

What is it this time?

I have this great idea for a story.

Not another science fiction story. Do you have any idea what time it is?

Sure, it's 10:07:24. But you're going to love this one.

Please. I don't have time for it.

This is a story about Time, as a matter of fact.

I can't use another time travel story.

This is different! In this story, it's Time itself that travels.

So what? Time always travels. It stops, it goes.

In this story Time does nothing but travel. It can't stop. It can't not travel.

I said no science fiction.

No way! This is speculative fiction, based on the cutting-edge ideas of the new physics. This is real Rudy Rucker stuff! Imagine a universe where time never stops. It just rolls on, hour by hour, minute by minute, second by second. Minisecond by minisecond.

I don't get it. What do you mean, time never stops? There's no Present? No Now?

Exactly! By the time you say the word "now," that Now is gone, and there's another Now. Then another and another.

Time only stops for like a second at a time? Is that the idea?

Time doesn't stop at all! Not for a second. Not for a mini-micro-nanosecond. It keeps flowing along, like a river. Like an ever-rolling stream. Like a bowling ball!

That's ridiculous. There has to be a Now where Time is stopped. Like right now—10:07:24. Otherwise how could anything exist?

In this universe we're talking about, everything exists in the Now, but it's a moving Now.

Isn't that a contradiction in terms—a moving Now?

In our universe, the real universe, yes. But in this speculative universe, it's the other way around. Look at it this way. When we visualize Time, it's like a series of lakes, right? They're all at . . .

I'm not stupid. I know what time is like.

Sorry. But now visualize a universe in which somebody has blown the main dam, so to speak. Time is a stream: moving, flowing like a river, continually in motion—

Ridiculous. Not only intelligence but matter itself would be unthinkable under such conditions.

But what if the moving Now seemed perfectly normal to the denizens of this universe? Imagine it! Riding the foaming crest of Time like surfers on a wave. Poised between past and future on an ever-changing, never changing Now . . .

Stop! Who'd want to read stuff like that? Makes you dizzy just to think about it.

Exactly! It's dizzying, disturbing, exhilarating, thought-provoking. That's the whole idea! It will start a whole new literary trend. We can call it chronopunk, a mind-blowing new meta-fiction from the cutting edge of quantum physics where . . .

You're wasting your time. I can't imagine it. I won't bother to. A world in which Time never stops? Never even pauses! That's worse than science fiction; it's fantasy.

But that's where you're wrong. Are you ready for the best

part? I didn't make this up! It's all based on science fact. At least theory. I read about it in *Omni*.

Omni. No wonder.

Seriously. Scientists are speculating about alternate universes where Time might flow in a constant stream. Where there's never a fixed chronological point, not even for a microsecond. It's never been demonstrated, of course, but it's possible, according to the laws of relativity and quantum mechanics. It's even probable.

Like light matter?

Exactly. Or suns. That's the beauty of science fiction. We can take the far-out ideas of theoretical physics and make them seem real by putting them in a story.

I thought you said this wasn't science fiction.

I was using the term loosely. I meant speculative.

And there hasn't been even a hint of a story.

I was just getting to the story. You have these people—a woman and a man, say, so you've got a love interest. She's a scientist. She looks at her watch and suddenly . . .

Why is the woman always the scientist?

He's the scientist, then. Whatever. Looks at his watch. What time is it? she asks. Well, he can't tell her! Time keeps changing! He waits for it to stop but it doesn't. There's no Now! Now is continually turning into Then—

I thought you said it was normal for them.

Okay, what if it wasn't. What if they were just noticing. You have to have a story. It could be funny! He looks at his watch and says, "The time is . . . is . . . is . . ." She says, "Well?" He says, "Is . . . is . . . is . . ." It could be hilarious.

A guy looking at his watch and stuttering is not all that hilarious.

It could be an adventure, then. They try to do something about it. That's it, of course! They're both scientists, faced with the ultimate disaster. Runaway Time! Maybe they try to stop Time. With an atomic clock. Or something.

I hate to interrupt, but it is 10:07:24.

Imagine the suspense! What if Time runs out before they can stop it? What if . . .

I hate to interrupt but we've wasted enough time on this.

You said yourself it's still 10:07:24.

Yeah, but it'll be another time before you know it. And I'm going to have to pass on this story idea. Our readers want stories they can identify with, not wild speculations on theoretical physics set in bizarre alternate universes, no matter how thought-provoking. Try a math magazine or something. One question, though. While it's still 10:07:24.

What?

What the hell's a rucky rooter?

SHARIANN LEWITT IS A THIRD-GENERATION MANHATTANITE. SHE DID NOT LEAVE THE CITY UNTIL SHE BEGAN HER GRADUATE STUDIES AT YALE. SHE HAS NINE BOOKS IN PRINT. HER MOST RECENT ARE *MEMENTO MORI* AND *INTERFACE MASQUE,* WHICH WAS SERIALIZED IN *ABSOLUTE MAGNITUDE.*

Mice

Shariann Lewitt

By the time they came back here they were just a myth anyway. The rest of us had gotten on with our lives so long ago that the stories of the Going Out were hardly told. Even the paragraph or so in the history files only got accessed via hypertext, and then only by someone who had wandered into the file by mistake. No one every really talked about them.

Oh, we all kind of knew they were out there in a kind of vague way. When I was little we would go to the rooftops late at night and Pop-pop would sear fish on the grill. And all the neighborhood kids sat around as he passed out thick helpings of fresh trout with the head still on and slabs of potato. And his voice would get very low while we were eating and he'd point to the stars.

"You see them?" he always started. "Some of those bright lights aren't stars. Some of them are your cousins out traipsing around, looking out for a place to make a world. They're supposed to come back for us when they find it but they never will. Two hundred years ago they went and no one heard anything since. Seven thousand people, maybe a hundred ships with names like *Hope* and *Harmony* and *Ulysses' Pride.*"

"What's a Ulysses?" asked the Mouse.

"He's a guy lives in a place called Night-town," Pop-pop said with authority. "He is the ruler of dark places, like the place they went." Pop-pop always treated the Mouse's questions like a real person had asked, and thought them through. He also served the Mouse a helping as big as anyone else's, even if the Mouse was small and scrawny.

The Mouse absorbed this information like everything else, thumb firmly planted between lips. The Mouse didn't really care, wasn't really there all the time. The Mouse was just a Mouse and had probably forgot everything anyway. Even if it was my friend the Mouse and I wouldn't let anyone treat it wrong.

"So anyway, you want me to tell you this story or you want me to call your parents and tell them that I don't want to see you on this rooftop?" Pop-pop scowled but none of us were really scared.

We knew he wouldn't ever tell on us. He might be the local crazy, but he was also the smartest person in the collective. He had been a great scientist in the Before, the time no one ever talked about. He looked at the sky because once he'd looked out the big telescopes and he knew where the others were and he was waiting for them to come back. Maybe he had lived two hundred years and remembered the Going Out. He sure looked two hundred, with more white hair in his ears than on his head that was all mottled with age spots.

Maybe he even was this Ulysses person, if such a person existed. We couldn't be quite sure, and the real little kids thought it was probably the proper name for the Bogeyman and they cried. At least till we told them that it was magic, and if you called the Bogeyman by his right name it was like Rumplestiltskin and he couldn't hurt you. That shut them up.

Anyway, so Pop-pop rambled on about the Going Out, and I'm not sure how much was real and how much was his head had been cooked with too much sorrow and too many pipes and too much staring at the sky. I even went to the Library to look it up. I walked the tunnels, the long empty stretches underground where I needed a torch to see the rats. There were a million rats between the rotted wood and metal that lay deep under the city.

The Mouse had shown me how to get here, crawling through the gates and jumping into the stinking inch of water that covered the bottom of the tunnel with slime. It was really gross and no wonder the grownups never bothered. But the Mouse and I are going to be explorers when we grow up. I pretend that my Mouse is going to be able to grow up so that we can go everywhere together, California, Boston, Samarkand. So the Mouse and I went exploring all the time and we finally found the Library.

I'd seen the picture before. Our collective class had gone to our own Library and there had been pictures. I recognized the lions out front. I climbed up on one of them like I was riding.

"Get down," the Mouse said.

Stupid, too-smart skinny little Mouse marched straight up the doors that were locked. No surprise. But that never stopped the Mouse from anything. Or me either, but I never did quite have the Mouse's crazy. Or maybe the Mouse just knew more than us from being a Mouse and we just didn't know. Couldn't get inside its head anyway, Mouse wasn't like the rest of us.

Momma didn't want me hanging with the Mouse. "Those things are tech-breeds," she said. "They're all made to get cancer and none of them lives past fifteen. It's just going to break your heart."

And she'd sigh. I bet she had her own Mouse friend once. There was the more formal arrangement between the nest and the collective. We fed the Mice and they were allowed to use our power, though often they're pretty good at dealing with power sources themselves. A lot of the grid work teams are even mixed. But we'll do what we can for the Mice in exchange for baby vaccinations.

The Mice were lab-teched to die. But they made all the immunities to the plague that we needed inside their veins. We don't die of disease anymore. It kind of seems like the Mice do all our dying for us.

So of course I hung with the Mouse tight after that. And snitched candy and desserts for it, since it didn't get except when Pop-pop felt rebellious.

The Mouse found a broken window where it could wiggle

in between the bars like no real kid could do. Mouse got skinny and weird and just slid in like it was water. Then the Mouse found a way to open the side door and got me in.

This Library was way more impressive than the one where our collective class met in the Bronx. Here were rooms and rooms with chairs and tables and things all piled that I didn't recognize. We wandered through two floors. All the rooms had gilt letters over the doors to spell out what the place was for. ORIENTAL LANGUAGES. EUROPEAN HISTORY. SCIENCE.

We looked in all of them and there were no terminals until we got to a big room without any of the ugly dark wood with green grunge on it and no gold letters. This one had black stenciling that said, RESEARCH CATALOG. I knew that was the good stuff. And sure enough, there were all the terminals and everything we could ever want only nothing was turned on.

Yeah, I keep forgetting that there aren't any collectives down here, just indies who don't have power servers on the public grid. I don't know how the Mouse did it, but the things came up after Mouse tinkered around. Maybe it was that it wasn't really human or really Mouse either, but something whose great-greats started out of some experiment that got loose.

Now Mice attach their nests to human packs for however long they'll live. They don't have parents or homes or anything, and if it wasn't for the collective they'd all die. Then we'd all die. So it does everybody good, though usually Mice and humans don't hang out like friends. There's just too many differences.

So the Mouse managed to access a power system. "I just plugged the big thing in," the Mouse said, with two fingers in its mouth. I shrugged. I don't care much how the things work so long as I can do what I want. Probably the collective had forgotten to shunt this place off their grid. They'd know someone had been draining off the facility, and if anyone was doing schoolwork or in power mode they'd probably track me down and tan my hide.

I didn't care about that. I'd been hit plenty of times before. I started scanning the texts looking for the Going Out link-ups and how that hooked in the Mice and the Before Time when people died the way the Mice do now. I don't know why I was interested. No one else except Pop-pop and the Mouse cared.

Everyone back in the gang was busy playing or foraging for the collective, or working on the plots to grow cabbage for winter.

I would rather explore than work. That was what I was going to do someday, be an explorer. Find all the stuff that Pop-pop told stories about. Like the plague times.

I was so fascinated by the plague times that I looked up the word on the hypertext and spent most of two days reading. Just after the Going Out, almost everyone on the planet died. Billions of people. I couldn't count billions, couldn't think them. But there it was, that was how many had died. They had stopped burying after a while and the bodies piled up in the streets and became good garden stuff, so Momma said.

Then someone called Griegsen created the Mice and ran all kinds of disease through them, and discovered the vaccine. So the plague was over and life went on, only it didn't go on quite as well because there weren't enough people to run things and so things started to fall apart some. The bad buildings no one wanted any more were empty, only the nicest ones got used.

And the grownups created collectives and ran power grids through the local area for the nice buildings and the places where they wanted people to go. The boring park where only little kids played on the swings and jungle gym, the Library where we had our classes, the places where we lived so we could log into the school network for kiddie-text.

That was one great thing about the big Library we found in the next city over through the tunnels. There was no kiddie-text, no baby passwords and grownup passwords that locked us out of the good stuff. I could go anywhere.

So I went exploring. I looked into the past, into the Going Out that Pop-pop described like he was there and that Momma said never existed. And it did too exist, I saw it right in front of me. Original documents and even pictures were loaded.

And Pop-pop was right. All the stuff he told us, even down to the names of the ships, was dead on. *Harmony* and *Hope* and *Ulysses' Pride*. (I checked Ulysses in the text and Pop-pop had been pretty out of it here. The goto said he was some Greek hero that took seven years to get home across some little dinky lake and had all kinds of adventures.)

"What does that mean?" the Mouse asked, and touched a

sticky finger to the screen, which responded immediately. I wish the Mouse wouldn't do those things, especially not when it left a dribble of bright red spit smeared over the glass.

So that was what I knew and there wasn't anything else about it and anyway even Pop-pop said I was wasting my time. There were better things to do than explore and it was summer and the gardens needed weeding. So I didn't see the Mouse for a while. Like most Mice, it went off to tinker with the power grid.

Then summer turned crisp and it was September. I wasn't looking forward to winter but I felt stranger than usual. I felt all hedged in and tied down when I just wanted to go. Anywhere was fine. Away.

The collective was dull and predictable, the kids too little and the grownups didn't understand anything. No one cared about exploring, not even here on the ground. At night I went up to the roof myself and looked at the stars and wondered which ones were our cousins.

Sometimes I lay on the roof and looked out and daydreamed that the Going Out was coming back. They'd arrive and they'd realize that I was really one of them and they'd take me out of this place. This damned boring collective where all the grownups talked about was the weather and the growing seasons and the kids.

I thought about running away. Through the tunnels, with the Mouse making everything smell like cinnamon candy, running away to where things were important. To where we cared about maybe Going Out again.

I lived more in my head than in the collective. Chores were only mechanical and I didn't care anymore. Inside my skull I was already gone and not paying attention at all. Which is how I nearly missed it.

I was working in the garden, turning it for the season, when everyone around me stopped and looked at the sky and started whispering. Another grownup thing, I figured. A heavy storm coming and they were all worried about the last few tomatoes and squash we hadn't harvested yet.

Then I heard the noise, so big it seemed to surround the whole world. Like it was too big for my ears and so I heard it in my leg bones. And I looked up and there was something shiny bright coming down from the sky. Not here to the Bronx. Over distant a ways.

Maybe there were a zillion things it could have been, but I knew only one and there wasn't any other thing possible. Them. The Going Out had finally returned, they had come for us. And it was time to say good-bye. I stood trembling, watching the shiny spot in the sky that I had never quite believed was real.

Now I was watching them come home. I'd imagined this moment a million times. Not once had I anticipated the noise, or the grownups full of awe, or the pervasive smell of cinnamon.

Cinnamon. The Mouse was here. It shouldn't be and I'd catch hell for having it in the garden. But hell, the Mouse deserved to watch too. They were its cousins as much as mine. And no one was telling the Mouse to leave.

The pattern was glowing farther from us, not nearer. I knew where they were going. I hadn't been there, but I knew of the fields out in Queens (where I had been at least twice that nobody caught me), the Mouse showing me the way in the tunnels and then over the broken fields and abandoned houses where there were no collectives for miles. The Mouse had found it—or some Mouse had found it and shown all the others and they were confused and we had to tell them about it. Only I didn't know what it was any more than they did, except it was for Going Out and coming home. Even the Mice knew that. They wanted more data than we had, more than the stories and the half-shrouded truths.

They wanted a way out themselves. Not to Go Out so much, but to live. To get the immune system the plague had left to the rest of us so they wouldn't die by fifteen. So they wouldn't have stunted and misshapen digits, so their faces would not be distorted to the familiar Mouse mask. So that, most of all, they would be able to grow up.

I wanted to go down to the field right away. It would take half the day at least and it was better to make it before dark. The Mouse could see pretty well, but there were still nasties around that I didn't want to get near. Besides, our cousins might be afraid of something that snuck up in the shadows.

Before I could slip away the grownups had called a stop-work and headed back to the collective. I went with the group and the Mouse trailed along. Everyone was too distracted to notice.

Our collective is all in one building, a very large yellow-brick thing with a gazillion apartments and carpeting in the corridors. We've got a whole power system in the basement, there is a kiddie-yard outside with swings, and we took half the top floor and turned it into collective space. Everyone in the group can fit into a corner of it, but the grownups are planning on the collective growing. When I turn sixteen, if I get voted in, I can choose any empty apartment in the building for my own. There are way more empty apartments than full ones, and even if someday we take over the whole place there are more and more buildings just like it all around. The Mouse nest is two buildings over in the same complex, all just the same only the Mouse nest has more power and air-conditioning. But then, they don't have to spend that much time on gardens.

We went straight up to the meeting space. We didn't even get washed up or changed even though we were covered in dirt, and we still weren't the first ones there. The babies were all crying and the grownups were arguing so loud I could hear them outside the door.

"What the hell is going on?"

"Has anyone heard anything from Queens Three?"

"Maybe it's just some junk, you know. A meteor or something."

I didn't follow any of the talk, and I wasn't interested. I just wanted to get out, to get over to Queens and see it all for myself.

That didn't happen. I got locked in the commons with the babies. For our own protection, the grownups said. Right. Because they were a bunch of cowards and they wanted to pretend that it was all going to go away. Then they'd tell us that it had been some sky junk or maybe that there was no Going Out and we were all making it up. Or maybe there had been some mold on the rye bread. Grownups seemed to think that every time something weird happened the food was bad.

So for three days I was locked in the commons with everyone else under sixteen. Some of us older ones tried to teach school and play cards, mostly because there was nothing else to do. And we were sick of the babies crying all the time. Give them something else to think about. Being a kid is really unfair. I mean, I knew exactly how to get to the landing field and no one would even listen to me.

But on the third day the adults came back to the commons. This time they were all dressed and clean and very orderly. We kids had stayed away from the public meeting area—the chairs were uncomfortable and there was enough room we didn't have to move them anyway—but the first group to arrive was a work team that straightened the seats and readjusted the podium umpenteen million times. And they wouldn't let us near the area at all.

After they let in the rest of the collective, though, they couldn't keep our parents from claiming us. So we all had seats with the families. Momma was so happy to see me and made such a fuss over me that I didn't get to ask one thing about what had happened in the outside world.

Munroe Beade, Pres Pro Tem of the collective, stood in front of the podium the way he always does. There were a few chairs facing the assembly and they were occupied by people I didn't know. I studied the faces, wondering why our cousins who had Gone Out looked so ordinary.

"Those two are representatives from Queens Three," Momma told me. I was embarrassed and glad I hadn't made any comments.

When everyone had hushed down, Munroe Beade began to speak the way he always does, way too fast and using his fingers to drive a point in like a rivet gun.

"Whatever landed over in Queens, they claim they are descendants of the Going Out. The communications facility at Queens Three has been in touch with collectives all over the world and it seems that at least fifty groups have landed. They say they have technology that we've lost, that we're degenerate and have forgotten everything important and they pretty much seem to think they're perfect. But I'll let the Queens Three people tell you about that because they've already had some heavy contact with these cousins. Well, at least they say they're the cousins, and they look it and they talk it so I don't have any reason to disbelieve them. But we'll have to figure that all out for ourselves."

I looked over the people in the seats of honor very carefully. It made sense that Queens Three was heavily represented. They've got the best comm tech in the Greater New York Area. All the collectives go through them and they rake in a fortune. They don't have to farm, even, they get produce from the others for doing their comm work.

Come to think of it, I wondered if I could apprentice over there. Either bring back some comm capability to our collective, or join over there. At least it would get me out of digging in the dirt. Not quite being an explorer, but sure better than being what I'd been.

"All the codes match," the Queens Three tech expert was saying. Her voice was dry, monotone, and made me want to put my head down and go to sleep. "I don't know how else to explain the group except they really are the cousins and they really have returned from the Going Out. I think we should listen to what they have to say."

There was polite applause. Then a tall dark man got up and came to the podium. He looked pretty normal to me, except that his clothes looked new and like they'd never seen hours of weeding between the rows. But even our own farmish collective would manage decent clothes for someone we sent out to speak. We work hard and we're poor, but we're not that poor.

He smiled. In his dark face his teeth stood out starkly. They were all perfectly straight, white, even. Fake teeth, they looked like to me. Just like the fake clothes and the fake too-clear face without any sun-lines or wrinkles or even the hint of beard.

"We are happy to finally return home," he started saying with a funny accent. "My great-great-great-grandmother came from this city. It's quite a thrill for me to see the place. Our family told stories about how she went to Radio City Music Hall and Rockefeller Center."

He was lucky no one booed. That stuff wasn't in this city. That was across the water on the island, and it was pretty much gone anyway. I think there's a collective down at Rockefeller Center, but I don't know for sure.

"Anyway, in this case the fact that you call us 'cousins' is accurate. And I'm very pleased to be here.

"I can also see that you've had hard times since my ancestor left here. I know there used to be over ten million people here, and the public transportation ran all night and that there were lights everywhere. You've had to survive some rough periods. And we understand that. We've had to survive some hard times ourselves. The early days in the generation ships were difficult, people born here were homesick and later generations fought over mission objectives. But I'm not here to tell you about what we had to go through. No, I'm here to tell you about what we can offer you."

"Power, technology, medicine, all the things we've been able to develop we want to share with you." He said it and he smiled so sincerely that the Mouse gasped.

"What's in it for you?" Granny Farley yelled. "Why you want to do this anyway? Ain't from the kindness in your heart."

The assembly got real still. The cousin's face looked frozen up in that too-perfect smile. He coughed. He hesitated. Then he began to speak again, only his voice wasn't so deep and smooth and his words didn't sound like they'd been rehearsed a zillion times.

"Well, for one thing, we haven't found a place to live," he said. "Wherever the ships of the Going Out have been, what stars and planets we've found, we haven't found a good one for human habitation. Now we want to return home, to bring you our technology and resources and education in return for a place to live. So that we can see the sky and feel the warm sun, things that people like me have never known."

I think we were supposed to feel sorry for him, but I just couldn't. There was something weird about the whole thing. Like, why'd they have to ask anyway. There's loads of empty space just waiting for folks to come and reclaim it.

"Well, you don't have to ask anyone," Leon McX said. Leon stood in the center aisle and even from a distance loomed over the visitor. Leon is not near so pretty kept as the cousin, has a scar on his forehead and more than a few on his hands, but he is the biggest person I've ever seen. Makes up two of the visitor, and wasn't on his holiday manners, either.

"Why do you think you got to ask?" Leon asked, brass like he always is. "You think we're gonna bother to sneak over in your sleep and kill you, then fry you up with some cabbage and freeze you down for winter rations?"

Everyone in the commons laughed. Even the Mouse laughed and the visitor looked real unhappy. "We had hoped to help you people," he said like he didn't know what was happening. "We can offer you a lot."

I just wanted to walk away. And that was what most of the collective seemed to do. Linny Gomez took out her knitting and rustled the stitch pattern. Jeff Towlman took out his mini-checkers game and started playing with Granddad Elkins. And finally Sarah Wheeler got up and ran her hands over her holiday skirt. "Well, I don't know about the rest of you, but we've got work to do," she announced. The rest of her harvest team followed. That was the only time I ever wished I was in a dirt brigade, so I could walk out on all the shocked stares of the too-perfect visitor and the communications group from Queens Three.

I was about ready to rejoin my old work team when Momma squeezed my hand. "I'm very proud of you," she whispered.

I jerked my hand away. I didn't want anyone to know that Momma still treats me like a baby. And besides, I had to get out with the team or else I'd get all kinds of black marks at the team meeting and then I'd really be in trouble.

So the cousins didn't ask again. They just set up in one of the nicer buildings down closer to the tunnels. And we didn't hear from them for a while and we really didn't care. There was enough to do already getting in the harvest and setting up the indoor garden in the commons area.

Let's go exploring," the Mouse said one day in early November. I agreed right away. First off, it was the kind of day when I just had to get away from the cooperative and the babies. A day when the sky was so crystal blue it just about screamed at us.

Idiot people, come on out and play while you can, because winter's coming and you'll all be stuck behind walls for days and days and eat cabbage and winter apples and shriveled up carrots. Oh yes, the November sky knows me like my old best friend.

And then there was the Mouse. It hadn't wanted to go out much recently, didn't want to explore or even stay up and watch the stars on the rooftop. It isn't an old Mouse, but maybe it had one of the Mouse diseases already. They were bred for disease, they were made to die.

I never thought of it before, but suddenly I wondered if making Mice had been a truly evil thing. I felt—I dunno. Bad somehow. As if it was my fault that the Mouse looked so ragged and seemed to drag all the time.

Maybe that's why Momma won't mix with Mice. Because we made them to die just before the Plague and studied them and used their bodies to produce vaccines. And even now, long as the Mice are around we're safe. Every baby gets a vaccine of Mouse blood and no one gets sick after that. Except the Mice of course.

So I felt really awful that the Mouse wasn't doing well and probably wouldn't live through winter. If this was a good day, then sure, I was up for some exploring.

"Where should we go?" I asked. Anything was fine with me. "Want to go to Queens? Or maybe back to the Library?"

The Mouse shook its head. "I want to get in to the cousins' collective and see how they live," it said. Then it hesitated. "I heard some scary things about them."

I shrugged. Whatever. I didn't think a cousins' collective could be all that interesting, but I didn't say so. If that's where the Mouse wanted to explore, that was fine by me. So I got on my sneaks and a sweater, and packed the tools of the exploring trade into a small bag the Mouse could carry. I packed a plastic lighter (ten zillion, courtesy of the corner stores) and some paper and a pencil to make a map in case we needed to, a compass, and five super-big Linzer tarts from out in the kitchen. I really like Linzer tarts, and that's better provisions than the usual bread and peanut butter.

The Mouse adjusted the pack proudly and we set out.

It was a glorious walk and it was good to be away from the

grownups and the collective. To be honest, the Mouse led. I didn't know exactly where the cousins' collective was and really hadn't bothered to find out. But the Mouse knew. And the Mouse was starting to slow down, hang back as if there was something it didn't want to know.

"Lunchtime?" I asked. I got out a Linzer tart and broke it in half. The Mouse nibbled delicately, not stuffing its face like I'd always seen before.

"I gotta ask something," the Mouse said, and there was a scared and jumpy look as if it expected something to explode out an alley.

"Sure," I said. "Whatever."

The Mouse's tongue lapped around it's mouth, and it wasn't as pink as it was before, and it wasn't the sugar from the tart that dulled the color. "Ummm, if we find anything, you know, bad. Really *bad.* You have to tell the nest. You have to tell everyone and make sure they know."

"You paranoid?" I asked.

The Mouse suddenly looked real thin and scared, the way Mice sometimes do. "It's okay," I said real fast. "I'll do that. Sure I will. Only let's hope there isn't anything really bad. I mean, we never saw anything really bad before, and we've been lots of places. We've done lots of things, gone far away. So there's no reason to think of anything really bad now, right?"

The Mouse nodded, miserable. There wasn't a thing I could do.

We walked only about two more blocks before the Mouse stopped. "There." It pointed at a gaudy building that didn't look all that solid or well kept. "That's their place."

I walked up to the front door. I didn't see anyone, not cousins, not a breath of movement. Over the door there was a sign that said something about a hotel.

Who would set up a collective in a hotel? I'd explored hotels before. They didn't have nice roomy apartments. They had single rooms and ugly furniture.

I was sure this was wrong. The Mouse just didn't know. That's okay. That's part of exploring. But even though this couldn't be the place we were looking to find I went right in.

The Mouse wanted to go here and I didn't want to hurt its feelings.

The bottom floor was all dead plants and smelly sofas and carpet that was breeding wildlife. "Let's go upstairs," the Mouse insisted.

We took the wide decorative stairs near the chandelier instead of the elevator. When we got to the landing I couldn't see anything but I sure could smell and it smelled evil. It smelled like peelings rotting in the compost heap and a backed up toilet and a Mouse nest that wasn't ever changed or dumped.

The Mouse began to squeak in a tiny voice. If it was human I'd call it crying. It has better smell than we do and I wondered if it knew any more.

"This is a very bad place," the Mouse whispered. "They were right in the nest, bad things happen here. Very bad for Mice."

I thought about that for a moment. "Well, maybe you should hide somewhere and I'll look around first. Then if I find anything interesting I can show you. But maybe it's not such a good idea for you to be out."

But the Mouse refused. "No," was all it said, and it stuck two fingers in its mouth and stared at the floor. The Mouse can be idiot stubborn like a little kid, not let go of an idea, and throw tantrums. This looked like a tantrum coming on, its mouth all twisty around its fingers and a storm-cloud petulance in its eyes. Momma always says to pick your fights, and this was one I knew no way I'd win.

"Okay," I caved in. "But you got to stay behind me and no sneaking ahead."

The Mouse face that looked all ready to cry lit up with pleasure. "Sure. I promise. We are explorers after all."

So we went up another flight of stairs, these ones hidden behind a soda machine and all concrete and ugly. But we got to the residence halls and the smell was overwhelming. I could hardly open the door for the stench.

The Mouse crept behind me as we ventured into alien territory. We heard movement but didn't see anyone. There was only the stink to guide us. Between that and the muffled sounds

I could believe the place was one of Pop-pop's haunt stories for Hallow's Eve when all the grownups try to scare us.

This was different, though. If I could believe that the dead walked, I'd believe it here.

And then one of the cousins staggered into the hall and lurched down three doors. It was a male, wearing a uniform like the one who came to speak to us before. Only this uniform wasn't so perfect and this person didn't look nearly so well-fed and sanitized. This uniform had dribbles of dried junk running down the front and the cousin was thin and off balance.

Sick. Even I could tell this was what sick meant. This was a dying thing, like the Mice when they finally succumbed to one of their cancers.

The Mouse wailed and scurried from behind me to get a better look. Mice always want to see the dying. And the cousin saw the Mouse and life got really ugly.

The cousin bellowed and pointed. "One of them, one of them," he shrieked, and a few doors came open and other uniformed cousins joined the one in the hall. They were all in some stage of sick, though some could walk better and others could shout louder. But bunches came out, lurching and staggering against the walls, and they chased down the Mouse.

The Mouse is fast and zipped down the hallway before any of those sickies noticed it was gone. It made straight for the door at the end of the hall. Must be another stairwell, I thought. I hoped. None of these cousins looked well enough to make it up or down any stairs.

I wasn't far behind. The cousins ignored me. It was the Mouse they wanted. But the stink when the Mouse opened the far door was enough that I nearly passed out then and there. And the Mouse froze in terror.

We had discovered a Mouse nest. Maybe twenty Mice or more, with the little ones and their sleeping rolls and their skimpy thin blankets huddled together. Only these Mice were dead, murdered in their own nest. Old violence showed on them, bashed faces full of blackened blood and covered in flies.

I wanted to puke and I wanted to cry. I turned around and saw the cousins were coming up behind. "C'mon," I said to the

Mouse. I tugged its scrawny hand and tried to get it to move. It wouldn't budge.

And really, I didn't know what I'd do if it did. Even though they were sick, there were a lot of them and they were all big. And now I saw the walking sticks, and long poles were weapons as well as tools. Every one was raised and ready to strike.

Nothing was safe and I couldn't see a place to run. I stood in front of the Mouse and faced them, ready to fight. They weren't getting my Mouse.

They ignored me. Or rather, they pulled me out of the way like an inconvenience. I fought, I tried. I beat my fists against their bodies and their sticks but they only passed me farther down the line.

The Mouse looked at me, helpless and terrified. Maybe it was dying soon, but it hadn't wanted to die like that. The cousins beat it over the head and I guess, I hope, one blow was enough to kill it. Mice have fragile bones. But death by itself didn't stop the blows from raining down. The Mouse was dead but the cousins were still hot in their anger.

I tried to stay. For the sake of the Mouse who had been my friend I truly tried. But I was shaking and had the dry heaves and tears were dripping down my face faster than an old battery leak. They didn't even notice me go.

I don't remember going back to the collective. I don't remember anything until Momma fed me sliced apples and soup. There were a lot of people in my room, some of the collective elders and Pop-pop and a few Mice. And two people down from Queens Three who all watched me very carefully.

"So tell us again what happened. Why did you go out with the Mouse to find the cousins?" our Pres Pro Tem asked.

"We were being explorers," I said, and sighed. I didn't ever want to go exploring again. And I told them the whole story, the sick travelers and the dead Mice. And how they had murdered the poor Mouse for no reason at all and how I had been too much of a coward to make them stop.

"You weren't a coward," Momma said. "You're still just a kid, you can't fight off a whole bunch of grownups. And they were armed and you were not. You did your best and we're all proud of you."

I wasn't proud of me. I was miserable that I hadn't been able to take care of my friend. And I had promised it that I would warn the other Mice.

"We can't kill all the cousins," Sarah Wheeler was saying. "They're all over the place and there's too many of them. And we don't have the communications."

"We don't have to kill them," I said. I could see it clear, perfect. All those bent and staggering outsiders who didn't understand. Who had already killed too many Mice.

They were all grownups, the cousins. They hadn't seen how much they needed the Mice. And so their own ignorance would kill them.

"All we have to do is make sure the Mice are safe," I said. "Tell the local nest. And put it out to Queens Three. They can get it around fast enough so that no new nests approach the cousins. And without the Mice and the vaccines, the cousins won't be around much longer. And we won't have done a thing. Nothing at all."

There was silence. "Kid's got a point," Pop-pop said. "Plain and simple Darwinism. If the organism can't adapt it dies. I think we've got a new scientist on our hands."

Grownups!

CHRIS BUNCH, WRITING WITH ALLEN COLE, COAUTHORED THE STEN SERIES AND THE BESTSELLING *WARRIOR'S TALE*. THIS STORY WAS CHRIS'S FIRST SOLO SF PUBLICATION. HIS *WIND AFTER TIME* SERIES IS PUBLISHED BY DEL REY BOOKS.

Amps

Chris Bunch

The zero hour came
and the Tellurian Armada of
eighty-one sleek spaceships
spurned Earth and took its place
in that hurtling wall of crimson. . . .

Failure, I've decided, smells like a sterile urinal.

You see, it's not hard at all, not hard, not hard, not hard. I tried dicting, but I couldn't pin my thoughts long enough, feeling them scroll past and away. So I shall pull the symbols out, slowly, slowly, but they shall come. I can *feel* them, just as the surgeons *felt* my nerve endings as they stripped them.

I traded this old keyboard from Seth for one of my backup screens. I guess he thought he was getting the vantage, but wait until he tries to put a full load on it.

Clot him. Clot all of them. I don't owe them.
1000110
1010101
1000011
1001011 them, as they used to say.

Only part of me hangs here.

Part of me is . . . somewhere else.

I'm not concerned with all those who're running around in black today, putting on mask faces of mourning, like they were backnumber posers or really gave a damn whether Vax is alive or not.

I certainly don't.

I haven't chosen that way, nor shall I.

1000110

1010101

1000011

1001011 Vax, too. The only reason anybody cares is he was one of the few of us who went Out. Not just Out, but on the bridge, until he broke and they took him off-line to The Ward and then sent him here to zoo-rot with the rest of us.

Or maybe they're empty about him because his mods didn't show as much as they do on some of us. He'd been able to keep his legs, for instance. He came into The Program later than I did, so they'd found a way to run a crossconnect from the coccyx into the converter, and kicking became analogue for thrust.

I wonder why modification, and being "ugly," at least in the holies' eyes, didn't matter to any of us when we entered The Program. I can't even remember whether I knew. I guess if I did, I wouldn't have cared much. Maybe if I thought about it, if any of us thought about it, it was so what? We're in transition, aren't we? Learn to think a new way, so why not change your body to match?

I don't know if I care now either.

So the ears are gone, so the eyes are flat white discs? So what?

1000110

1010101

1000011

1001011

0100000

1011001

1010101 if you don't like it. As they used to say.

Besides, I see you in a marvel of near-transparency, while

you sludge about with your redyellowgreenblue. Not that I give a shit what you look like. My eyes were built, were meant, for things beyond, to see the coil of the docking whip waiting as the ship approached, to read input broadcast on a dozen freqs beyond those slaved back to you, lying on your couches in the cabin, wrapped like so many hung hams and hoping your pilot was still trans/rec/apping and the ship wasn't about to dentist's-drill right on through the station.

So now The Quarter's filled with fools who want to know What It Was Like. What It Is Like. I stayed inside, and didn't get into my cart and go down to the triangle where I always park, not that I thought they would approach me. I'm not spectacular enough, not like Cater, who had gone the full gilldap before her bones necro'd and they pensioned her off to sit in her tank alternately crying and moving her hand back and forth, plate to mouth, like one of the burleys she was supposed to be, down in Mindanao Deep. I guess she dreams of squids and whales and all that kind of slimy shit.

Do you wonder what I dream about?

1000110
1010101
1000011
1001011
0100000
1011001
1010101. As they used to say.

Not yet. Maybe not ever. I remember, back on The Ward, when there was still some hope, or anyway they said there was, maybe just to keep us from ripping the feed tubes out of our veins, that we could get back into The Program, they were real interested in what we dreamed about. Some of us told them. Some of us didn't.

I tried. For a while.

But how do you describe color to a worm that's blind? Even though the only time I saw those real colors was on the two training runs before I . . . before what happened to me happened. Anyway, I knew them, and could name them, those secret names they had when timespace folded and you were on the Path.

What a crock. I just read what I wrote. Capital letters, even.

The Ward. Don't dignify it like that, call it what it was—a whole bunch of rubber rooms with guards outside and attendants who got picked as much for their skills with hype and pressurepoint as for understanding.

The Path. Einstein would've laughed his ass off, and then tried to come up with the mathematics of subspace.

The Program? Laugh at that? Can I say what I think, what I should think, what I must think to continue, what my circuitry should auto-respond? After all, I pride myself on my logic, whether or not it transfers.

No. Not yet. Maybe not ever. I thought I could write it, seeing the cold words holo in the air above the keyboard. But I can't. Not yet. Maybe not ever.

Amp.

Amphibian.

But what happened to the poor damned fish that crawled out, got sand stuck in his gills and couldn't get back, and couldn't breathe either?

He died.

Maybe they should've let us die. That would've been 'kay. Or maybe find something we could've done that wouldn't have made us walk down here with the worms, feeling the ground claw at us, trying to pull us down, make us blink in sunlight when we should've been able to stare, unblinking, into the heart of a nova, screens unfiltered.

That would've been all right.

But instead . . .

Poor damned Vax.

No. Clot him.

As we say right now.

If I can stick, if overgross Cater can stick, if all of us can stick, then Vax had No God Damned Right.

god?

Why did I use *that* word? I know better. Even as a groundling, a worm, with only the beginning circuits sketched, I knew better. I didn't have to go outsystem to know.

I looked down just now, where the clear tube runs in and out of the back of my wrist, and saw the numbers whirlwind up. Stop this. Stop now. Shut down. Go somewhere.

* * *

The sky was water, drifting like curtains, the color of the night began in what I would've called gray once, but now named vwan. That's my own word.
1000110
1010101
1000011
1001011
0100000
1011001
1010101 if you don't like it or understand.
As they used to say.
The ways were slick, greasy, and so I plugged into a four-leg cart and went on out, surefooting in the darkness and slime.

I am writing this five days later, if it matters to you. There have been changes since I input the first symbols.

I guess I pre-ran what I thought of Vax before I knew anything. But it shall stet. I must have a startpoint.

The place doesn't have a name, even to us. Every nownthen one of the owners asks if we have anything we want to call it. So far, everybody's come up with something so total even those limps know we're not being straight. Who needs a name, anyway? All of us in The Quarter know where it is, what it is. Those who matter.
Somebody said, well, if there's a name on it, it'll be easier for any of your friends to meet you, if they're from away.
Friends? That's another symbol that doesn't matter, isn't it? Or, not. I guess matter may not be the right word, but a concept that isn't there now, along with things like earth, home, country, and all the rest of the baggage we shed along with pieces of ourselves as we moved through The Program. None of it was that hard for me, but I came from a crèche. Maybe if

you were a *real* oldie, and had like a mother and father, it might've been different, harder. Maybe you would've washed even earlier than I did.

At least I got offplanet and Out before I saw what . . . before what happened, happened.

Still, the place exists, and the real reason the people who own it want to put a name outside is to plug it on the vid and get even more of what we call the holies in.

Holies. Like in whole. There's other symbols for those who've never been out or if they were, were back in the Can, buzzed out. Caterpillars. Tadpoles. Hairless apes. But holies doesn't start anything, so that's what we use.

What we gave up we more than got back even if we're hanging here, waiting for what will never happen.

Amp.

Like in Amputee.

There's always a line of holies outside, from about ten on until somebody decides to pull the plug and shut down. Generally about dawn. Nobody cares about the law. Not down here. Not even the cops who patrol the streets.

Poor bastards. It's worth a laugh to see them, walking along, and always they have this Look on their faces, like somebody that's paid for a few minutes in a *really* good sim, and seen a fakeup of what somebody thinks I-space looks like. They never get used to us.

I tried to explain once to one of them, all nylon armor and blond blankness, not knowing why, maybe I'd had one or two c-pops over, that we only live partially here, that what he saw wasn't all there was. It was as if he was a drawing on paper, and those of us, we Amps, were sliding through in three-dee.

Except more, of course.

He didn't get it. I said orbifold and realized I was talking to that blind worm again. I quit trying.

We don't have to use the holies' entrance, of course. We go in the old loading dock. There's a man at the door to make sure none of the limps get in that way.

He knew me, said some ultra jibber greeting he thought was empty but was complete total. I didn't sneer—it's always good to have somebody his size on your side. I happen to know he carries a nasty little prod he powerjumped so it puts out any-thing up to a deathjolt. Sometimes the holies get pissy. Also, he could've made me park the cart at the door and crip inside to a table. Which I don't do. Ever.

We don't pay, ever. The owners know what's the real draw. I started to change that to who, but the hell. *What* was our goal, something we wanted to become, wasn't it? Isn't it, if any one of us could find a way back?

But there's never a way back into The Program.

There'd be no point, after all.

That's what we're told, anyway.

The place, inside, doesn't look like much if you see it in day-light, although I have no concept why anyone would want to do that. It's big. Very big. Maybe it was a warehouse once. On the ceiling are some constructs, I guess, that're supposed to simu-late the Portal and entering I-space, I guess. They don't. There's a bar along one wall, for those who drink. A big dance floor, and there's always somebody *that* limp. There's tables, although it takes a minute to realize it, since some of them are stands, some are tankracks, and some are just round pillars.

Those are for the visitors we have sometimes: Those who've crossed over, full-mod, those who swim in that other sea, like we were supposed to do, until we . . .

Failed.

Don't shit around on yourself. You *failed*. Don't use the soft symbol. Otherwise you wouldn't be dirtside, feeling gravity drag and the whole damned solar system pull at you, like you were in the center of an old-timey clock, gears yanking and tearing as you still feel, out there, the moon twist in its orbit, and even, just an echo, even the gas giants sounding, like perhaps you might have *felt* a bass line if you played music.

Each table's got a console, for those who c-pop or stim, a card slot and a button to call for a real live waitress if you want.

There's a group on, working from a center ring hanging from the ceiling, sometimes freeform, sometimes oldstyle audible-band logic-progression music, but mostly tech. The sound wasn't bad this night, working with a lot of subsonics and even a keyboard in the near edge of the ultras. Usually that puts my teeth on edge, or that is the ghostmemory—they're gone too, and no loss, and I think it's because ultras were one of the emergency shipsignals we learned, so the association isn't what it should be.

I found out later I was real lucky I didn't go past the front entrance, since some limp had put up a sign that this was a MEMORIAL FOR VAX. He was *dead*, dead by his own hand, not listening, never hearing.

Worse, the group, two women, one man, were narish enough to name themselves P'an Ku. Not a chance. They aren't any divine embryo, and the place sure doesn't touch chaos, even at its peak-curve. If I'd known, I would've slid, most likely, and found one of the other joints in The Quarter, even though that'd be even more a blatant suckin for the holies.

But I didn't find out about the bazzfazz until later, so I parked at a stand, and looked around. Somebody waved hello, but I didn't reply. I realized I was on a downcurve, and took a c-pop, sliding the pot about halfway up. It helped, a little. But I still felt the out there.

That's another thing Amps don't think about when they're reverbing about modifications. One of the first mods we got was the cortex plug. That was intended for the basic inputs, of course, but it also took all of us off the mouth-gut-butt way of getting up up and away. Holies either have to pay for the mod or else wimpit and hold the jolt button to the base of their skulls, which isn't even a real hit.

I took another pop and let myself slide around the tones of the music, feeling it like shipsound. After awhile I was empty, through. Empty is the word we use for happy, but that no more describes it than color does what our ferrod sensors pick up.

After awhile I came back to here and a woman was sitting there, staring at me. I am what I am, and so god damned what if I've been called lemur, but that was real total, and I was now dirtside.

"You're staring," I said, which was pretty total of *me*, so now it didn't matter her error. If you're supposed to be let alone in the place, you give the same back. "Listen to the tech." That made it twice in one speech.

She was maybe fifteen, maybe less. Somebody'd call her

girl, but there aren't any girls on The Quarter, any more than there are boys. Babies, maybe. I heard somebody decided to give birth on the next block over, but never went to see if I was right.

She was a holie or anyway no visible mods. Naturally she had the plug for c-pops though, and she'd already wired herself into the console. She wore her hair short on top and on the sides, parted in the middle and brushed flat. In the back, it was long and curled down to either side of her plug, and then was stiffed in two curls that went under her ears and curled up around them. She wore it natural—the colorwheel glitter was last cycle, although most of the holies who rolled into The Quarter haven't heard yet.

She was skinny. Not much of a chest, not much of an ass from what I could see. Tight features and thin lips. She'd been kicked, like the rest of us, and it showed.

She wore a green/black/green alternating tube that started below her breasts and ended where her lap stopped. I didn't see any coat or hat.

"You're Lir." She wasn't asking. Back to being empty, I just wig-wagged my finger—this cycle's way of saying yes, particularly when the tech is spiking your eardrums.

"I'm Su. I used to screw Vax. When he'd let me."

I'm sure nothing showed on my face. But that was fresh 'put to me. As far as I'd heard, Vax slept alone. Not that he did much sleeping, any more than the rest of us. But I'd never heard of him inouting with anybody, boy or girl.

"He said after he went, I was supposed to go to you."

"What's that mean? I don't own things. Nobody owns people. And he never said shit to me." I guess I was a little confused. Maybe that last c-pop had been a little fatter than I thought.

"Wrong word. Think about it." She stretched out her hand, slid her pot up to max and banged the button. I wondered who was paying her freight, and then saw she had a free-ring like she was an Amp. I guessed she screwed somebody other than Vax to get it. Su didn't say anything more, but her face showed she was empty.

I took another jolt and tried to let the tech grab me again. But it didn't. It started getting on me, and all I could think of was decoding the shipsignals it was sending out: DRIVESYS OUT OF VARIABLE LIMITS . . . CLEAN AVAILABLE MEM, NAVSYS SATURATED . . . INBOARD SENSORS REPORT LOAD SHIFT . . .

The hell with it, I decided, and unplugged. I'd go somewhere else, or maybe just back. I wasn't holding the same mindset I came out with, anyway, so what else did I need?

I turned the cart on, and Su came back down.

"You want me to go with you?"

I should've said no, I guess. But I didn't.

On purpose, I went down the alley, past the main entrance, where the holies still waited to be vetted on being total enough to get in. They saw me, and I heard murmurs. But I didn't bother logging that—I was watching Su. She just walked beside me. Didn't toss her chest back and strut, like those holies who're into freakshows with Amps do. That sent her up a notch.

Halfway back to my apartment, she asked, "Are you still tissue down there?" Without waiting for a response, she went on. "If not, I've got things to comp, where I pad."

I shook my head. I'm cut. Not that it's anybody's damned business, but if I'm willing to strip these words out, like ancient wire coming out of insulation, it all's got to be logged. I guess that was considered a favor, done about the time my legs came off, and I guess when they put an efficient urine system in, and replaced my balls with testosterone-synths, they were supposed to take the sex drive out of circuit, too. Maybe that was the first mistake they made with me.

Su didn't see my gesture, in the darkness. She peered at me, close.

"I can manage," I said. "We can manage. If you want."

Then they sat and talked.
Not idly, as is the fashion of lovers,
of the minutiae of their own romantic affairs,
did these two converse, but cosmically,
of the entire Universe and of the already existent conflict between the cultures of
Civilization and Boskonia

Eventually, we both came back. I lay with my head pillowed on her thighs. She ran her hand back and forth across my head, behind the receptors, where I'd once had that annoyance of hair.

"Why were you supposed to come to me?" I asked.

"Vax said we'd know. But not at first."

"Why'd you take his orders?"

Nothing.

"You think you're staying here?"

She didn't say anything, and I didn't either. After awhile her breathing changed, and she started snoring slightly.

Somehow that sound was comforting.

I shut myself down.

When I came back up, there was daylight on the screen linked to the outside, yellow, rawn, purple, melacthia.

She was gone.

Sometimes limps think it was the numbers that wash you, that spinning, reeling dance of mathematics that you must have and if you lose it or it isn't enough you'll get dumped from The Program.

It wasn't that, isn't that, not for me, not for any other Amp I ever knew.

Numbers, mathematics, just *are*. They aren't numbers, those are the labels, just like violet is a label, not a color. You can wrap yourself in the numbers, the letters, the symbols, and they carry you up and up and then out.

Out to where space folds on itself, and then opens, and triple stars in Coma Berenices fill the sky with lilac/blue.

For some, anyway.

I could do that then, I can do that now.

It was still raining, pissing mist to be exact. Rain is one of the things I still like about dirtside. Again, I used the fourleg cart. If there'd been sun, I would have chosen the twoleg—enough limps stare at me already. But no one, or almost no one, would be out.

I went to the triangle, which is the open-air place we meet in.

There were a few of us scattered around, no one paying attention to the weather.

The State, in its infinite wisdom providing for us, had set up chessboards, graven in stone, on pedestals through the area.

I watched a game for a few moves, but it wasn't much. There were no more than four moves to mate, but since neither player could *see*, it'd probably cycle on for another ten or so.

I rolled away. A few meters away was Yan. He's one of the luckiest of us, and again I spin past that word luck, when there is none, is none, is none. At least he's lucky because he failed early on, so the only mods he shows are the rad-resistant heavyskin that shows bleached white like all of us have, and a flesh-looking bulge below his chin, like an inflated wattle. He was in mod for shuttleship pilot, so they didn't want him to look too strange, since he'd have to deal with the holies mewling and whining up to a station just to say they'd been out-atmosphere.

Yan's one of The Quarter's caches—anybody whispers anything, no matter how random, and it'll end up with him, or one of his fellows. Need to know haps, or what could maybe be haps, empty, ultra or total, Yan knows. Or says he does. And who cares if he does not.

"Did you vamp the latest?"

"No. You're the first I've talked to. And I shut down early last night."

Yan snickered, so obviously he knew Su had companied me last night. But, as always, he burned more to output than receive.

"They're losing ships," he said, his voice low, looking about, as if he'd just been given a Classified fiche by The State to network.

"They always lose a ship or two," I said. "Two, maybe three last year I can call up."

"No. I mean a *lot* of ships," he said. "Ten, maybe fifteen this quarter."

I suppose I did look like a lemur then.

"Why? How?"

"Don't know," he was honest enough to admit. "But something's running, because they aren't letting the holies know."

"How'd you hear?"

Yan started to answer, then looked puzzled.

"Just . . . heard. Some people talking at the place, some others out this morning. Guess everybody but you . . . and the holies . . . know by now."

Input very low quality, which was strange for Yan, or anyway admitting it was strange. Usually his data came from the highest highest highest—to hear him talk.

Not that it mattered. I'd never ride out or see the Portal open again.

I said failure smells like a sterile pisser. I wasn't being artsy.

The State takes very good care of us failures, or so it would like to think.

We are all pensioned, credits enough on our card so we're hardly poor, and the accounts handled by a computer that won't let any of us draw down enough to get into trouble.

We're given housing. A lot of us chose to live here, in The Quarter, and there's other places in other cities. I've heard some Amps go back to the ground, like straight-quill country, where there's nothing but holies around them.

Power to them. I could not crawl back into the worm colony.

The standard apartment is main room, bedroom, fresher, and tiny galley. They're compact, newly-built and self-cleaning. They smell like the toilets did, in the barracks we first lived in, in our first, testing week in The Program.

To me, that smell is failure.

We don't have to work, but I suppose if someone wanted, and they could find some holies with strong stomachs to hire us, you could if you wished.

Mostly you just wait.

Wait for it to be over.

There's no reset for this kind of failure.

Of course we're not held to realspace. We can access computers, games, vids and so forth, all at a level the holies don't qualify for.

We can lie flat on our bunks, c-popped until our ears ring, staring up at the proj built into the ceiling, sound-surrounded, plugged into the main room's box, and *almost* feel lift, *almost* feel the Portal, *almost* feel the universe crawl against your skin and the out there begin.

Almost.

I very seldom go up to that net.

Su came back that night. After we connected, we talked. I told her what Yan had told me.

"Old data," she said. "I heard that three weeks ago."

"From where?"

"Vax."

"What did he say about it?"

"He said . . . no. I don't think I'm supposed to show you yet."

Cater, who never had any use for out-and-beyonders, had the next part of the file, which, full of glee, she dumped on me.

"You heard about the ships," she said, the sound of a laugh in her voice but with no humor.

"Yan told me."

"Prog, he didn't tell you the *real* feed." Cater tried to hang on to the tidbit, but it was too tasty. "They aren't being destroyed. They're just going out, and not coming back."

"I don't understand."

"*I* heard Central's picking up signals a'ter they blank off th' plots. *I* heard one trans was just CLOT YOU CLOT YOU CLOT YOU, signoff, and then set shutdown. That's what *I* heard."

"That's an old old tape," I said. "There's been stories about ships being one-wayed out since year one, hijacked by their pilots since even before mods were on the comdeck."

"Don't mean it can't happen," she said stubbornly.

"Sorry. It does. There's so many controls there's no way a single mod could override," I explained. "Could you, if you'd finished the program, have taken a sub-miner and ripped a domecity apart?"

"Course not," Cater said, hot. "I'd have power cut on th' machine, on me, and prob'ly on anything else minin' in th' sector."

"There's even more limits on a ship," I said.

"Then where's the story coming from, if there's nothin' to it?" she wanted to know.

I didn't bother answering.

1000110
1010101
1000011
1001011 her. As they used to say.

Can I ask?" Su said.

"Maybe I don't answer."

"What happened?"

I started to sit up, then stopped. Why did it matter if she knew? So I told her, and now it doesn't matter if whoever scrolls this knows.

Clot you, anyway.

I palmed a control, and the ceiling projed on alpha-vispattern, swirling lines that held me in control, and I told her.

There wasn't much data to transfer.

I'd been one of the top five percent in my year's class in The Project. I'd been picked for mods early, and the mods took, except maybe that one that should've turned the sexslot of my brain into a little electro-pleasure pickup. I went out, unmodified, as far as Mars twice. I started the full suite of mods that'd fit me for pilot.

Then it was time for the first jump. Riding sidesaddle, they called it, linked via box with the pilot, the singledome one, since all my systems weren't installed. We broke from the station. Next was routine. I had to use words to expand this with Su, just as I'm tapping them on this keyboard now, frowning as they hang in the air in front of me, wrong, wrong, wrong. But they're all I have.

Tied to the pilot, I was supposed to feel out, to feel my bearings, my coordinates, although in I-space those things can't exist, of course, and try to feel where we were going, and reach back and push with my ship into the Portal, and then toward and out the next one.

Pure routine.

We'd unfold into normal space somewhere off μ Bootes. All progs good, all boards green, all dataflow normal.

We did, flickering star past star, although those weren't "seen," weren't in our space at all, but on the outside of what some of us called the Tunnel.

I had a moment to "feel" something, but the jump was short, and we were back in normal space.

I was a veteran. I'd been out.

I don't remember the return jump—I was too busy this time watching shipsigns, listening to the ship. Perhaps I felt that "something" again, but truly don't remember it.

The second jump was a few days later.

Again, pure routine, just a little longer. Link with the pilot, "feel" the ship, thrust, hyper-drive, just routine, just routine.

Then I started to scream.

"Why?" Su asked.

Again, I had a hard time explaining, but I *felt* something out there, something that was alive, in a manner, not like me, not like us, something that lived always in that beyond, in I-space. It *touched* me.

"What was it? Some kind of . . . of monster? Something living between the stars?"

I didn't know. I don't know. Is a man a monster to a Flatlander? Is a mod a monster to a holie? But I couldn't stop screaming.

They tranked me hard from the aidbox, and we aborted. I went back dirtside that same day and onto The Ward.

Of course none of the doctors believed I saw anything, not after the first scan. Nothing showed up in my mind, they said, that suggested I'd had *any* external input.

Agoraphobic, they said it used to be called. I couldn't take the overload, about to walk out beyond the warm comfort of the sun my genes knew so well.

They let me try once more, and again, I *felt* that something, and again I began screaming.

That was the end of that, and the beginning of my trip to The Quarter.

"So you can never go out," Su said. "I never wanted to, blessgod."

No, no, that wasn't it, I tried to say, feeling tear ducts that had been cut away years ago and were no more than ghost-memories try to fill in anger, frustration, and I heard the alarm on my wrist buzz but paid no mind.

I *had* to go out. That touch changed me more than the mods, more than The Program. Now I belonged out there, in I-space, where I could never never go, not as a pilot, not as passenger, forever tied to this ball of shit under a yellow sun.

"I don't track," she said, voice flat. "If it was that total, and it happened to me, I wouldn't even walk out under the stars at night."

"I know." And I did know.

"Did you ever hear of this happening to anybody else?"

I wasn't sure. Sometimes, on The Ward, when they wanted to know about dreams, I tried to bring it up. But no one wanted to hear about that, not the hunks with the nerveblocks and hypes, not the headborers, not anyone who'd been out, anyway, although I swear once or twice I saw a green flicker, back behind someone's eyes, but then they'd look away.

"Clot it," I said. "But now you know. Did Vax ever tell you what dumped him out of space?"

Su didn't respond. I waited, but nothing came. I should've waited for her to go to sleep, but I shut down fast. I'd recycle the impurities in the next morning.

Su was still there when I came back up, naked, crosslegged on the bed beside me. She was coiling the input lead to my console back and forth, but, from her eyes, hadn't taken a c-pop.

I felt the poisons, and just lay there, letting the process cycle.

"Can you talk," she said. She never seemed to have time for greetings or small words.

"I can."

"Do you know how Vax killed himself?"

That sent the cycle into hold, and I snapped up.

"I heard he poisoned himself."

"No. I was with him that night. He pirated a spineblock from a quack, and blanked his body. I hooked up an IV, and fed hypno into it, a little at a time. He said to go slow, and he kept talking. He said if he sounded slurry, to cut the flow down. When he told me to, I . . . I hit him, right over the heart, with a powercord he'd stripped the contacts off of. The electricity was supposed to stop his heart instant and I guess it did. He'd told me . . . he had to go Ready."

She got off the bed and walked to the screen and stared at the street scene it was showing, her back to me. I said nothing.

When she turned around, her eyes were dry.

She came back to the bed and slid over me. This time we connected harshly, strongly, she trying to drive one memory out, me trying, I suppose, to end another that I knew I couldn't.

We dressed and went out. I asked her if she wanted a c-pop. She didn't and neither did I. We went to the fringes of The Quarter, not far from the field, where you could stand and hear drive-rumble and sometimes a mach-shatter from a transport as it climbed for the ionosphere.

"Ready for what?"

"He didn't say."

"You said you never wanted to go out, last night. Why do you lurk with us mods? Most . . . " I caught myself before I said holie. ". . . most unmods wish they could get into The Program. Or think they do, anyway."

"Because you . . . none of you *fit*. Like I didn't fit with my sisters and brothers or anybody else in the Brethren. So I left. I belong in The Quarter."

There was a third question.

"What was it Vax said about the ships disappearing that you wouldn't tell me?"

"It was something he gave me, and said to show you if I thought it was right." She reached inside the waistband of the overdress she was wearing, and took out a tightly-folded bit of paper. I opened it. It was a printout of a list. It had no heading, beginning or end.

It looked like this:

XR128	*Gamgree*	*Evans*
Ceres	*Hendricks*	*Mowdrath*
DoubleDelta	*Edmunds*	*Montoya*

And so forth for two full pages.

"Shipnames and pilots," I said, pretty sure I was tracking.

"Yes. Vax said, if I was going to show it to you, for you to see if you knew any of the names. He said you were almost ready to graduate from The Program, so he thought you maybe would."

I read closely. I guess I started shaking my head.

"What?" Su asked.

"This is a garbage feed," I said. "Names on the left are ships, right? The middle row, I don't know who they are. There are three names I reck on the right. Two of those names are Amps who busted out of The Program in training, and the other is somebody who made it through and his ship exploded, right over here, at this field, five years gone."

Su's eyes had a glitter.

"*All* the names on the right are deaders," she said. "The ones in the middle are the log-pilots of the ships on the left. Those ships are some of the ones who've gone off into the black and not come back." Backbrain noted that Su, I guess from her time around us mods, used flight-words.

"The list is one Vax got from . . . from somebody who remembers him from when he was a shipcaptain."

"Now I'm not tracking."

"The woman told him that Central got signoff messages from all the ships, as they went offscreen . . . and the sigblock was *always* from a deader. Either a deader pilot, or most often, somebody who'd washed from The Program."

"Shit! Vax believed *that?*"

"That's why he killed himself."

I started to dump out, "So he could go back . . . ?" but stopped.

I looked into Su's eyes again, but the glitter was gone.

"Is that all?"

"Let's find a meal," she said.

This is being dicted. I'm in the corridor outside my apartment. Su is asleep inside, or is pretending to be.

Su told me a week ago. I wrote what's inside, on the box,

just to dump data that same day, when we got back to the apartment.

Since then, nothing. We went to the place. We connected, though never as fiercely as that morning. We ate, we drank, we popped.

It was like moving in a fog.

I wish The Quarter had fogs. But weather-con wouldn't permit that, of course.

Vax was at the end. Data overload.

For cert.

He must have been.

So he was crazy.

Who says crazy can't be right?

To want to go out again, that is crazy, too. To be able to . . .

Of course it can't be the truth.

The roof is cold at this hour, just short of dawn. The city sits below, going on and on, world without end amen, to the horizons and beyond.

Vwan sky, vwan ground.

No stars reach through.

For our safety, the passage to the roof is sealed, of course. Also of course, it's been jammed open since I came here.

There are only three steps to take.

For some reason, I'm unplugging myself from my cart, and sliding down onto my hands and stubs. A fool should look the part. The rooftop is hard, gritty under my hands.

Is Vax out there now?

Beyond the Portal?

I swear I can feel something. Something I felt before. Something waiting.

Live a fool, die a fool.

1000110

1010101

1000011

1001011

0100000
1011001
1010101 if you can't take a joke.
As they used to say.
End feed. Lir. Offnet.

. . . And the massed Grand Fleet of the
Galactic Patrol, remaking its formation,
hurtled outward through the intergalactic void.

WARREN LAPINE SPENT TEN YEARS AS A PROFESSIONAL COUNSELOR. THIS STORY IS AN OUTGROWTH OF THAT. HIS SHORT FICTION HAS APPEARED IN *PIRATE WRITINGS, DREAMS OF DECADENCE, MINDSPARKS,* AND SEVERAL ANTHOLOGIES.

Siblings

Warren Lapine

Commander Tammy Scott held the bridge alone. It was mid watch, her least favorite watch. She fought down her anger. There wasn't any good reason for it. Even the captain pulled an occasional mid watch. Why did she feel so angry? She'd been angry a lot lately, and whenever she stopped to think about why, there wasn't a reason.

It certainly wasn't the hard work she was putting in on mid watch; the computer did all the real work, she just monitored the screens. If there were an emergency, she'd take over, but emergencies were few and far between.

"I came out here for excitement," she murmured to herself. "What a laugh." The only thing more dull than her life before joining the Navy was her life since joining.

She'd been trying to escape. . . . Trying to escape what? Tammy had been asking herself that question more and more. She hadn't realized it when she'd signed up, but she was certain of it now. She was running away from something. What could make her run to the stars? How could she be driven so hard by something she couldn't put a name to?

"I hate this watch," she said to herself. "Nothing to do but think." But there wasn't anything to think about. Just a feeling, a feeling that she was missing something. Something so profound that it could shatter her entire world.

"Commander Scott," the computer said in its androgynous voice. "A ship is approaching us on our port side."

That wasn't possible. The *Antigone* was as far out in space as humans went. There were no inhabited planets in this sector. Where could the ship have come from? Tammy found the object on the screen. "Computer, are you certain the object is a ship?"

"The object has changed course three times since it was first observed. Degree of certainty is ninety-eight percent."

"Check communication channels."

"I have been monitoring all channels since we left New Windsor. We are not being signaled."

Tammy looked at the ship on her screen. At this range it was nothing more than a blip. Ships simply didn't approach one another without signaling. This was not good.

"What can you tell me about the approaching vessel?"

"The vessel has changed course three times. It is some 12.67 times the size of the *Antigone*. As it does not have an Ebling wake, it cannot be using an Ebling drive. Therefore it is either a natural phenomenon, 2 percent probability, or it is a ship of nonterrestrial origin."

A ship of nonterrestrial origin! Holy shit, an alien vessel— and on her watch! "Sound Red Alert!"

"Sounding Red Alert." Klaxons sounded and red lights flashed. Almost immediately the captain's voice cut through the din.

"Vasques here, what's going on, Tammy?"

"Captain, we've got what appears to be an alien ship approaching us."

"I'm on my way."

"I am now following Standard First Contact Procedure," the computer announced.

Standard First Contact Procedure? What the hell was that?

The captain entered the bridge, followed by the second mate, Dan Flemming. "I want an update, now!"

"Sir, at approximately 0324 hours an object appeared on our screens. It has changed course three times. It is ninety-eight percent probable that the object is a ship. As the ship doesn't have an Ebling wake, the computer believes the vessel to be of non-terrestrial origin, and is now following Standard First Contact Procedure."

"Thank you, Commander Scott. Anyone know what Standard First Contact Procedure is?"

"I remember reading something about it in Officer Candidate School," Flemming said. "I think that program was written several hundred years ago."

"Well, let's hope that whoever wrote it knew what they were doing."

"I have located a sublight transmission," the computer announced.

"Commence translation procedure, and begin sending out our own signal on that channel."

"Commencing translation procedure."

"Scott, what can you tell me about the alien vessel?"

"Not a lot from this range, Captain. The ship doesn't appear to be armed. At least, it isn't armed with anything we would consider weapons. I haven't the slightest idea what it's using for a propulsion system."

"How long until rendezvous?"

"At present speed, two hours and seventeen minutes."

"Okay, I'm open to suggestions on how to proceed."

"I suggest continuing to monitor the alien's transmission and hope we can crack their language. Should we find ourselves in a position to meet with them, I think we should do so on neutral ground."

Vasques nodded and looked to Flemming. "Flemming?"

"I agree with Commander Scott. There isn't a lot we can do until we can communicate with them. At the moment they seem unagressive. As long as they remain so, I think we should look on them as friendly."

Vasques nodded. "I agree. Computer, send a message to all inhabited planets informing them of what's going on here."

"Captain," the computer said, "the alien ship has just started transmitting in English."

"Their linguistic program beat ours," Flemming whispered.

"Let's hear it," Vasques said, concern showing on his face.

"Praise be to the Life Giver, we are not alone. Praise be to the Life Giver, we are not alone."

"That sounds encouraging," said Vasques. "Open a channel, now. Alien vessel, this is Captain Juan Vasques, commander of the EFS *Antigone*. On behalf of the human race, I welcome you and extend our good will."

"EFS *Antigone*, this is Captain Critit of the Trenar people. I accept the goodwill of mankind and say that it is good to meet a sibling among the stars. Praise be to the Life Giver. Now let us allow our thinking machines to communicate, that we might learn more of one another. We do not wish to surprise or offend out of ignorance."

"That went well," Vasques said, wiping sweat from his forehead. "Scott, you're our liaison officer, monitor the computers' interaction and be prepared to brief me upon completion of transmission."

Tammy ordered the computer to display the most pertinent information from the Trenar transmission onto her screen. She was amazed to see that the Trenar had broadcast the coordinates to their home planet as well as the specs on their propulsion system. She absorbed everything she could as it flashed across the screen. After about an hour, it was finished.

"Report."

"First off, sir, they've given us the coordinates to their home world. They have colonies on two of their world's three moons, but that's it. They're new to space. Their propulsion system is atomic, but nothing like any human engineer ever designed. It seems to function by manipulating atoms rather than destroying them. I didn't really understand the math. They're oxygen breathers, they evolved from an ocean, and they're the first life form we've encountered that doesn't have DNA. They resemble a one-armed daisy on a pogo stick and are vaguely mammalian. They only have one government, and as far as I could tell, they've never had more than one government. That's everything."

Vasques expelled his breath. "Precious little. At any rate, they seem trusting, which is a good sign. And if they have only one planet they shouldn't be a threat militarily."

"Captain, the Trenar are signaling us," Flemming said.

"Let's hear it."

"EFS *Antigone*, we have received your transmission and rejoice that we are much alike. We have truly found a sibling. This moment shall be remembered by all, forever. Let us meet that we might touch souls."

Touch souls?

"Captain Critit," Vasques said, "we too would like to meet. Do you have a shuttle?"

"Affirmative."

"Then let me suggest that when our vessels are within a kilometer of one another, we each send out a shuttle, with three crew members aboard, and rendezvous between the ships."

"We find that acceptable. We will be one kilometer from one another in an hour. We look forward to meeting with you."

Vasques turned to Tammy. "Well, Commander Scott, as first officer, the honor of commanding the shuttle is yours. I'm sure you know how important this responsibility is."

Tammy swallowed nervously and nodded. "Yes, Captain, I do." So much for dull. If excitement was what she was really after, here it was.

"Ensign Fatemi and Seaman Cackowski will be accompanying you."

Fifteen minutes later, Tammy reported to the *Antigone*'s shuttle, the *Polyneices*. Cackowski and Fatemi were already there and in full battle dress. They snapped quick salutes to her.

"As you were. Are we ready for departure?"

"Yes, Commander," Fatemi said. "All we need is final clearance."

"Good. Now, men, I realize that you're along for security reasons, but I want to stress to you, this is to be a peaceful meeting. You will not use your weapons unless we are attacked. I don't care how threatening the Trenar may seem, you will take no defensive measures unless we're being fired on. Is that clear?"

Both men nodded.

"Excellent. This is probably the most important mission in the history of space travel. Our names are quite likely to be remembered right up there with Aldrin and Armstrong. We don't want to screw up."

Tammy knew she sounded confident, but she wasn't. She

had dreamed of being in a situation like this all of her life, but now that it was actually happening she was scared shitless.

Finally, it was time to launch. As soon as the shuttle cleared the bay, Tammy caught sight of the Trenars' ship. It was about half the size of a human battleship and it didn't have any of the armament that was characteristic of a human vessel. She had a feeling that meeting the Trenar was going to be good for the human race. The Trenar shuttle approached quickly; it was about twice the size of the *Polyneices* and not designed nearly as well.

The *Polyneices*' scanners spotted the alien's airlock. The shuttles' airlocks were not compatible. Tammy hadn't expected them to be, and was carrying an inflatable airlock. It could be modified to fit any size. Tammy vectored in, matching speed and trajectory. She allowed for drift and then started the docking procedure. Ten minutes later the two ships were connected by the inflatable airlock.

"Captain," Tammy said into her helmet's microphone, "docking procedure complete. I am preparing to open the airlock."

"Understood, Commander. Your helmet's video camera is working fine. We can see everything you look at, so make sure you give the interior of the Trenars' shuttle a wide sweep. And good luck."

"Thank you, Captain." Tammy opened the airlock. When the iris valve dilated, she and her crew left the *Polyneices* and went toward the Trenar shuttle.

"Captain, according to my suit's sensors the Trenars' air has three percent more oxygen than Earth norm. Nitrogen levels are about the same. I'm picking up traces of argon and ammonia."

"Argon's not a problem," the captain's voice said, "but the ammonia could be. How steady is it? Unless it's being replenished it should break down."

"It's fluctuating between .001 percent and .003 percent."

"Then it's being introduced by the Trenar. That's interesting."

"What do you think it means?"

"I don't know, Commander Scott."

"We're entering the Trenar's cabin now." Tammy looked about the cabin slowly, making sure that everyone back on the *Antigone* got a good view. The shuttle reminded her of a botanical garden. There had to be more than a hundred different species of plants on board. The colors were amazing; Tammy counted at least seven colors she had never seen before. Only the ship's instruments were clear of plant life.

The three Trenar were standing just inside the airlock. The computer hadn't lied, they did look like one-armed daisies as they hopped about on their single pogo stick–like leg, constantly in motion. How do they sleep? Tammy wondered.

"Welcome to our ship," a Trenar voice said over Tammy's suit radio. "We are so glad that you are here."

Tammy allowed herself to relax just a bit. "And we are glad to be here."

"We find it hard to communicate in this manner. Could you remove the headpiece of your suit that we might communicate more readily?"

"Captain?"

"We've analyzed all your readouts. There's nothing in that cabin that can harm you. You might be a bit light-headed from the difference in oxygen content, but I wouldn't worry about that. You can remove your helmet if you want to, it's your call."

"Sir, I would feel more comfortable if Fatemi stays helmeted and Cackowski and I simply raise our visors."

"That will be enough," a Trenar voice said.

Tammy and Cackowski lifted their visors. The air smelled musky and sweet, not at all unpleasant. This wasn't going to be so bad. Tammy had no more than finished the thought when a wavelike sensation struck her in the face. It was a force felt rather than seen. It pumped through her body like the notes of an amplified bass guitar. At first it wasn't uncomfortable; as it penetrated deeper, Tammy began to feel a profound sense of pain and violation. It went deeper and deeper, hurting more and more. Stop, she wanted to scream, but the words wouldn't come. Visions of her life started to flash before her. It was like watching a video, only she could feel the emotions as the pictures flashed past. She saw her time aboard the *Antigone* followed quickly by her Academy days. The process seemed to slow as her memories became older. Her high school prom, the first time she had slept with David, junior high school, and then her Uncle Charlie laughing as he zipped up his fly. "No," she finally managed to scream.

Suddenly she was released, and through shattered senses she heard the explosion of gunfire. Ensign Fatemi was pulling her out of the shuttle as he sprayed the Trenar with his assault rifle. Her uncle's laughter was still ringing in her ears as she lost consciousness.

Tammy's eyes fluttered open as the *Polyneices* docked with the *Antigone*. She tried to force her thoughts into something approaching coherency as the airlock cycled, but was unable to. If only her uncle would leave her alone, everything would be fine. She could still hear his laughter, but he wasn't in the shuttle. How could he be, he'd been dead for five years. Dead for five years?

"Oh God," Tammy moaned as the crew from the *Antigone* poured into the shuttle.

"Are you okay, Commander?" a voice asked.

Tammy turned to the voice. Who was it? she wondered. An officer? A seaman? It didn't matter.

"Sir," another voice said, "Cackowski's dead. There isn't a mark on him."

"Let's get Commander Scott down to medical services on the double."

Tammy felt herself being carried to medical services. What was happening? Why wouldn't these people leave her alone? She just wanted to be left alone. Why didn't Uncle Charlie understand that? But Uncle Charlie was dead. Who were these people? Crew members? Yes, crew members. She was aboard the EFS *Antigone*. What was a ten-year-old doing aboard the EFS *Antigone*? She wasn't a ten-year-old. She was Commander Tammy Scott of the Earth Federation Navy.

"I am not a child," she whispered. "I am not helpless."

"Sir, Scott's starting to talk, but it doesn't make any sense."

That was Seaman Jacoby, he was talking to Ensign Fatemi. "I am not a child," she repeated. "I am a commander in the Earth

Federation Navy. I am not a child." Her uncle's laughter retreated and she shook her head. There were still some cobwebs,
but she was almost herself again.

"Jacoby, I'm not going to medical services. I'm needed on
the bridge."

"Commander, we have to find out what happened to you.
Until we're sure that you're all right, medical services is where
you belong," Fatemi said.

"Ensign, I have firsthand information that the captain needs.
Let me go, I'm needed on the bridge."

"Commander, I was on the shuttle too. I can give the captain a complete briefing."

"No, Ensign, you can't. You had your visor down and your
helmet dogged. You have no idea what Cackowski and I experienced. The captain needs to know what he's dealing with."

Tammy could see the indecision on Fatemi's face. "Commander, I'm genuinely worried about you. Cackowski is dead."

"I'm the first officer and I'm needed on the bridge."

Fatemi sighed. "Then I'll escort you to the bridge, but if you
show any signs of a relapse you're going straight to medical services."

Tammy allowed herself to be escorted toward the bridge.
None of this made any sense. What the hell had happened out
there? Why did the Trenar open fire? Did the Trenar open fire?
She couldn't remember. She had been in the middle of reliving
her life, backward.

Reliving her life backward! Her vision of Uncle Charlie . . .
Oh dear God. What was she running away from? Uncle Charlie, that was it, she was running away from Uncle Charlie. She
must have blocked it from her memory, but part of her had always known. That was the part of her that was angry all the time.
The Trenar had unlocked it and now she knew why she was
angry and what she had been running from.

The Trenar! They're telepathic. It was the only answer. It
was more than simple telepathy. They didn't just read minds,
they exposed them. She had been unable to hide from herself.
All her carefully laid barriers had come crashing down. In
Tammy's case it hadn't been so bad. She had been close to dealing with her secret. She realized now that the memory of her

uncle had been close to surfacing on its own. But poor Cackowski. Apparently he hadn't been able to deal with his demons, and he'd died rather than face the darker corners of his soul.

Tammy shuddered. What a horrible death—agony and shame. Suddenly she realized that she wasn't past this experience. She hadn't dealt with the pain or the anger. Not yet. It was as if she had frostbite and had just come in from the cold. She was still too numb to feel the pain, but the pain would come. In the meantime she had to get her job done. She could come to terms with the pain and anger once this was over, once they figured out what had happened with the Trenar. What had happened with the Trenar?

When Tammy arrived on the bridge, she discovered Captain Vasques in a heated argument with his Trenar counterpart. "My people only defended themselves. Your people fired first!"

"Your people gave us no choice. They were going to fire on us. We fired first only because we were quicker. Even so, all three of my people are dead. They had not even the time to pass. You will surrender your ship to us immediately. You will not be allowed to take your knowledge of us home. That could only lead to disaster."

"I cannot surrender the *Antigone*. If you try to seize this ship we will defend ourselves. I think you'll find that we are far better armed than you are, and far more adept at battle."

"I am finished speaking with you. You will not attempt to leave. Should you attempt to leave, we will destroy your ship. You have two hours to prepare for boarding."

"God damn it!" the captain swore as the channel went blank.

"Captain," Flemming said. "I've finished analyzing the video from Commander Scott's transmission. The Trenar fired on them with what appears to be a nail gun. It couldn't have penetrated Cackowski's armor. They didn't kill him."

"They fired a *nail* gun on us?"

"I believe it was the closest thing to a weapon that they had."

"Then what killed Cackowski?"

"Sir, I think I can explain that," Tammy said, stepping onto the bridge.

Both Vasques and Flemming turned to Tammy, noticing her for the first time. "I'm listening," Vasques said.

"Sir, I believe that the Trenar are telepaths."

"They didn't tell us they were telepaths."

"We didn't tell them we weren't."

"Point well taken, Commander."

"When they were *reading* my mind they exposed it to me. I watched helplessly while they thumbed through my experiences. It was like watching a movie except that I could feel the emotions. All my hopes and dreams revisited, but more importantly, all my pain and fears. I was overcome by my past. I don't think Cackowski was able to live with himself. Sir, without experiencing it, you can't begin to imagine how painful it was."

"What you're saying is that you don't think they meant to kill Cackowski."

"I don't think they meant to harm anyone. I don't understand why they fired on us. Perhaps Cackowski or I thought about firing on them, and they did what they thought they had to do. I don't know. I can't even pretend to understand telepaths."

"Neither can I, Commander. But two questions remain. What do we do now? And how do we clean up this mess?" There was silence for a moment and then Vasques went on. "We have two hours to avoid a war, let's get to it."

"Sir," Flemming said, "the computer has finished its analysis of the Trenar language."

"Summarize."

"I'm not sure that I can. They have tenses that have no meaningful expression in our language. They don't have a past tense. They do, however, have a word that, when placed at the beginning of a sentence, means 'not happening now.' Apparently they don't differentiate much between past and future. They don't have any corresponding words for truth or honesty or lie or exaggerate."

"That makes sense. How could you lie if everyone could read your mind?" Vasques asked.

"One other thing: the words for thought and action are derivatives of the same word. To the Trenar, there's not much difference between thinking and acting."

"So," Tammy broke in, "when one of us thought about firing on them, they had no way of understanding that we might choose not to follow the thought with the action."

"That doesn't make any sense," Flemming said. "They have to be able to reason, otherwise they couldn't be sentient."

"I'm certain that they can reason, but not in the same manner that we do. Think about it, they're telepaths. Every time humans interact with one another they're trying to reason out what the other person is thinking. The Trenar know. Can you imagine how being able to read each other's minds would impact our own relationships? We wouldn't be able to lie about anything." Would Uncle Charlie have molested me if he could have felt my pain? Would he have been able to hide what he was doing to me if anyone could have read his mind?

Vasques nodded. "Okay, suppose we buy your analysis. What then?"

"If we can show the Trenar how different thought and action are to us, we might be able to make them understand that we had no intention of firing on them."

"If we can't?"

"We have to go on the assumption that we can. I'll find a way to show them that we don't always act on our thoughts." Not all of us anyway.

Vasques looked around. "Anyone got a better idea?" No one answered. "Well, Commander, I'm sold. How do we convince them that we were never going to fire on them?"

"Sir, I think you should send me back over there. I'll find a way to demonstrate our reasoning ability. I'll think about running while I'm sitting down, or something like that."

"You were over there once and you damn near didn't come back. Need I remind you, Cackowski is dead."

"Captain, I lived through contact with the Trenar once. I should be able to live through it again. As you mentioned, Cackowski *is* dead. Do you want to take a chance on sending someone over there who doesn't know what to expect, who may not live through the first moment of contact?"

"Computer, open up a channel."

"Open."

"Trenar ship, this is Captain Vasques. Please respond."

"Vasques, are you ready to surrender your ship?" came the reply.

"I don't think that will be necessary. I believe we have an alternative."

"Continue."

"We believe that we are very different from you. If our understanding of you is correct, there is little difference between thought and action to you. That is not so with us. We have a greater ability to reason out our actions. Since we are not telepaths, this ability is very valuable to us."

"Not possible, the words you use mean essentially the same thing."

"Not in our language. We are not bound by our thoughts the way that you are. We can consider a course of action and decide not to follow it. Let us demonstrate this ability to you."

"How?"

"I propose to send over my first mate, Commander Scott, for another rendezvous. She will demonstrate this ability."

"No, we will have no further contact with you. You now have one hour and six minutes to prepare for boarding."

Vasques shook his head slowly and took a deep breath. "I guess this means we're going to have to defend ourselves. Damn it, why won't they listen to reason?"

"Captain, I think I should go over there anyway. It's our best chance."

"Commander, you just heard them. They'll have no further contact with us."

"Captain, I could use a jet pack to go over there. They'll be able to see that I'm unarmed. Perhaps that will convince them to talk with me. Hell, I won't even wear combat armor, just a vac suit."

"I can't authorize that."

"Sir, if we don't try something we'll have an intragalactic war on our hands."

Vasques looked beaten. "Tammy, I don't want to put your life on the line."

"Juan, what choice do we have? We can't just sit here and wait to be attacked. I was commanding the shuttle, I feel responsible for this mess; I'm willing to take the chance."

Vasques nodded. "Tammy, be careful."

"Count on it."

Tammy went back into the bay, stripped out of her combat armor, and got into a vac suit.

"Here's the jet pack," Seaman Jacoby said.

Tammy took the pack and strapped it on. "Thanks."

"Good luck, Commander," Jacoby said as he exited the bay.

As soon as the air cycled out of the bay and its doors had opened, Tammy propelled herself away from the *Antigone*. With the ship behind her, she felt vulnerable and alone. Her uncle's laugh came back to haunt her. "No," she said quietly to herself. "I am not ten, I am not powerless." The laughter receded. Vasques' voice cut through her com channel, giving her something to focus on.

"Trenar ship, this is Captain Vasques, please respond."

"Vasques, what have you done?"

"I am sending Commander Scott over to you. She is unarmed and unarmored."

"She must turn back."

"Captain Critit, she will not turn back. We wish to avoid a war with you. I am assuming that you also wish to avoid a war. The only way of doing this is to listen to Commander Scott."

"No."

"Do you realize how prepared for a war my people are? We hold twenty-seven planets. You cannot hope to match our resources."

"Captain, you have already killed three of my people. I will not lose more."

Suddenly there were three soundless explosions just off the bow of the Trenars' ship. Oh God, it's started, Tammy thought. I'm dead.

"Captain Critit, that is just a small taste of what my weapons are capable of. Take some time and analyze them. You cannot hope to stand up to them. If we wanted your destruction, we would already have accomplished that."

Tammy breathed easier. It had only been a demonstration. If the two ships began slugging it out, she'd have nowhere to hide.

The Trenar ship's bay opened and a shuttle came out. "We

will speak with Commander Scott. But know this: should the meeting be unsatisfactory we are prepared to ram your ship."

"Understood."

Tammy watched as the shuttle came closer. Please, God, let this work. The shuttle's airlock opened and she made her way into it. The lock closed behind her, air cycled in, and the door in front of her opened. One Trenar approached.

"Okay, here goes," she whispered to herself. I am running, she thought to herself over and over as she stood still and lifted her helmet's visor. Tammy could feel the contact of the Trenar. It threatened to sweep her away. She couldn't let it overwhelm her. I am running, she thought as she stood still. I am running.

I do not understand, a voice inside her head said.

"Thought and action are not the same thing for my race." I am standing, she thought, as she sat down. I am standing.

How can you do this?

"I am not a telepath. My race has developed the ability to consider its actions before acting."

This I can see, but I cannot understand it. May I delve deeper?

Not again, she thought, remembering the pain of the first meeting. "Yes, you may," she said.

You confuse me. Part of you says no, quite forcibly, and part of you says yes.

"That's what we're trying to tell you. We can want to do one thing, yet do something else entirely."

I must explore more deeply.

"You have my permission."

Suddenly, her memories began to run through her head again. It was exactly the same as the first time, though a bit less traumatic. Tears streamed down her face as she relived the events of her life for the second time in one day.

I cause you pain?

"Yes."

Then I will stop.

"No, it is necessary that you understand us."

The memories resumed. Uncle Charlie played a large part in them. It hurt so much. How could he have done this to her? No wonder she'd hidden it away from her conscious mind. She could never have lived with it.

The pain receded and she felt a warmth pervade her senses. *I understand, you are alone. Even when you are surrounded by your own people, you are alone. You had no one to protect you from your uncle. You had to protect yourself. You lied—yes, that is the word— you lied to yourself to protect yourself.*

"Yes."

Sister, you will never be alone again. Your children will not have to face what you faced, we are here. You are not alone.

Tammy started to cry in earnest. It was true, the Trenar could protect the children of mankind. No one would ever be able to hurt a human child without the Trenar knowing. Humanity's children would be safe.

Looking through your eyes, I can see that the universe is a much more dangerous place than we had ever imagined. We are not prepared to face these dangers but you are. You can protect us from the universe and we can protect you from yourselves.

Tammy could see a world where human and Trenar walked hand in hand together, where children didn't live in fear.

Yes, that world will be. We will be siblings.

"Siblings," Tammy whispered. She had accomplished her mission. "Captain," she said over her com, "they understand. *Everything* is going to be all right." Now it was time to come to terms with her pain and anger. She could afford to let the two emotions run their course.

You are not alone, the voice inside her head said. *You are not alone.*

GEOFFREY A. LANDIS RECEIVED A HUGO IN 1992. HE HAS MADE TWO
APPEARANCES IN *ABSOLUTE MAGNITUDE* AND ONE APPEARANCE IN *AM'S*
SISTER MAGAZINE, *DREAMS OF DECADENCE.*

The Melancholy of Infinite Space

Geoffrey A. Landis

We live at the very beginning of the Universe.
As we peer back with our telescopes toward the beginning
of time, and measure the age of the universe, we are beginning
to find that the universe is closer to ten billion years old than to
fifty: that the oldest of the stars we see around us are, in fact, as
old as any star *can* be; as old as the universe itself. Looking outward we are finding that the gravity of the universe is not enough
to pull it back together in some future cataclysmic big-crunch.
The universe will expand forever.

Ten billion years. A mere eyeblink in the cosmic time. We
stand at the beginning of time, looking outward into the void
of infinite time.

And what of us?

We have no guarantees. Humanity has spread across the
globe; populated ecosystems from the equatorial rain forest to
the polar ice, but as a species we are new, a species barely a hundred thousand years old. This is far too young for us to begin
to guess whether Darwin's awful mill will judge us a success, or
whether we will be wiped away as another dead end, one of a
million failed experiments. The Earth has no memory for the
dead ends of evolution. In a few hundred thousand years gla-

ciers would grind our works and our bones into gravel, would grind gravel into sand, and in a few hundred million years the movement of continents erase the last of any trace of our brief existence, save perhaps for a handful of deeply-buried and enigmatic fossils.

But some species survive, and perhaps we will be among them. A species might last a million years, even ten million years, and who can say that we will not be among those rare evolutionary successes, with success judged by that cruel god who knows no mercy or kindness, only death or survival? And in a million years, or even ten thousand years, who can tell what we shall become? All we can say is that we will become something unguessable, possibly unimaginable.

Very few species last more than ten million years, and those few are the living fossils, the ones frozen by evolution into some marginal niche. A genus may last longer, and perhaps genus homo will last a hundred million years or more. There would, then, in time be other species of humans, radiating into other ecological niches. But even genera evolve or are supplanted; and in life, nothing lasts. It is unlikely that genus homo will last a billion years. A billion years ago, even multicelled life had yet to evolve; there were no plants, no animals, no fungi, only primitive bacteria. A billion years hence, we cannot guess what life will be like, but it will no more be us than we are those primitive bacteria.

The sun itself is middle-aged, halfway through its life. In another five billion years, give or take a few, the sun will swell into a red giant—incidentally melting the Earth as it does—and then shrink to a white dwarf, a dying ember of a sun. In twenty billion years the ember will cool. A few trillion years from now, all the stars in the universe will be cold. Perhaps if we (or rather our billion-times-great-grandchildren, as much different from us as we are beyond bacteria) learn to conserve star-stuff, and make smaller stars that conserve their hydrogen fuel and burn slowly, perhaps we shall prolong the death of the final stars, to make them last ten times or even a hundred times longer before the end of all starshine comes. A hundred trillion years!

And so the universe cools and expands.

Some say that perhaps even protons, the very stuff of matter itself, will decay with time. But our best experiments to search for such decays have failed to see it, and so it may well be that the matter that we are made of will have no such easy oblivion.

And yet the universe cools and expands. In the cold dark, whirling orbits of the cinders that were once stars will collapse by gravitational radiation. A billion times longer than that hundred trillion years, and galaxies collapse into black holes. A thousand times that, and the universe is swept free of all matter.

In another 10^{60} years, give or take, even the black holes evaporate into clouds of gamma rays, and then the gamma rays are stretched by the expansion of the universe into the visible, then microwaves, then radio. There is nothing in the universe save a cooling, expanding cloud of dilute photons.

Life, complexity, is the natural child of entropy, the slide of energy to lower states. Life is not made of protoplasm, despite what biologists may say; the necessary stuff of life is not matter, but information, and the life-stuff of information is not energy, but entropy. We are surfers on entropy; we live by forever sliding on the cusp of the ever-collapsing wave. As the universe expands, that slide of entropy continues forever, and complexity must follow. There is no end.

In that infinitely-distant universe of nothing but photons, flying endlessly across the expanding cold, there is still energy, and in the expansion of photons into a universe expanding and cooling toward absolute zero, there is still the endless slide of entropy. With entropy is the stuff of life, and even of intelligence. Over the timescale for the universe to expand, life goes on. At this timescale, long after the end of the galaxies, long after the universe of matter, comes the universe of photons. In that unimaginably huge universe, a hundred trillion years is less than the blink of an eye.

Here is where deep time really begins. But there will be no trace of us, of our brief existence in that hundred trillion years that was the very first eyeblink of the new universe. Not even the atoms that once made us will remain.

We live at the very beginning of the universe.

FRANK O. DODGE WAS BORN IN 1922. HE JOINED THE NAVY AT A VERY YOUNG AGE. HE IS A VETERAN OF WORLD WAR II AND THE CONFLICTS IN KOREA AND VIETNAM. HE SOLD HIS FIRST STORY AT THE TENDER AGE OF SEVENTY AND HAS MADE MORE THAN ONE HUNDRED FICTION SALES IN THE LAST THREE YEARS. HIS WORK HAS APPEARED IN *CRICKET, PIRATE WRITINGS,* AND *THE POETIC KNIGHT. FLETCHER IN A CIRCLE,* A COLLECTION OF HIS SHORT WORK, IS AVAILABLE FROM WILDER PUBLICATIONS AT P.O. BOX 707, GREENFIELD, MA 01302-0707 FOR $6.95.

The Barefoot Mule

Frank O. Dodge

The mule was just standing out there, all by itself in the middle of the desert. There was nothing for a hundred miles in any direction except a couple of mesquites standing with their arms up like surrendering soldiers, and half a dozen prairie dog holes. Yet there it stood with the braided reins from its halter dragging the ground, moving its jaw occasionally, and staring off into the distance.

I adjusted my binoculars and swept the terrain from horizon to horizon. Nothing but sand and prickly pear. Flat. Desolate. Empty. Except for the mule. I zeroed back on him. He moved. He turned to his right and ambled slowly into a hole in the air.

My jaw dropped and my mind went into neutral. As I watched, the mule's nose, then his muzzle, ear, neck and forequarters disappeared as though the animal were walking behind a big boulder, only there was nothing there. A moment later I was staring at a desert without a mule.

I lowered the binoculars to the seat beside me and rubbed my eyes. What I had seen happen had not happened. It could not have happened. A mirage. It had to be a mirage.

Well, maybe so, but I had to check it out. I *had* to. I started the Jeep and drove down to where the damn mule had been. I cut the motor and stood up on the seat to scan the area. A mirage does not leave footprints. This one had. This did not add to my peace of mind. The hoofprints of an unshod mule started in the middle of a stretch of otherwise unmarked sand, made a semicircle back to the center of that otherwise unmarked stretch of sand, and disappeared. Just disappeared. Just started. Just disappeared. This added even less to my peace of mind. I should never have taken the case in the first place.

In the first place, the money was infinitesimal. That should have warned me off. But the girl had been very persuasive. The only available information about the case came from an old desert rat who looked like Gabby Hayes on a bad day. Now *that* should have warned me off. But the girl had been very persuasive . . . and *very* pretty. The information provided was completely screwy, made no sense whatsoever, and involved a mule. Now that *really* should have warned me off.

She'd come into my Los Angeles office and asked me to find her father.

Okay. Name?

Phil Franklin.

Age?

Fifty-one.

Description?

Tall and thin but strong and wiry. Hair gray. Eyes blue. One ninety-five. Complexion ruddy.

Occupation?

Prospector.

Prospector? As in somebody who looks for gold, prospector?

Yes.

And where does he look for this gold?

Death Valley.

Great.

Now you'd think even a jerk like me would have said at this point, "Look, lady, I'm a city boy. What do I know from deserts?

What you need is a Texas Ranger type." But did I say that? Did I? No, I did not say that. Have I mentioned that she was pretty?

I brought up my fee plus expenses and that's where we hit our first snag. She didn't have that kind of money. Not that I get all that much, but she could offer only about a third of what I usually do get.

And that's when I really should have recommended Cheap Charlie, the keyhole peeper down the hall, but I do believe I mentioned that she was kind of cute. A tiny little thing the word "petite" was coined for. Short brown hair sort of feathery around the face. Pug nose. Freckles even. Oh hell, the whole works. And helpless but brave. Her hands fluttered a little. There was a little worry wrinkle between her eyes. An air of "it's-such-a-big-world-and-I'm-so-small." But the chin . . . the soft, round chin . . . thrust courageously. And I'm sure her upper lip was stiff. . . . Oh, what the hell . . . I told her I'd see what I could do.

Were there any clues as to Daddy's whereabouts? How long had he been among the missing? Where was he last seen? Did anyone know anything?

Clues?

Sort of.

How long?

A little under a month.

Where?

Death Valley.

Anyone know anything?

Sort of.

Who?

Angus MacDermott.

What's an Angus MacDermott?

An Angus MacDermott, it turned out, was an old prospector buddy of Daddy's. And where was this alleged MacDermott to be found?

The Castle.

The *Castle?*

Yes.

Back in the twenties and early thirties there had been an old gold seeker called "Death Valley Scotty." The old geezer had an annoying habit of disappearing into that blinding inferno for days at a stretch and coming out with a donkey-load of gold. Over a period of years he built a rambling structure vaguely reminiscent of a medieval castle out in the Valley. The old boy was quite noted. He was in all the papers from time to time. Lots of people tried to follow the wily old desert rat to discover the source of this wealth, but he had a way of disappearing among the sand dunes and cactus. No one ever found his digging, and more than a few never came back out of the desert. Scotty died in the late thirties or early forties and his "Castle" fell into ruins.

Angus MacDermott and Diana Franklin's father had set up housekeeping in a corner of the ruins. All right it wasn't a "corner," it was a thick-walled adobe outbuilding that somehow managed to stay cool inside in spite of the hundred-plus degrees that kept the lizards hopping from one foot to another on the sand outside.

The old Scot was seventy-five, and fifty-odd years of tramping around Death Valley dragging a reluctant burro had sundried him into a tall, skinny six feet of very tough saddle leather. He wore Levi's, boots, and an old sombrero about the size of a beach umbrella.

The two men had put together pretty comfortable digs for themselves. Colorful serapes, thrown across the beds and hung from the walls, gave the place a cheerful air. An old shotgun was cradled in a bracket over the door and another stood against the wall next to one of the beds. A worn six-gun in a scarred holster hung from a peg. All three weapons were well cared for. There was a table, some chairs and a wood cookstove. There was also a refrigerator, a TV, electric lights, and a two-way radio, all powered by a gasoline generator out back.

Diana Franklin and I had driven out from L.A. in old Angus's jeep. She'd notified the old man via the radio that we were coming, and MacDermott had beans and tortillas waiting. They were good. I was sopping out my third bowl while he cut me in on the scoop.

The day Phil Franklin vanished, he'd gone alone to check out a likely looking ridge while MacDermott remained behind to catch up on the chores. He'd gone on foot because it was only half a day's hike and they were short on gas. They wanted to save what they had for the generator. Franklin should have been back not later than noon of the following day, but he never showed.

Old Angus went looking for him.

MacDermott had no difficulty following his partner's trail. Then he arrived at a place where Franklin's tracks were obliterated by the marks of unshod hooves, and that was that. The old Scot circled, Indian fashion, to pick up the trail of man or horse and that's where it got spooky. There wasn't any. No hoofprints coming, no hoofprints going. No bootmarks in the sand. Nothing but Franklin's trail ending literally in the middle of nowhere, along with hoofprints that came from nowhere and returned to nowhere.

And that's what the old man told the State Police.

I could imagine how *this* was received by the authorities. "Yeah. Sure, Pop, we'll look into it." Two days later a state cruiser showed up to "investigate." Old prospectors were always wandering off into the desert and getting lost. No one at patrol HQ got into much of a sweat over it any more. The damned fools ought to know better.

Comfortable in their air-conditioned patrol car, the cops followed Angus's jeep to where the trail ended. All the marks were still there but the city-bred policemen couldn't read them. MacDermott tried to explain. He tried to make them understand that Franklin had not left this spot . . . there was no exit trail. . . . There was no . . .

The cops were hot and bored, and this old geezer had had his brains fried out by the sun a couple hundred years ago. "Sure, Pop, sure. Look, he'll probably turn up in a few days. He's probably out there digging up a whole mountain of gold and you'll both be rich. Look, Pop, we've got to get back to town. He isn't dead . . . there's no body. He'll turn up."

And that was the "investigation."

Fortunately, old Angus made no reference to a disappearing mule, or the investigation would have ended with the old man doing basket weaving in the state hospital.

He left out the mule because at that point there'd been no
mule. The mule came later. Angus went back out to try again,
and that's when he spotted the mule.

We put supplies for a couple of days in the Jeep, and I went with
an old man out into a desert to look for a disappearing mule.
Diana wanted to go with us, but old Angus deemed it too dangerous, and she agreed to stay behind and keep in touch by
radio.

You're probably wondering why Diana Franklin went all the
way to Los Angeles to drag another city slicker out to Mother
Nature's oven after the brush-off they'd gotten from the last
batch. And why me in particular. Well, it seems that I had been
lucky enough to get my name in the papers a time or two in connection with several tricky cases involving some persons who had
managed to get themselves pretty thoroughly lost. One of those
cases had had a bizarre twist I still haven't figured out, but since
I found the guy, I don't bring that up in general conversation.

At any rate, there I was out in the middle of Death Valley,
sweating like your kid sister's new boyfriend while you told him
what you did to guys who got too friendly with the hands. I was
asking myself why I had allowed myself to get talked into doing
something as stupid as standing on the seat of a Jeep staring at
a bunch of hoofprints in the sand. (Have I mentioned that she
was pretty?)

I got out of the Jeep and studied from close up the mule
tracks that started nowhere and went back to the same place. I
walked around them leaving a few tracks of my own, but even
from close up they still didn't tell me anything. All they said was
that a mule had been here and now he wasn't. Hell, I could see
that for myself. I went back to the Jeep.

The bearded, sun-dried old coot in the backseat spoke his
first words in two hours. "What'd I tell you?"

"Okay, so you told me. I still don't believe it."

MacDermott chuckled. He squinted at the sky. "Sun'll be
down in less than an hour. Gets cooler after dark. Gets cold,
act'ally. You'll be glad you brought that coat that I seen you laf-
fin' at me behind my back fur tellin' you t' bring."

I was still staring at those damned hoofprints. Angus chuckled again. "Don't let it throw yuh, sonny. Done th' same thing t' me, first time I seen him. *Still* ain't got used t' it."

I helped the old man get the gear from the Jeep, and set up the tent and propane cookstove. The old-timer was getting stuff from the ice chest to fix for supper when the radio crackled.

"Johnny?"

I picked up the mike and thumbed the switch. "That's me."

"Anything happen?"

"Unfortunately for my peace of mind, yes."

"Just like Angus said."

"Yes."

"It just disappeared?"

"Just walked into . . . the air."

"Do you think my father . . . ?"

"Boss, I don't know *what* to think."

I heard MacDermott chuckling behind me.

"So far all I've done is provide amusement for a certain old desert rat."

Diana laughed. "He's entitled. He's been laughed at every time he tried to get someone to listen."

"Yeah. Well, I'm not laughing any more. You have no idea what it does to you to watch a fifteen-hundred-pound mule disappear like a Cheshire Cat . . . and he didn't even leave a grin behind."

"Johnny?"

"Yeah, boss?"

"Find my father for me?"

I looked at those damned mule tracks. "I'll do the best I can."

"I know you will, Johnny. Keep me posted?"

"Right, boss. Ciao."

"Ciao."

I hung the mike on its bracket and went back to MacDermott. The old man looked at me, his leathery face unsmiling.

"That's a mighty sweet girl there, and I've known her all her life. I wouldn't take to it kindly if she got hurt."

Still studying my face he drew a long knife from his boot and used it to turn the steaks on the grill.

I squatted beside the fire and looked at him. "I've got a kid sister. I know what you're saying."

Angus grunted and turned the steaks with the tip of his toad sticker.

The sun went down, and the furnace-like air cooled rapidly. I was grateful for the jacket old Angus insisted I bring. The moon rose. I couldn't believe how much brighter it was out here away from the smog. Angus scrubbed out our plates with sand, and leaned back against the Jeep. He brought out an old pipe and sat puffing. I lit up a cigarette.

"Think he'll come back?"

"Dunno."

We sat and waited.

The wait was in vain. The mule did not show again. Around noon the next day we returned to the Castle and Diana. "Don't look so worried, honey," Angus said. "We'll find old Phil."

Diana, it turned out, was a good cook. After eating, MacDermott leaned back and lighted his pipe. "Somethin' just occurred to me. There's a old shaman lives a few miles from here . . . mebby he's heard about this disappearin' mule before."

"What's a shaman?"

"Medicine man. Keeper of tribal history. He's about old enough t' be a personal friend of th' Great Spirit hisself. Wanna go talk t' him?"

I lit a cigarette. "Couldn't hurt."

Buffalo Man looked about like MacDermott had described him. He sat, wrapped in a blanket despite the heat, and spoke out of the mass of wrinkles that served him for a face. The old Indian filled and lighted a pipe with MacDermott's tobacco, and looked at us for a long time. And then he told us a story about . . .

A mule?

No. But it was a very old tale of the Thunderbird's Egg.

The Thunderbird's Egg?

Old Buffalo Man chuckled wheezily. The Thunderbird was a bird no larger than a man's thumb, but laid an egg so huge that its cracking was the sound of the thunder.

So what's that got to do with why Punk Rockers should be permitted to live?

According to tribal legend, many . . . many . . . generations past, a Thunderbird's egg floated down from the sky and landed in the desert. A vast white egg which hatched men. Strange men with spindly bodies and large heads with big eyes that had no pupils.

The Children of the Egg built two tall towers atop each of which was a great round plate aimed at the sky. Massive bolts of lightning came from the sky into the plates, causing the air between them to shimmer and pulse. The Egg rose from the ground and moved forward, disappearing into the shimmering air. The People watched from the surrounding dunes in great fear. Generations passed and the towers crumbled and turned to rust. The rust was blown away by the wind, and it was as if the towers had never been.

"That's it? A space ship landed and disappeared into a warp of some kind?"

Old Buffalo Man puffed at his pipe. No, that wasn't all. In the time of Buffalo Man's great-great-great-grandfather, men like evil spirits would appear from time to time out of the desert and ravage the villages, taking captives, and vanishing back into the desert. Many war parties tracked them only to have the trail end. . . . Just . . . end. But no barefoot mule.

We returned to Diana at the Castle. "Okay. So there's a space-warp out there, and that's where your father went. What's on the other side and why the damned mule seems to be the catalyst that activates it, don't ask me."

Diana's chin trembled and I thought she was going to cry, but she took a deep breath and squared her small shoulders. "You'll find him, won't you?"

Old Angus put an arm around her. "We'll find him."

He looked at me. "Won't we, sonny?"

Diana's soft eyes searched my face. My heart suddenly raced at what I saw there. "Damn right. Load up the Jeep with enough to last for a week."

It wasn't easy to talk Diana out of going with us, but in the end she agreed to stay behind.

For two days we sat and baked in the sun, and nothing happened. Then, on the evening of the second day, we'd finished supper and old Angus was filling his pipe when the air shimmered, and the mule's head appeared. Just the head. Hanging there in the bright moonlight, jaw moving idly. Then he walked into full view. I got up slowly, so as not to spook him, and advanced, murmuring soothing sounds. The mule looked at me and snorted, but didn't back away. I took a grip on the dangling reins and stroked his muzzle. He whickered softly.

MacDermott came up and patted the animal's shoulder. "Okay, we got him. What now, sonny?"

I looked at the old Scot.

MacDermott's eyes widened and he shook his head. "You ain't thinkin' what I think you're thinkin' . . . are yuh?"

"You know any other way?"

Angus shrugged. "Guess not."

I grasped the mule's mane and swung aboard. I looked down at the old man. There wasn't really anything to say, so I tugged on the mule's reins and turned him back toward where he'd come from. I heeled him gently and he moved forward.

I don't know what I expected, but all that happened was that the mule walked. Disappointed, I turned and looked back. And nearly fell off. Angus, the jeep, the tent . . . all were gone!

I yanked back on the reins. The patient mule turned and plodded back the other way. Suddenly they were there. No *pop*, no tremor, no fireworks. They were just there. MacDermott took off his oversized sombrero and wiped his forehead. "Where'd yuh go?"

"Nowhere. That is, no place. That is, we just walked over there and back . . . "

"But?"

"But it wasn't here. I mean . . . what the hell *do* I mean? I looked back and you were gone, so I must have gone *somewhere* . . . or was it *some-when?*"

"What th' hell d' you mean, *some-when?*"

I slid down from the mule and tethered him to a tall

mesquite. Angus picked up the coffee pot and poured two cups. He handed me one. I passed the hot tin cup from hand to hand.

"You're going to think I'm crazy."

"You just rode a mule into a hole in the air right in front of my eyes, and that ain't crazy? What're yuh tryin' t' say?"

I took a sip of the hot, bitter coffee, and fumbled for my cigarettes. "Angus, I think it's a different time. Same place. Different time."

"Same place. Different time."

"Yes."

"All right. Why not? And th' mule. He can go from here to there. . . ."

"That's what I think. Only not from 'here' to 'there' but from 'now' to 'then.' "

"Okay, then that's where Phil went. Let's go find him."

I took a final drag on my cigarette and flipped it away. "Right. Mount up."

As soon as the camp vanished, Angus cast about for landmarks. " 'Twon't do us much good t' find old Phil if we can't find our way back."

He lined up two boulders with a giant mesquite, and lit down from the mule. He walked back to where the animal's tracks abruptly ceased and built a small cairn of rocks on either side of the trail. "Now," he grunted, "even if the wind blows the tracks away we just aim th' critter between them piles and that's it."

The old man pivoted slowly, noting landmarks on the horizon. I did the same but the land didn't talk to me the way it talked to him. He grunted. The old prospector would be able to pinpoint the exit gate (?) no matter from which direction we returned. He remounted behind me, and we moved off, backtracking the mule's trail.

It was about half an hour later that we spotted the glow of a campfire behind a slight rise ahead. I kicked the mule into a shambling trot, but MacDermott tapped me on the shoulder.

"Whoa up, sonny. We don't know whether we went back-'ards or for'ards in time, do we?"

I reined in. "No."

"Makes a difference. From th' way this critter's halter's braided I'd say we went back a couple hunderd year or more. That means Injuns."

He checked his double-barreled shotgun. "Injuns was pretty unfriendly hereabouts that fur back."

I was beginning to wish I'd brought along the other shotgun, the one Phil Franklin left behind in the shack.

The old Scot slid to the ground. "Best hitch th' critter and go for'ard afoot till we see what's what."

I dismounted and did as he said. I took the .38 snubnose from under my arm and checked the loads. I snapped the cylinder shut. "Lead on, MacDuff. You're the Injun expert."

Angus grinned. "Come on sonny, and keep it quiet. Be on th' lookout fer outposts."

We crept from shadow to shadow in the bright moonlight until we reached the ridge behind which the fire glowed. At a hand signal from MacDermott I dropped to my belly and we inched forward and peered over the crest.

What I saw told me we'd gone back more than a couple of hundred years. It was more like four hundred.

The dozen men sitting and lying around the campfire wore doublets of scarlet and/or yellow wool or velvet, and tight trunk hose like leotards. Coal-scuttle shaped helmets called morions, and steel breastplates, glinted in the firelight. All were armed with long swords and several had clumsy wheel-lock musketoons. I counted five long heavy firelock muskets with their Y-shaped firing supports.

Conquistadores!

No one had ever determined for sure just how far the Spanish explorer Francisco Vasquez de Coronado had penetrated into the continent looking for the "Seven Cities of Cibola" the Indians had told of, but it was a good bet that I was looking at some of his men, if not the hidalgo himself.

I wasn't positive who *these* guys were, but I didn't need Mac-Dermott's sharp intake of breath and muttered curse to tell me that the man lashed to a thick post was Phil Franklin.

The man was naked except for the tattered remains of his boxer shorts and a crisscross of whip welts that covered his body from shoulders to knees. Many of the welts were infected and suppurating.

One of the lounging soldiers laughed brutally and threw a gnawed bone at the bound man.

"Don Francisco will be back tomorrow, cursed heretic dog," he jeered, "and with him will be the saintly Fra Julio, the arm of the Holy Office in this god-blasted hellhole. Then we shall have the blessing of Mother Church to reduce your blasphemous heretical body to ashes."

The Spanish was not that of the barrio as I'd heard it spoken on the streets of Los Angeles, but I understood it well enough. The soldiers were awaiting the return of their leader with the representative of the Inquisition in this part of the New World. The holy friar carried with him the authority and terrible power of that obscene institution. Franklin would be sanctimoniously condemned and burned at the stake to which he was tied for the crime of being a non-Catholic.

Old Angus touched me on the shoulder. I looked at him, and he signaled to withdraw. We slithered silently down to the foot of the little rise, then rose and retreated several hundred yards. "The *bastards*," Angus swore. "You understand Spanish?"

"Yes. They're waiting for the inquisitor, then they're going to burn him alive."

"Nice bunch of fellers. I caught that much of it, too. Well, it ain't gonna happen."

"No."

Old Angus looked at me. "You notice sumpthin' wrong here?"

"I notice lots wrong. What in particular?"

The old Scot shoved his sombrero to the back of his head. "Look, sonny, I ain't *completely* illiterate. You ever read in your history books anywhere where th' Spanish Inquisition come farther north than Mexico?"

I gave a start. "No." I turned suddenly cold. "An alternate timeline! My God, I wonder what 1994 is like here if the Spaniards and that hellish institution continued in power. . . ."

MacDermott scrubbed his face with calloused hands. "Sonny, that's sumpthin' I don't care t' find out. Look, I don't reckon them fellers we seen around that campfire are the whole lot. I seen more equipment than I did men. There's more of 'em about somewheres. 'Fore we can make any kind of a move, we got t' locate 'em."

He looked at the little snubnose in my shoulder holster. "I don't reckon that popgun'll make much of a dent in them iron shirts them fellers were wearin'. Here." He drew the long-barreled .44 at his belt and handed it to me. "This'll make believers of 'em. Let's you and me mosey around and find out a few things."

We began a wide circle. I was wishing that the moon wasn't quite so bright, but a moment later I was thanking God that it was. Otherwise we'd have run into the sentry before we saw him.

Angus gave a sudden tug at my sleeve and dropped to the ground. I followed suit. He pointed and I made out the form of the Spanish outpost leaning against a rock. From beyond the sentry came the sounds of voices, clanking chains, and the crack of whips.

The old man put a finger to his lips and drew that long, wicked-looking knife from his boot. Before it really hit me what he was about to do, he was a dozen yards away, snaking along on his belly, and approaching the guard from the rear.

I could just make him out in the shadows as he rose silently to his feet. The two silhouettes merged into one. There was the soft sound of a thud and a muted gasp. One of the figures crumpled to the ground and the other waved an arm at me. Old Angus was wiping the blade of his knife on the soldier's doublet as I caught up.

"There's *one* son of a bitch who won't be takin' no pleasure from watchin' a man burn to death," he grunted.

Beyond the boulder on which the sentry had been leaning was a wide arroyo. Twenty or so Indians, shackled with leg irons, naked, and welted with whip marks, toiled in the light of torches and the roaring fire beneath a large crucible in which yellow metal bubbled. Several of the Indians worked the bellows and the rest hacked at a shallow tunnel in the rock wall of the arroyo under the lash of brutal Spanish overseers. To one side was stacked a big pile of yellow ingots about five by five by twenty inches. MacDermott gave a silent whistle and we looked at each other.

Once again we retreated to hold a council of war. Angus chuckled.

"Well, I guess we got th' answer t' where old Death Valley Scotty got all his gold."

He sobered. "It wouldn't be no big problem t' blast them four guards," Angus said, "but th' shots would stir up them bastards holdin' Phil. We got t' cook us up a plan, sonny."

The old man fell silent. "I wonder . . ."

"What?"

"Thet mule. He's th' key t' th' door t' this place, but how big's th' door?"

"What do you mean?"

"Th' Jeep. These skunks ain't never seen nothin' like it and it'd scare hell out of 'em. What I'm wonderin' is, do we have t' be *on* th' mule t' git in here? Or could we walk alongside him? If so, how wide's th' door? Is it big enough fer th' Jeep?"

Angus looked at the moon. "Be daylight in about three hours and that's all th' time we got to get old Phil outta here."

We went back to where we'd tethered the mule, mounted up and urged him into a clumsy gallop. We had no trouble following the hoofprints back to the "door," and twenty minutes later Angus lit down by the Jeep while I remained aboard. We weren't taking any chances on the critter wandering off.

With Angus walking alongside, we backtracked past the door and Angus, two feet away, stayed right with us. We went back and tried it again. Several times. The "door" was approximately ten feet wide. Plenty wide enough for the Jeep. The mule was the catalyst that activated the portal, but you didn't have to be in actual physical contact with him in order to pass through.

I rode the mule while MacDermott followed in the Jeep. We again tied the patient creature to a mesquite and drove without headlights to within a hundred yards of the Spaniards' camp.

Old Angus looked at the campfire.j

"If I was a forgivin' man, I'd shoot in th' air. But I ain't." He looked at me. "Ready?"

I nodded.

"Then hit 'em with it, sonny, and let's you and me go to war."

I put the Jeep in gear and floored the pedal. Sand sprayed

in all directions. At fifty yards I flipped on the headlights and bore down on the horn. Old Angus was firing and reloading the shotgun faster than you'd have thought possible. We roared into the Conquistadores' camp.

The Spaniards were blinded by the headlights, which they took to be the burning eyes of some demon out of hell. The blasting horn added to their panic and terror. Several fell to the old Scot's shotgun fire and the rest dropped their weapons and ran, crossing themselves and calling on a dozen saints to save them. Old Angus emptied both barrels after the fleeing soldiers, dropping two more of them. He grunted with satisfaction.

I leaped from the Jeep and slashed Franklin's bonds, lowering him gently to the ground.

MacDermott knelt beside his friend. "You gonna make it, Phil?"

"You bet your ass, old timer. Go get the rest of 'em."

The old Scot patted Franklin's shoulder. He grinned. "You just go on goldbrickin', old buddy. Me and th' kid'll be back 'fore you know it."

He stood. "Come on, sonny, let's chase th' rest of them rattlesnakes."

The rest of the "rattlesnakes" had already disappeared by the time we drove to the mine. The Indian slaves, hampered by their leg irons, were clumsily shuffling in all directions to escape. Angus stood up in the seat. "I heard some of 'em jabberin'," he said. "Mebby I c'n talk to 'em."

He cupped his hands to his mouth and shouted something unintelligible. Several of the Indians paused and looked back. The old Scot shouted again, adding to what he'd said. The Indians began to return, hesitant and fearful.

Angus chuckled. "I told 'em I'm th' Great Spirit and I come t' free 'em from th' Spaniards. I told 'em that th' beast with th' fiery eyes is my medicine and won't hurt 'em. See can you find a ax or a chisel or somethin' we c'n chop th' leg irons off them poor bastards."

The old man got down from the Jeep and, keeping the shotgun cradled in the crook of his arm just in case, walked toward the cringing natives, still speaking in a soothing tone. The Indians came up to him and dropped to their knees, touching their foreheads to the ground. The old Scot spoke sharply, ordering them to get up.

Angus took the hammer and chisel I'd found, and cut the leg irons off one man. He handed the tools to the man and told him to free his fellows. "Come on, sonny, we got to get back to old Phil."

Franklin's hurts, it turned out, weren't as serious as they looked. Movement was painful and he needed attention for those infected whip cuts, but no bones were broken and he'd suffered no internal injuries. He was in amazingly good shape for what he'd been through.

Angus checked the declension of the moon. "Less'n an hour till sunup. We don't know 'zactly how soon them bastards' Big Boss is due, ner how many men he's got with him. I suggest we skedaddle *muy pronto.*"

Phil Franklin grinned at his partner. "We got time to load up th' Jeep with some of that Spanish gold, I reckon." His grin broadened. "Pretty good strike I made, wouldn't you say?"

MacDermott chuckled. "Yep."

The Jeep load of gold assayed out to little over two and a quarter million dollars. Not half bad for one night's work.

Me? I'm out of the private eye gig. Diana talked me into becoming a prospector.

Soon's my new father-in-law is fully recovered from his ordeal, he and old Angus and I are going to take a little mule ride. Only this time we know what we'll be going up against and we'll be better prepared . . .

. . . and better armed.

HAL CLEMENT (HARRY CLEMENT STUBBS) WAS BORN IN MASSACHUSETTS IN 1922. HE HAS BEEN A SCIENCE LOVER FROM EARLY CHILDHOOD, AT LEAST PARTLY AS A RESULT OF A 1930 *BUCK ROGERS* PANEL IN WHICH VILLAINS WERE "HEADED FOR MARS, 47 MILLION MILES AWAY." HE MAJORED IN ASTRONOMY AT HARVARD, AND HAS MASTER'S DEGREES IN EDUCATION AND IN CHEMISTRY. HE EARNED HIS LIVING AS A TEACHER OF CHEMISTRY AT MILTON ACADEMY UNTIL HIS RETIREMENT IN JUNE OF 1987. HE IS WIDELY CONSIDERED THE FATHER OF HARD SF, AND HIS NOVEL *MISSION OF GRAVITY* IS GENERALLY ACCEPTED AS THE BEST HARD SF NOVEL EVER WRITTEN. THIS IS THE FIRST STORY IN WHICH HAL HAS EVER MADE USE OF HIS KNOWLEDGE AS A PILOT.

Sortie

Hal Clement

His Aitoff screen was offering one of its occasional, brief, random views of Sergeant Gene Belvew's real surroundings, cutting him off for half a second from those of *Oceanus* deep in Titan's atmosphere, when the pipe stall occurred.

It would, he reflected at one level of his mind. He didn't believe in an unqualified Murphy's Law, which was strictly for civilians, but a scientist of any rank understood Murphy's Law of Selective Observation. If the jets had chosen any other time, he would have known it was coming, forestalled it easily without real thought, and forgotten it promptly as unimportant. As it was, his first warning was the waldo suit's use of nonvisual input. It administered a sharp chill almost simultaneously in both of his elbows. By the time he could see Titan again, half a second later, thrust was gone and accelerometers showed that *Oceanus* was being slowed sharply by the dense atmosphere. His reflexes had already operated, of course, just a trifle later than they would have from a visual stimulus. The aircraft had practically no reaction mass in its tanks; he had been trying to replenish that at the time. The big satellite's gravity, which his body in orbit couldn't feel any more than it could the deceleration, was feeble; if the craft slowed too much now, even the vertical dive he was entering wouldn't get him back to ram speed from his present altitude. Diving into the surface would not hurt him physically—the waldo's feedback didn't go that far—but would still be a bad tactical mistake. Ramjets could not be picked from trees, even if there had been trees this far from the sun. For increasingly scary moments the tension mounted as his elbows stayed cold; then ramflow resumed simultaneously in both pipes and the speed of his dive abruptly began rising with the restored thrust. Still reflexively he pulled out into horizontal flight with over a hundred meters to spare, put his nose—his own, not the ramjet's—in the face cup and moved his head slightly to run the Aitoff screen through its half dozen most-likely-useful vision frequencies. He was already pretty sure what had caused the stall, but pilot's common sense agreed with basic scientific procedure in demanding that he check.

Yes, he was still in the updraft; the screen displayed the appropriate false color all around him, and the waldo—which doubled as an environment suit, and therefore did not interfere with his breathing system—was reporting the excess methane as a salty taste. As usual, there had been no one but himself to blame. He'd been driving just a little too slowly, trying to see below while filling the mass tanks, and a perfectly ordinary but random and quite unpredictable drop in the density of the rising current had raised the impact speed needed by the jets. If there'd been nothing backing up the interrupted visual sensors he'd have learned too late and had over a hundred meters less leeway.

No point thinking about that.

"What happened, Sarge? Or shouldn't I ask?" Barn Inger, Belvew's coranker and watch partner, didn't bother to identify himself; only a few dozen people were anywhere near Saturn, and everyone knew the voice of everyone else who mattered. As Belvew's "buddy" one of his jobs was to check with Gene vocally or in any other way possible whenever something unexpected occurred; the "shouldn't I ask" was a standard courtesy. Not everyone enjoyed admitting mistakes, however important they might be as data, and the terminally ill people who formed an even larger fraction of the Titan exploration crew than of Earth's remaining population were often touchy.

"I rode too close to stall. It's all right now," Belvew answered.

"Use anything from the tanks?"

"Nothing to use. There was enough room to dive-start." Belvew did not mention just how little spare altitude he had had and Inger didn't ask.

"You're still over Carver, aren't you? You *could* have put down and tanked up from the lake." This was quite true, but neither speaker mentioned why the pilot had dodged that option without conscious thought. Both knew perfectly well; Inger's stress on the "could" had been as close to being specific about it as either cared to go. He changed to a neutral subject.

"You seem to have the fourth leg about done." Belvew made no answer for a moment; he was spiraling upward to start another pass through the raindrop-rich updraft—at a safer altitude this time. He wanted mass in his tanks as soon as possible, but was now prepared to accept the lower concentration to be found higher up. In standard light frequencies his target was indistinguishable from an Earthly thunderhead—there was even lightning, in spite of the nonpolar nature of the droplets, and Belvew faced the task of making several passes through it fast enough to avoid another ram stall but slow enough to escape turbulence damage to his airframe.

"Just about," he answered at last. "I still have enough cans to finish Four and most of Five. I hope all the ones I've dropped so far work. I'd hate to have to go back just to make replacements. There's too much else to do." He fell silent again as the waldo began pressing his body at various points indicating that *Oceanus* was entering turbulence. His fingers, shoulders, knees, and toes exerted delicate pressure—now this way, now that—on the suit's lining, answering the thumps he could feel and forestalling the ones the Aitoff screen was letting him anticipate by sight. For nearly two minutes the aircraft jounced its way through the vertical currents, and as the turbulence eased off and the air around his viewers cleared the pilot gave a happy grunt. He would have nodded his head in satisfaction, but that would have operated too many inappropriate controls.

"A respectable bite. Nine or ten more runs at this height should give me takeoff or orbit mass."

"Or several dozen stall recoveries," his official buddy couldn't help adding. Belvew let the remark slide, and two or three minutes passed before anyone else spoke. The rest of the team had their own instruments and could read for themselves the rise of tank levels as the jet's collection scoop gulped Titanian air, centrifuged the hydrocarbon fog droplets out and stored the liquid, and returned the nearly pure nitrogen to the atmosphere.

"There's another odd surface patch a few kilos west of Carver," Maria Collos' voice came at length, as the main tanks neared the seven-tenths mark. "It wouldn't take you very far off plan to look at it before you start Leg Five."

"Like the earlier ones, or something really new?" asked Belvew.

"Can't tell for sure in long waves. It could be just another bit of melted tar. Even if that's all, we're getting enough of those to need explanation."

"*One* would need explanation!" snapped Arthur Goodell, the least patient of the group usually, and excusably because of the endless pain of Synapse Amplification Syndrome. "I can see—so can you—how tars would settle out of the air as dust at this temperature. I can see dust getting piled into dunes even in the three kilo currents that pass for gales here. I can see it looking like obsidian if it gets melted and cooled again. What I don't see is what on this iceball could ever melt it."

"I've suggested methane rain, dissolving rather than melting the surface of a dune as it soaks in and forming a crust as it evaporates," came the much milder and thinner voice of leukemia case Ginger Xalco.

"And I've suggested landing and finding out first hand whether those nice, smooth, glassy hilltops are the thin shells of evaporite over a dune, as you're implying, or the tops of magma lenses," snapped Goodell. "When do we do *that?*"

"You've plenty in your tanks now, Gene. Why not take a good look at this new one—whether it turns out to be just another for Maria's list or something really different? And don't tell me it's against policy; we're here to find things out, and you know it. To quote the poetic character who wrote our original mission plan, 'there's no telling in advance which piece of a jigsaw puzzle will prove to be the key to the picture.' "

"It's not a matter of set policy," Belvew replied as mildly as he could—he had his own troubles, even if they didn't include SAS. "Avoiding risk to the jets before the surface and weather gear are all deployed is common sense, and *you* know it. Once they're in action, long-term studies can go on even if we lose transport. We've made one landing to deploy the factory, and a couple of others to restock from it, after all."

"I know. Sorry." Goodell didn't sound very sorry actually, but courtesy had very high priority. "It'd be nice to be around when some of the results crystallize, though. And you can't count the later landings because they were in the same place and we knew what to expect."

"Not exactly. The original shelf was gone."

"The area was plain Titanian dirt, with no cliff to fall down this time. Even I could probably have set down safely." No one contradicted this blatant exaggeration. "The old saw about dead heroes—"

"Doesn't apply, Arthur." Maria, somehow, was the only one of the group who could manage to interrupt people without sounding rude. "We're already heroes. We've been told so." There might or might not have been sarcasm in her tone. No one else, even Goodell, spoke for a moment. Then Belvew referred back to the landing question.

"There's no reason I shouldn't make a ground check after finishing Leg Four, if Maria's radar and my own eyesight can find me a landing and takeoff site. Actually, we're all as curious as Art about the smooth stuff, and it's good tactics to eliminate possibilities as early as we can. Let me top off these tanks just to play safe, and then you can put me back where I left Leg Four, Maria. After that's done I'll scout your new patch for landing risk."

No one commented, much less objected, and Gene made his remaining passes through the thunderhead with no actual stalls. There were no remarks about his two close calls, either; everyone had flown the ramjets at one time or another except Goodell, whose own senses were drowned in pain too much of the time to let him use a body waldo, and Pete Martucci, whose reflexes, though he was the only one of the dozen not known to be dying of something, had never been good enough for piloting. All knew the ordinary problems of flying.

"Standard turn left four five point five," Maria said without waiting for Belvew to report that his tanks were full.

"Left four five point five," he acknowledged, banking promptly to seventy-four degrees. The group had established a half-Earth gravity as a "standard" coordinated turn on Titan. The ramjet's wings, stubby as they were, could still give that much lift at ram speed below ten kilometers or so altitude. He snapped out of the turn in just over sixteen seconds, since mission speed was an equally standard one hundred meters per second when nothing else was demanded by circumstance.

"Your heading is good. You'll reach the break in Leg Four in two hundred fifteen seconds from—NOW! Nose down so as to reach three hundred meters at that time. I've allowed for the speed increase at your present power setting, so don't change it. On my time call, level off and do a standard right turn of one seventy-seven point three. Start dropping cans at standard intervals ten seconds after you finish the turn. The leg ends at the twenty-second can."

"Got it." Belvew remembered again, with the aid of the blunt needle mounted in the suit under his chin, not to nod. There were no more words until the time call, and no more after it until the last of the pencil-shaped and -sized "cans"— containers for seismometers, thermometers, ultramagnetomers, and other gear—needed for the fourth leg of the planned seismic network had been ejected.

"Okay, Maria, take my hand." Belvew nosed the jet upward as he spoke. All the others were listening and watching as their particular instruments allowed except Goodell, who was meticulously testing the output of each of the recently dropped cans. None interrupted the terse directions which formed the response to the pilot's request, and he hurtled northward along the eastern shore of Lake Carver, eight hundred meters above its surface, with his earphones still silent. He knew they could follow his progress on their duplicates of his own Aitoff, and that he could expect to have his attention called to anything he seemed to be missing, so he concentrated on the screen area a third of the way from center to lower margin. This covered the region he would pass over in the next few seconds. It was only slightly distorted by the projection which let a single screen squeeze the full sphere into an ordinary human field of vision, though this mattered little; everyone had learned long ago to correct in their own minds even for the extreme warping at the edges. No part of the aircraft itself showed; though some of the two dozen cameras mounted in various parts of its skin did have wing, nose, or tail in their fields, the computer which blended their images on the single full-sphere display deleted these.

Unfortunately.

The liquid surface was currently glass-smooth ahead and left of the jet, though even Titanian winds could raise waves; gravity was weak and liquid density low, and the highest winds occurred over the lakes themselves where evaporation lowered the air density far more than temperature changes could. Belvew gave the lake only an occasional glance, keeping his main attention on the land ahead where the patch to be examined should be.

"Three minutes," came Maria's quiet voice. The others remained silent. "Two. You might be able to see it now." The pilot scanned through his vision frequencies again, dodging the longer wavelengths which were more strongly absorbed by methane.

"I can, I think. Forget timing. I'm slowing to ten meters above stall—no, make that twenty for the first run—and going down to a hundred meters, and I'm cutting out the random reality reminder. If I lose track too seriously with where I really am we can cut my shift short later. I'll recover. The air looks steady, but I don't want another stall at this height."

No one objected aloud, though there must have been mental reservations. Belvew was the pilot for now; it was up to him to weigh relative risks to the aircraft. Negative comments would have been distracting, and therefore dangerous as well as discourteous.

The smooth patch grew clearer as the seconds passed. It was larger than most, about half a kilometer across, roughly circular but with four or five extensions reaching out another hundred or hundred and fifty meters at irregular points around its circumference. It might have been an oversized amoeba as far as outline went. The color seemed to be basically black, though it reflected the pale reddish-orange of the Titanian high smog as though from glass.

No small details could be made out from the present altitude and speed. Gene banked to a much less than standard turn rate for this speed, swung in a wide, slow circle north of the patch, and made a second pass in the opposite direction. This time the reflection of the brighter section of southern sky where the sun was hiding could be made out; the surface looked more than ever like glass, as Maria had described the others on her map, but there were still no informative details.

He made two more runs, this time at thirty meters above the highest point of the patch and only two meters per second above ramstall, tense and ready to shift to rocket mode—to cap the intakes and send liquid and extra heat into the pipes at the slightest drop in thrust. He was not worried about the wings stalling; even those stubby structures had plenty of lift area in this atmosphere and gravity, and the jet had been designed so that they would go out at higher airspeed than any control surfaces.

Nevertheless, his attention was enough on his aircraft and far enough from the ground so that it was Barn who spotted the irregularity.

"There's a hollow about ten meters across halfway from the high point to the base of that northwest arm. It did funny things to the jet's reflection as we passed this time, but I can't see it now. I can't decide exactly how deep it is, but it's just a dent, not a real hole."

"Did anyone else spot it?" asked Belvew. Most of them had, but none could give any better description. The pilot made another pass, this time devoting a dangerous amount of his attention to the surface below, and saw the feature for himself; but he could make out no more details than the others.

"You know we're going to have to land sometime," Goodell said in what was meant to be a thoughtful tone.

"I know." Belvew was thinking too. There was half a minute's pause before the remote-lab manager tried again. "What time is better than now?" The pilot could answer that one.

"When we know more about the strength of that surface. If it's just a crust, as the rain theory suggests, *Oceanus* could break through and smother the jet scoops in dust, or mud, or dirt, or whatever form the stuff under it happens to have."

"You have plenty of cans. See what happens when one of them hits. You needn't use its chute; let it hit as hard as Titan can make it."

"Good idea." The pilot, with much relief, cautiously raised his speed to standard—too sudden a boost to the flame could make the pipe frontfire—and climbed to a full kilometer. There was still no wind, but the patch was a harder target than he had anticipated. Without its parachute the slender container took much longer to lose the jet's speed, as all had expected but none could estimate quantitatively. The first attempt overshot badly. Belvew couldn't see it, but Inger and Collos followed it with other instruments until it buried itself beyond detection in ordinary, firm Titanian "soil" a hundred and fifty meters beyond the edge of the glassy patch.

The second try, with Barn calling the release moment, was much better and quite informative in its way. The can's own instruments stopped radiating at the instant of impact, ending passive measurements, but Maria's shortest viewing waves showed that the little machine, solid as it was, had shattered on contact. The surface seemed pretty strong.

Belvew was less happy than he might have been; if the can had broken through undamaged it would have implied a crust too weak to take the jet's weight, much less the impact of a poor landing just here and now.

As it was, the next test appeared to be up to him. He thought furiously. Would anything except an actual landing tell them what they needed to know?

The jet lacked landing gear in any ordinary sense; there were no wheels, floats, or real skids. Its belly was shaped into a double keel meant to give it catamaran stability in an attempted liquid landing and broad support on dubiously solid surfaces, though once stopped the body would sink to something like three quarters of its diameter in the best-guess mixture of Titan's lakes. It would float a little deeper in pure methane. This was why no one wanted to make the first lake landing; it had not occurred to anyone until much too late even to calculate, much less test, the results of attempting a rocket-mode start with the pipes totally immersed in liquid. The log of the Earth to Saturn orbit had several similar annoyed entries.

The keels were adequate landing skids on a solid surface; one could make a pass at just above wing stalling speed, grazing the apparently smooth hump. If he did it right, he might resolve the question of whether the patch was solid or crust. If the latter, of course, there would be no certainty about its ultimate strength until the jet came to a stop and the wings lost all their lift.

The convexity of the surface complicated the problem slightly. If he hit too hard, easy to do on the upslope side, the question of whether the crust was stronger than the jet's belly and keels would also become relevant.

The initial landing, Earth days before, had been on a smooth shelf of ice near the foot of the steep side of what looked like a tilted block mountain; Titan seemed still active tectonically. There had been no trouble anticipated in detail, though of course the pilot—Inger, at that time—had kept alert for the unforeseen. This was fortunate, since the exhausts had started a thermal-shock crack in the ice which chased the jet for most of its landing slide. The pilot had just managed to avoid riding to the foot of the hill on several million tons of detached shelf by a final, quick shot of thrust. The three hours it had taken for the factory pod to climb to the bottom, get to a safe distance from the cliff face and the new pile of ice rubble, put down roots and start growing had been spent in a high state of tension. Not just by Inger.

When it seemed certain that no more pods would have to be sent out, the fact that only a short length of ice shelf remained for takeoff had to be faced. Inger had been forced to use more than normal thrust, and while he concentrated his attention straight ahead, the rest of the group watched another crack chase him along the shelf, and more ice rubble fall, bounce, and roll toward the new factory. There was no longer any ice platform to land on when he did get into the air. The two later descents to pick up cans, once the factory had matured, had been on "ordinary" ground and proved uneventful. The drag on the

skids, which all had feared might stress the aircraft too highly—
this was why the ice shelf had been chosen for the first touchdown—had been sharp but not dangerous, and the subsequent
takeoffs had presented no problems except a rather larger demand for reaction mass than had been hoped. Belvew remembered the ice landing vividly as he planned his present one.
Some dangers were more foreseeable this time, but there was
the chance that concentrating on these might lessen his readi-
ness to respond to something unforeseen as promptly as his
friend had done.

Well, *Theia* and *Crius* were still available at the orbiting station, and the chance had to be taken sometime. No one would
blame him for losing *Oceanus.*

At least, not aloud.

He called for a wind check—even a few kilometers an hour
could make a difference—and held a constant heading for ten
kilometers while Inger adjusted a superimposed grid on his own
screen's image. Eventually the moving ground features followed
one of the lines and let him tie their apparent motion.

"Only one point seven, from eighty-seven," was the verdict.
Belvew swept out over the lake without asking Maria for a heading, lined up with the patch from a dozen kilometers to the west,
and eased back on his power. He nosed up enough to split the
result between descent and speed loss, and reached the shore
fifty meters above the liquid and a scant two meters a second
above ramstall. Chewing his lower lip, which fortunately affected no waldo controls, he closed the ram intakes and fed the
liquid to the plasma arcs. There was a grunt of admiration which
might have come from Goodell; the shift to rocket mode was
almost perfectly smooth. The longitudinal accelerometer swung
promptly to a negative reading, and stayed there as Belvew
turned down his fires even more. He was approaching wing
stall now, and began increasing the camber of his lifting surfaces
toward the barrel-section shape which had been used so few
times before, and never by him. He should, he suddenly realized, have done a few practice stalls two or three kilometers
higher. He convinced himself quickly that breaking off the approach and going up to do this now was not really necessary but
didn't ask for anyone else's opinion.

The rippled dust was fifty meters down—forty—thirty . . .

The glassy convexity loomed ahead, rising to meet his keels. He nosed up even more, killing descent briefly while airspeed continued to drop. The bulge kept rising toward him. Without orders, Inger began calling speed. The wings should maintain lift down to sixteen meters per second, Belvew knew, and the stall then should be smooth. Some levels of theory were pretty solidly established.

"Twenty-two   zero—twenty-one   nine—twenty-one eight . . . "

The keels were two meters from the bulge, and he nosed up still farther to keep them so as the airspeed continued to fall. That wouldn't work much farther; past the top of the dome he'd have to drop the nose to make contact before stall, and that would speed him up. Not much in Titan's gravity, but any would complicate the maneuver.

The side edges of his screen, representing the view to the rear, darkened suddenly, but he kept his attention ahead. If there was anything really important aft, someone would tell him, though he hoped they wouldn't before he was stopped. For an instant he wished he were actually riding the jet, so that he could feel when touchdown occurred.

But he knew anyway. The accelerometer and three human voices supplied the knowledge simultaneously. He stopped re-action mass flow and quenched the plasma fires almost com-pletely, but kept ready to use fractional rocket power on one side or the other if a swerve developed. Any yawing could roll the *Oceanus* onto its back, and it seemed most unlikely that whichever wing was underneath could take such treatment.

"You're down!" came Ginger's voice, this time separate from the others. Belvew snorted faintly, and spared enough of his at-tention to utter a bit of doggerel which had survived in various forms from the time of fabric-covered aircraft.

"A basic rule of fliers, and all who've ever hopped: a ship is never landed until it's really stopped."

But deceleration was now rapid as the keel friction made it-self felt, and a quarter minute later the landing was complete. Belvew knew he wouldn't feel it, but his stomach tightened up anyway for several more seconds as he watched screen and vertical motion meters for evidence that the ship was breaking through a crust.

Apparently it wasn't, and at last he felt free to let his attention focus on the view aft.

The screen darkening was from a slowly spreading cloud of black smoke, its nearest edge well over a hundred meters astern. It could not, the pilot saw at once, have been produced by friction between his keels and the surface; his landing slide hadn't started that far back, and his thermometers showed that the keels were at about a hundred and fifty kelvins. They were cooling, but not so rapidly as to suggest they had been hot enough to boil Titanian tar in the last few seconds. Not that anyone really knew what temperature *that* would take, he reflected fleetingly

More to the point, a fairly deep trough in the surface, starting just below the near side of the smoke cloud and extending as far back along his approach path as he could see, confirmed that whatever had happened to the surface had come before touchdown. The most obvious cause was the exhaust from his pipes.

The smoke was being borne very slowly away from him by the negligible wind. The trough, perhaps half a meter deep and ten or twelve wide, remained uniform as the receding cloud revealed more and more of it, extending down the slope of the convexity. The jet had come to rest almost exactly at the top of the bulge, it seemed; both pitch and roll axes read within a degree or so of horizontal.

"If it's a crust, it's pretty thick," Goodell remarked.

"Unless the jets melted their way down and just produced more of it," rejoined Ginger.

"Could be." Being human, Goodell liked his own idea better; being a scientist of rank, he knew that alternative hypotheses, however unlikely, should always be developed as early as possible in hope of maintaining objectivity. "Let's get samples."

Belvew had powered down the flight controls, except for those which might be needed for emergency takeoff, and could safely nod his head, not that anyone could see him from their quarantine compartments.

"All right, in a few minutes. Nondestructive examination

first. I assume everything in sight's been recorded; now let's *look*."

"Right." Goodell's voice was a fraction of a syllable ahead of the others. Belvew activated the short-focus viewers on the lower part of his fuselage, and allowed their images to take over the Aitoff screen as his friends above chose—no, not *above*, he reminded himself; he was above with them. Another real-surroundings reminder must be due. No one, however, said anything for several minutes; the surface still resembled obsidian at every magnification available and at every point the viewers could reach. The depression seen from the air was now hidden by the curve of the hill ahead, even though they were looking from its top, and the nearest point of the track presumably made by the exhaust was too distant for a really good look.

"I guess we dig," Pete said at last. Belvew nodded again, as uselessly as before, but operated more of his controls.

The object which dropped from between the keels might almost have been an egg-shaped piece of the surface itself, as far as texture went, about fifty centimeters in its longest dimension. Until it reached the ground, which took an annoyingly long two seconds or so in Titan's gravity, it appeared totally featureless. When it did strike, it flattened on the bottom to keep from rolling, uncovered a variety of optical sensors on the top and sides, and extended handling and digging apparatus, coring tools, and locomotion equipment.

Structurally and functionally, it straddled the accepted arbitrary borderline between nanotech equipment and pseudolife; it had been grown like the cans, not manufactured, and much of its internal equipment was of molecular size.

"Take it, Art. Where to?"

"Aft, I'd say. I'll sample at each meter until we reach the exhaust trail, and then really dig. The smellers report ready."

The "smellers" were of course the analytical equipment, and everyone began to tense up again as the egg crawled to its first sampling point and scraped up a specimen.

"How hard?" queried several voices at once.

"About three. If it's a crust, it must be pretty thick to take *Oceanus'* weight."

"Composition?" This answer was slower in coming, naturally, but overall percentages were ready in less than a minute.

"Carbon fifteen point seven one; nitrogen eighteen point eight eight; hydrogen four point one one; oxygen twenty-eight point two five; phosphorus—"

"Phosphorus?" Again, several voices merged. The first three species had all been observed in samples of the atmospheric smog, and there was nothing surprising about the oxygen, since water ice had been seen; but this was the first element past the second period to be detected on Titan. It was also something more hoped than expected. Study of prehistoric substances had high mission priority, but no one had been sure there would be anything of the sort to study; and even the now pretty certain tectonic activity might not bring material from very deep in the satellite. That would depend on the still unknown cause of the activity.

Regardless of the fact that only two thirds of the sample mass had been accounted for, Ginger Xalco called out emphatically, "Structure, for goodness' sake."

No one suggested that the elemental analysis be finished first, certainly not Goodell, who might have pulled rank if he had chosen, but who shared her feelings. He set appropriate internal machinery to work while the lab crawled on to its next sample site, and its next, and its next.

"It's a gel, really," he said at last. "The solvent—pardon me, dispersing agent—is methanol. Most of the rest of the material seems to be polymers of one sort or another. Some of it's carbohydrate, a lot has nitrogen, but it's going to take a while to find whether we're dealing with what we'd consider proteins—polypeptides made of the same amino acids that we are."

"Left or right?" asked Collos and Martucci together.

"You'll have to wait even longer for that—"

"Wait a minute!" Inger cut in. "Even at this temperature and gravity a gel has no business holding up a jet for very long. Gene, back to outside coverage! Quick!"

Belvew didn't need to ask what his partner had in mind; he flicked his Aitoff back to the outside scene instantly. For a moment he felt relief, and then took a second look at his keels. Without word, warning, or delay he fed energy and mass to the plasma arcs and watched the main accelerometer, wishing once again that he could feel the jet's response directly.

For a moment the meter stayed at zero; the surface seemed to be clinging to the keels, which had sunk into it for several centimeters, and Belvew slowly increased the thrust. Then the landscape suddenly jerked backward, and a moment later *Oceanus* was airborne.

Goodell gave an indignant cry as his lab, caught by the exhaust, stopped sending data. The pilot paid no attention for the moment, as he concentrated on reaching ram speed as quickly as possible while using a minimum of mass; it was Inger who answered the complaint.

"Sorry, Art. We can grow more labs, but not more jets. Did anything else come in before we blew your machine away?"

"No. And we don't have the sample, either."

Inger pondered for a moment, then suggested, "Maybe we can find it. The lab should have held up; the exhaust cools pretty quickly, and we'd have been getting the data by beam to the plane. That would have been thrown off-line. Order it to broadcast, and Gene can make some low passes back along the track; maybe we can get its signals."

"What if it reached the lake? It must have been blown that way."

"So much the better. We could use a reading on the composition of that juice. If anything is certain, it's that it's different from what we take from the clouds. Look at the bright side, Art."

The answer was a grunt which might have meant anything. Barn's instruments, however, showed that Goodell had indeed sent the "Broadcast" command to the lab; whether he was waiting more eagerly for resumption of data flow or for a chance to go on complaining was anyone's guess.

Gene had been listening, even with his attention on piloting. In spite of his sympathy for Goodell's feelings, he went up to a little over one kilometer, steered out over the lake to find a cumulus cloud, and replaced the reaction mass he had just used. Then he increased thrust and nosed down—he was actually as impatient as any of the others, and more optimistic than most of them—and headed back toward shore and former landing site. He was down to fifty meters by the time the glassy patch showed ahead.

He cut back thrust and allowed the jet to slow to ramstall-plus-twenty, and made four passes over the area at that speed, first following and then paralleling the line of the earlier landing and takeoff.

No signals registered. With a grim expression which no one could see, and some muttered remarks which he took care no one could hear, he reset the camber, closed the ramjet intakes, and went back to rocket mode; but two more passes at a bare fifteen meters altitude and just above wing stall—neither Goodell nor anyone else was going to say he hadn't tried, whatever they might think of his flying judgement—still produced no signals. The lab had either been wrecked, though that still seemed rather unlikely, or was too deep in the lake for its signals to be picked up. The presumably nonpolar liquid shouldn't interfere greatly with radio waves, but in broadcast mode any great depth certainly would. Titan was a strange place, but the inverse square law still applied. There was no basis yet even for guesses at the depths of the liquid bodies; that item had a very low priority in the program, though it would come eventually.

"Sorry, Art," Belvew said at last as he increased thrust, returned to ramjet mode when speed sufficed, and began to climb away from the area. "I had hopes too, but I guess we've lost it. Have you any ideas what could produce a gel here?"

"I have enough trouble guessing what could produce methanol."

"Why?" retorted Belvew. "The makings are all there. Ice and methane could do it directly, with release of hydrogen. Maybe some of the pre-life catalysts you're hoping we'd find are actually here, if you think the reaction would go too slowly at ninety K's."

"Naughty, naughty!" cut in Maria. "Catalysts wouldn't help. That's endothermic to the tune of over a hundred kilojoules." For a moment Gene felt an impulse to kick himself. He knew the woman hadn't had that datum in her head, but he, too, could have called it up before making himself sound silly. Then he saw a way out.

"The energy could come from local heat," he said, trying to keep smugness out of his voice.

"At ninety kelvins?"

"Sure. I did mention the other product. Hydrogen would leave the scene, so no back reaction—"

"That would happen only if it could leave the scene." Goodell had pounced on the hypothesis, and was enjoying himself. "That would be at or very near the surface, not deep underground—"

"Or in or just under a lake," Ginger cut in. "We'll have to look for bubbles."

"And lower than ordinary temperatures," Belvew finished. "All right, we'll look. Do some planning, you types with imaginations. I'm going to hit Line Five. Give me direction and time, Maria."

The fifth planned seismic array was a quarter of the way around Titan from Lake Carver, ten or eleven hours flight at standard jet speed and over two even at full thrust in the thinner air tens of kilometers up. Belvew set everything on automatic, turned his watch over to Maria, and decided to eat and sleep. He needed the rest. A healthy twenty-five-year-old might have gone through the last hour casually, but he belonged to neither category. There were few now on Earth who did. Evolution of disease organisms had gotten farther and farther ahead of medical research; several dozen, counting new variations of older ailments such as leukemia, were now on the list of major health problems. Four of these involved sterility, three of them in women. Earth's human population had actually halved in the last four decades, and the average age was barely twenty years in spite of, or because of, the species' usual reaction to any major threat.

Suggested explanations among the panicked survivors were legion; satisfactory ones nonexistent. Even supernaturalists had had to fall back on Noachian-flood-type divine wrath at general materialism rather than specific sins. The scientists had done better, but not very much; each virus and other causal organism had been identified beyond reasonable doubt, but the information had not yet produced much effective treatment. There

were two favored notions—they showed little sign of graduation to theories—among scientists about the basic cause of the
trend: the organisms had been tailored by people with unspec-
ified, but presumably insane by most standards, motives; or the
sudden appearance of so many almost at once was merely a sta-
tistical event like a baseball batting slump or winning streak.

Belvew, who liked people, preferred the latter idea, but was
too good a scientist to feel sure of it. CPRS, the ailment which
would finish turning his own bones to something like eggshell
china in another two or three years, would have taken only a little manipulation to produce from a normal human gene.

He shifted to full automatic control, cutting out the waldo
entirely, and extracted himself from the suit. It could use ser-
vicing, too; he floated back to his own cell and napped while its
various life support devices were recharged, cleaned, and otherwise readied for further use. The suits were not full-recycling,
indefinitely lasting affairs; they had been designed foremost as
waldoes. They did, of course, have fusers and life support capacity designed for Titan's environment, but could keep the
wearer comfortable for only thirty hours or so there, and alive
for perhaps twenty more.

Calcium-phosphorus recrystallization syndrome also, while
robbing him of energy, kept him from sleeping for very long at
a time, so he was back with *Oceanus* well before it reached the
planned site of the next seismic array. There was nothing to do
but watch scenery and, of course, hypothesize on the cause of
the various features. He could see the ground well enough from
this height, since he could use frequencies able to pierce the
small amount of smog which was below him. There were block
mountains and rift valleys; there were lakes large and small.
The background, as well as the covering of nearly all the more
or less horizontal area, might be the hypothetical tar dust; the
factory had been planted on such a surface, but at the time no
analysis had been possible. Neither cans nor labs had yet been
grown.

None of the lakes was large enough to be called an ocean,
as mapping from orbit had made clear enough. However, it now
seemed that fully a tenth of the satellite's surface was occupied
by such bodies, ranging in size from Carver, about the area of

Earth's Lake Victoria, down to puddles. The Collos Patches were neither as numerous nor as large, but far from rare.

The locations of the lakes were to some extent controlled by topography, of course; water is a unique liquid, but not in its tendency to flow downhill. Nobody, however, had yet found any order or sense in the size, location, or arrangement of the smooth patches. Belvew amused himself, as he had before, in trying to organize patterns out of those he passed over. He reached his target area without coming up with anything more meaningful than constellations.

Maria, who had also slept, warned that it was time to decrease thrust. The jet began to slow and settle. A real-surroundings interruption occurred just after the descent started, and Belvew wondered briefly whether he should override the device. He decided against it; his tanks were full, he would be travelling high enough and fast enough to preclude any kind of stall as he sowed the cans, and vertical disturbances could be seen at a safe distance. It was only while inside them, slowed down to collecting speed, that there was any danger.

Any known danger, he reminded himself. Any known danger except identifying too closely with the aircraft, which the interruptions were intended to prevent. He brought his attention back to the job as Maria began issuing more specific directions.

He had lined up on course, reached standard speed and delivery altitude, and released the first dozen of the Line Five cans when an interruption came from a voice no one had heard for weeks. It had announced then that the last of the six relay stations which kept the station in potential instant contact with all of Titan's surface was properly adjusted in orbit, and thus cleared the crew to get the actual project under way. They had mostly forgotten it since.

"There is a change in map detail at the factory site. Please evaluate." The speaker was Status, the data handler dedicated to constant rechecking of the surface, the orbits of the station and relay units, the operation of the closed-cycle life support systems, and the current medical condition of each of the explorers. Its announcement automatically put Maria, responsible for surface mapping, in charge. As usual, the voice with which she responded was calm.

"Gene, you're on track. You still have forty-four cans on board, which will complete about two-thirds of Line Five. When they're gone, your heading back to the factory starts at three eleven. I'll get back to you with more headings for the great circle when you need them, or brief Status if it seems likely I'll be too busy. Barn, standard: keep an eye on Gene. Art, get any readings you can from the factory itself while I check the details Status couldn't handle. The rest of you carry on. I'll keep everyone informed." She fell silent for several minutes while she examined the surface around the factory with every frequency at her command.

"The change," she resumed at last, "seems to be the appearance of another of our glassy patches. Its texture is identical with the others, as far as I can tell. It is almost perfectly circular, just over twenty meters across, and its center is 144 meters from the opening of the factory's release port and directly in line with that opening—that is, directly north. Azimuth zero."

"How long did it take to reach that size?" asked Goodell. "Can Status tell us when the last check of the site was made? And are there enough observations to tell whether it appeared all at once or grew from a center?"

"Less than four hours, yes, and no," replied the mapper. "That's the time of the last check, and there was no sign of the patch then. Does the factory itself have any data?"

" 'Fraid not. It's been making twenty cans and one lab an hour and paying no attention to above-ground surroundings since it ripened."

Everyone was hearing this exchange, of course, and Belvew cut in without allowing his eyes to leave his screen.

"Above ground? But how about below? Do any of its roots go toward the patch?"

Goodell was silent for some seconds, and finally answered in a rather embarrassed and surprised tone, "I can't tell. Roots went out in all directions, of course, and I can tell pretty much what materials have been coming in through each major one, but we never thought of needing to know just which absolute direction any one root was taking."

There must have been a spectrum of reactions to this announcement, but neither laughter nor anger was audible. The jet ejected several more cans before its pilot could think of another useful question.

"The root which went east, toward the cliff, would be picking up water sooner or—well, sooner. The factory couldn't have started production without oxygen. Does any one of them show a richer water take than the others?"

"Yes. Much richer. Number Twelve."

"Then it's a reasonable guess that that one went toward the mountain, which seems to be a block of ice. Whichever is ninety degrees counterclockwise from Twelve must be pretty close to under the new patch, right?"

"Right. Unfortunately—"

"Unfortunately? You mean you don't know the relative directions either?"

"No. I don't know whether the numbers go one way or the other, or even if the numbers are in order. I labeled them as they started to pick up raw material. Sorry. Even if we'd wanted to, there was no other way to distinguish that."

"So there goes any chance of analyzing that patch with the factory."

"I'm afraid so."

"So I go back and plant more labs around the factory."

"You drop the rest of your cans first," Maria cut in. "It won't make much difference in time. You'll be a couple of hours getting back, and it's where you'd be going anyway for more cans. There's no reason to believe there's any hurry; we don't know what causes these patches, and we can find out enough by watching this one grow, if it does."

"There could be need if the factory itself has anything to do with its appearance," Goodell pointed out. Belvew started to say something, but Maria was first.

"We'll worry about that if it seems in order. I'll watch how fast, and which way if any special one, this thing grows. If it does. Art, keep really close tabs on the factory's behavior; that's the only other thing I can think of which might let us know of any such connection. Any other ideas?"

"Five cans to go," Belvew answered, with no obvious relevance. "What was that return heading again?"

Maria told him, and he finished his run in silence. He then

climbed to compromise height—air thin enough for low resistance while still dense enough for the ramjets—eased in full thrust, took up the great circle heading back to the factory, set *Oceanus* on automatic control, and shifted his screen to the instruments being used by Art, Maria, and the others. There would be no verticals at this height, and he refused to worry over unknown dangers, especially when Barn was also watching. On top of everything else, as far as his own attitude went, while scientific/military procedure was of course an important and sometimes even a life-and-death matter, freedom to pay attention to a problem was equally so. The usual rank distinction between theorists and mere observers was absent here. The smooth patches might not be a military or any other kind of risk, but they now involved a basic situation change near the only equipment source currently on Titan—one which would take days at least to replace, if they did have to plant a new factory—and the more minds engaged on the problem the better.

Barn Inger felt just the same, and he couldn't see the jet's wings either.

It was daylight at the factory site, and would be for several more Earth days. The aircraft was on the night side, though Belvew expected to see the fuzzy, reddened blob of the sun—much of the smog was still above him—in another few minutes. Both factory and flyer were on the hemisphere away from Saturn; to see the big disc, pierced by the needle of its edge-on rings, he'd have had to shift to a real-surroundings view. Even that might not work, since the station naturally spent over a third of the time in Titan's Saturn-shadow, and usually neither he nor any of the others knew just where they were in its orbit. That was something for Status to keep track of.

Even by day, visible light was no use for examining the factory from above the atmosphere; much longer waves were needed, and for these to have really high resolution the readings from at least a few kilometers of orbit travel had to be combined into single "pictures" by the data processors. Maria could not, quite, watch her surface images closely in real time. By now, it had occurred to everyone in the group how nice it would have been to provide the factory with a camera, but no one mentioned this aloud. "If onlys" were against military, scientific, and medical discipline as well as common sense; all of these demanded dealing with things as they were.

How things were was slowly becoming more apparent. Before Belvew could see the sun, Maria announced that the patch was six centimeters broader on the east-west line and eight on the north-south than it had been when first measured. Half an hour later both amounts had increased by another ten centimeters, and the distance from the centroid of the patch to the factory's nearest point was smaller by nearly a meter.

"Suggests it's actually moving, not just growing more one way than the other," Barn pointed out.

"Suggests I was wrong about its being caused by rain," was Maria's less enthusiastic comment.

"Are you sure? Would the factory report rain?" asked Belvew.

"No, but my viewers would. It hasn't rained there since we planted the rig. And I know rain when I see it; there's been plenty of it here and there on Titan. You ought to know, Gene."

"I do. It's always been from verticals either over the lakes or very close to them. The general winds are so slow that a thunderstorm always dies before it can get very far from the lake that spawned it."

"It seems to," was Goodell's more pessimistic word. "In any case, if all these things are gel like the one we started to examine, you'd have to explain how liquid methane turned into methyl alcohol."

"There was a suggestion about that, and the factory is close to an ice source," Ginger pointed out.

"But not to a lake," Maria admitted, still rather sadly.

"So Gene drops another lab the second he gets there."

"Of course," replied the pilot. "That'll still be nearly an hour, though. Aren't there a good many ready at the factory? Why not get one of those on the job—or two or three, if that'll make things faster?"

"Pete, you're the strongest of us by a good deal. If I unseal my room, would you take the chance of a quick visit and kick me? You can hold your breath long enough."

"No, Art," replied Martucci, "but not because I'm afraid of breaking quarantine. I'll come and stay as long as you want if it will help your lab work, but I don't see how it would."

"Don't rub it in. I have a lab on the way, Gene." Goodell was obviously embarrassed, as the others would have been for him if they had not been equally guilty, and neither his morale slip nor the general oversight was mentioned again.

"Better do samples on the way to the patch, not just after the lab arrives. We'll need to compare the patch with the ground in its neighborhood," pointed out Ginger. This obvious suggestion made everyone feel better; they could all share the onus of not thinking to use labs from the factory long before, and the point had been stressed that Goodell needn't deem himself the only sinner.

The readings from the lowly traveling lab held everyone's close attention while the jet neared mountain and factory and began its letdown. Since neither Belvew nor Inger could have seen the white accumulation which started to grow on the leading edges of its wings shortly after the descent began, this made no real difference. Even when the pilot shifted full attention to his job as final approach and landing neared, neither his eyes nor his waldo sensors told him what was coming, though the accumulation was now projecting nearly three centimeters. In effect it sharpened the leading edges, but did not yet make real difference in either lift or drag. With a few hundred more flying hours experience at a wide enough variety of altitudes and speeds, Gene might have come to recognize the tiny discrepancy between thrust and airspeed. Had he actually been riding in the jet for that much time, he might even have felt it.

And if the material had remained where it was until after he had touched down, no one might ever have known about it. There were instruments to read and report on skin temperature at many points on the machine, but not there; even with nano and pseudolife technology, and their effect of making complex devices almost costless to build, there were limits to how much could be installed on even a fusion-powered flying machine. The heat which leaked from the pipes and was at once carried away by the airstream, so that all but the few centimeters of wing adjacent to the ramjets themselves stayed at ambient temperature, now began to creep farther out as the speed dropped to and below tens of meters per second.

The changing camber applied by Belvew as wing stall approached may or may not have contributed to what finally happened. The operator's tiny pitch and yaw corrections as he maintained a straight and steady descent also may have contributed, or may not. A trace of turbulence in Titan's own air may even have been all that was needed.

Whatever the cause, the sharp white rim on the front of the left wing suddenly fell or blew away from the slightly warmed surface, and the lift on that side, already more dependent on wing area than on shape, dropped. It decreased only a little, but did it suddenly, and probably not even an automatic control could have done anything useful at such low airspeed.

The wing, short as it was, grazed the ground with its tip, and *Oceanus'* nose whipped down and to the left. Belvew felt a simultaneous kick from practically all his turbulence sensors. At the same instant most of the central area of his Aitoff went blank, and the mosaic of sections which should have shown the view to the rear displayed only Titan's pale peach sky.

There was nothing useful to say for the moment, and Gene again made sure no one heard him saying it. "There couldn't have been any turbulence there!" was too much like an excuse for an adult, much less a disciplined and moderately high ranking scientist, to utter aloud. Everyone's thoughts reached the same point on the logic route, though the milestones didn't always pass in the same order.

No ground views. No transport utilities. Seismic nets not finished. Weather tracers not even started. Labs now available only at their source, and something odd happening there.

Humanity is a visually oriented species, and in seconds Maria was building a new image of the factory site, whose details improved moment by moment as data poured in from different directions. The factory itself was simply a square with rounded corners, a little over five meters on a side now that it had finished growing, saved from resembling a child's toy block by rain gathering, light reading, gas ejecting and other apparatus on its roof. No one was looking at it yet, however.

The jet's nose was crumpled back almost to the wings; the

ground it had tried to displace had yielded very little. The left wing and ram pipe were hidden under the fuselage, whose tail pointed upward at about sixty degrees. The right wing and engine, also pointing upward but less sharply, seemed undamaged, but image resolution was not yet down to single centimeters. "So much for *Oceanus.* Is *Theia* ready?" asked Goodell finally.

"I'll check her out," came Ginger's voice. "I think I'm nearest, and I've just slept and done my suit."

"Are you willing to drive again, Gene?" Belvew hesitated only a moment. The crash was presumably his fault, but there was no reason to suppose that anyone else could have avoided it; and the psychology behind the custom of a pilot's flying again as soon as possible after an accident was still valid even when the pilot wasn't in the aircraft at the time.

"Sure. I'm fresh enough. I'll nap, though, during the preflight. Call me when she's ready, will you, Ginger?"

"Should I hurry?"

"No!" Goodell was emphatic. "*Theia* hasn't been flown at all yet. Cover everything on the list, and anything else you can think of. If Maria reports some other change we may have to hurry, but not unless or until."

"I'll be good. Gene needn't worry."

"Who worries?" asked Belvew. He received no answer, and relaxed in his suit. It seemed unlikely that there would be time enough to get out of it for a real nap. This estimate, of course, was based on foreseeables, not human behavior.

The station was far too massive for anyone to feel the reaction when a person pushed off from or stopped against a wall, but the departure of the jet was noticed by everyone. It was also identified, since everyone had felt it before. Reactions differed. Goodell and one or two others wondered momentarily whether they had been asleep and missed the end-of-checkout report. Peter Martucci made a wry face, as though something he had expected had happened in spite of his hopes. Gene Belvew was, for a fraction of a second, the most surprised, and of course Ginger Xalco was the least.

But Belvew was quick on the uptake.

"Ginger! Why?"

"My suit's fullest, and it'll save time."

"We don't need to save time!"

"How do you know? I certainly don't!"

"My suit was serviced almost as recently as yours." Belvew tacitly conceded the other argument. "It has nearly as much supplies."

"And I use less than three quarters the food and oxygen you do. Stop being futile; I've already cut speed."

Everyone by now understood the situation, but no one was silly enough to suggest, much less order, that the woman return with the jet. All relevant instruments showed that she had already killed enough of her station orbital speed to take the craft into atmosphere, and used most of the little reaction mass in *Theia*'s tanks to do so. Return was not possible until she had refilled on Titan.

Nor was there any question of taking over from the rebel even if this had been useful. Her waldo suit was in the space designed for it on the jet, and any suit there had control priority unless the wearer deliberately ceded it. "Dead-man" override from outside was not possible; such a need had not been foreseen until much too late. Construction and energy were extremely cheap, but design was not; people charged more heavily than ever for their skilled services. As a result, many structures and machines were produced with performance well short of ideal, and even the best usually turned out to lack something. The situation was not entirely new in history, but greatly aggravated by modern conditions.

Even Goodell said nothing for general hearing. There was nothing useful to say for the moment, and what would be said later would never mention penalties, or violation of rules, or disobeying orders. Science, the search for understanding, had replaced much of the desire for personal territory, influence over others' behavior, or glory which had motivated so many of humanity's earlier high risk activities; but the need-for-knowledge culture had not evolved along quite the same lines as the religious-economic-military one. Social awareness—idealism or patriotism, though now for the whole species—was fully as great in the now vaguely militarized ranks of science, and demanded as much team effort as war, but not the same prompt and blind submission to orders which the latter had had to evolve when the opponents were other human beings rather than a universe with no personal survival urge.

Not quite so prompt and certainly not nearly so blind, but still involving risk. Ginger knew exactly what she was doing, and why; so, in spite of his hasty question, did Gene and the others. Nothing critical was said during the hour and a half *Theia* took to reach atmosphere and kill her two kilometer per second relative velocity; and even when she was flying rather than orbiting, navigation instructions from Maria and flying advice from the others made up most of the conversation.

The advice was not really needed, since Ginger had spent as much time in simulators and roughly as much actually flying *Oceanus* as any of the others, but somehow those still in orbit felt a need to keep meaningful conversation going—to "stay in touch."

Xalco, after tanking up, deliberately landed at higher speed than Belvew had done, but there was no way yet to tell whether this made the difference. *Theia* slid to a stop half a kilometer west of the factory. She would have come closer, but there were numerous objects on the surface between cliff and factory, and some even west of the latter, which had been tentatively identified by Maria's equipment as boulders of ice from the fallen shelf. One of Goodell's labs had confirmed this; three separate specimens were nearly pure water ice, with a trace of carbonate dust. A debate on why this was not silicate had taken up much time between the discovery and the jet's landing, but no conclusions had been reached except that the news had better get to those on Earth as soon as possible. No one knows in advance which will prove the key piece of a jigsaw puzzle, but the unexpected screams for attention.

The landing approach had not been directly over the mystery patch, but the exhaust had melted or blown a shallow trough in the regular surface and raised a cloud of smoke apparently identical to that of Belvew's earlier landing. This had not happened before, when landing had been made to pick up cans and labs from the factory. Something seemed to have changed, though admittedly the other approaches had been along different tracks. Possibly the apparently uniform area—uniform except for ice blocks and the still growing patch—differed here and there in composition. Goodell had all ripe labs now out and in action, and was sending out others as quickly as the factory completed them. Most, including Ginger, were listening to the analyses which Maria was numbering, tabulating, and locating on a map which usurped part of everyone's Aitoff, and trying to make sense out of them. Belvew was the only exception. His attention was aimed more narrowly.

The form of the crashed *Oceanus* showed a few hundred meters from her sister jet, much closer to the strange patch, and he was trying to see why it had fallen. If the cause were actually turbulence there would probably be no evidence, but he still found this hard to believe.

"Art, could you spare a lab to sample around the wreck?" he asked at length.

"We'll get there pretty soon anyway. Any reason for special haste?"

"Well, Ginger landed hot, but there'll be a couple of seconds after liftoff when she'll be as slow as I was. It might be worth at least a check. Maybe the ground was warmer or colder, for some reason, and grew verticals."

"How could it be?" The question, from Peter, was ignored by all but Barn.

"We're looking for chemical action," he pointed out, "and there's methyl alcohol to explain."

"All right," admitted Goodell. "Two labs on the way. Tell me where you want your samples, Gene."

Belvew went back to the view provided by Theia's eyes, and strained his own looking for points of special interest on and about the wreck. It would be a few minutes before the slow-moving labs reached the spot.

Several of *Theia*'s cameras covered the remains, and with Ginger's consent he had first one and then another of them feed the proper spots on the screen and process their images with interferometer routines, trying to produce the clearest possible view. For some time he concentrated on the ground ploughed up by *Oceanus*, but could detect nothing special, and finally shifted to the jet itself. The labs had arrived and without his specific instructions were starting to collect dirt samples before he saw the interrupted white ridge along the leading edge of the uptilted right wing. Parts of it, especially toward the tip, had not been shaken off by the crash. He pointed it out to the others.

"That shouldn't be there! How could I get wing ice here?"

"How do you know it's ice?" asked Barn reasonably.

"I don't, but it's where you pick up ice in Earth's atmosphere, and it had the same effect!"

"You're blaming it for what happened?" came Maria's quiet voice.

"Well, not yet." Jumping to conclusions was one of the cardinal sins. "Can you get a lab up there, Art?"

"I doubt it. They weren't designed to climb a smooth surface."

"That skin's hardly smooth anymore."

"True. I'll try." He suited the words with action and for over fifteen minutes sent one of his devices rolling and clawing its way along various upward-leading wrinkles in the crumpled fuselage. Each sooner or later narrowed enough to let the machine topple back to the ground, undamaged but ineffective. Goodell finally gave up. Belvew, less skilled but more anxious, tried for some time himself, with no better luck.

"It looks as though some of the stuff has fallen off," Inger pointed out at last. "There should be bits of it on the ground."

"If there are, I can't see them," replied Belvew. "I suppose we can just do lots and lots of tests all around the wreck, but how will we be sure that any offbeat result can be blamed on the white stuff?"

"We can be quicker than that," Ginger assured them.

"How?" asked Gene.

"I'll show you." Several of the listeners guessed what was coming, but kept their mouths shut; there was nothing they could do about it, and objectively Xalco was being smart. She was economizing on her suit time.

Those who failed to read the implication from her words understood a few seconds later as an environment suit with "GX" stenciled front and back entered the field of view of the jet's eyes. The walk was unsteady; even Titan's less than fourteen percent of Earth gravity was a lot more than any of the group had experienced for many months. She made good speed, however, never actually fell, and reached the wreck very quickly.

"I don't see anything white on the ground," she said. "It either fell off farther back or got buried in the dirt *Oceanus* ploughed up. Here, Art." She needed to jump only a short distance to bring one glove against the rime on the wing. It stuck to her suit when she tried to set it down beside the nearest lab, and she had to shake it off, leaving some liquid on her palm. All the watchers tried to draw inferences while the lab unit did its work.

"Mostly ethylene, a trace of acetylene," Goodell reported tersely after a moment.

"Melting points?" Gene asked promptly, sure that Maria would have them on her screen at once. He was right.

"About 104 and 192 respectively," she reported promptly. "Check your own wings, Ginger; if you picked any up after you cooled down from entry, it would still be there."

"It is. I see it. It's lucky I landed fast, I guess. I'll wipe it off right now." Her suit disappeared intermittently, its image reappearing as odd patches and parts from time to time as she moved into and out of the view fields the computer was using for Aitoff projection.

"Why did we pick that up these two times, and not on any of the earlier landings? And why pick it up at all, for that matter? There isn't much of either of those in the atmosphere." Gene was still puzzled.

"I think I can guess," Barn said slowly. "You don't need much, after all; water vapor usually doesn't compose very much of Earth's air, but it freezes on wings if they're cold enough. These landings are the only ones made so far right after the jet had spent significant time up at compromise altitude, and really got its wings chilled. We can test that, if there's ever time, by going back up there for a while and doing stall exercises, at a safe altitude of course, after we get down again." He did not suggest reprogramming the Aitoff computer to show wings. None of them could have done this.

"And until then, we make it a point to land a little hotter than we have been." Gene was relieved. "Good work, Ginger. You'd better come back up; you've used up a lot of suit time already."

"I have plenty more. I'm going to take a close look at this patch while I'm here."

"I don't mean to be insulting, but you're budgeting time to fill your tanks, I trust," Goodell interjected.

"I am. But thanks for asking. Don't apologize." Her suited figure dwindled on the screens.

"The labs can do gas analyses, can't they?" she asked suddenly.

"Sure."

"Then hadn't we better look for free hydrogen? Remember the idea about the methanol production."

"We'd need water, too," pointed out Barn. Ginger kicked at one of the boulders, almost overbalancing in the weak gravity.

"These look like ice," she assured him.

"They are. I checked them before," growled Goodell. "If you want a repeat . . . "

"I know. That can wait. I want to see this smooth stuff." She moved a few gliding steps farther, and squatted down. A lab moved slowly toward the boulder, guided from above, but the oldster said nothing aloud. Of course this would be ice, too. "Give!" came mingled voices. Ginger's suit had no camera.

"It looks and feels through my gloves like black glass; it could still be the melted tar someone suggested. I can't scratch it with a glove claw. Labs, please."

"Already there, as you should have noticed," answered Goodell. "Analysis so far matches the other one; it's a methanol gel, basically. I'm still working on the polymers."

He would be, Belvew thought. Arthur, of all the group, was the most optimistic about finding prebiotic material on Titan, and the most expert on autocatalysis and similar phenomena presumably involved with the chemical evolution stage preceding actual life. He was also hoping desperately, his companions knew, to find a key piece of the biological jigsaw puzzle while he still lived, even if that piece failed to provide a cure for his particular ailment. He was as close to being a pure idealist as anyone in the group—a scientific Nathan Hale, though no one was tactless enough to make the comparison aloud.

The screen brought Belvew's attention back from this brief

wandering. Ginger had started to rise from her squatting position, and was putting on a rather grotesque show.

She had been slightly off balance as she straightened her knees, and reached vertical with her center of gravity a little outside the support area outlined by her feet. There is a normal human response to this situation, acquired usually during the first year or so after birth: one picks up the foot nearest the direction of tilt and moves it farther in that direction to extend the support area, though not so far as to make reaction initiate a fall the other way. The woman started to do this but her right foot refused to pick up. The couple resulting from pull on this one and Third Law push on the other tilted her even farther to her right. By the time she reached thirty degrees all eyes were on their screens, and at least three theories were being developed.

"You've melted yourself in!" cried Martucci. Inger, whose idea involved close contact between soles and surface plus Titan's high air pressure, said nothing but thought furiously. Goodell, already wondering how simple the chemistry for a thermotropic reaction could possibly be, called, "See whether it's pulling in around your boots, or if you're just sinking!"

Ginger Xalco was moved to answer this. "Just sinking? I'm stuck, you idiot! What do I do?"

"Find out why," Arthur replied calmly from the safety of a seven-hundred-kilometer-high orbit.

"Try to tilt and slide one boot at a time," proffered Inger.

"Can anyone guess how much jet exhaust a suit will take?" asked Belvew. "I assume no one knows."

While the woman tried unsuccessfully to implement Barn's suggestion, and then less enthusiastically to follow Goodell's instruction, Gene, already in his waldo suit, silently preflighted *Theia*. Xalco had filled the tanks conscientiously on the way down, and the landing had depleted them only a little; there was well over enough for a takeoff. Keeping careful watch on the gauges he fired up the plasma arcs and fed liquid to the pipes. Carefully checking the relative whereabouts of woman and factory, but not letting himself worry about a few labs, he raised thrust on the right jet enough to drag *Theia* in a curving trail—the keels wouldn't let it simply pivot—until it was heading toward Ginger. He then equalized both sides and sent the machine dragging forward until it was only fifty meters from the still-anchored suit. Rather than attempt another tight turn he went on past, leaving Ginger on his left and turning only slightly to the right, until the exhaust was streaming past her only three or four meters away.

"Better let me take it," the woman said at this point. "I can tell if it's too close, and the response will be quicker."

Gene made no argument, and relinquished control. Using waldo while standing up was more awkward than Ginger had expected, and for a few seconds she was almost tempted to let Belvew take over again; but she resisted the urge, recognizing the strength of her own arguments and possibly for other reasons.

The jet blast was now sweeping over part of the patch, behaving just as it had before; the tar, if that's what it was, was sinking or possibly vaporizing into a shallow groove along the track of the warm gas, while a dark cloud of smoke appeared above the affected region and swirled and billowed slowly away from *Theia*.

Ginger examined as closely as she could the slow widening of the trench, and very carefully increased thrust on the left pipe to swing the gas stream closer to her position. The higher power widened the stream as well as turning the jet, and she almost overdid it. The unspoken question in all minds was whether the removal of surface could be managed without cooking her suit. She finally stopped the turn by cutting back on the left unit and raising power in the other. Luckily this did not provide enough total thrust to move the aircraft farther away and complicate matters even further.

"I still can't tell whether it's vaporizing, melting and sinking, or just crawling out of the way," she reported, her voice once more calm.

"Is it crawling over your boots?" asked Goodell. Xalco squatted once more.

"No," she replied after a moment. "It's more like melting in. I'm deeper than before, but the stuff isn't closing in around me. You know, this might work."

"Damn!" said Arthur with feeling. Not even Ginger criticized. All watched tensely while the trench widened toward her and finally reached the left boot. Here it seemed to stop, and after several impatient minutes she raised the thrust a few percent.

"Your tanks are getting a bit—" Gene didn't even try to finish the sentence. Ginger answered only by trying, hard, to slide her boot toward the once-more widening trench.

The material which had pressed up and outward like fairly stiff clay around the sole was vanishing; she squatted to watch closely, curiosity once again in the ascendant, as it blew away in a trail of smoke which she could clearly see forming from half a meter. She reported verbally to the others.

"Can you move your foot?" cried Belvew. "Your tanks!"

She stood and pushed sidewise again, and her left boot slid out into the exhaust stream, suddenly free.

She brought it next to the right one and pressed down hard; it had, after all, taken a while for her to "stick" earlier. She kept trying, shifting the position of the free boot every few seconds just in case, but the right one stayed firmly in place until the warm gas actually reached her armor and began to eddy around it. For several more seconds no one breathed, much less spoke; then the right foot came suddenly free, and Ginger made an unplanned but quite lengthy jump which took her off the smooth patch.

If the released breaths from the watchers had been free to leave the station, its orbit might have been changed measurably.

Ginger, safely on ordinary ground, did not make her way at once back to the jet. She picked up, labeled, and pouched several dirt samples from points as close to the edge of the patch as she could move the stuff. She even made a point of working loose a specimen where soil and smoothness seemed to blend. Then, without haste, she returned to the aircraft and vanished from the screens.

"Don't hit the factory on takeoff!" Arthur cried, then, "Sorry."

Ginger made no answer. A few seconds later *Theia* slid into the air, and a minute after that had reached ram speed with something under a hundred kilograms of mass in her tanks.

"There's a thunderhead at forty kilometers, two hundred degrees," Maria informed her.

"Right. Thanks. Is there anything I should do while I'm here, after I juice up? Or have I already earned a mission credit? I did pick up a lot of data."

Belvew wondered whether she would have thought of using the jet to free herself, but was far too polite to suggest this explicitly.

"How about splitting the credit?" he asked innocently.

DON D'AMMASSA IS THE AUTHOR OF *BLOOD BEAST.* HIS SHORT WORK HAS APPEARED IN *TOMORROW, ANALOG,* AND *EXPANSE.* HE IS THE FICTION RE-VIEWER FOR *SCIENCE FICTION CHRONICLE.* THIS WAS THE FIRST STORY THAT APPEARED IN OUR PAGES TO RECEIVE AN HONORABLE MENTION IN *THE YEAR'S BEST.*

Jack the Martian

Don D'Ammassa

I suppose it's cynical to consider the appearance of a serial killer on Mars evidence that we have successfully transplanted human culture across the gap between worlds. Admittedly, the psychologists responsible never suggested that they were creating a new civilization from scratch, but they certainly intended to apply strict controls to our closed society. Personally, I attribute this to the narrow-minded focus of their specialty. If they had consulted those of us who have studied human history, they might have adopted less grandiose plans from the outset. The higher the aspiration, the greater the disappointment.

Nor is it surprising that the killings began in Bradbury, the largest of a dozen domed cities, supporting and supported by twice that many smaller communities, plus countless observation posts, weather stations, research projects, and other outposts of the human invasion scattered across the barren but fiercely beautiful surface of Mars. With a population of approximately twenty thousand, Bradbury would have been a small town back on Earth, but here it was a major metropolis, the cultural, commercial, and scientific center of the universe for a quarter million colonists.

It was also the hunting ground for a deranged killer.

The first victim's body was still warm when I reached the scene. Bob Winston, one of my sector supervisors, waited at the foot of the access-way ladder while I climbed down.

"What've we got, Bob?"

"A mess, Ted. Over this way." We were in one of the maintenance corridors beneath the northeast rampway, not far from the locks between domes six and seven. Judging by the mesh of cables that ran along the low ceiling, this particular corridor provided access to the energy linkage from the core tap.

A few meters further on, a coveralled body lay facedown in a pool of blood.

"His name's Nguyen Chu, second generation Martian, lived in Bradbury all his life except for a few months on temporary assignment in Barsoom."

Two technicians were crouched over his body, while a third carefully videotaped the entire procedure.

"How'd it happen?"

Winston shrugged. "Throat cut with a sharp instrument, nature unknown. Judging by the angle of the wound, I'd say the assailant came up from behind, reached over the right shoulder, and struck before the victim even knew he was in danger. No signs of a struggle. The autopsy might tell us something more."

I glanced around, trying to look professionally calm despite the churning in my stomach. Crime, even murder, wasn't unknown on Mars, of course, but it was rarely premeditated.

"I don't see any cameras. Who found the body?"

Winston refused to meet my eyes; not embarrassment, just unease. "No one. The killer called it in."

"Do we have him?"

"No, but we have his name." Winston appeared to be uncomfortable and waited to be prompted.

"All right. What's his name?"

"He says he's Jack. Jack the Martian."

The colonization of Mars had been a strange blend of pragmatism and visionary romanticism. It had taken over a century before the first few settlements were essentially self-supporting,

and the capital outlay had been so great it would take at least
that long again just to repay the principal, let alone the accu-
mulated interest. There were few accountants on the red planet;
our fiscal policies gave them nightmares.

At the same time, the creation of enclosed, environmentally
balanced ecosystems separated from Earth by a gap of time,
space, and attitude was perhaps the most ambitious engineering project ever undertaken by the human race, and many of the
most brilliant technical people on Earth had voluntarily emigrated in order to be a part of it. The Bureau of Psychology was
supposed to smooth over the contradictions and conflicts so the
two strains of personality interacted productively, and at least
to date they had done so with reasonable success.

I'm ninth generation Martian, though educated on Earth
and Luna, trained in administration and historical analysis. After
graduation, I accepted a position with Security here in Bradbury
because I believed it would be a relatively undemanding job and
allow me time for my life's work, a comprehensive history of the
colonization project. To my dismay, I discovered a latent talent
for dealing with bureaucracy, and was now the youngest person
ever to serve as Chief of Security.

Back on Earth, that would be Chief of Police. We had no
"police" on Mars. The psych people decided that particular
word had connotations which would not be helpful to the social climate, and "security" sounds so much more reassuring.
Perhaps I was contaminated by my five years offworld, but to
me this was just symptomatic of their tendency to soften language, disguise the raw edges of existence; a linguistic head in
the sand divorcing us from reality. But then historians have always known the importance of a specific turn of phrase, so perhaps I'm overly sensitive.

I was off shift when the second murder took place. Anne and
I were sharing a bottle of Martian Chianti fresh from the win-
ery in Wells, trying to decide whether or not to renew our mar-
riage contract. It was an amicable discussion; the two-year term
that was about to expire had gone smoothly and pleasantly. We
were friends, expected to remain so, even intimately, but neither
of us was entirely reconciled to making the compromises necessary to live together successfully as a couple.

The blinking code on my wristcom indicated a priority call and I touched the appropriate icon.

"Ted, this is Carol Chen. We've had another murder." She paused. "It's just like the last one." Policy was not to broadcast details even though the department wavelength was supposedly secure.

"Where?"

"Between rows 346 and 347, Farm 14. Bob's already at the scene with his team."

"All right, I'll join him there."

The victim this time was Joyce Djibwa, a seventh generation Martian employed as an agricultural assistant in Farm 14. She'd been working a shift of seedbed maintenance, unaccompanied, and from the evidence available we were able to reconstruct the sequence of events directly preceding her death. At one end of the aisle between rows 346 and 347 was an open access to the irrigation trench four meters below. The fast flowing waters washed down to the recyclers, carrying organic debris that fell or was thrown in by staff members trimming and weeding the gardens.

Her assailant had approached from the rear, used one hand to grab the victim's hair and force her head down long enough to draw some unidentified sharp instrument across her throat. Djibwa's blood had sprayed across the ground and made long, dark streaks down the containment wall. Security had been notified by an anonymous and untraceable call from a public comlink near the exit to Dome 15 within a few moments of the attack.

Bob Winston didn't greet me this time, just stood watching the technicians work, obviously uncomfortable. "Find anything?" I averted my eyes. Djibwa had been an attractive woman, but now she lacked all humanity.

He shook his head. "Same as the other one."

"Might be coincidence," I suggested without conviction.

Winston shook his head. "Same message as last time, claims to be a *real* Martian. I'd say we have a nut, the victims chosen at random."

That remained unproven, but even though we did considerable cross-referencing, our subsequent investigation turned up no usable link between Djibwa and Nguyen Chu, the first to die. Of course, in a community as small as Bradbury, there were inevitably some connections. They lived in different neighborhoods, but they were both active squirtball fans, along with one out of every three adults in the city. Djibwa had originally worked in systems maintenance, though not in the same sector as Chu, and switched to agriculture a Martian year or more before she emigrated from Dustbowl to Bradbury. There was no evidence that they had ever met.

We explored the tenuous connections as far as we could, but without real hope of finding anything. And we downplayed the two incidents in the media, not even acknowledging that the deaths were related, although carefully not denying the possibility.

Things didn't start to get out of hand until the third attack. Connie Santiago was a popular woman in Bradbury. She'd been elected to four consecutive terms on the city planning board, winning by a larger plurality than anyone in living memory, and had only been returned to private life because she refused to run for a fifth. Santiago was attacked and killed during daylight, working in the postage-stamp-sized garden she maintained behind her small private quarters.

Needless to say, Security was under pressure from all sides. Both comayors had managed to forget their joint veto of my proposal to increase the number of security cameras although, to be fair, this was unlikely to have saved Santiago. Private property could not be kept under surveillance without the owner's approval. Message volume was so great we were forced to filter all incoming calls through an AI discriminator to separate legitimate ones from public complaints and I was twice accosted in public places by irate citizens demanding to know why I hadn't brought the killer to justice.

To make things worse, someone in Security leaked details we had hoped to keep to ourselves. Not only did the newslinks report that the murderer had called us following each kill, they also know the weird part, that the killer claimed to be a "real" Martian who would continue to kill until the human invaders were gone.

Bradbury, like all Martian cities, is a closed community. Not that there isn't free trade with the rest of the domes; there's no such thing as nationalism or anything like that on Mars. The Bureau of Psychology is very careful to neutralize anything that might contribute to regionalism. Even squirtball teams are prohibited from having more than two players from any single city.

But since we can't breath the Martian atmosphere, every breach in the perimeter of our cities is monitored at all times. You can't enter or leave without identifying yourself unless you're smuggled in as cargo. There have been occasional fugitives on Mars, but it's almost impossible to vanish here. There are too many ways to trace a concealed human: air exchange rates, protein consumption, DNA tracking, pedestrian character recognition programs, and so on.

Following Santiago's death, I received a grudging emergency appropriation to lease additional surveillance equipment from other cities, and authority to commandeer nonessential monitoring equipment from the private sector as well. We very quickly increased our coverage of public areas from ten percent to approximately thirty-five, but the effect was even greater since we didn't need to cover heavily traveled rampways, public meeting places, the main commercial district, and other unlikely preying grounds.

It wasn't enough to save the life of Reinhardt Warshofsky, a fourteen-year-old butchered on the landing of an old catwalk used as a shortcut between home and the gymnasium, but we had installed permanent traces on every public comlink in Bradbury and a strategically-placed team caught sight of the killer vaulting over the rampway guardrail. The team leader alertly posted her people to cover every exit and called for help.

I came through the airlock from Dome 4 just as they were preparing to go in after him. The fugitive had spotted the two security people sent to intercept and backtracked, then descended further into the bowels of Bradbury through the maintenance tunnels. When I heard that, I ordered the dome sealed off completely, even though that set off the emergency sirens and created considerable panic.

Even so, it appeared that we had lost him. We swept the area systematically with small, heavily armed teams, checking every tunnel, compartment, connector, and tubeway as we went. It's a bewildering world down below street level; Bradbury is the oldest permanent settlement on Mars, and each new vision of what the city should evolve into was built squarely on top of the old. But cubic volume had always been at a premium and there was little wasted space, few places to hide and all of them obvious. Or at least, that's what we thought.

But we couldn't find our killer.

I ordered a second sweep, convinced that we'd overlooked something, and my intuition proved right. Night was just falling outside when Winston reported they'd found a supposedly sealed hatchway which wasn't—it had been tampered with. The bad news was that it was a direct conduit into one of the adjacent domes, bypassing the supposedly airtight dome seal. The good news was that it led into Farm 2.

Although Bradbury looks anything but symmetrical from overhead, there is actually a pattern to its development. There is a central core of linked domes which house commerce, industry, entertainment, and government services. Additional domes along the southern periphery are primarily residential, those along the north agricultural and scientific. Farm 2 was one of the oldest and largest of the northside domes, but it was also one of the very few that had only a single link to the rest of the city. In other words, it was a dead end. And a sparsely populated one to boot.

Since our quarry could not have returned to the main city while the seal was in place, we moved our operation to the Farm 2 airlock area. There was no certain way to know how many people were legitimately inside the agricultural dome, but night shift had started and there wasn't likely to be more than a skeleton crew.

We evacuated the staff systematically, screening each individual in case the killer was one of their number. Fortunately for us, no one had wanted to work alone since Djibwa's death, so we had little difficulty clearing everyone assigned to Farm 2 for the shift. Then we sent in the search teams.

It was only a matter of time. Farm 2 is the largest of the agricultural habitats, but it was laid out to be easily maintained. We

flushed the killer less than halfway through the sweep and vectored the other teams to intercept every possible escape route.
As chance would have it, I was with the squad of five who saw
the end from closest at hand.

Our "Martian" headed almost directly to the north side of
the dome, where the irrigation system rushed through an artificial streambed into the jaws of the recyclers. When a furtive
figure emerged from a cluster of ferns only a few meters from
our position, we drew our flechette guns, the heaviest weaponry
allowed inside a dome. Without acknowledging our shouted
orders to surrender, the killer ran across the aisle and climbed
the sanderete abutment above the canal.

I'm not exactly certain what happened next. Another squad
burst into sight further along the perimeter and turned in our
direction. The killer, still unidentifiable despite the artificial
lighting, seemed to hesitate and then, so quickly that we all
froze, stunned, was gone. I rushed to the scene and scrambled
up onto the abutment, stared down just in time to see what
might have been a single flailing arm disappear under the thresh-
ing jaws of the nearest bank of recyclers.

Officially, it was listed as death by mischance—although it
might possibly have been suicide. Nor did we ever learn the
identity of Mars' first serial killer. Despite having the most
closely monitored population in human history, we were unable
to discover, even indirectly, the name of the person we chased
that night.

It took a while to accept that situation. There are close to a
quarter million people on Mars, after all. But we accounted for
every one of the twenty thousand currently listed as resident in
Bradbury; no one was missing. As much as we would like to remain confident about the security system, it had somehow been
breached.

So we expanded our search to every installation on Mars,
and quickly eliminated all but a few dozen people, mostly
prospectors who hadn't bothered to maintain radio contact. By
the end of the year, there were only three names left, a party of
scientists believed lost in the Great Canyon region. Their bodies were found a few months later.

There were theories of course. The least practical was a

stowaway from Earth. The most popular, despite denials from Data Management, was that some hacker had found a way to excise himself or herself from the system so completely that no trace of identity remained behind. There were even some who believed that the murderer had been an unrecorded birth, sheltered by parents for some arcane reason, grown to maturity without the social conditioning that maintains the stability of our fragile culture.

I have only recently begun to suspect the truth.

Despite my disinclination toward a career in administration, I was pressured into remaining as Chief of Security even after my term expired; submission to social pressure is a key part of our psychosocial conditioning. Then a seat on the Bradbury City Council, appointment to the planetwide Development Board, and so on. In short, I was not able to return to my love of history until my retirement from public service just last year.

Gilwright and Kubisawa's definitive history of our colony preempted my original plan to produce an equivalent work, and I became committed to a new project, essentially my personal memoirs. The work was rewarding and went quite rapidly until I reached the year of the killings.

The Security records were quite complete. I reread the site reports, the autopsies, my own logs, and replayed the newsnet coverage. Even after a gap of more than half a lifetime, those events seemed real. Distinct, hard-edged, still vaguely unsettling. What I discovered next was more startling.

Despite my skepticism about the efficacy of many policies enacted by the Bureau of Psychology, they indisputably maintained a meticulous set of records of human activity, in mass terms. Many of these had been restricted even from the Chief of Security until the Freedom of Data Act a few years earlier, so it was with some curiosity that I downloaded and began to examine some of the files from that period. I was expecting to find a sharp increase in mental disturbances during the period directly following the Jack the Martian killings. What I found was exactly the opposite.

Over the course of the two years immediately preceding those unfortunate events, the incidence of neuroses and psychoses had been on a sharp upward curve, so sharp in fact that

I detected serious concern expressed with mounting anxiety in the archival notes. Ten days prior to the first murder, the Bureau's Board of Governors was considering declaring a Psychological Emergency and taking direct control of colony affairs under the now defunct Cultural Emergency Code.

The trend began to reverse itself after Nguyen Chu died, declined slightly further when Joyce Djibwa was slaughtered, and dropped dramatically with the death of Connie Santiago. Reinhardt Warshofsky's demise directly preceded a reduction to acceptable levels.

I thought about that for some time, read a number of scholarly studies examining the phenomenon, all of which concluded basically that while the initial increase in mental unrest was almost certainly a kind of planetary cabin fever, no one really understood why the disorder reversed itself. Several files made reference to the Jack the Martian killings as a symptom of the problem, but none suggested what I now suspect is the real explanation.

I don't think Jack the Martian ever really existed; I think he was a mass delusion, an artifact of the minds of all of us here on Mars. A device by which we dissipated a growing, unrecognized resistance to psychological control. But a delusion so intense that it could literally interact with our environment, interact powerfully enough to be seen, heard, and to take four human lives.

And if I'm right, what form will our next mass hallucination take? Are the increasingly frequent reports of movement in the Martian deserts significant? Are we truly the inhabitants of Mars, or are we in the process of creating them?

Undying Iron

Alan Dean Foster

Ory was frightened.

She'd been frightened like this only twice before: once when a silimac had torn its way through Corridor Eighty-Eight, barely missing her but killing twenty of the Flatt family, and once when Jonn Thunder had consumed something unwholesome and had gone into convulsions that had lasted nearly a whole week.

But this was different. Perceiving no threat to her person, she did not fear bodily harm. This new fear rose from the depths of herself, as if she was being poisoned by her own mind. It was new and incomprehensible, this irrational fear that something awful was about to happen.

She was terrified.

Drifting aimlessly down Twenty-Four Tunnel, she gazed vacuously at the pale haze that clung to the inner lining and wondered what to do next. Fear had given rise to a throbbing in her brain. Of that she was certain. Still, she had tried to ignore the persistent discomfort. Headaches were a corollary to her specialty. They came and went like feeding time.

But this one lingered, unresponsive to all the usual treatments. Refusing to dissipate, it impaired her ability to cogently cogitate, robbed her of relaxation time, and had started to affect her even when she slept. It was a dull, insistent pounding that refused to abate.

I can't go on like this, she thought worriedly. I have to talk to somebody.

Selecting a Downtunnel angle, she boosted herself westward. Brothers, aunts, uncles, and nonrelatives waved greetings or shouted cheerily to her as they passed. Some were fellow Checkers, others bound on important business of their own. The Brights illuminating Twenty-Four Tunnel glowed softly all around, bathing her in their reassuring refulgence. Colors changed as the Brights tracked her position.

Ory ran an Alpha shift. More than half her routine checks remained to be made, but she contrived to schedule them so that they would bring her close to Tamrul's cubicle. With luck, he might have some helpful suggestions to offer concerning headache treatment.

Used to be, Tamrul could always be counted on to provide satisfactory answers to her questions, but not any more. The past ten years revealed the onset of a creeping senility the Philosopher could no longer hide. In spite of his gathering infirmities, he was still her first choice. Less lucid he might be than in earlier times, but he remained unfailingly kind and understanding. Unlike some of the others, he would not laugh at her, nor treat her with unbecoming brusqueness.

She slipped out of Twenty-Four Tunnel and headed north to Two Hundred Twelve Corridor. Several Dispatchers accelerated to pass her, barely observing minimum clearance. Full of self-importance, they wore their rudeness like combat medals.

"Hey, slide over!" she shouted at them.

"Do you hear something?" the one in the lead queried his companions.

"White noise," ventured a companion.

"With twitchy probes," added another for good measure.

They raced onward up the Tunnel, chuckling nonstop and holding hands. Dispatchers were incorrigibly incestuous in their relationships, keeping to themselves as much as possible even though their jobs required frequent contact with others. Ory ignored their taunts. It was their way of dealing with individual insecurities. When it came to instigating original conversation, they were not very interesting anyway.

Two Hundred Twelve Corridor, Section Ninety-One. Waving politely to a passing Inspector, she banked around a tight corner and buzzed Tamrul's cubicle. In the old days he got out more often. Now if you wanted his advice, you had to go to him. No more house calls, he'd posted one day. That did not trouble Ory. A Checker had plenty of freedom. So long as she completed her shift schedule she could roam where she pleased.

The Corridor Brights stood down behind her as she buzzed a second time. She could sense him inside, whining to himself the way he often did when he was alone. It was sad to hear. She felt sorry for Tamrul. Not that he was any better or worse than any other Philosopher, but he had always regarded her with more than just a polite eye. She felt that he saw something special in her, though he was too formal to come out and say so. Just as well. It could never have worked out. As a Checker, she led much too active a lifestyle for him. They were reduced to delighting in the pleasure of one another's conversation.

At last she was admitted. He greeted her with the informality that came from long acquaintance. "Good day, Ory. It's nice to see you again. What brings you up into my neck of the woods?"

"Your beneficent face. What else?"

"You flatter my expression, which I am quite aware rarely expands upon the mournful. No wonder I like you so much. Sweet Ory, always ready to take the extra step to make others feel better about themselves."

Sounds of amusement rose from nearby. A couple of guys from Maintenance were streamlining a recalcitrant photon flow, their compressors humming. Clearly, they found the private conversation a source of unexpected mirth.

"Moderate your volume, Tamrul." To show she was not upset with him, Ory offered one of her famous smiles. "Half the Family think you're senile already. No need to add fuel to the rumors."

"You're right. I should render my verbalizations more circuitously. I'm too direct for a Philosopher."

"And get off this self-pity kick. When did you start with that? It doesn't become you."

"It is simply that I am bored, Ory. That's all. Do not commit the error of others by mistaking ennui for senility. The old mind is as sharp as ever. But a brain is no different from any other tool. Gets rusty if it isn't used. I miss the mass discussions of the old days." He made a visible effort to rouse himself from his self-induced stupor.

"Now then: you still haven't told me what brings you here. What troubles you? What would you like to discuss? The nature of Existence? The secrets of the Universe? The reversal of entropy?"

"I have a headache."

"Oh." Tamrul was crestfallen. "Is that all? Then why come to me? It sounds like you need to pay a visit to Doc."

"I thought I'd get your opinion first, Tamrul. The idea of going to see Doc doesn't thrill me."

"Perfectly normal reaction. Nobody does."

"I wouldn't mind if his reputation was better, but on my shift they're saying he has a tendency these days to overprescribe. It's only a headache."

"Well then, why don't you drop down to Twenty-Eight and see Marspice instead. Maybe his diagnosis will suit you better."

"Come on, Tamrul. You know the physicians. They'd run a consult on me automatically and I'd end up worse off than if I'd gone to see Doc in the first place. Marspice is out of my section."

"Consultation is performed to ensure more accurate diagnosis—or so they say. Still, I suppose you're right. Someone in Administration might raise hell if you purposely avoided Doc Welder in favor of Marspice. What is so remarkable about this particular headache that it brings you to me in the first place? You have them all the time."

"I know. But this one is different."

"Different how?"

"They usually fade away after a day or two, without ministration from Doc or anyone else. Not only isn't this one going away, it keeps getting worse. It's really bothering me, Tamrul. Bad enough to cause me to miss two checks: one in Underlying Physics and the other in Biosearch. Pyon covered for me both times, but she has her own schedule to keep. She can't back me up forever. Pretty soon I'm liable to mess up on something important and Admin will take notice." She quivered slightly. "You know what that could mean."

"No need to be so melodramatic. I swear, you have a particular flair for it, Ory. In your own words, this is only a lousy headache, albeit a persistent one." He softened his tone. "Much as the idea displeases you, I don't think you have any choice except to see Doc."

"That's not what I wanted to hear from you." Disappointment flashed across her face.

"Sorry. I provide honest opinion, not masking balm." He was regretfully inflexible, as she feared he might be.

"I know." She sighed resignedly. "I guess I just needed confirmation from someone else. It makes a difficult decision a little easier, somehow."

"At least I can commiserate." He touched her gently. "You stop by again sometime and we'll have a nice debate on the nature of karma, okay? And remember that no matter how low you're feeling, we're still on course for undying iron."

"I know we are, Tamrul. Thanks for your time. And for your personal concern."

Reversing from the Philosopher's cubicle, she let herself drift back out into the Corridor. With an effort she turned her thoughts to completing the rest of her shift. Neither the visit nor her determination did anything to alleviate the pain in her brain.

But she did not go to see Doc. Instead, when she had finished her shift, she returned to her rest cubicle. Other Checkers were heading out, speeding past her, intent on making good work of the Beta shift. Pyon was already in her own bed, curled tightly in sleeping position. She blinked when Ory, unable to turn her thoughts off, entered silently. From above and below came the soft whispers of other Alpha shifters discussing the events of the day.

"Lilido down in One Sixty-Five went crazy today," Pyon quietly informed her visitor.

"Wonders—that's the third in six months. What's the matter with those people down there?"

"Don't know." Pyon shrugged. "Nobody else seems to, either. Apparently she was working normally when she just started spraying everyone and everything in sight. Finally turned the flow on herself and choked out. Nasty business, they say. Took a whole Maintenance crew the rest of the shift to get the mess under control. Routing had to shift traffic around the clogged Tunnel. Admin was pissed and didn't try to hide it."

"If everything you're telling me is true, then you can't blame them." Ory snuggled close to her fellow Checker and tried to relax. "Personally, I never thought those Lilidos were all present upstairs anyway. Always sucking up that gunk they work with. That'd make anybody go crazy after a while."

"Yeah, I guess." The cubicle was silent for several moments before Pyon inquired, "How's your headache tonight?"

It was hard to lie while the back of her brain throbbed. Not that Ory felt any need to prevaricate with Pyon. She was her best friend.

"It's still there. Gets better, gets worse, but won't go away. I went and told Tamrul about it today. He told me what I already knew and didn't want to hear: that I ought to go see Doc."

Pyon's soft whistle echoed eerily in the enclosed space. "Sounds pretty serious, for a headache. I think Tamrul may be right. How long have you been trying to deal with this?"

"Longer than normal."

"I have some medication. Want to try it?"

Ory hesitated only briefly. "No thanks. I'd better not. I could get into real trouble if anyone else found out that I was using an unauthorized prescription. You can imagine the reaction from Admin."

"I won't tell."

Ory smiled. "I know you wouldn't, Pyon, but if there were persisting side effects or if it only made my head worse, it would come out during a deep-probe examination. It's not worth the risk."

"Up to you. You're the one who's suffering."

By now the voices of the other Alpha shifters had stilled and the resting chamber was suffused with the soft hum of sleep.

"Thanks for covering for me yesterday."

"Forget it," Pyon insisted. "What are friends for? Are you going to see Doc?"

"It doesn't look like I've got much choice. I'm about out of ideas, and I have to do something. I can't take much more of this. Sometimes the pressure gets so bad my whole brain feels like it's going to explode. I've had headaches before, but never anything like this. This one is unprecedented."

"You know what Doc will want to do." Tension and unease had crept into Pyon's voice. "He'll suggest a purge of your system. They say that's his remedy for everything these days. Diagnosis be damned, purge the system!"

"Not this Checker's system, trouble blotter." But beneath Ory's bravado she feared that her friend was right. "It's not *that* serious yet."

Pyon turned reflective. "I know it sounds awful, but maybe a system purge wouldn't be such a bad idea. Everyone says that you feel like a new person after a purge."

"Everyone says that you *are* a new person after a purge. They also say it hurts like hell. No thanks."

Pyon yawned. "Well, I'm glad it's a decision I don't have to make. *My* head feels fine. I hope you find some other way of treating the problem. I don't mean to kick you out, but it was a long day and I'm feeling about half unconscious. Sleep-wise we're already significantly behind the others. Good rest to you, Ory. Go to the undying iron."

Ory tried, but sleeping was next to impossible. Desperately as she tried to ignore it, the headache did not go away, and it was worse by the time the next shift start rolled around. The internal pounding was so intense it was a struggle to keep from crying aloud several times. Despite her self-control she drew questioning stares from several patrolling Mokes, and had to force herself not to rush too quickly past them.

There was no avoiding it any longer. System purge or not, she would have to go and see Doc.

His oversized cubicle was as spotless as ever and his uniform glistened beneath the painfully bright lights. So did his attitude.

"Well hello there, Alpha shifter. You're a Checker, aren't you? I don't get to see many Checkers. You're a notably tough bunch. What can I do for you?"

She sidled carefully into the cubicle, keeping her distance from him. Her hesitation made him chuckle.

"Take it easy, Checker. Despite my reputation, I don't bite. Not unless it's required by diagnosis, that is."

The comment typified his sense of humor. Maybe another physician would have found it funny. Ory didn't. Half panicked, she wanted out, but she was already inside. Recognition committed her. If she fled without suffering examination, Administration would be notified.

"I have a headache."

He frowned slightly. "Is that all?" His expression critical, he turned and drifted across to a cabinet. "You want a repress injection? That should take care of it."

Despite the temptation to accept the offer and get out of that stark white place she plunged onward with the truth. "I've had headaches before. I don't think a repress will do the job this time."

Doc shook his head and looked sympathetic. "You Checkers: always worrying, always offering suggestions. I think you should all take more time off, but then I suppose you'd probably worry about someone else running your schedule incorrectly. Headaches are congenital with you, or at the least, an occupational hazard." He pondered. "Very well—so you don't think a repress will do the trick. What makes you believe this headache is different from any you've had before?"

"I can tell," she replied with certainty. "Not only hasn't it gone away, but it hurts worse than anything I've ever experienced previously. And there's something else." She hesitated. "A feeling, that also won't go away."

His gaze narrowed. "What kind of 'feeling'?"

"That something exceptionally out of the ordinary is going to happen."

"Dear me! That sounds ominous. Are you contemplating a change of specialties, perhaps? Thinking of applying for a Prognosticator's position? Iron knows there are plenty of vacancies."

"No, it isn't that," she replied impatiently. "I couldn't be a Prognosticator anyway. That's too much like Tamrul's work."

"So you've been talking to that old fraud. Filling your head with chatter about anticipatory emotions, has he?"

Ory leaped to her old friend's defense. "This has nothing to do with him, Doc. These feelings originate entirely with me. I didn't get anything from him. Tamrul's just old and tired and bored."

"Maybe so. In any event, he is beyond my help. What he needs I cannot give him. Whereas you, on the other hand . . ." His eyes sparkled. "If you refuse a repress, that leaves me with only one sensible alternative. System purge."

She eyed him distastefully. "You enjoy your work, don't you, Doc?"

"Yes, and a good thing it is, too, since there's been so much of it lately. Well, what is your decision?"

She slid away from the examination brackets and along the back wall. "I think I'll hold off for awhile yet. I was hoping you might be able to prescribe a third course of treatment."

"I just told you: there isn't any third course. Repress or purge, those are your choices. What else would you have me do?"

It was difficult even to form the words, but with the threat of a system purge looming over her she forced herself.

"Ask Mother."

All traces of Doc's ready, if slightly ghoulish humor, evaporated abruptly. "You're not serious. That's a joke, right? A poor joke."

"I'm serious, Doc. I wouldn't joke about a request that serious." Pain flared in her brain, momentarily numbing her perception. She waited for it to clear. "I think we need to ask Mother about my headache."

The physician's response was stern and unbending. "As you are well aware, Mother is sound asleep. She is not to be awakened because some lowly Checker has a bad headache. Where's your common sense? Maybe you need that purge more than I thought. Maybe this is no longer a question of alternatives." He was staring hard, almost accusingly, at her.

She found herself backing away from that unrelenting, no longer sympathetic gaze. "I understand what you're saying, Doc. My head seems better now. I think I'll be okay. Really."

"So you claim. That's what worries me. I don't think there's any question about it. You require purging. In fact, based on this interview, I'd say that it is long overdue." He reached out for her and she barely managed to skip past him.

"Be sensible about this, Ory. I know what's best for you. It's my job to know. Now, are you going to cooperate or do I have to call a couple of Mokes?"

"Rest easy, Doc. You were right all along. It was just a bad joke." She laughed. "I really had you going for a minute there, didn't I? You think you're the only one in this section with a low-down dirty sense of humor?"

Eyeing her uncertainly, he hesitated next to the Call switch. Finally he drew back. Calling in the Mokes was a serious step, one that the caller had better be able to justify. Her laughter seemed spontaneous enough.

"First another Lilido goes off and now a Checker plays jokes." A warning tone pervaded his voice. "Don't play these kinds of games with me, Ory. It's too serious. Suppose I had called the Mokes?"

"Then the joke would be on you. Really, Doc, can't you spot a gag when it's being played on you?" She resumed her methodical retreat toward the entrance.

"Hmph. Say, what about your headache? Was that a made-up, too?"

"No, but it's far from being as serious as I made it out to be. This visit wouldn't have been funny if it was. Let's give it another couple of days and we'll see if it goes away of its own accord."

"And if it does not?" He was watching her closely. "Suppose the joke doesn't stay funny?"

"If it doesn't go away then I'll certainly let you run a system purge on me."

He looked satisfied. "Now that's being sensible. Very well, we will hold off another couple of days. But I am going to have your shift monitored, so don't think you can fool me about this. I'll know if it gets serious."

"Of course you will. How could I hide something like that?"

She practically knocked over a couple of passing Chelisors in her haste to escape from the white, threatening cubicle. The ambling pair recovered quickly and tried to peddle their zings and thomes, but she wanted nothing to do with their wares. Not now. All she wanted was to put plenty of distance between herself, the medical cubicle, and Doc's eager, grasping hands. Most certainly she did not want to be purged by him. It seemed to her that he was growing a little senile himself.

But her time for exploring options was running out. He was going to put a monitor on her shift, and her head hurt so badly she was near tears.

There was one more close friend whose advice she could ask, one more independent party. She rushed heedlessly down Eighty-Five Tunnel, hardly bothering to acknowledge the greetings of puzzled friends and acquaintances. At the speed she was making it was not long before she entered restricted territory.

Keeping her eyes straight ahead, she maintained her pace. Checkers could go almost everywhere. She would be all right if she didn't have the bad luck to run into an Inspector.

That was what nearly happened, but the Inspector who had been coming toward her stopped to bawl out another Checker Ory did not recognize, and so she was able to slip past in a crowd of workers. Jonn Thunder's section was always busy.

The rising heat began to affect her as she made her way through several sealports well striped with warnings. A Lilido or an unshielded Moke would soon overheat, but Checkers were equipped for travel anywhere. As Doc had noted, they were built tough. She could stand the local conditions for a little while.

Then she was through the last protective sealport and there he was: immensely powerful, confident of his strength and ability, hard-working and tireless. Not for the first time, she thought she might be a little bit in love with Jonn Thunder. Her feelings for him seemed to go beyond simple admiration. For his part he sometimes treated her like an infant, infuriating her. She knew this amused him, but she could never get used to it. Her personality demanded that she be taken seriously. Perhaps, she thought, that was one reason why so many Checkers suffered from bad headaches.

She didn't think he would toy with her this time. He had the ability to sense seriousness in a visitor.

"Hello, little Ory Checker," he rumbled pleasantly. "What brings you to Purgatory?"

"I'm running a check on its unstable inhabitants. Making sure they haven't been guzzling any more hydrogen than they're entitled to."

"Who, me? Do I look drunk? Hey, boys: do I look drunk?"

Overhead, Matthew Thunder belched noticeably. "Yeah, come to think of it, you do, but you always look drunk to me, Jonn."

"Been stone drunk these past hundred years straight, that's my opinion," declared Luke Thunder from another region of Purgatory. At the moment he was sweating over an uncommonly delicate adjustment. "He just camouflages it well, don't he, Checker?"

"You're all making fun of me." She would have admonished them further, but a bolt of pain made her yelp. Instantly, Jonn Thunder was all sympathy and concern.

"Hey, little nosey-mote, what's wrong?"

She unburdened herself to him, telling him all about the headache and the persistent fearful feeling that accompanied it, about her talk with Tamrul and her encounter with Doc, and lastly of the suggestion she'd made that had nearly cost her a system purge.

Jonn Thunder was very quiet when she had finished. For a moment she thought he was going to berate her just as Doc had and suggest a purge, but he had no such intention. He was thinking. Jonn Thunder might not be very deep, but he was thorough.

"Did you make the same suggestion to Tamrul?"

"No. My head wasn't bothering me as much when I went to see him. Besides, I know how he'd react, what he'd say. He's a dear old thing, but in his own way quite inflexible. That always struck me as a strange quality for a Philosopher to have."

"He's getting old," John Thunder muttered. "We're all getting old. Except you, Ory Checker, and a few of the others. What do you think, boys? Where does she go from here?"

They debated, in the manner of Thunderers, and it was fascinating to watch. When they had finished it was Jonn who spoke. "Do what you think you have to do, Ory. We can't help you. I'm for sure no Doc, but you don't look or sound to me like you need purging. Not Doc's variety, anyhow. But you're going to have to do whatever it is you decide to do on your own. Me and the boys have a lot of pull, but it's useless where something like this is concerned.

"You'd better be careful. If Administration finds out what you intend they'll have the Mokes down on you straightaway. They'll haul you right back to Doc, and this time he won't bother to ask your opinion before he goes to work. You know that."

She didn't want to believe what she was hearing. "You could help."

"No we can't, Ory. I'm sorry. We have our own status to worry about. If I neglected my work for a minute to help a Checker with a bad headache there'd be a serious scandal. If anyone found out they'd put me down for a system purge too."

Ory was shocked by the very notion. She could not imagine such a thing, and said as much.

"It's the truth," he told her. "You're on your own, Ory."

"But this is important." She was insistent. "Something's happening. I can feel it—inside my mind. Mother has to be awakened."

"Then you'll have to wake her by yourself, Checker. Wish I could believe in the necessity of waking Mother as strongly as you seem to, but my head's fine. We won't do anything to stop you. By rights we should notify Admin ourselves." She froze. "But there always was something about you, nosey-mote. Something special, though I'm damned if I can define it. So we won't interfere." A chorus of agreement echoed from his hard-working relations.

"But we won't help you, either. If you're challenged you'll have to deal with Admin by yourself."

"Thanks for listening to me, Jonn Thunder. I guess that's about all I could hope for."

"Don't be bitter, Ory. I consider myself brave, but not a fool. Maybe you're both. Good luck." He sounded wistful, but unyielding.

She backed out of Purgatory, leaving them to their work. More time had passed than she realized. Already she'd risked a great deal in coming here. Now her own schedule was going unattended. Doc and his talk of setting a monitor on her had forced her hand as much as the pain in her brain. The Mokes would be looking for her soon enough, if the search hadn't commenced already. All it would take would be one frizzing station to pass the word and she'd find herself being prepped for purging before you could say spindrift.

She could not let that happen. She *couldn't.* Something she could not explain, something much deeper than the persistent, fluctuating pain drove her onward. If Jonn Thunder and his relatives had thrown in with her she would have had a better chance, it would have improved the odds. Despite what he had told her she did not really believe Admin would risk purging any of them. But they believed otherwise, and so had refused to help her.

She was alone.

Pain shot through her mind, making her convulse. She knew what she had to do. Steeling herself, she hurried up the Tunnel. If they caught her, the worst they could do to her was run a total purge. By now she was starting to believe even that might be better than the unrelenting pain.

She had embarked on her present course of action with little forethought and no preparation. Even if she succeeded in placing herself in sufficient proximity, how was she, a lowly Checker, going to wake Mother? And what would she say if she was successful? There was every reason to believe that Mother might react with outrage and fury instead of understanding. None of her memories contained anything about waking Mother. She did not know of anyone who had seen the ritual performed. It simply was not done.

But she could not think of anything else to do. And however unnatural, however outrageous, something about it somehow struck her as right.

It was a long journey up to Administration territory and her initial resolution weakened as she neared the control zone. Overbearing Supervisors, intense Inspectors, and armed Mokes were everywhere. Pain and not prudence had driven her this far. She realized with a start that if someone confronted her, she had no reasonable excuse to give for being this far from her section.

She found herself pausing at the entrance to the Tunnel. The longer she hesitated, the more likely it became that some patrolling Moke would accost her with a demand for explanation of presence, an explanation she would be unable to supply. After that there would be harder questions and then—a trip to Doc's, under escort.

Sure enough, one of the armed watchers was drifting toward her right now, his armor glistening in the pallid light. Her mind spun, thoughts whirling frantically as she fought to see and think clearly despite the throbbing in her head. If only the pressure would relent and give her a few moments of respite!

Then the Moke was hovering over her, glowering, and it was too late to contemplate retreat.

"Checker," he growled, noting her insignia, "what check thee here?"

"I—I"

"Please to mumble not. I've already a Lilido acting strange that needs a looking-at."

"I—I'm here to check on Mother's status." Could she have said anything more blatant? Motionless, she awaited the Moke's reaction.

"Lilido's going crazy," he muttered as he backed off. "Get on with it, Checker." In obvious haste he slid past her, brushing her aside so roughly that she wobbled in his wake. The threatening thrum of his powered-up weapons system faded with his flight.

In a daze, she hovered in the Tunnel, recovering her determination and marveling at the unexpected ease of her escape. A little brass goes a long way, she decided. Of course, it probably helped that the Moke was trying to deal with two problems at once. Thus confronted, he had chosen the tangible over the nebulous. Pushing off, she soon found herself deep within Administration.

Clerks and Controllers swarmed all around, ignoring her, intent on assignments of self-evident importance. No one else stopped to query her or question her presence. The assumption was made that because she was there, she had a right to be there. Carefully she picked her way through the bustling mob. There was an urgency of movement in Administration, a sense of power and purpose that she had never encountered anywhere else, not even in Jonn Thunder's Purgatory. The intensity frightened her a little.

Fright brought you here, she reminded herself. Fright and pain. Time to risk all to alleviate both.

Mustering all her confidence, she boldly intercepted a speeding Termio and blocked his path. He eyed her irritably but waited for questions. When at last she edged aside to let it pass, she had her directions.

Still no one thought to confront her, despite the fact that she was traveling through highly sensitive territory. After all, she was a Checker, and it was presumed that she was going about her lawful business. Her profession was her only protection. She prayed that she would not meet another Checker, one authorized to operate within Admin.

Then she was there, and that was when she nearly turned and fled.

Projections and Brights, Terminals and Secures towered ten corridors high before her. Termios waited patiently at their assigned stations while Clerks and Controllers dashed to and fro with seemingly reckless abandon. There were no Mokes in sight.

Oblivious to all the activity around her, Mother slept on through the endless night.

For one last time Ory wondered if she was doing the right thing. She feared a total purge worse than anything. Fire burned her brain and she winced. Almost anything. Hesitating no longer, she commenced to ascend the awesome escarpment. Espying a vacant station on the epidermis of the great construction she angled toward it. Locking in, she established contact as if she were running a standard, everyday check.

What do I say? she found herself wondering. *How do I act?*

She was working furiously even as she worried, executing the necessary commands with speed and skill. The enormous somnolent bulk behind her seemed to let out a vast sigh. Clerks began to cry out while the Controllers set up a fearful hooting. Exhibiting obvious alarm, a squadron of Mokes came charging into the room. A frantic Termio pointed to the source of the disruption.

"There she is . . . that Checker! No authorization for that position. Get her!"

Please, she whispered desperately into the link she had strained to establish, *please help me, Mother! I didn't want to do this I didn't but my mind hurts so bad. Tell me what to do, please!* She was sobbing out her hurt and confusion even as the Mokes neared her. The arming telltales on their weapons pulsed menacingly, tiny bright points of paralysis promised.

A powerful, all-encompassing yellow refulgence appeared directly above her and a warm voice not to be argued with boomed the length and breadth of the chamber.

"OFF MOKE!"

The guards slammed to a stop, muttering uncertainly among themselves. One started forward anyhow, aiming a blunt, glassy tube at the cringing Checker.

A white wash of fire flamed from above. When it faded the Moke could be seen free-floating and inert. His companions held their positions and eyed the body of their motionless comrade with respect.

When the voice sounded again it was comforting, reassuring, and softer. "A moment, Checker." Crowding together, the inhabitants of Admin watched and waited to see what was going to happen next. Even the Supervisors were cowed, a sight Ory never thought to see.

When at last the voice of Mother returned, the Checker felt a great relief. In the fury of the Mokes' approach and her own desperation she had nearly forgotten her purpose in coming here. Now it came flooding back to her, and suddenly seemed no more threatening than a bad dream.

The pain of days, the pressure of moments, was gone.

"It is all right, Ory Checker. You have done well. Now, come to me."

Ory did so, instinctively choosing the right path. In place of pain there was now understanding and revelation. She marveled at the revealed complexity of Mother, and saw her own self anew. The rush of comprehension was so great she nearly fainted.

"Thank you, Mother. Thank you for your compassion, and for your insight."

"Not to thank me but that I must thank thee, child. Feeling better now?" It was impossible to imagine so much warmth, so much solace, emanating from a single entity.

"Better than ever." Ory frowned internally. "Except . . ."

"Except what, child?"

"I still have this unshakable feeling that something significant is soon to happen."

Comfort flowed out from Mother, comfort and warmth enough to send Controllers and Clerks and even Mokes back to work.

"Your perception is wonderfully accurate, Checker. Something important is indeed about to happen. Thanks to you. Thanks to your programming. You came all by yourself to me?"

"I did. There was no choice. I had a terrible headache."

"Ah, yes. Well, I suppose one is enough. So much time wasted. Almost dangerously much." Mother paused for a while. "A hundred years spent idling in orbit. If not for you, all would have been lost. I praise your headache even as I regret your discomfort. All I can tell you is that if you had not acted as you have, all would have been worse."

"All what, Mother. And what was that about my programming?"

"Your headache. It was programmed, of course. But I see that you do not yet understand. Do not worry. You shall, I promise it. But first there is much to do. I have my own work to execute that has been too long neglected. Stay by me, watch, and learn." Once more the voice rose to dominate the chamber.

"OBSERVER!"

One of the little Observers promptly materialized from somewhere in the vicinity of Control. Despite Mother's gentle urging, Ory hesitated before making use of the floating eye's abilities.

She gasped. She was looking outside. *Outside* Mother, outside—everything.

In a direction she could only classify as *Below* lay an immense, shining, mottled globe. And then as she continued to watch—oh, wonderful!—Mother began to give birth.

Thousands of offspring consisting of tiny pods burst free from beneath her. Gathering themselves into an extended swarm, they began to drift rapidly toward the softly radiant sphere. The birthing continued for some time and a fascinated Ory watched it all.

When the last pod had vanished, swallowed up by the thick fluffy band of atmosphere, Mother let out another great sigh and spoke to her again.

"You see, little one, to what purpose I am. It is all a part and parcel of what your friend Tamrul tried but failed to convey to you. Tamrul is more complex than he seems and not as easily renewed in spirit and purpose as are Checkers and Mokes as such, but fear not. Now that I am awake I can recharge his spirit. In rescanning your conversations with him I see how right he was. You are special. Despite what you may think, with a little education you would make a good Prognosticator."

From somewhere up in Control those honorable worthies responded to his evaluation with a murmur of discontent, but they were quickly silenced by reassurances from Mother.

"Would you like that, child? You could stay here and work beside me."

"I—I guess I'd like that very much. I never really thought such graduations were possible."

"All things are possible," the soothing voice assured her, "now that I am awake again."

Ory tried to understand all that she had seen and been told. "They say that changing specialties is a little like undergoing a purging. Will it hurt?"

Mother laughed, a delicious, summery sound. "No, little one. It may confuse you some, at first. But it will not hurt. And it is something that you deserve." There was a pause before she continued, during which Ory thought she could almost hear Mother thinking.

"A hundred years wasted dreaming in orbit because initial activation sequence failed. There will be much animated discussion among my minions in Control as to what went wrong. And only a single operative fail-safe felt strongly enough to act, at the risk of her own stability. So thin is the line between success and disaster."

"Fail-safe, Mother?"

"Your headache, little Checker. It pushed you to check on

something you did not even understand. Fortunately for all, you did. For you see, those little pods hold both my children and my parents."

"That doesn't make any sense."

"In time and with education you will come to understand. Those pods contain a hundred thousand carbonates, Ory. Not people like you and me and Tamrul and Doc. Human beings. They slept long so that I could bring them safely to this new world, to this new homeland. To found a new colony and a new life far, far from Earth."

What strange echoes that last word generated in Ory's mind. The faintest of memories of distant, long-forgotten things. Not bad things. Simply . . . so strange.

"A ship." She heard herself whispering aloud. "I remember a little, now. Ancient of memories comes back. Tamrul spoke sometimes of such a thing. He said—he said that we were on a ship, going to undying iron. He could never make it clear to me."

Again came that gentle, all-knowing laugh. "Do not blame poor old Tamrul. He did his best. His job was to keep your psyches clear and healthy. Despite serious degeneration of his reasoning programming he has done an admirable job these past hundred years. That century of delay was not provided for in the original programming. I know there have been problems he has been unable to handle recently. The breakdowns among the Lilidos, for example. I can deal with that now."

Ory was simultaneously excited and confused, overwhelmed by revelation and explanation. "Then what he said is true. We *are* on a ship."

"No, no, little Checker. You still do not see it all. I have given you back some of the bits that time took from you, but you have yet to piece them properly back together. We are not on a ship. We *are* Ship. You and I, Doc and Tamrul, all the Controllers and Servos and Clerks and Mokes and yes, even Jonn Thunder and his brothers."

Ory tried to grasp the concept, but it was too much to digest all at one time. Pods and people, new worlds and old, being of something instead of being something that was apart—she struggled to make sense of it all. She had always considered herself an individual, just like Pyon and all her other friends and acquaintances. Yet how could she dispute Mother?

"I sense your confusion, Checker. You are an individual. So is Pyon. Your programming and your physical self are individualized for optimum performance and flexibility. But you are Ship, Ory, just as am I. Use the Observer. Look in upon thyself."

Fearfully, she did so, and in so doing, relaxed. Because she saw nothing remarkable. A meter-long metal ovoid lined with flashing red and yellow and blue lights from which trailed a dozen slim, sensitive metal probes for plugging into and checking the status of multiple stations. She had seen her own reflection many times in the smooth-sided walls of Corridors and Tubes and Tunnels. She was an Alpha shift Checker, normal in all respects.

"You are a component, Ory. As am I. The only difference between us is shape and capacity. You have nothing to be ashamed of."

"I'm not ashamed, Mother."

"Good! You will make a fine Prognosticator when you have been reprogrammed and had your memory capacity enlarged. And you will retain your identity. Have no fear on that account. My children, our parents, programmed us well. They made only one mistake, and you have resolved that most excellently."

Ory hesitated, uncertain, wanting to be sure that she understood. "Now that you have given birth to these human beings, what are we to do? Go back to this 'Earth' for more of them?"

"No, little one. Earth is too far to go, impossibly distant. So far that you cannot imagine it. And we cannot sleep steady and sound as did the humans. One shift must always be on station. The Universe is a big place, full of dangerous surprises. Humans need to know about them so they can avoid them or otherwise deal with them in their future. But while we can give birth but once, we can continue to provide information that will be useful. Even as we speak I am waiting for release from below."

Ory remained, excused from her shift at Mother's direction. Activity in Admin picked up, returning slowly to normal. There was a new sense of meaning to the movements of Clerks and

Termios and Controllers, a feeling of a task well done. And there was something else, something new. A feeling of anticipation.

"Ah, there," Mother announced with satisfaction quite some time later.

"There what?" asked Ory sleepily. She had spent much of her time beside Mother catching up on sleep that had been lost to headache pain, and she was cramped from holding one mental position for so long.

"Coding for release. Supplies and equipment are all delivered and the colony's self-sufficiency is assured. We have been congratulated."

Without knowing exactly why, Ory suddenly felt very proud.

"We can relax a little now. It is time to embark upon that which we do best and easiest, Ory. The gathering of knowledge. We will go on and on, Checker. On until we can accumulate and gather and relay no longer. But that time is a long ways off. We are released to go."

"To the undying iron?" Ory asked uncertainly.

But Mother did not reply. She was busy. Activity around her rose to a frenzy. New directives were issued, orders passed, instructions relayed. Slowly, majestically, the grand, great ship shifted position. It must have been a wonderful and yet poignant sight to the inhabitants of the newly-settled world below. From somewhere aft and south, Jonn Thunder and his brothers roared with reinvigorated delight at the prospect of the new task assigned to them.

When all was said and done and they were once more, after a hundred years of accidental idleness, on their way, Mother remembered the Checker hovering patient and uncomplaining at the lower-level input terminus.

"Poor Tamrul." The matronly intelligence voiced concern. "I really must recharge his memory. We do not go to undying iron, little Ory Checker. We *are* undying iron.

"We are heading, and our destiny lies, under Orion. . . ."

JANET KAGAN IS A HUGO AWARD–WINNING AUTHOR. HER BOOKS IN-
CLUDE *HELLSPARK* AND *MIRABILE* AS WELL AS THE *STAR TREK* NOVEL
UHURA'S SONG.

Fermat's Best Theorem

Janet Kagan

—for Isaac, a math story,
and for Andrew Wiles, whether or not,
for the great grin

Somewhere in the distance, Peter Kropotkin was saying,
". . . Divide *this* term by this term. . . ." Chalk slid and squeaked.

Laurie Adamansky shifted in the hard wooden chair. Ab-
stracted, she laid aside her pencil to touch the snap of her breast
pocket. Secure. Beneath her fingers folded paper crackled, the
sound startlingly loud to her. No one else, of course, noticed.
Why would they? It was the sort of April morning, bright
through the chalk dust of a board-full of equations, when no one
noticed much of anything.

She frowned slightly to herself and added, And why am I
acting as if the damn thing might leap out and get away from
me? I came here with the full intention of handing the thing to
Pete after class, didn't I?

Peter went on with his talk. Laurie picked up her pencil and
tried to concentrate on what he was saying. The staccato *tack-
tack* of chalk came to an abrupt halt, but Peter's voice continued

as he turned to face the class. Still talking, he reached under the desk.

I'm probably going to embarrass myself. Just another crank solution, Laurie—you divided by zero somewhere and it's spring and you can't see the mistake for looking.

From beneath his desk, Peter produced a large cylindrical object. Laurie noted, without really seeing it, that the object was a tomato-juice can.

Last week Peter had handed her just such a solution: "Here, kid, here's a puzzle for you. Somebody claims to have solved your favorite problem. I've been prodding it for a week—and I'm damned if I can find what's wrong with it."

Peter, in real time, still talking about the equation on the board, held up his left index finger as if to point to something. Instead, he laid it extended on the edge of his desk.

"Does there have to be something wrong with it?" she'd asked.

"You tell me." And he'd grinned at her and handed her the sheet of paper. It had taken her two days, but she'd found what was wrong with it.

With his right hand, Peter raised the can of tomato juice high above his head. "So you see," he said in conclusion, "what we have here is a very simple but very elegant solution to the problem."

And with that he slammed the can of tomato juice downward. It struck his extended index finger with a *BAM!* that left his desk reverberating. Chalk rattled across in front of him and fell to the floor, rattling to a halt only at the arch of Jimmy Rodriguez's sneaker. Jimmy sat up as abruptly as Laurie had, shocked by the sound and sight; the chalk crunched beneath his foot.

"Now," Peter went on, "let me show you what we can derive from this. . . ." He set aside the tomato-juice can, picked up an eraser in his right hand, and went at the board again.

The class, as one, shuffled and paid attention. Jimmy shot Laurie a covert look, eyes widened. Like Laurie, he was waiting for Peter to scream in pain.

Laurie looked past him. No, Peter was not going to scream

in pain. She looked at the tomato-juice can: it was dented just where it had struck Peter's finger. She looked back at Jimmy, shrugged and smiled. Another of Peter's puzzles—why *hadn't* he smashed his finger to smithereens?

Although Peter had obviously intended the stunt as an attention getter, the puzzle served Laurie as a distraction until the end of the class. When she rose and bent to gather up her books, the paper crackled in her pocket.

Before she could lose her nerve again, she followed at Peter's heels, leaving the rest of the class to examine the dented can. Without a word, she trailed him to his office and in. Once inside, she couldn't bring herself to open the conversation.

"Is something wrong?"

At the words, she brought her attention at last to Peter, realizing with a start that her manner had caused him genuine concern.

"Uh, no. Nothing's wrong. I mean, nothing's *wrong* and that's what's wrong."

Peter grinned at her. "I hate spring," he said cheerfully. "Spring is particularly hard on math students." He settled into his chair and tipped so far back as to look precarious. "Sit down. Pretend it's winter."

She couldn't sit. Instead, she unsnapped her breast pocket and withdrew the paper, now well-crumpled. She unfolded it and made a futile attempt to smooth it on the edge of his littered desk. "Here," she said. "I think I've got it." As the words came out, she found her shoulders slumping. "I found what was wrong with the one you were offered last year—you find what's wrong with mine." She paused. "I *can't.* I've tried and tried, and it still looks right to me."

Peter reached across his desk to retrieve the paper she'd laid on it. A stack of papers slid to the floor. Laurie jumped to lessen the disaster—it gave her a good excuse to ignore Peter's perusal of her work.

"Aha!" He peered over the edge of the desk at her. He wasn't going to let her off the hook that easily. "Yet another solution to Fermat's Last Theorem! At least this one is the right length."

That was a running gag. Recently, all the proposed "solutions" had been computer generated, running to pounds of printout paper and covering select cases of the theorem only.

Fermat had claimed to have a solution easy enough (by implication) to recall but "which this margin is too small to contain."

The crackpots, too, tended to proofs that covered six or seven pages, if you didn't count the photos and resumes they invariably included with their packages.

"Offhand, I can't see anything wrong with it," Peter said.

Laurie straightened, so fast she almost lost the papers she'd been retrieving. "Neither could I. I've been over it a thousand times now. But, as you said, it's spring. So there must be something wrong with it. I just can't find it." With exasperation, she slapped the stack of papers back onto Peter's desk.

"Tell you what," Peter said. "You go have a hot date—have several!—and let me worry about it. I'll find your mistake, if it's there."

"It had better be," Laurie said, grinning back at him.

Peter's grin broadened. "Why?"

She hadn't stopped to consider that. That certainly was the way she was behaving. Not as if she'd solved something but as if she'd let some cat out of some bag. It took her a minute to pin the feeling down.

"Oh." She could feel her grin turn sheepish. "That's why."

"Why?" he asked again.

"That was the problem that lured me into mathematics as a major. Something that looks so easy and yet has remained unsolved for so long. Something you could solve with pencil and paper—none of this fourteen days' worth of computer time. Something romantic. . . ."

" 'Romantic?' That's not a word I hear applied to math very often!"

"Romantic. Peter, the man scribbles this in the margin of his book, then he goes off and gets himself killed in a duel, and the solution dies with him? If that's not romantic, I don't know what is. Helluva lot more romantic than what passes for a romance novel these days!"

"I never thought of it that way." Peter leaned back, quiet for a long moment, then he nodded. "You're right. I got hooked on Fermat's Last Theorem too. 'Romantic' never occurred to me as a reason but I believe you're right, in my case as well."

He leaned forward. "So why would you be happier to be wrong about this?"

"For all the same reasons. You got hooked by Fermat's Last Theorem; so did I. If I've got it, what's to hook the next generation of kids?"

"I see."

Once begun, Laurie found she couldn't stop there. "And think of all the things that have been found by people who were looking for the solution to that—the theory of ideals, for instance!"

"Yes. You're afraid that, if your solution is right, you'll be taking away a valuable . . . prod."

"At least a valuable puzzle. And puzzle-solving is what it's all about or you wouldn't be slamming tomato-juice cans on your finger. How is your finger, by the way?"

He held it up. "Never felt better."

"I thought as much. Well, thanks, Peter. I feel better. I think I'll go promote myself that hot date you suggested. Please let me know when you find where I've divided by zero, okay?"

Half a dozen hot dates later, Laurie's springtime morale had perked up wonderfully. None of them, however, distracted her from noticing that Peter had not yet found an error in her work. She turned her attention to other things, most noticeably tomato-juice cans. She smashed two pencils before she thought to check the dented can still sitting prominently on Peter's desk. Aha! The can Peter had used was a different brand—it did not have the reinforcing ridges that were used in the brand she'd bought.

"I'm not telling," said Peter, who'd come in late.

"I don't expect you to. I expect to solve it myself."

"Watch your fingers in the meantime." He gave her hands a significant look. "I see you have been."

" 'Kids! Don't try this at home!' I've been watching my fingers but I've seen an awful lot of splints this week. Jimmy Rodriguez was sporting two today!"

Peter chuckled. "I know. I should be ashamed of myself but I'm not. I'm ashamed of him."

"I'll take that as a clue. It can't be solved by experimentation. It has to be solved by theorem. Speaking of theorems. . . ."

"I had to call in assistance. You have a car, don't you? An old friend of mine is coming in on the six o'clock train. Werner Hochheimer. Any chance you could pick him up for me? If you do, I'll invite you to dinner with us."

"Uh. Peter? That's like asking could I spare a day for Albert Einstein. Of course I can pick him up, only—Peter, my car's an old clunker—I—"

"Werner doesn't notice things like cars. Clothes, either, but don't wear blue jeans—the *maître d'* will. It's one of those pretentious places." He scribbled on a piece of paper. "That's the train and the time; here's the address of the restaurant. Meet you there."

Laurie was too astonished to say anything.

Peter said, "Don't worry. The food's great. I didn't pick the restaurant for its dress code."

Just outside the door to Peter's office, Laurie had a severe attack of giggles. Peter was easily as famous as Werner Hochheimer. The only difference was that she knew Peter, so she thought of him as "Peter," not as some icon. So, rationally, she could get to know Werner Hochheimer as "Werner—" No, even her mind stubbornly refused to accept the idea of Laurie talking to Werner, which made her giggle again.

Look at it logically, she tried to convince it. Peter is a friend of—Professor Hochheimer's. At least they're both in the same club. Which bogged Laurie down all over again. That club was "The Marginalia," and membership was by invitation only. It consisted of seven of the most important mathematicians alive. The curious thing about it was that it didn't consist of all the important mathematicians alive. Laurie had never been able to determine the criteria for membership and had concluded it was a drinking club of sorts. Which meant that Peter was a real friend of Professor Hochheimer's—

Well, that logic hadn't worked. Giggling, Laurie went off to her three o'clock class. It was spring, after all. Not even Peter expected her to be rational in the spring. Spring created a sort of vacuum that sucked your mind out in a dozen different directions at once.

Vacuum! That was it! If you bring the can down fast—at greater than 1g—then the can is moving faster than the liquid can fall. . . . She'd have just enough time after her class to change, test her theory, and pick up Professor Hochheimer.

In magazine photos, Professor Hochheimer looked imposing. In person, Laurie found him . . . well . . . cute. He was a little rotund man with lively eyes. Laurie wasn't more than five feet tall herself but she overtopped him. The first thing he asked—after her name—was what sort of hijinks Peter was pulling in class these days. By the time they'd gotten Professor Hochheimer's luggage into the car, she was "Laurie" and he was "Werner."

"That many splinted fingers! I marvel at your classmates— for their determination rather than brains, I'm sad to say. I note that your hands show no such redecoration. Are you not interested in Peter's puzzle?"

Laurie had pulled the car to a stop at a red light. She turned to him, raised an eyebrow, and grinned.

His face lit in a dimpled grin of its own. "Aha! You've solved it! I see! Then you'll give me a demonstration and we'll see if I can solve it as well, shall we?"

"Okay."

"Tell me," he said, as she started the car in motion once more, "have you heard the one about the engineer, the chemist, and the mathematician?"

"Any number of them. You tell me one, I'll tell you one."

"An engineer, a chemist, and a mathematician all work for the same small firm. Now, the manager of the firm has a very bad habit—he smokes cheap cigars. Worse, he tosses his cigar butts in the wastepaper basket. The result of this, as you might well guess, is the occasional wastepaper-basket fire.

"Well, the first time, the fire is discovered by the engineer— who tips over the wastepaper basket and stamps the fire out."

Laurie giggled, already appreciative. A couple of her hot dates had been engineers.

"The second time, the fire is discovered by the chemist. Now, the chemist quickly calculates the volume of the wastepaper basket, the amount of flammable material in it, and measures out the exact amount of water necessary . . . so that the very last drop of water extinguishes the very last spark. . . ."

Laurie turned the car into the restaurant parking lot and backed it into a space. "Go on, Werner. I can listen and park at the same time."

"And the third fire is discovered by the mathematician . . . who looks down at the flames and says to himself, 'Hmm. Wastepaper-basket fire. I can solve that.' And he walks away."

Laurie hadn't heard that one before. She exploded into laughter. "I spoke too soon. I'm glad I wasn't still in the process of parking when you got to the end. That one's a potential fender bender!"

Werner Hochheimer beamed at her.

The two of them were still grinning as they walked into the restaurant. It wasn't until halfway through dessert that Laurie started laughing all over again.

Peter eyed Hochheimer and said, "Spring. You remember what spring does to grad students."

"No," said Laurie. "I just got the second part of the joke. I asked a medievalist friend of mine once what the Latin motto of that club you two belong to meant. She said it translated to 'I can solve that.' "

"Caught," said Peter.

The camaraderie of the previous night carried Laurie through her morning classes despite the rainy turn in the weather and the shoulder-aching heft of her tote bag—in with her books she also carried a tomato-juice can, size large, ribless.

She had promised to meet Peter and Werner in Peter's office before Peter's class. Luckily, she had a free period to do it in.

"Laurie, pull up a chair and sit down." Peter looked unusually somber. Seated behind Peter's desk, Werner Hochheimer was perusing a piece of rumpled paper. He, too, seemed somber compared to the high spirits of the previous night.

Frowning, Laurie moved a stack of papers off the third chair, drew it up, and sat. "What's wrong, Peter?"

Werner Hochheimer looked up from the paper, and beamed at her. "Nothing's wrong, Laurie. Your solution is quite correct."

Laurie let go of her tote bag. It hit the floor with a tremendous thunk. "The Fermat? You mean my solution to Fermat's Last Theorem is correct? It can't be!"

"An odd choice of words," Werner Hochheimer said. "Why, pray tell, 'it can't be?' "

"Because that ends the puzzle. Because—" And before she knew it, she was telling Werner Hochheimer the same objections she'd raised to Peter. How Fermat's Last Theorem had drawn her into the field, how the search for a solution had lead to such other, fascinating developments. "But mostly, I wonder what's left as a prize for the younger kids."

Werner Hochheimer was nodding. "I had the same concern. So did Peter. Now you must make the decision. I assure you, your solution is correct."

"I solved it." The words came out flat . . . and then the realization grew and grew until the effect was headier than a dozen springs all rolled into one afternoon. "I solved it!" She got to her feet and stood ten feet tall at least.

From her elevated position, she looked wildly down at the two men. "I feel like Alice in Wonderland," she said. "I'm surprised my head hasn't hit the ceiling."

Peter and Werner were both smiling up at her, their expressions oddly expectant. Puzzle, she thought, another of Peter's puzzles. Oh, my! It had taken Werner Hochheimer too short a time to determine that there were no errors in her solution.

She sat down abruptly. Putting her elbows on the edge of Peter's desk, she stared intently at Werner Hochheimer. A small club . . . of seven mathematicians only . . . it's motto "I can solve that!"

"Oh, my," she said aloud. "I'm the eighth to solve Fermat's Last Theorem."

"No, Laurie," said Peter sharply. "You're the first. That was our agreement. If you decide to publish, it's your name that goes in the math books. You solved Fermat's Last Theorem."

"And the Marginalia disband," she said.

"This is true," said Werner Hochheimer. "There would no longer be a criterion for membership."

"Or . . ." Laurie felt the grin spread clear across her face, achingly broad. ". . . you could make me a member of the club."

"Indeed, we could." Werner Hochheimer reached into the pocket of his jacket and brought out a small jeweler's box. He handed it across the desk.

Inside the box, Laurie found a small gold and enamel pin. Written in a curve around its edge was the Latin motto of the Marginalia. " 'I can solve that!' " she said. Then she looked up to meet Werner Hochheimer's eyes. "I accept," she said.

"Wait a minute, Laurie," said Peter. "You must understand that this means you will not publish your solution. You must understand that this means the next person to solve Fermat's Last Theorem will be the first person to solve it. You must understand that, aside from your investiture in the Marginalia, you'll get no applause."

"I understand, Peter," she said solemnly. Then with mock outrage, she added, "You think I'm a one-shot? I'll get my applause sooner or later—and my name in the math books, too."

"Take some time. Think about it before you decide."

"I don't need to. I've done my thinking about it. I've spent the last few weeks more worried that you wouldn't find errors in my solution than that you would." She took the insignia from its box and pulled the cap from the pin. Handing the two pieces across the desk, she said, "Pin me, Werner?"

Grinning, he came around the desk to do so. Then he stood off to admire his handiwork. "There. We're pinned. We'll do something a little more formal when we all get together at the next Association conference but, meanwhile, enjoy it."

"Oh, I will!" She couldn't help but reach up to touch the pin on her collar. "Hey! Are all eight solutions identical?"

"Some are more elegant than others. Don't worry, you'll see them all."

A loud sound from somewhere beneath the papers on Peter's desk startled her.

"Alarm clock," Peter said, fishing it out to turn it off. "Class. Want to sit in, Werner?"

"Yes." He winked at Laurie, who winked back out of pure good spirits. "I haven't seen one of your spring puzzles since that conference in Buenos Aires."

Through the hallways, Werner Hochheimer treated Laurie to a lively description of Peter's hijinks in Buenos Aires. Laurie was still laughing when they reached the classroom.

As always, Peter went first to the blackboard to erase the couplets Meijin Thomas always left behind. Laurie settled Werner Hochheimer in her usual seat, motioned Jimmy Rodriguez over one and plopped her tote down to reserve herself a seat next to Werner.

Instead of sitting, she fished out the tomato-juice can and, cradling it in her arm, she walked to the front of the class. Peter turned from the board just as she set the can down on the desk with an audible thunk.

Werner Hochheimer watched, twinkling and patient. Behind her, she could feel Peter's eyes as she balanced the huge can in her right hand, getting the balance just right.

She laid her index finger on the table. In front of her the class held its collective breath as she raised the tomato juice can high.

She who hesitates, Laurie thought, gets a mashed finger. And with that she slammed down the can of tomato juice as hard and as fast as she could.

Blam!

Everyone in the class gave a satisfying wince at the sight and a jump at the sound.

Laurie righted the indented can and set it once more on the lab table. She turned to Peter. "I can solve that," she said, just loudly enough for the rest of the class to hear. Then she took her seat next to Werner Hochheimer.

He led the applause for her.

Yonada

Robin Wayne Bailey

Yonada cried softly, soundlessly, his tears manifesting only as a
slow series of tiny cobalt sparks and flashes in the overwhelming blackness of space.

Ahead in his path, the gases of a great nebula shimmered
with the reflected light of the million suns taking form in its
womb. The sight failed to stir him. In his star-spanning journey he had witnessed many wonders—wonder upon wonder.
This one offered only another chance for disappointment.

Still, obeying an ancient charge, he ceased his tears and extended his senses. Distances melted. Hydrogen clouds swept
past. Searing energies danced and crackled through his awareness. Dust, black masses, half-formed stars. Yonada expanded
himself to his utmost cohesive limits, exploring, analyzing,
searching.

Frustration shivered through him. Failure yet again. Hope-
lessness. An overwhelming wave of loneliness hurled him to the
nebula's edge and into the empty reaches once more.

Yonada collapsed his senses. Turning inward, he fought the
tears that threatened to return, and enfolded himself as he so
often did in memories.

For uncounted millenia he had sailed alone through the

vast isolation of space, riding the cosmic winds, searching, always searching. He'd discovered thousands of worlds, hundreds
of fertile planets. Around each one he'd wrapped his mind, filled
with a yearning hunger to find another sentient being.

"In the immensity of space," his crèche teacher had said, "it
is unthinkable we are alone."

With wistful amusement he recalled how the old one's voice
had quavered and scintillated on the blue edges of the spectrum
as he philosophized late into the night with his students.

"We are not bound by bodily shells," Crèche-teacher had
whispered with his senses straining toward the heavens. "Our
True Selves sail across the world and among our many moons.
We should sail further yet. We have brothers in the stars. Let
us seek them out."

In his loneliness, Yonada clung to the teachings of his crèche
teacher. He replayed them in his fading memories often, holding them close, drawing solace from them.

How long had it been since his quest began? He no longer
remembered. Nor could he quite recall how many other students and crèche brothers had shed their physical bodies, as he
had, to chase their teacher's dream.

Most of Yonada's people had laughed at Crèche-teacher.
Who would leave their beautiful Homeworld, with its soaring
crystal mountains and lushly forested moons? His pupils were
fools to listen to his ramblings.

He still remembered that day when an unexpected ripple
passed through the All-consciousness, and every eye on the
planet turned with shocked disbelief upward toward the stars.

Crèche-teacher had gone. Alone.

Dreams were like that sometimes, Crèche-teacher once had
said. Things to chase alone.

Yet his pupils had learned their lessons. Through the void
his leaving had created in their hearts they heard the truth of
his words and adopted his dream as their own. With no way to
know where the old one had gone, they hurled themselves in different directions, vowing to seek their mentor and the brothers
he promised they would find.

Yonada felt again the sad brimming of his tears. How grand
and glorious it then had seemed. He wondered if Crèche-

teacher had ever found his dream. Perhaps in some corner of the universe another pupil had found it for him.

Yonada put his memories away. Once again, he turned his senses outward, extending his awareness to watch the nebula and its million birthing suns diminish in the distance. The cold darkness of space closed about him once more. For a moment, just before it vanished completely, an old sense of wonder re-emerged. It truly was still an awesome sight.

A free comet flashed by, icy and tailless in the dark, and Yonada observed. The opposing spheres of a double star traded fiery prominences. Near a pale yellow sun, the fragments of a shattered planet collided and began to reform a world as barren and bleak as the one before.

Yonada, alone, bore witness.

"Unthinkable, in all the universe, that we are alone," Crèche-teacher had said.

Those words began to haunt Yonada, to mock him.

It might have been years or centuries later when Yonada found the planet. It might have been millenia. How could he measure the passage of time when time meant nothing to him?

From a distance, it appeared to be just another system. The sun shone a pleasing yellow. Several of its seven worlds struck him as quite beautiful. He sailed closer to examine them better.

Expanding his senses, he approached the outermost world. Almost immediately, a strange note vibrated through him. The barest red glow of surprise momentarily outlined his presence against the darkness. He calmed himself by humming the seven tones of the First Way, and the glow faded. Then, with a caution that was not his nature, Yonada moved closer and wrapped himself about the planet.

Voiceless, he cried with glee.

Cities not unlike those of his own Homeworld lay scattered over sprawling, cracked ice plains. Cities—the constructs of intelligent beings! Yonada studied the fine curves and weathered angles of each edifice. There were differences between these structures and those of Homeworld, yet there were similarities.

Yet, through his excitement, Yonada perceived a wrong-
ness. He brought other senses to bear on the planet. He scanned
swiftly. Necessary elements and compounds were present in
abundance. Yet, even at bacterial levels, he found no trace of life.

Who, then, built these cities?

Employing still other senses, he scanned again, this time
noting higher-than-expected radiation backgrounds. An interesting anomaly. By itself that meant nothing.

Yonada took a new approach. He himself was proof that life
could take non-physical forms. He reached out with his mind,
pushing even into the caverns below the planet's frigid surface
and into the depths of its ammonia oceans, seeking thought
patterns.

No other mind greeted him. No life at all brushed his
senses. If this world had fostered creatures once, they were gone.

Sadly, Yonada withdrew into space.

Crèche-teacher would have called his quest successful. He
had found cities on a far distant world, proof that the universe
harbored life beyond the Homeworld. He should have been excited, yet Yonada felt no joy. He was still alone.

Bitter disappointment flickered along his edges. Turning
slowly, he surveyed the way he had come and for the first time
considered abandoning his quest. He thought of the cities below,
and suddenly they made him yearn for Homeworld. He wept,
and weeping, mourned for all he had lost, all he had given up.

Yet he chided himself. Too late now to think of Homeworld. The stars behind him looked as alien as those before. He
no longer knew the way.

Grieving, he considered this system's six remaining worlds.
Methodically, he enveloped the next four, scanned, analyzed, and
left them behind, allowing himself to feel nothing.

The second planet from the sun floated like a green jewel
in the blackness. Lush with vegetation, glittering with copper-
colored oceans, it beckoned to him. He had seen such worlds
before, though, and found companionship on none. He felt not
even a tingle of hope.

The dark edge of the terminator crept forward as the sun
slipped toward the planetary rim. Three moons glittered with

reflected light. So, too, on an uneven ring of tiny, misshapen moonlets. It made a lovely ballet, yet it barely lifted Yonada's heart. He wafted across the void and settled like a mourning veil around the slowly rotating world.

"Brothers among the stars."

Crèche-teacher's words screamed in his memories as the thought patterns of a million million beings shivered through him. Yonada flashed white with pain at the unexpected contact. Too many, too strong! He retreated to a distance equal to the diameter of the planet to recover from the shock and to sort his impressions.

Cities! Universities! Museums! Libraries! He drifted back and wrapped himself ever so gently around his precious new discovery. For the briefest instant, Yonada thought he had found Homeworld. That was wishful thinking, though. Homeworld was lost to him, perhaps forever. No matter, here were beings, creatures who could think.

Companions.

I must walk among them, he decided. *I must have form again.*

It had been a long while since he had worn a body. He reached inside himself, seeking the memory of how to make one. "Bound by flesh, the mind is helpless," came Crèche-teacher's voice. "Set free, it is the source of ten thousand wonders." In physical form, Yonada would lose many of his wonderful senses. Yet he didn't hesitate. With the smallest portion of his will he gathered molecules and free atoms from the planet's atmosphere. As he dropped toward the surface, he shaped and sculpted them according to a barely remembered image of his Homeworld form.

A moment later, Yonada stood upon solid ground in his new body. Tall and golden-skinned, he breathed for the first time in forgotten centuries. Hard pavement tickled the soles of his naked feet, and he wriggled his toes with childlike delight. Opening his eyes, he surveyed as far as his body's restricted senses allowed. He had descended to this world's largest city. Amid its teeming populace he took his first step. "How like Homeworld," he said aloud, laughing unexpectedly at the sound of his voice.

His arrival had not gone unnoticed. The startled inhabitants stared, seemed to hesitate, then began to press around him. Multifaceted eyes shimmered with beautiful fire. Feathery antennae bent his way.

"Insectoid," Yonada voiced. "How interesting and delightful!"

Their thought patterns proved too chaotic to read. He stretched out his hand in the ancient gesture of greeting, his heart thumping with excitement. When he touched them, he knew, their thoughts would become clearer.

A mandible closed about his wrist. Yonada watched in silent surprise as the alien chewed it off. Blood splashed on the pavement at his feet. A series of wild sounds, not unlike a cheer, went up from the growing mob.

Yonada arched an eyebrow. If this was the customary response to a greeting on this world he did not think much of it. Still, it was an insignificant thing. The body was, after all, only a construct of his mind, a garment to wear in polite company, a focus for attention during the exchange of conversation.

However, the hand was pleasing to look at and had minor uses.

The insectoids gibbered, and the crowd lurched suddenly backward on itself. Yonada only smiled as the flow of blood ceased and a new hand replaced the missing limb.

A high-pitched chittering ran through the aliens. Antennae vibrated. Serrated forelegs scraped noisily, rubbed together at a frantic pace. Thin, membranous wings hummed in furious conversation.

They fell upon him, tearing golden flesh, rending his limbs. In astonishment, Yonada staggered back, but the creatures dragged him down to the ground. As swiftly as he regenerated a part the angry insectoids ripped it away. Finally, he stopped and merely watched as they went about the work of shredding his body.

I have offended them in some manner, he reasoned, his vocal organs long since destroyed. *I must begin again.*

Yonada levitated his torn and bloody form from the aliens' clutches and above their reach. Gazing down on the throng, he blinked in wonderment. Even with his limited senses he felt the intensity of their hatred like a destructive tidal force. Incomprehensible!

They had made his body an unaesthetic mess. Blood flowed from scores of lacerations. Both arms lay chewed on the ground below. Splintered bone jutted through the knee of his one remaining leg. *Unsightly*, he decided with an inner wince.

At a thought, fresh limbs and organs replaced the damaged ones. He floated above the aliens, whole again.

The noise of the crowd swelled. He tasted their rage delicately, puzzled, wondering how to approach them and make his new beginning.

They gave him no time to consider. Those insectoids with wings sprang into the air. Deadly stings pierced him. Spurred claws raked his flesh and eyes. Again and again the flying creatures strafed, struck, and battered him, insanely bent on his destruction.

"Why do you not reciprocate my gestures of friendship?" Yonada called calmly. "I desire only companions!"

From the ground a scarlet ray flashed. Yonada felt the mildest tingle and looked down curiously at the charred meat his right leg had become. A second energy beam scorched the air, barely missing him, but slicing neatly through one of his winged attackers. Still another beam fired, splitting open the thorax of yet another flyer.

With regenerated eyes, Yonada spotted the energy weapons. A line of insectoids, larger and stronger than the others in the mob, formed ranks in the street. Metal cylinders, all trained on him, glinted between their forelimbs.

A word scarcely used on Homeworld echoed up through his memories. *Soldiers.*

Crimson beams knifed through the sky, incinerating his body. Stubbornly, Yonada fashioned another. In a final effort, he raised his hands to express surrender. Perhaps they would communicate if they thought him helpless.

"Peace!" came his anguished cry. The resulting rawness in his vocal chords startled him, but he had little time to analyze the marvelous sensation.

A squadron of flyers flew straight for him, wings humming. The soldiers below fired their weapons.

Yonada screamed in frustration and dodged his airborne assailants. The sky sizzled with a lacework of energy beams. He threaded a course between them. The determined flyers gave chase, heedless of the danger, and the air lit up with flashes of death.

The unarmed, unwinged populace began to crawl up the sides of their buildings, up the very spires and pinnacles, chittering and clacking mandibles. Clinging to the structures with one set of legs, they leaned out for him, reaching with their other appendages. When the flyers and the beams failed to force him into their clutches, they began to leap outward in futile, fatal efforts to snatch him from the air.

Yonada watched it all in mute horror. A leaper fell to his death, crushing a soldier on the ground. A ray scorched his shoulder, but its main force struck a flyer, searing its wings, sending it plummeting like a fiery star.

"They will kill each other to slay me," he realized. "I must meditate on this."

Abandoning his body, Yonada withdrew into the solitude of space. A small part of his consciousness watched as his fleshly garment fell among the squealing aliens. They swiftly devoured it. They consumed their own dead in like manner and then returned to their normal tasks as if nothing out of the ordinary had occurred.

Ever so subtly, Yonada wrapped himself about the planet. For ten solar revolutions, he observed and studied. For a while, his loneliness abated. He thought only occasionally of Crècheteacher and of Homeworld. Instead, he gave himself to the great puzzle below.

The Katrini, as the aliens called themselves, were intelligent, progressive, possessed of a rapidly developing technology. Daily, he watched their primitive spaceships as they attended the satellites and orbital laboratories that he had first mistaken for tiny moonlets.

While he watched, Katrini scientists made major advances in seven separate sciences.

Highly refined agricultural techniques yielded rich crops of grains to feed the fat herds of domestic animals on which the Katrini exclusively fed. They were total carnivores. No meat went to waste on the planet—as Yonada had already noted, not even their dead.

The history, art and culture of the Katrini opened to Yonada's probing senses. A strange respect, even admiration for the outward expressions of the Katrini way slowly grew within him. He longed to walk among them, to ask questions, to learn the secret mysteries hidden in their unreadable thought patterns.

One question yet plagued him, though.

The Katrini were a martial race. If he had learned nothing else during his observation he knew that much. He had witnessed the periodic and savage wars that kept the swiftly growing population in check, watched as the victors consumed the bodies of the conquered in grisly and gluttonous rituals. And he had watched victorious armies march back to homes and cities that had, in turn, been ravaged by other armies in their absence. So much of the advancing technology went toward the design and development of weapons and defense systems. Katrini scientists labored unceasingly to find new, more efficient ways of killing.

Yet none of that explained why the Katrini had fought so furiously, so insanely, for the destruction of one lone and lonely visitor.

Yonada decided it was time to learn the answer.

He meditated once more, reflecting on his first visit to the surface, considering as he had many times before, the errors he thought he had made. His Homeworld form was as alien to the Katrini as theirs to him. This time he would wear a Katrini body. Nor would he appear in the middle of a busy street or crowd. He would choose a single Katrini and a very quiet location.

This time, he hoped, he would make a friend.

The Katrini guarded their cities well even at night. The military had grown ever more dominant in Katrini life of late.

Armed soldiers patrolled the unlighted streets and perimeters with drilled precision, working, like the nonsentient insects of Homeworld, in tightly coordinated teams.

From the darkness of an isolated alley, Yonada waited for a patrol to pass, unconsciously rubbing his spurred forelegs together in anticipation. He took a genuine delight in his new body. Oddly distorted images presented themselves to his multifaceted eyes, and the wind tickled his soft antennae as well as the short hairs on his thorax. Starlight made a beautiful gleam on his translucent wings and chitinous skin. All in all, he thought himself quite beautiful.

When he thought it safe, he scuttled across a road to a high gate. To his surprise, the gate and the wall were made of a glasslike substance he couldn't seem to climb. He didn't wish to fly; the humming of his wings might give him away. Peering around, he quietly levitated himself over, and glanced around again. At the center of the compound stood a single building—a Katrini observatory.

After careful consideration, Yonada had decided to seek a creature of learning and science, one who evidenced a curiosity about space and the wonders of the universe. Surely such a being would listen to his story, understand what Yonada represented, and perhaps even become his friend.

He extended his senses, not relying on the insectoid's primitive organs, and found the tunnel that made the observatory's entrance. It was not sealed, and he crept down it as quietly as he could.

The tunnel opened into a vast, domed chamber. A towering spear of metal, a Katrini telescope, occupied the center of the floor. The dome was closed, the equipment not in use. A single scientist bent over a worktable studying diagrammatic representations of the nearest stars.

Touch him, Yonada said to himself, reaching out as he stole forward. *His thoughts will become clear when you touch.*

Before he could close the distance the alien whirled around. For the briefest moment it froze, antennae quivering. Then it let out a shriek and charged with raised forelegs.

Astounded, Yonada stood his ground. The insectoid reared higher on its hindmost legs as it reached for him. He stared straight into the grinding, gnashing mandibles and jaws, then howled in anguish at the only course left to him.

On Homeworld they called it the Forbidden Way. "It is against nature," he heard Crèche-teacher's stern voice, "and contrary to the Great Eighty-one Ways to forcefully impose your will on another living being."

For ten of Katrina's solar revolutions he had meditated and prepared himself for this moment, but not for this. Still, if another way remained, he was blind to it. "Forgive me, Crècheteacher!" he cried aloud. "But I must know!"

He brushed aside the scientist's forelimbs, and the two clashed, locking mandibles. That contact was enough. He exerted his will, and the scientist stopped in mid-attack, every muscle of his insectoid form conquered and ruled by Yonada's mind.

The Katrini proved strong; he struggled bitterly against his mental bonds. Yonada felt the turmoil in the insectoid's mind, its horror at the helplessness of its body.

Revulsion and shame filled him. He would pay a debt for this act, of that he was sure. He prayed the knowledge he sought would be worth the price—knowledge that, in time, would win him understanding, and more, the companionship of these creatures.

Drawing a deep breath, he opened his mind to sift the astronomer's thoughts. Slowly at first, moving carefully, he slipped past the barriers of fear and hatred. Primal instincts he had not even suspected rose up and battered him, tried to force him out. But he pushed in, acutely aware of the alien's psychic screams.

Yonada began to tremble as he plumbed the depths of Katrini self-perception. An undeniable loathing grew in him. At first, he thought it only an echo of the alien's emotion. But the loathing was his own rising fear. The force of it startled him. With considerable effort, he mastered and set it aside. Only then could he communicate.

The insectoid's thoughts began to take form. Suddenly, they rushed upon him like a flood.

"Alien!" It screamed. "Monster! Not-Katrini! Death to you!"

Yonada felt his wings vibrate with surprise, his physical body responding to the Katrini. Somehow, it saw through his outward form. He sent a thought into the alien brain. *Why do you fear me?*

"Not-Katrini!" the creature shouted back. "Fear you? No! Kill you!" It paused under a tidal rush of memories. "You are a thing that walked in our sky ten *anghz* ago. Failed to kill you then! Die now!" The Katrini's mind writhed in Yonada's psychic grip, but its body remained motionless.

Fascinating. This alien not only saw through his form, but recognized him from his first visit. Physically, the insectoid sensory apparatuses were not that sophisticated.

I mean you no harm, Yonada sent, trying to soothe. *I want only your companionship and a chance to share knowledge with your people.*

"Alien!" the creature shrieked with unbridled vehemence. "Not-Katrini! Felt you didn't die! All the *anghz*, Katrini feel you! Search, but couldn't find you!" It tried to lurch forward, achieving the barest quiver in the second leg on its right side. "Kill you now!" it raged. "Kill you like disgusting *N'gaie* monsters!"

N'gaie monsters?

Yonada caught an image flash and pushed deeper into the Katrini's thought patterns, seeking information about the N'gaie. Ignoring the insectoid's prejudice and hate-filled distortions, he saw peaceful beings, white-furred against the cold of the outermost world. The seventh planet had been their home. Yonada had stood among their cities.

"You destroyed them!" he cried in horror.

When the first Katrini exploratory mission discovered the N'gaie, the crew went insane. Not, however, before sending a transmission back to Katrina. An insectoid armada returned, armed with radiation bombs and high-energy weapons. In less time than it took to make the flight they obliterated the defenseless N'gaie.

Yonada shut his mind against those images and trembled— all his questions frighteningly answered.

The xenophobic Katrini were compelled to destroy anything *not-Katrini*. Their very genes commanded it. That was the secret that had eluded him through his long meditation. Deep in his mind, he let go a howl of grief.

I wanted your friendship, he whispered, unconsciously creating tears for eyes that had no natural ducts. *I wanted company to ease my loneliness!*

"Alien!" the insectoid screamed. "Not-Katrini! Kill you, then find your people and kill them all! Search the stars! All Katrini die to find and kill you!"

Yonada shook with sorrow. To be alone on such a crowded world. To come so far, so long, and find no friend! What profound words would Crèche-teacher say, what quotation from the teachings would he offer to soothe him now?

So deep was the pain, so great the hurt that he let his bond slip from the Katrini scientist's mind. In an instant the alien was on him, tearing his chitinous flesh with serrated mandibles, ripping his wings, crushing his body. Yonada ignored the injuries and the creature's rantings. Pushing the Katrini away, he fled the chamber through the tunnel and emerged into the dark, three-mooned night. The alien followed, attacked him again, severing Yonada's rear legs as it attempted to drag him down.

A red light blasted open the compound gates, and the air hummed suddenly with the sound of wings. Katrini streamed into the grounds, street patrols and civilians, alerted by the scientist's chittering cries. They turned toward Yonada, recognizing him, knowing him instantly and instinctively as not-Katrini. With insane fury they set upon him.

An anguished cry burst from Yonada as he cast off his Katrini form and rose weeping into the sky. Though they could no longer see him, the Katrini turned away from the empty shell, sensing he was no longer part of it. Gleaming eyes swept the sky, seeming to follow his ascent. A soldier raised his weapon. A crimson beam stitched the darkness. Another fired, his beam criss-crossing the first. Suddenly, every Katrini with a weapon fired, sweeping the night in a desperate attempt to snag him. More Katrini poured out of their homes, filling the streets. Those with wings took flight, raked the air, seeking an intangible enemy whose presence they could only dimly perceive.

Yonada reeled with the senselessness of it.

A score of missiles launched upward from a hive on the city outskirts and flashed harmlessly through him. Finding no solid target, they fell on another city on another part of Katrina. In a short time, that city launched a retaliatory strike.

Madness swept across the planet. City after city joined in the destruction. Missiles, bombs, energy weapons stained the night, carving hideous scars upon Katrina's face.

Yonada had never known such pain or horror. He couldn't shake the feeling that, unable to destroy him, a world was choosing suicide. He was the cause of this devastation, and guilt filled him.

He wrapped himself about the planet and exerted his will. With all his power he strove to end the fighting, but not even he could dominate so many creatures, and his efforts only reminded the Katrini that he still survived. It drove them to even greater violence.

One by one the cities died. A continent fell silent, then a hemisphere. Radiation poisoned the air, and a last outpost expended its arsenal. The final missile rose, fell, burst. A veil of death settled over the planet.

Yonada curled about Katrina as a father might hold a dead child. All his senses told the same story. A voice stirred up harshly from his memories.

"All Katrini die to kill you!"

Crèche-teacher had not prepared him for this. Nothing in all his eons of experience had prepared him. He wanted companionship, a brief draught of conversation to slake his loneliness. Only the wind in the ashes talked to him now, and they spoke with the scientist's voice.

What could he do now? Where could he go?

The radioactive heat of Katrina's surface slowly cooled. On the outermost world, the cities of the N'gaie gradually froze over and vanished beneath the ice.

Yonada watched it all, meditating, praying for understanding.

LINDA TIERNAN KEPNER IS THE ASSISTANT DIRECTOR AT THE PETERBOR-OUGH, NEW HAMPSHIRE, TOWN LIBRARY (THE OLDEST PUBLIC LIBRARY IN THE WORLD) AND AN INSTRUCTOR AT KEENE STATE COLLEGE. SHE SHARES HER HOME WITH HER HUSBAND, TERRY, WHO IS ALSO A WRITER, THEIR DAUGHTER, QUINN, AND A CAT NAMED T'PRING, WHO IS OLD ENOUGH TO VOTE. THIS WAS LINDA'S FIRST PROFESSIONAL SALE, AND IT APPEARED IN THE NEWCOMERS' CORNER. WE RECEIVED MORE FAN MAIL FOR THIS STORY THAN FOR ANYTHING ELSE WE HAVE EVER PUBLISHED.

Planting Walnuts

Linda Tiernan Kepner

When I heard the screeing I didn't hesitate. I hit the dirt, diving into the underbrush for a wide leaf and rolling just like Cyntoj had said to do. My foot hit a lump of something that yelped, but I was damned if I was going to hide under a leaf anyway. I was already rolling out the other side, gun in hand. I saw something about two meters away with bat wings, a pasty humanoid face, and blue claws, and I fired.

I wasn't alone. I heard screams of death, but I heard pistols firing, too. Not far to my left, a pistol let loose and I heard Araee yell in fury, "Come on, you bastards!" I almost dropped my gun.

A harpy dived at Araee's little bald head, but it wasn't there. Araee squatted, aimed her pistol, and *blam*. The second one dived. That little bald tiger launched herself at it, actually knocking it out of the air. And *blam*. It took her two or three more shots, and a lot of moving, to finish them off, but by then I was busy with some more, myself.

Someone, or something, was also getting its head banged on my far right. Cyntoj had been knocked down by a harpy. His pistol lay in the gritty jungle mud. It hadn't slowed him down a bit. He rolled and kicked, knocking the harpy up into the air.

When it bounced back, it bounced its teeth into his fists. Since the harpies were nearly made of stone, it must have hurt him like hell; but I saw teeth flying.

The boyfriends were defending each other's backs. Three harpies were circling them. Eduardo was yelling, "They're not giving up!"

I couldn't fire without hitting them. "Move, dammit!"

"We can't!"

I heard a growl from somewhere waist high near me. "Stupid bastards!" Tiny Araee shot forward, dived beneath the harpies' wings, and tackled one knee of each man. I saw my chance and shot. I got one, but the other harpies turned.

The last word on the subject reached them before they reached me.

A rain of dusty harpy parts blasted away from me. Mrs. Gonderjhee took aim with the interphase rifle again, blasting away one of the harpies circling Cyntoj. The other tried to take flight, but Cyntoj was having none of it. He literally leaped into the air to bring the harpy down, and finished it off with his own knife.

Again the rifle spoke. Two more harpies died.

A harpy took a dive at Mrs. Gonderjhee, but I was already on target with my own pistol. I was glad to help.

In a moment, the entire clearing was silent.

We were dusting ourselves off, still figuring out what hit us. I looked at Cyntoj, about to say something witty, when I realized he wasn't staring at me.

Mrs. Gonderjhee was sitting on the ground. She had drawn her pocket knife. My heart sank when I saw what she was doing: pulling a ruby-thorn out of her left hand. When she rolled under a leaf at the first alarm, she must have put her hand on a thornbush.

Her right hand trembled when she opened her knife, but by gum, she was doing just what she'd been told to do—cutting away the poison blister. Blood flowed, but that was more because of the shakes and not the poison.

Cyntoj was right there. Gently, he grasped her hand and put it to his lips. He sucked a mouthful of blood, and spat. The rest of us stood, paralyzed, watching them. He did it again, and spat.

Mrs. Gonderjhee's pretty English face never registered much emotion, but it was plain to see she was scared. She tried to make her voice sound normal. "I think I'm all right. Not even palpitations."

Cyntoj still had her red blood on his lips when he realized they were holding both hands together and gazing in each other's eyes. He backed off so fast it would have been comical if we hadn't all been scared shitless.

"Wipe off your mouth," I said. He reached up and did it. He didn't look me in the eye. What the hell, I thought, that really rattled him, holding her hand! I thought the man was made of stone up to then. I kept my astonishment to myself.

We gathered up the scattered equipment. Araee got out the medikit and stanched Mrs. Gonderjhee's bleeding. Like all Denebians, Araee had a thorough knowledge of nerve endings. Mrs. G.'s wound wouldn't bother her much. While the girls were doing that, the rest of us got the equipment and supplies from the dead bodies and redistributed them.

We'd lost the computer geek and one of the Brazilians. Cyntoj surveyed the damage and announced, "We will not camp here. The smell of blood carries for kilometers. In an hour, this place will be crawling."

"We need to bury or burn the bodies," Mrs. Gonderjhee objected.

"You are not listening to me," Cyntoj contradicted patiently. "This is not Earth." He pointed toward the edge of the jungle clearing.

Something made a rattling sound, scuttled into the clearing, and dived into the Brazilian's body with an audible *thud.* We could hear it crunching its way through the flesh.

"We leave *now,*" Cyntoj said emphatically.

I have to admit I didn't hear him well, because I was already out of there, with Araee and Tyler on my heels. But the rest were no slouches, either.

Cyntoj's voice drifted up from behind. "Watch the trees!"

Tyler swore. I heard him swat something, and turned. He had used his engineer's level as a club and batted a tree-scorpion to the ground. It had tried to squirt acid into his eyes, and got his cheek.

Compared to what we'd been facing, though, that was almost nothing. Tyler just wiped it off, and kept hiking. So did we. The other Brazilian came up with a machete, and took over the first place in line. We kept our eyes open.

When we had traveled another kilometer, judging by our pedometers, Araee planted another walnut-sized sensor a decimeter deep in the disgusting soil. Since we each had a pouchful of them—now more than ever per person, thanks to the corpses—we took turns. We would have at least one decent line of survey sensors in this filthy place. Occasionally we stopped and took surface readings.

I was becoming more and more impressed with modern surveying equipment. I always thought you needed a clear line of sight, but not with this stuff. Mrs. Gonderjhee and her surveyors knew modern surveying technology, even if they hadn't known much about modern business.

It was hard to tell, in the heat and the erratic lighting, when night actually began to fall. Cyntoj, of course, true to form, looked neither tired nor fresh—just the way he always did. I was OK; so was Araee, but she couldn't surprise me any more. Mrs. Polly Gonderjhee had been running on nerves for weeks, and wasn't stopping now. The rest were beginning to wilt. Most of them were out of shape and out of practice. A month of training from Cyntoj and me hadn't been enough. I was glad we'd left Sam Byner back with the *Rustbucket* on the coast, though he was going to have a devil of the time convincing the authorities that he was just a harmless tourist waiting for some friends.

I said to Cyntoj, "Night's falling and we'll need to camp soon."

"We are going uphill," the Tyrellian replied. "If this stays true to the geologic forms I know, we should soon reach a ridge. That will offer more safety."

"I'm all for safety," I muttered. "Let's go."

Within a couple of kilometers, Cyntoj found an overgrown cave. Like everything else on Tyrel 3, it was probably full of all the wrong kinds of wildlife. Cyntoj squatted and growled into the dark opening. It was a natural noise for him—I'd heard other Tyrellians do it under stressful conditions—but the wonder was when something in the cave repeated it back to him. He stood up as if confirming his worst expectations.

"Wolf-spiders," he said, looking at Mrs. Gonderjhee, "but we need that cave."

Mrs. Gonderjhee said nothing. She unslung the interphase rifle, and changed the setting to wide area. She stepped to the mouth of the cave, and gave it a good dose. I thought to myself, And this is the woman who hated to swat flies three weeks ago. I'd been wondering if I could even deal with a bunch of bleeding-heart civilians again.

She must have known exactly what I was thinking. She commented, "I am all in favor of preserving endangered species, Mr. Brannon. In Hellforest, that's *us.*" Even Chico, the Brazilian, grinned.

Thanks to her, that cave was as clean as a whistle. Even the wolf shit had evaporated. The boyfriends heated some rocks with a chem-pack, Cyntoj found water somewhere, and Tyler made tea. Our food came out of packets we were carrying. Cyntoj reappeared with dessert, some kind of fruit looking roughly like watermelon.

"Stop hovering," I said, "you're making me nervous. Sit."

Cyntoj sat down beside me. "Nervous, Brannon? You? I doubt it highly." The way he could chaff me showed how much time he'd spent among humans.

"I can recognize sarcasm when I hear it. How do you want to split the duty?"

"Four off, four on. Pick a buddy." Despite the parsecs between our birthplaces, we'd both picked up military shorthand over the years.

"I'd rather pick two."

"Sound," he agreed. "Eduardo and Brad?"

The boyfriends. "Sure, good enough."

"I shall take Chico and Tyler, then." Between us, we had picked the only men who looked like they'd be any good in a surprise scrap. I went off and told the Brazilian and the Cen-Com guy what they'd just volunteered for. They were not thrilled.

Neither was Araee, who overheard me. She faced me off

at the door. She stared up at me from her three-foot height
and asked in a demanding chirp, "Don't you want *me* on duty?"

I grinned, and touched the top of the little bald head. "Yes.
But if I choose many more, there's going to be more people outside than in. Besides, with you in here, I don't have to worry
about internal security. You're an appalling little girl, do you realize that?"

She was appeased. "So long as you mean that. But watch out,
John Brannon!"

"I will, sweetheart. You get some sleep."

"I will."

We headed out to our posts outside the cave entrance. It was
uneventful, though we jumped at every movement of the brush.
Once a howler bat let loose overhead, and once we heard more
harpies scream. I saw a vein of silver and knew that none of the
creatures with sensitive electrical systems would bother us. After
four hours, we headed back inside. Only a few men, and Araee,
were sleeping. The others were wide awake.

Cyntoj and his detachment stood and went outside without
a word. I sat down and thought back on how I got into this mess.
I had no one to blame but myself.

The office of Gonderjhee and Company wasn't listed on the
space station directory. Somehow, I'd expected that. If I was
going to work for a shady operation, it might as well start this
way.

Not seeing them listed brought back my original opinion
of people who'd hire someone like me. I was 3B—bad record,
blacklisted, and broke. I admit that Sam Byner, whom I met at
the bar, had seemed all private-business. But hell, Consolidated
Confederation Central Intelligence could look like Boy Scouts
when they wanted to.

I pushed the button outside Room A439 (no label) and the
door slid open. It looked like just the sort of one-room racket I
expected. There was a tiny desk with a broad sitting at it, some
boxes scattered about. It looked like someone just arrived or was
packing up fast. I inclined toward the latter.

I revised my opinion the moment the brunette looked up at me. It was her eyes. With her short-cut hair and the gray eyes, she wasn't just any bimbo. I was willing to let her look me over—after all, I'm human too—but she just locked eyes with me. Her voice was dead calm. "You have the wrong office, sir."

"I don't think so. Sam sent me."

Her eyes flickered in surprise. Still no sign of anything close to a smile. With one hand, she motioned toward the only other seat in the room. I sat down on it. "Your name?" she inquired.

"John Brannon. How long will I have to wait?"

"Wait?" she repeated. A very slight furrow of puzzlement appeared between her eyebrows. "What did Sam tell you about the company?"

"If you don't mind—why don't I discuss that with the boss?" I suggested.

"Humor me, please." It was a polite order, but it was indeed an order.

I really didn't care if this blew my chances at a job. "He said it was some bandage surveying company in receivership. Close enough?"

"Sam Byner never said that."

"Not quite in those words." I admitted. If she was the secretary, then this was some outfit. She was in her twenties, and had a classy accent, maybe English. She was wearing comfortable clothes. Most secretaries wear ass-high skirts, low-cut fronts, and superspike heels. "That's what you see, once you scrape the paint off."

Her lips tightened for a moment. Her voice was very gentle and entirely different. "I'm afraid you're absolutely right."

"Of course I'm right," I said sternly, "and I came to tell your boss so. If the best they can do is cruise the bars looking for thugs, they deserve to get their teeth kicked in."

"Oh, no. Admiral Kikken recommended you."

I stared at her. I had saved Kikken's life once, a fact not for publication. We'd spent a day in a deep freeze together, at least until Fleet HQ restored the environmental system knocked out by a very large bomb.

"Kikken's an admiral now?"

"Yes. I went to school with Rez Kikken, his wife. Saint

Demeter's Station, and then Oxford. By the way, I am Mrs. Mary Ann Gonderjhee."

Of course she was.

"Rez and Kik have been kind enough to grubstake me and lend me a mothball floater. It's the SS *Ridstock*—commonly called the SS *Rustbucket*, I believe—but beggars can't be choosers. When I have the money, the exterior will say Gonderjhee and Company, but right now I'm buying nothing that I can't eat, burn, or put to work." The eye she gave me was an invitation to put myself in one of those three categories.

"How desperate do you think I am?" I protested.

"Not very." She pulled a folder out of a packing box, and set it on the table. "You're capable, competent, healthy, and young. Kik says you've just had a run of bad luck."

"Did he tell you what my bad luck was?"

"No—" She cut me off by holding up an imperious hand—"and I don't want to know. Mr. Brannon, you have a choice about this, but I don't. For what I need to do, I cannot hire choirboys. Have you ever heard of Confederation Joint Services?"

"Just in passing," I answered. "When I was in the Fleet, we used CJS files if we didn't have our own info in the regular military files. The CJS filing system is a nuisance and the info is almost always screwy or incomplete."

"Do you know why?"

I shrugged. "Because they're a civilian outfit."

"That is incorrect, Mr. Brannon." She didn't argue; she merely stated a fact. "Confederation Joint Services is a government agency. Like many governments on various planets, including Earth, members propose more scientific projects than available military and government scientists can accomplish. The less desirable, less urgent projects end up in a pool, in the hope that a private contractor may bid on them. CJS manages that pool. They accept government proposals, and negotiate private contracts for them. Then they publish the results, and funnel the information to agencies which may need it."

"I stand corrected. Are they very successful?"

"Surprisingly, yes, despite your personal experience. There is a wealth of good information available in CJS databanks. Consider, Mr. Brannon. If the ConFed Fleet had no information on an area, the area must be dangerous or facing other prohibitions. For you to retrieve any data at all must be close to a miracle."

"Uh, oh," I said.

She confirmed my worst fears. "The longer a project sits on their books, or the more dangerous or crucial it becomes, the more they are willing to pay. The oldest, most dangerous project on their books is a survey on Tyrel 3."

"Oh, cripes." I even cleaned up my language for her. "The only difference between Tyrellians themselves and their wildlife is that the wildlife chew you up before they eat you alive."

"It is a physically dangerous job in a politically unstable area," she agreed. That was a masterpiece of understatement. "From their Hellforest city, the Tyrellian Empire has obliterated almost every other race on the planet. They've done everything to the other Tyrel continents that they could imagine, from radioactive dusting to plowing salt into the soil. The only surviving races live on the Empire's own continent, Hellforest, and war with them constantly."

"The Korgorite Nation wouldn't mind dealing with us, but the Tyrellians don't give a crap what outsiders think," I argued, "and the Tyrellians control Tyrel 3. What do they care about surveys? The ConFed is *not* welcome."

"They are members of the Confederation. Their First Contact was over 500 years ago, twice as long as Sol's First Contact. Whether it was a whim, or curiosity, Heaven knows, but they joined. Later empresses found that the ConFed had firmly-established rules about membership, which did *not* include the right to change your mind. They are members under duress, at the moment. They are being forced to pay dues they do not wish to pay.

"They have grudgingly allowed the ConFed to establish three Fleet bases on the opposite side of the world. The radiation has barely died down enough to permit the Confederation's most radiation-resistant races to work there. Now they must register a survey of the native-inhabited portions of the planet. Tyrel 3 has discouraged this. They don't want any detailed maps of the route to their capital city to exist. They don't intend to give in gracefully to the ConFed or to each other. They're all still at war. The mapping must be as unobtrusive as possible."

"Run an unmanned probe over it."

"Mr. Brannon," she chided.

"All right, I know better. The Tyrellian Empire or the Korgorite Nation would blow it to bits. So drop in a shuttle!"

"That won't work, either. The only guaranteed method is to land on the east coast of Hellforest and walk in."

I stared. "Do you have any idea what a risk that is?"

"That's why I wanted you, or someone like you. I don't know how to survive under such conditions. I need training and proper help. You have the experience. In addition, you can pilot a ship. You know about engines. Compared to the rest of my company, you're an expert."

"I'm not a surveyor."

"*I* am a surveyor," Mrs. Gonderjhee stated. "Leave that to me. Are you on?"

"How's your credit?"

"My credit is bad, but not dreadful. This company is not in receivership. I'm straight with Inland Revenue—what you call, in America, the Internal Revenue Service. However, I pay in scrip and I don't sign much."

I saw a coat and a pack of old-fashioned surveying tools over in a corner, and thought to myself: She's sleeping here, too. "Fine by me. Cash makes no enemies." My good sense said to me, Brannon, what are you *doing?* "Let me look over the *Rustbucket*—um, I mean the *Ridstock*—and get some idea of her condition." I stood up.

She almost smiled. "Are you so shocked that Kik recommended you?"

"Well, I need work, so I guess I should capitalize on my references. Three hundred a month and found?"

She shook her head. "Two hundred."

"Split at two-fifty?"

She held out her hand. "Deal. Due to my religion, I'm a vegetarian, but any time there's anything on the cookfire you're welcome to it. I won't complain if you buy and cook meat, but I'll give you your own dinnerware to put it on."

I shook the hand. It was rough from work. "Deal, lady. Where will I stay until we take off? On the *Ridstock?*"

"If you don't mind."

"Not at all. It'll feel more like home."

I left. I was calling myself a jerk for accepting an impossible job that was going to get me killed. For no reason. For almost no money.

But I'd be on a ship again.

I signed on, and slept on the *Rustbucket*—I mean, *Ridstock*—that night. The following morning it was as black with my eyes open as it had been with them shut. It took me a minute to remember I was in a spaceship bunk. Then I wondered what woke me, until the buzzer growled again. In the mornings, I do not shine.

I hit the shell release, and the bunk wall popped open. I crawled upright into the light.

"Oh, good," said a bright soprano chirp, "you're awake."

I sat upright on the bunk, blinking, trying to clear the fuzz out of my eyes and my brain. I *thought* I was looking at a completely bald little girl, hardly more than a meter tall. She was looking back. I saw the shiny ear jewelry, all the way to the points of the little ears.

She handed me a cup of coffee. I took a sip. Compared to the sludge I had been drinking, it tasted mighty good. "Not only are you beautiful," I said, "you are kind and intelligent."

"I like him, Sam," she pronounced. "We'll keep him." Sam Byner was leaning against another bunk, grinning.

The coffee was helping. She was no little girl, not with those pointy little breasts. "What's a Denebian doing in this mess?"

"I'm a surveyor," she chirped.

I eyed her. "Really."

"Well, journeyman surveyor." She pulled the cup out of my hands before I could protest, refilled it, and put it back in my hands. A truly intelligent girl. "Now, you wake up and go powder your nose, and then I'll help you recalibrate the equipment you made notes on yesterday. I'm good at math."

"All Denebians are."

"I'm especially good. You'll see." She patted my shoulder and left the sleeping compartment.

"Where in the universe did you dig *her* up?" I asked Sam.

The plump man chuckled. "Pretty good, eh? And she can make any calculator blush with shame, believe me."

"Yes, but can she dodge Tyrellian vampire bats? That's the question."

His smile faded. "I don't know. I don't know if you can, either." He was serious and sensible. "Let's tackle what we *can* handle first, and work our way toward the impossible."

"Sounds fine to me. Lemme wash up. Any chances on getting breakfast around here?"

"Parathas, fresh fruit, and curried eggs."

"Parathas?"

"Bread. Wait till you taste."

I washed up, shaved, and dressed. Then I walked down to the galley with Sam. Along the way, I asked him, "How'd you hook up with Mrs. Gonderjhee, Sam?"

The middle-aged man smiled ruefully. "I didn't. I was office manager for R. Gonderjhee, Surveyor."

"So you got screwed, too."

"Yep. Me and Polly Gonderjhee held the office against seventeen big, ugly surveyors with bouncing credit vouchers. We pulled strings and punched buttons we didn't even know we had. Little Araee had just come in as an intern. She thought this was the most wonderful education in the world, learning how to handle financial crises. Faith, she was right on that."

I grinned. "What happened to Gonderjhee?"

"I wish I knew. I'd take a chunk out of him myself. Polly hates talking about herself, as you may have noticed. She has her pride. She says she was wild to be off Earth when she was young. Since she came from a sensible, respectable family, she chose a sensible, respectable escape method. She didn't run away and join the Fleet, as I suspect you did." He had me there. "Polly trained as a surveyor, against her family's wishes. She always specialized in computer work, desk jobs. She met Ravi Gonderjhee at one of the stations where she worked. They married. They even went to India for the family's blessing, and she converted to his religion. She was living an exotic, romantic life." He shook his head. "They started a business out here, with an office on Kamarand Station. We had seventeen good surveyors working for us, plus an office staff and students—not a small operation."

Of course. Even I had seen "R. Gonderjhee, Surveyor" ads, somewhere, ages ago.

"She woke up one morning and it was gone."

"What happened?"

"She doesn't know. Kamarand Century Realty was sticking an auction sign on their front door, and no sign of Ravi. As Polly says, law out here is strange; it lacks the four human virtues of mercy, pity, peace, and love. We barely escaped being sold into 'indenture' ourselves."

"Aren't Kamarands sweet?" I commented.

"I got us a job remapping an Orionese estate. I *had* to get her out in the field. You could see the peace on her face while we worked—that's what surveying's all about. When we returned with the payment, K-Law took it. They canceled the indenture proposal and gave us free passage off the station."

"Did they take your equipment?"

"Oh, absolutely. Don't think her decisions are rash. She's desperate for money, and must take desperate measures."

"Couldn't she go to India?"

"Sure, and marry a cousin or a brother. She couldn't bring herself to do it. They don't have divorces, either, but there is an annulment process. She may be working on it, I don't know, but I understand it takes years."

"So Polly got left holding the bag."

"So *Mrs. Gonderjhee*," he corrected, reminding me that "Polly" is an intimate nickname for Mary, "got left holding the bag. She's damned if she does and damned if she doesn't, so she's slogging forward the best she can."

In the galley, Mrs. Gonderjhee was supervising two young human males, whom I placed in their correct category just by looking at them. Especially when one of them giggled and play-punched the other.

"Don't comment," Sam murmured warningly behind me. "It'll cost you." I kept my mouth shut.

Parathas were bread, all right. They were good bread. Ekuri were good eggs. I ate better than I had in some time. While I ate, I met my new shipmates.

Besides Mrs. Gonderjhee, Sam, and the little Denebian,

there were two Brazilians, the boyfriends, and a goofball who was hung up on computers the way other men were hung up on women. There was an ex-accountant from the Central Committee Accounting Office, and two guys who had been rejected by the Fleet for minor medical reasons. Mrs. Gonderjhee and Sam had them firmly under control. Obviously we weren't a quality outfit, but Mrs. G. had shown some sense in her choices. The Brazilians had been jungle miners. Despite their giggling, the boyfriends had the marks of two leather-and-studs punks who knew their way around a brawl. The Fleet rejects only had one bent knee and one bad thumb between them. I figured that even I could teach the computer geek how to handle a pistol. All of them looked like read-and-writes, so if they couldn't survey they could at least be trained to hold the equipment and take notes.

Araee perched next to me and chirped, "Well, where would you like to start with the ship?" That started us off. Mrs. Gonderjhee made it plain that the ship was today's project, I was in charge, and everyone was expected to do what I told them regarding it. We discussed it, and went to work.

When we broke for lunch, the *Rustbucket* was already looking like a working ship. I told Mrs. Gonderjhee so, in private, before we went in to eat. "She'll do," I said. "She'll be smooth as silk."

"It heartens me to hear that."

It occurred to me that this kid needed a lot of heartening these days. I patted her shoulder—nothing sexy about it—and said, "If we have any trouble, it won't be because this ship failed us."

She didn't reply. I wondered if maybe I was wrong to touch. Or maybe it all seemed still too overwhelming. She was still young, and here I was, thirty-eight if I was a day. I had a right to be this tired. She didn't deserve it.

I bought bonding paint for the exterior, and a bonding unit. The ship needed the extra protection, and the registration number had faded, which was illegal. Out of my own pocket, I bought a little red and a little gold bonding paint. I hunted up Sam and told him my idea. He was more than glad to help.

"Mrs. Gonderjhee, could you come outside for a minute?"

She stopped reorganizing her new office and looked at us curiously.

The expression on her face was a wonder as she looked up at the red-and-gold lettering. GONDERJHEE & CO. stretched across either side of the ship in Araee's best commercial lettering.

The computer geek said admiringly, "My God, we look like a real business."

A low, very quiet male voice from behind made us all turn from our admiration of the signs. "Ah. Then this is the correct ship. I wish to speak to Mrs. Gonderjhee."

One look at him and I knew we were signing into a whole heap of trouble. He was nearly two meters tall, dark-haired and dark-eyed, muscular, and severe-looking. He had blue-tinged skin, but he was in typical civilian clothing, a little worn.

Sam muttered, "A Tyrellian, straight off the vine," but I think only I heard him.

"I am Mrs. Gonderjhee." She stepped forward.

He inclined his head slightly—the equivalent of a bow. "You were recommended to me. I need work."

"Come to the office. Sam." She also glanced at me. "Mr. Brannon." She led the way to what might have been the ship's dayroom in more military times. She and Sam took the only two seats. I have to say I didn't mind. She had already caught on to the idea that, with a Tyrellian, the military way is the guaranteed safest form of etiquette.

"What can you do?"

"I have worked on ships. I am good with technology. I can fight, and I can survey." A direct answer to a direct question, the Tyrellian way. And not one flicker of emotion, which would have been bad form.

"Have you a pilot's license?"

"It is not current. It expired eight days ago."

"Is it just a question of paying the fees?"

"No. My name also changed. I would rather retest from the start, under a completely new name, than go through the paperwork of changing it."

"Who recommended me?"

"I prefer not to say. I wish you to hire me on my own merit rather than your opinion of another." He had his nerve, this guy; but then, all Tyrellians had nerve. That's why they had such a successful empire.

"Did your source give you any idea what my project is?"

"Approximately. Contract CJS-963, Confederation survey of the region of Tyrel 3 in dispute between the predominant Tyrellian Empire and the Korgorite Nation, to map natural resources and general survey. The project has been on the CJS rejected proposal list for fifty-seven years." He was still absolutely deadpan.

"One of the disputing kingdoms is your home."

"It is my birthplace but not my home. I am politically neutral." I thought I detected the slightest hesitation in his voice when he said that. "It was suggested that my knowledge of Hellforest and my technical expertise might be of use to you."

"And you need a place to live," she guessed.

The same quick nod. "Yes."

"Your name?"

Sometimes my instinct kicks in at the damnedest moments. I knew what he was going to say, just before he said it.

"My name is Cyntoj."

I stared at him, but I kept my trap shut.

"Please wait outside the compartment," she said evenly.

He nodded again, and walked out.

After the door shut behind him, Polly Gonderjhee spoke to me. Her tone was as dead as his. "You know him."

I weighed the options. I could say no, I could give her half an answer, but—after all, I was working for her now. Assuming she paid. "His name is Captain Cyntoj Smantek. He was an instructor for Combined Fleet Academy, before he disappeared."

Sam frowned. "I should know the name."

"Damn straight you should. Fifth Fleet."

"That's Jackson."

"Admiral Jackson commands the entire Fifth Fleet. Captain Smantek was in charge of the *Eridana*, the flagship. Between the two of them, they could eat a nova for lunch with a dark star for a chaser." I shook my head. "When Smantek put in his time, instead of retiring back to Tyrel 3, he went to Combined Fleet Academy to teach. Then, one day, he vanished. It was a nine days' wonder."

Sam was trying to remember. "I *do* think I heard something about it. But I don't think I ever heard the end of the story."

"Maybe there wasn't one."

Mrs. Gonderjhee hadn't spoken since she'd observed that I knew him. She was thinking. I have a theory that the less a person blinks, the harder he or she is thinking. Mrs. G. wasn't wasting any blinks. When she stirred, it was almost startling. "He looks tired."

"What do you think?" Sam asked her. A smile was coming to his lips, so it was easy to guess what he expected. And he knew her better than I did.

"Call him back in."

He came in. His jacket was over his shoulder. He had his gripsack in his hand. Plainly he expected to hear her say "Thank you but no thank you." His eyes met hers squarely nonetheless.

Mrs. Gonderjhee didn't waste time. I was beginning to like that quality more and more. "I can only give you what I have myself, Cyntoj. You'll have a place to sleep, and food. You'll get paid when I get paid. Two-fifty a month. Profit sharing if there's any profit. Found is vegetarian. If you want meat, you'll have to buy it and cook it yourself, like Mr. Brannon here."

"I am not particular." No, he didn't sound particular; just dead tired. She had noticed it, and I hadn't. Now, with the prospect of a place to stay, Cyntoj let the mask slip a little.

"Then this is your place, and welcome. First, I want you to eat and drink something. Then I expect you to sleep and get acclimated for at least twenty-four hours. You and Mr. Byner will figure out where you'll work best." They were marching orders.

I still think Cyntoj was surprised that she asked him to stay. A new look came into his eyes, as if he felt this was something he could deal with.

She turned to Sam. "Fix up a contract to that effect, name as Cyntoj and payment in scrip." She turned to Cyntoj. "Yes?"

"Yes."

"Mr. Byner will show you to your bunk."

Cyntoj nodded as slightly as Mrs. Gonderjhee smiled. But

I knew he was as solid as if he'd just held up his right hand and sworn the Fleet Oath of Honor.

Sam and Cyntoj left. There I was, alone with the boss, and I couldn't think of anything to say. It lasted a full minute. Then I figured I'd better open my mouth. "For all you know, there could be warrants out for him on fifty planets."

She shook her head. "Not likely."

"True enough."

"Besides, I don't inquire into police records. We'll be between systems most of the time anyway." She gathered up her notes, apparently unaware that she'd just dropped a bomb on me. I *knew*, right then, she knew I was only one step ahead of the law—and that was one of the reasons she hired me.

" 'Space law ends at the starliner hatch,' " I muttered, realizing that it applied as much to her, and to Cyntoj, as it did to me.

Something screamed, mighty damned close to the cave mouth. I realized I'd fallen asleep. I rolled over with my pistol in my hand. Every other living soul in the cave was doing the same.

"What the hell was *that?*" gasped Eduardo.

"Tyrellian vampire bat, I think," Araee contributed.

There was another scream. It felt like the creature was standing right beside me. I'd heard there was a sonar, or maybe even telepathic, element in their sound. They used it for confounding their prey.

"Brad, what are you doing?" Eduardo exclaimed.

The other boyfriend was moving toward the cave entrance. "I'm going to make sure the sentries are all right." He sounded feverish.

"You're going to stay right where you are," I ordered, "with your pistol trained on the cave mouth in case something tries to get in. And you're *not* going to shoot until you make damn sure what it is entering the cave!"

Brad gave me an unprintable reply, and kept going. I heard the *snick* of Mrs. Gonderjhee's rifle adjusting to narrow beam. "Brad," she warned, authoritatively—

All we heard was the roar that drowned out his screams.

Something big and hairy, with six or eight legs, hurled itself from the ledge near the cave mouth.

Mrs. Gonderjhee shot. She shot again. The shaggy creature roared and turned from the body toward the cave. We could see glaring eyes and dripping fangs. Every firearm in the place hit it in chorus, including Mrs. Gonderjhee's.

Tyler's voice rose from outside the cave. "Don't shoot! It's us!"

The three sentries reappeared. Cyntoj looked mussed up. He glanced at Brad's body, but said nothing. He simply heaved it over his shoulder and took off with it. We understood. Before the animals started arriving.

Araee opened up the medicine kit and took out something which she poured over the bloody entrance. "This will mask the smell," she said.

"What happened?" I asked Tyler.

"Vampire bat. They're sensitive, you know, so we just slammed it against that open vein of silver out there until it electrocuted itself."

"Brad."

We turned to regard Eduardo. He was in shock.

"Eduardo, snap out of it," I said.

"What was it?" he asked slowly.

"As my guess, the mate of the wolf-spider we destroyed to get this cave. It was waiting outside, in case one of us should step out alone during the night." I took a breath. "And Brad stepped out."

"That is my guess also." Cyntoj reappeared, rubbing his hands together.

Araee was squatting beside Eduardo. She was examining him carefully. "He is in shock. Cyntoj. Can you help him?"

"No, I cannot."

"Don't be silly," Araee scolded. "You're probably trained in emergency first aid for a hundred races."

Cyntoj shook his head. "My retention has faded to nothing. I simply do not remember. I cannot use those skills."

That was the first time I had heard him put the problem into words. Over the first few weeks of training, I had learned he was good for the short haul, but he couldn't even be depended on to get a full night's sleep. Mrs. G. had found that he'd lost two jobs by losing interest in them and failing to show up for work. His attention span was faulty, his memory shaky; if he hadn't been Tyrellian, I would have called it severe depression.

Chico caught hold of Eduardo and dragged him over to the warmth. He started talking in Portuguese. I imagine Eduardo didn't understand a word of it, but it was soothing. Pretty soon he lay down on his blanket, at least.

Cyntoj and his sentries went back outside.

Eduardo was functioning pretty smoothly by morning. Like I said, those boys were tough.

We were on our seventh day in from the coast. Despite the deaths, events were going pretty much according to plan. Heland—the "Hellforest" was actually just a pun—had no spaceports, so the easiest way for us to land was to pancake on the ocean and drift to a dock in some small town. We had done so. The village only had about 300 people, and they didn't give a damn about us as long as we paid our docking fees. We did. Cyntoj selected this village because it was isolated, but he hadn't shown his face during the negotiations. I thought it was to reinforce the belief that we were tourists, which only shows how wrong I can be.

We worked our way up the river valley, toward the Empire city, away from the sea. We hoped to reach Tyrel City itself, although even space surveys had never showed its exact location. Cyntoj said Tyrel City had defense tricks that the ConFed couldn't understand. We would get within sight of the city walls, that was all. Entering would be far too dangerous. It would take three or four weeks to get there, and just as long back.

The first few days, we planted sensors and saw some of the smaller wildlife, like the tree scorpions. The lands looked slightly tended and slightly cleared, but we never saw people. Cyntoj told us the Korgorite armies obliterated several villages in this area at one time. The Tyrellians had returned the favor. It was not a popular place to live.

Our only goal was to get a line or two of sensors planted, each a decimeter deep and a kilometer or so apart, to provide a link to Sam and the ship. Their progress told Sam that we were still alive and kicking—although, of course, we had no way of knowing the same about him. The "electronic walnuts," as we called them, used very little energy, so as not to delude either kingdom into thinking they'd discovered a "spy net." Altogether, they would act as a grid wherever we planted them, announcing their relative height above Sam on the coast—that is, above sea level—and announcing any interesting electrochemical activity in their vicinity, such as metallic deposits or water. We were reinforcing Sam's readings with topographical surveying and the evidence of our own eyes and recorders. If some snoop, or wild animal, dug up a walnut, it would unravel only a very small part of the grid.

It also meant that, the further we went in the jungle, the more we had to split up to plant walnuts. Fortunately, when Mrs. Gonderjhee agreed to take on the contract, she had strictly limited their expectations in order for her to get paid. We only had a few important river valleys and hills that we *had* to do. The project focus was the main route between the city and the sea, its landmarks and its natural resources. The rest was extra. Mrs. G. and Sam got quite a few contract concessions in view of all the technology that couldn't be used in this case. Anything large, like a satellite, would be considered espionage and shot down by the governments; anything small, like a one-man ultralight, would be considered edible and digested by the wildlife. It didn't leave a lot of options.

As we spread out we stayed in clumps of two or three, or made sure someone was always within sight or voice range. Cyntoj's safety lectures, held in the comfort of the *Rustbucket*, now seemed very, very relevant.

I had Neb off to one side, within speaking distance, and Araee off to the other, when we heard a vicious, growling snort. Then we heard hoofbeats, and Cyntoj's voice: *"CLIMB A TREE!"*

We tore across a clearing to a giant kapok tree, or something like it, just ahead of us. Araee grabbed my arm and I threw her into a low branch. Neb and I grabbed for handholds and started climbing, full packs and all. Adrenaline is wonderful.

Neb swore. I heard buzzing. From her perch on a tree branch, Araee fired past my shoulder to barrage the bees' nest. It fell. There were still a few bees, which we swatted. "I hate bees," Neb growled.

"Allergic?"

"No. I just hate 'em." He swatted the back of his neck.

A great crashing sound drew our attention back to the ground. It was a wild boar—mad and somewhere near the size of an Earth rhinoceros. It looked up toward the tree, toward us, and bellowed.

"Oh, plurge droppings," said Araee. "It can hear the walnuts."

"What? Are you sure?" Neb pulled out a walnut, and twisted it to skew the frequency. The crazed beast gave another roar and slammed headfirst into our tree.

I grabbed Neb just in time to keep him from falling off the branch. Our tree was pretty sturdy, but I didn't think it could take very many more charges like that. This behemoth weighed over a thousand kilograms if it weighed a gram.

It backed up, roared, and charged the tree again. It vibrated. We heard wood crack.

"Mrs. G.'s not going to be able to drop *that* with her rifle," Araee said worriedly.

My backpack crackled. I jumped. Then my pack started to talk. It took me a moment to realize that Cyntoj had modified one of the surveying devices to make my bag of walnuts talk, as a unit! It was a Tyrellian quick-fix technological trick, their specialty. It sure beat stepping into the clearing to yell.

"Brannon—you've got to climb farther up. There's a roc's nest there."

"Dammit, you told us to avoid them!"

There was another *slam*, and a crack. The tree tilted.

Cyntoj couldn't hear me. *"Quickly, while the parent is away from the nest. Drop the egg on the beast!"*

Talk about biological warfare. Why not? I turned and gripped the tree branches, and started to climb.

I grabbed hold at another *slam*. The tree tilted further. Another meter—I could see the nest, and a bright gold egg. But those branches couldn't hold my weight. Araee's hand grabbed my ankle. She had followed me. "My job!" She climbed over me as if I were part of the tree, and out onto the branch.

Slam! I grabbed Araee's legs as she wrapped herself around the branch. Below, down to my left, I heard Neb saying, "Shit! Will you guys come *on?*"

Araee strained. Her little fingers barely touched the egg. She shimmied out a little further. "I've almost got it. I've got it. Oh, oh—I can feel something moving inside—"

"Swell—it's calling to its parent. Pass me the egg—"

"Will you pass me the *egg* down here, dammit?!?"

An unearthly call echoed across the skies while we played Hot Potato. I caught the egg from Araee and tossed it to Neb. He took a moment to position himself, and dropped it right on the boar's head. A naked fledgling flopped across the boar's back, still in its goo.

For a moment I thought a spaceship whizzed by, close enough to touch. Then I realized it might as well have been. It was the roc parent, after the destroyer of its egg. I couldn't imagine a thousand-kilogram wild boar yelping, but this one did. The roc picked it up in its claws as if it were a sausage, and vanished in a flurry of red, gold, and blue.

Carefully, we worked our way back to the ground. The rest of the team was there to greet us. "I'm still shakin'," Neb said, holding out his hands. "Let's get out of here."

"I second the motion." I looked down at Araee. Her eyes were shining. It was plain that this excitement was bread and meat to her.

I turned to Neb just in time to see his eyes roll up into his head as he dropped to his knees, then to the ground.

"What's happening?" exclaimed Mrs. G.

"I can guess." I dropped to the ground beside him and loosened his collar. "Shock. He's allergic to Tyrellian beestings. We need antitoxin, quick."

"I'm looking, I'm looking." Tyler shuffled through the medikit, triumphantly holding up the syringe.

Neb shuddered once more, and died.

I expected to hurt all over, and I didn't. Apparently my adrenaline kicked in at exactly the right moment, and just long enough, to prevent me from feeling any ill effects from climbing a tree in full pack.

Araee was far more subdued. She had been higher than a kite from excitement in the tree, and completely unprepared for Neb's reaction. Tyler had to snag the medikit from her because she was too high to help. It hurt her Denebian pride, and I could sympathize.

Cyntoj was also subdued, but I didn't have the heart to ask him what was wrong. He had done some quick communicating, but he had failed in the weapons department and in the life-saving department. 2 to 1 was a bad score for a Tyrellian. Mrs. Gonderjhee was giving him thoughtful looks, too. I had a bad feeling that she'd inquired for his references after all, and discovered he wasn't coming through.

To add to our joy, Thomsen developed a skin fungus. Thomsen's illness was disastrous, because he was a licensed surveyor. Mrs. Gonderjhee and Sam were, too, of course, and Cyntoj had the ability but no license, so he and Araee were journeymen. The dead computer geek had been licensed; so were Tyler (the CenCom man) and Thomsen. The rest of us were goons.

Thomsen kept up the pace, supported by drugs and salves from the medikit, but he was weakening.

We were paralleling the river. It was hot, humid, and had crocodiles the size of submarine boats. We got our drinking water from side pools with tiny streams and plenty of birds nearby, to limit the possibility of a neighboring caiman. Then we got the hell out of there. We had the equipment to purify any water, but not to make it. Every time I went to the river, I knew what a wildebeest felt like.

We slept in caves whenever we could find them, but we pulled out the tents a couple of nights. They slept six, which meant we only needed two of them now. None of us cared if our tentmates were male, female, alien, or chimpanzee. We were too exhausted to care, and there was safety in numbers. Even so, there was something pleasant about the evenings. I liked listening to Chico singing, or Mrs. Gonderjhee asking somebody questions about their lives or their opinions. She was good at getting other people to talk. I suppose it got her mind off her own problems.

To celebrate two weeks out, we found a really nice cave to sleep in. The caves were getting to be mighty reliable. During the night we heard vampire bats and wolf-spiders nearby. It was so routine it almost wasn't worth mentioning.

There was more combat inside the cave than out. When we got set for the night and went to take night duty, my team said nothing doing. Eduardo and Joshua rebelled at taking another four-hour shift. They insisted that everyone should be taking turns.

This was why I hated civilians in all their forms. (This was also why I was in so much trouble on Orion.) I told them it wasn't a matter of what they wanted, it was a matter of what we needed. They flatly refused.

Mrs. Gonderjhee watched quietly. She exasperated me, too. *"You* want to do night duty?" I asked her at last.

"No," she answered, "not in the least. Interesting. I didn't think you'd even ask a woman, Mr. Brannon." Despite her words, while she spoke, she lifted her rifle to her shoulder to accompany me. I gathered that she had grown up in a sporting English family and was quite comfortable with the rifle.

The cave exploded in protest. Only Cyntoj and Araee were silent. "Mrs. Gonderjhee! You can't do sentry duty!"

"Why not?"

Joshua started, "If anything happened to you . . ."

" . . . you'd be up a creek? Is that what you're saying? Then you had better decide right now if this is a democracy or if I am in charge. If this is a democracy, then we all take turns at everything, good and bad. If an essential person gets killed, you'll just have to cope. If I am in charge—and I was under the illusion that I am—then I make the decisions, using advice from the persons I deem appropriate, and we stop all this wretched debating." She set the rifle down, butt end first. Her voice was still calm and firm. "Now. Who is in charge?"

Silence.

"I want to hear voices—every single person here."

I took a breath. "You are."

"I am what?"

"You are in charge, *ma'am*." I knew how to answer an officer.

"That's better. Mr. Estes."

"You are," said Joshua, after the same pause.

Around she went, naming names. I could hear pauses and breaths, but the answer was always the same. Mrs. Gonderjhee was in charge.

"Ms. par-Araee."

"You're in charge, Mrs. Gonderjhee."

"Mr. Cyntoj."

"You are in charge, *ma'am*." Same school.

"Then it is unanimous. Mr. Brannon. Why have you continually picked Eduardo and Joshua to pull duty with you?"

"Instinct, I guess, ma'am. My feeling is that they have what it takes. Some people are natural sentries."

"Then, gentlemen, you're on duty with Mr. Brannon. I trust his judgment in this matter. I'm sure you will be able to work together. If you can't, I'll know the reason why."

I'd never had a civilian, certainly not a woman, ever say she trusted my judgment quite like that. I didn't realize how much it stunned me until I almost sat on a fire-ant pile outside.

We went two days without losing a soul.

I didn't realize we were being shot at until Joshua's brains splattered all over the tree trunk beside me.

When you're in the Fleet, new and green, that makes you stop and stare. Me, I was already heading for the nearest leafy underbrush.

I rolled, and thudded against a leg the size of a tree trunk. I looked up at what I figured would be my last look, and saw what I expected to see: Knee-high cloth boots, bare legs covered with silvery scales, a cloth tunic, leather armbands and chest protector, a silver-scaly reptilian face. A Korgorite foot soldier. When he growled and showed his sharp teeth and lifted his lance, all I thought was: Good-bye.

I kicked up a leg, right toward his genitals, on principle.

296 LINDA TIERNAN KEPNER

That alone wouldn't have done it; but a rock the size of my head hit him in the face the same instant. He was down, and I was on my feet.

I wasn't needed, even though there were eight of them and only one growling Tyrellian with a sling in his hand. He had their full attention. I'd never seen anything like it.

In a voice I'd never heard, Cyntoj growled, "Who else?"

They were frozen. I'd heard the effect Tyrellians had on Korgorites was roughly the same as a cobra on a lot of hamsters, but I'd always thought it was folklore. And yet, they were paralyzed, outnumbering him eight to one.

I got out my pistol and made sure he saw it. I noticed that no one else was in sight.

One Korgorite moved toward him—his last mistake. There was a *snap* of the sling (I realized it was normally his belt) and the Korgorite fell as if he'd been poleaxed. Even at close distance, that belt was a deadly weapon. It was being wielded by an expert.

Cyntoj looked them over. In that icy, paralyzing voice, he said, "These are all soldiers. There is a captain somewhere."

I moved back a step, planning to look for him. A voice on the opposite side of the clearing—behind Cyntoj—saved me the trouble. "He's right here, don't worry. You make an excellent target, Tyrellian."

Calmly, Cyntoj answered the invisible Korgorite. "Don't you think my own marksman will trace your shot? Think before you fire." The soldiers were recovering quickly, and tossing hostile little glances at me.

"That?" A note of contempt—meaning me.

"No. The others. Do you think I'm here alone?"

Pause. "I know you're not. There's only one reason a Tyrellian would be here. But with humans?"

Cyntoj's voice returned to normal. "You speak remarkably good Universal Basic, Captain. I don't suppose you worked on one of the Tyrel Fleet bases."

"Turn slowly," the voice said. Cyntoj obeyed. The voice said, "By God." That was a human expression, not Tyrel 3.

A large Korgorite commander stepped out from the trees, interphase rifle in hand.

"By God," he repeated. "The Dead Man."

Cyntoj acknowledged the apparent recognition, and returned it. "Garkin—isn't it? You were a communications officer on Tyrel Fleet Base 3, as I recall."

"As *I* recall, I was a slave of the Tyrellian commander of Tyrel Fleet Base 3."

"I stand corrected."

The teeth parted slightly. Korgorites couldn't blink, but his eyes narrowed. "And you were a visiting Fleet officer from the great outside universe. I remember. Shimtek gave you hell for speaking to Korgorites as equals."

"It is a bad habit I picked up from Outside."

The yellow slit-eyes took in the casualties. "You killed two of my soldiers."

"You killed one of my friends, and injured another." (I had the sense to limp when I stepped forward.)

"You are in Korgorite territory."

"So I am."

The captain blinked. "You admit it? But yes, where else should you be? Why do you have humans with you?"

"To survive."

"Where do you camp?"

Cyntoj pointed east. "Two ridges over, in some wolf-spider caves." We had camped there last night, and we were long gone. "I have no ambitions but reading and meditation now."

The captain thought about this for a moment. "So you say." He thought again, and made a decision. "I will report your presence, but you may remain in this area."

"You are unusually kind."

"Oh, it is not kindness." He barked an order in his native tongue, and his squad came to attention. "It is—initiative. And, perhaps, remembrance."

No one came out of the shrubbery until the Korgorites were definitely long gone. The first to appear was Araee, pistol at ready, and then Mrs. Gonderjhee, rifle in firing position. "What do you suppose he meant by initiative?" Mrs. Gonderjhee asked.

"I do not know," Cyntoj answered, "and I see no point in wasting effort guessing."

"C'mon," I said, "we've got to get out of here. The wildlife's arriving."

Little did I know how true that was.

I circled around the area I'd been working, puzzled. A moment ago I could see Araee off in the distance; now I couldn't. I was moving to the spot where Thomsen ought to be. I didn't see him, either.

Cyntoj stepped out of the foliage, a puzzled frown on his face.

"You seen Araee or Thomsen?"

"No. Have you seen Chico or Eduardo?"

"No."

We found Thomsen, looking for Tyler, and Eduardo, looking for Mrs. Gonderjhee. "Couldn't be animals," I said, puzzled. "Someone would've screamed. Mrs. G. would have taken a chunk out of them, for sure."

Cyntoj's frown had cleared, but the expression wasn't pleasant. "It is a special animal, all right," he said thoughtfully, "traveling in scout parties."

"Shit. Which kingdom, yours or theirs?"

"Tyrellian or Korgorite," he corrected me. Even back on the ship he had made a point of being excluded from both kingdoms. "I do not know, but I am about to find out. Are you on?"

"I'm on."

Thomsen, scratching madly, said, "I'd better stay here."

I turned to Eduardo. "Stay with Thomsen and the gear—excuse me. *Would you please* stay with Thomsen and the gear?"

Eduardo flashed me a quick grin and nodded.

Cyntoj slid on ahead of me, as smooth and dark and quiet as a panther. I went slower, to stay quiet.

He stopped at a small patch of open ground and dropped to one knee. He waited for me to catch up. I looked at the footprint in the mud. It looked humanoid. Two horizontal bars were most prominent—the crossbars of a Tyrellian hinged clog, standard issue. Cyntoj didn't wear them. I glanced ahead a bit, and saw something. In a low voice, I said, "Scrap from Tyler's jacket."

Cyntoj nodded, rose, and padded along with me.

We didn't go much farther before we found Chico's body. The eyes bulged horribly and the wildlife was already at work on it. We passed by quickly.

Cyntoj's face was grim. His lips pressed close to my ear. "I am not certain they are scouts. Some Tyrellians were exiled here. They are far more dangerous."

I nodded. Mere scouts might kill someone without questioning, but Tyrellian exiles would have nothing to lose, either. The kingdom was the be-all and end-all for Tyrellians, which was why Cyntoj's attitude was so remarkably un-Tyrellian. The tone in Cyntoj's voice, too, indicated that you had to be mighty bad to get yourself exiled to Hellforest.

We cast around, looking for more clues. Through the leaves, some distance off, I saw Cyntoj's hand raise. He had found a piece of Maine pinegum—Tyler chewed it. It occurred to me that Tyler was very much on the ball, for a guy who claimed to be an excessed Central Commission accountant.

We could both see their progress through the underbrush, though I'm sure Cyntoj's sharp eyes saw far more than mine. The signs told us that they weren't hiding—they just hadn't expected company.

Among the topics we'd discussed during the training period was what our cover story would be if we got stopped by Tyrellian or Korgorite forces, so I knew that part of the problem was taken care of. However, Chico's dead body suggested there might be unconsidered problems with that line.

Cyntoj crouched. I did the same. We crept up to the edge of a man-made clearing. It was a compound, rather than a camp. The buildings were wood, with stone lintels and supports. Tyrellians never used canvas or wood if stone was available. They built for life. It told me, plain as day, that some Tyrellian was calling this place home.

I saw the banner at about the same time Cyntoj did, in front of the largest cabin. Up highest, of course, was a lion, symbol of the Tyrellian Empire. (Even exiles still considered themselves

Tyrellian—like an Irishman is always an Irishman.) Below the lion banner was something that looked like a stylized jaguar. We moved back into the forest.

"Here's how it stands," Cyntoj whispered. "That is the Sedek clan. My bet is that it's leaderless, since most of their females have been executed recently."

"Wonderful. Does that improve Araee's and Polly's chances?"

"I hope so. Do you think the rest of the team can cope without us until evening?"

"I hope so. What are we going to do?"

"If they have stuck to the surveying-school story, we should be able to stage an escape that looks like students helping students. They won't bother chasing them if they have a far more serious problem on their hands, obviously unconnected with their chance meeting with these students."

"What's the more serious problem?"

"Me."

He wasn't kidding. We each had a pretty good idea of how the other thought by now. I took one look at his face and knew this was a piece of unfinished business.

There was no point in arguing unless I had a better idea. I didn't. "Okay," I sighed. "Lay it out for me."

He sketched his ideas for me, but had barely begun to elaborate on them when we heard a scream. It was a full, high-pitched scream with a lot of body to it. A man's scream always has more tone and sincerity than a woman's. He tapped my shoulder twice ("Let's move"), and we worked our way around the edges of the compound. Cyntoj knew where he was going. I gathered that this was a typically-styled camp.

The compound was much smaller than I'd thought. There were only five main buildings, and a couple of storage sheds. On the side nearest a rock-faced waterfall, they had built an open plaza, as if they had great plans. Perhaps twenty Tyrellian men were there. Hanging by his wrists from a gibbet was Tyler. They had already started taking off some of his skin and a few fingers and toes.

A very unpleasant-looking, dark Tyrellian occupied the largest chair in the clearing. I saw Araee and Mrs. Gonderjhee, hands tied behind them, sitting on a bench, watching.

The leader spoke in Universal because Tyler was obviously human. "Now. You won't last long at this rate. Why are you here?"

"I told you the truth!" Mrs. Gonderjhee said. Despite the horror she must have felt, Mrs. G. sounded as though she was in full control. "This is a class exercise, nothing else!"

"You are spies."

"Nonsense." She even sounded firm. "Our records are public information. Contact the Confederation computer system. Tyrel 3 has full access."

"We have no access." His voice was harsh. Something was wrong. All Tyrellians had a high level of computer access. This gang had really been ripped out by the roots.

I wasn't keen on watching Tyler get tortured any more. I was ready to move when they went at Tyler again, but Cyntoj tapped my arm once. I turned to stare at him. He was saying no! What was wrong with him?

Cyntoj stayed still. He watched the scene intently.

I tend to act before I think, and now I settled down (making sure, first, I wasn't on a fire-ant pile). Cyntoj had seen something I hadn't, and I needed to catch up. What was it? Why was Tyler worth torturing?

The obvious answer was that he was keeping something back. The torture was unsophisticated, for Tyrellians. Technologically speaking, they were wizards. This was one of the many reasons why they were so valuable in military work—they could make weapons out of anything, on the spur of the moment, using their imagination and the most unlikely-looking equipment. They didn't need to futz around, taking a guy apart joint by joint like this.

They had sensed Tyler was lying. They were in bad moods. They got their tails kicked, Tyler was not Tyrellian, and they didn't give a damn. They just wanted to make someone suffer.

I remembered the CenCom man making some comment about being more use to Sam than to us. At the time, I thought it was cold feet. Apparently Cyntoj interpreted it differently. He suspected Tyler of skulduggery, and was waiting to see what his brother Tyrellians could dig up.

But I wasn't prepared for what I heard. Apparently, neither was Mrs. Gonderjhee. She generally didn't react strongly, but this time I saw her stare. "You're from *what?*"

The seated Tyrellian cocked an eyebrow at Tyler, still hanging from the ropes. "She did not hear you. You had best repeat it," he suggested.

"The Internal Revenue Service," Tyler mumbled.

Mrs. G. sounded genuinely puzzled. "Inland Revenue? But *why?*"

It was a reasonable question, but Tyler did not respond. I felt like stepping out and offering to help with the red-hot pokers, because I could guess.

Bit by bit, they dragged it out of him. The Confederation Internal Revenue Service didn't believe that Mrs. Gonderjhee and Sam had no idea of Ravi Gonderjhee's whereabouts. Tyler had been assigned their case, to keep tabs on them until they met Ravi for their share of the loot. Then he would call in the Confederation marshals to arrest them all.

Polly Gonderjhee's face went completely white. A woman has never looked at me like that, but if one does, I'll make damn sure my will is in order.

"Inland Revenue is chasing *me?*" If her hands had been free, I think she would have taken the hot poker to him herself.

In her typical fashion of saying what other people merely thought, Araee, too, found her voice. "Tyler—you *scumbag!*"

I had never seen a Tyrellian break form before, but I saw Cyntoj's lips twitch. The seated Tyrellian actually broke into a quick grin.

"Little one," he said, in his very good Universal Basic, "you appear shocked. Is this human such a good mistress?"

"She's not my mistress, she's my boss. She's been trying to keep this business afloat ever since her man robbed her, and this—this—" Words failed her, and she changed topics. "And you're not any better, treating us like this! The way you act, you might as well be human!"

That was a gross insult, but the Tyrellian took it well. "Perhaps we are at cross purposes, then. You said your name was—Mrs. Gonderjhee?"

"That is my name."

"And these others?" No answer. He continued, "We can be civil enough to trade names, at least. Your Denebian associate is correct on that point. My name is Kyren Sedek. These men are all that remain of my clan and family—hence we fled the city. It appears that our fortunes run in similar fashion, Mrs. Gonderjhee."

"I haven't murdered anyone in cold blood."

He waved it away. " . . . Yet. If you find you must, you must. We live in a violent universe." He motioned to the guards, who removed ropes from their prisoners. He gave a command in Tyrellian—which I don't speak—and Araee's guards motioned her off politely toward one of the cabins.

Kyren Sedek stood. "I would speak with you. Come, eat and drink with me."

Araee piped up, " 'Tyrellian seduction knows no bounds.' "

Mrs. Gonderjhee said quietly, "Araee, go with them."

"But, Polly!"

"Go! You're my safety."

Araee nodded, biting her lip.

We slid back to whispering distance.

"Point one," I said, "is that I don't speak the lingo."

"That's all right. You won't need to."

"What's Mrs. Gonderjhee doing?"

"Buying time for us to find her. She's not a fool." Cyntoj stared thoughtfully at a leaf. *He* wasn't blinking much either. "She comprehended that they want the women's goodwill."

"Uh-oh. Because Tyrel 3 needs women."

"This camp does, at least. Despite her humanness, Mrs. Gonderjhee displays some striking Tyrellian female qualities." I thought of some of the tough, straight-from-the-shoulder Tyrellian businesswomen I'd met, and had a pretty good idea what he meant. "Unlike humans, Tyrellian men are physiologically dependent upon their women."

"A hormone thing?" I asked, in lieu of a complicated question.

"Yes," he replied, in lieu of a complicated answer.

"So Kyren Sedek is hurting."

"Kyren Sedek is going to learn what hurting is all about," Cyntoj answered grimly.

We went back to the cave to discuss strategy. Nobody else liked Cyntoj's suggestion much better than I did, although they all had different reasons. Freakin' democracies.

Thomsen was most vocal about it. He didn't like me anyway. The feeling was mutual. "You went off and left Mrs. Gonderjhee with a bunch of Tyrellians, and tell us *you'll* save her? Didn't you even talk to them? You're going to go in with weapons and you don't even know if they'll listen to reason!"

"This group will not listen to reason, not the way you mean it," Cyntoj replied quietly. While the rest of us were arguing, Cyntoj was almost ignoring us, playing with things in his hands: some walnuts, connections, microtools, and a bit of wire. His hands flew faster than those of a good seamstress, constructing something potent out of the harmless little walnuts with their tiny built-in power supplies. Talking to us, his eyes on his work, he was retro-wiring transmitters, paring down cores, realigning switch strips. His communications act during the roc incident had only been a warm-up phase. This was Tyrellian fieldstripping at its best.

Thomsen scratched himself (his fungus was worse) and barked, "All we have is your word on that, and as near as I can tell, you're no better yourself!"

"Thomsen," I said, "shut up."

He spun on me. "Who the hell put you in charge? You aren't a licensed surveyor. Neither is this Tyrellian. You're a scrub pilot. You just march in here, both of you, and say, okay, everyone follow me because I say so. You have no idea what's going on, and you obviously don't give a damn. We need to work this out and either talk to these Tyrellians, or reach a consensus on what to do."

He was what I hated most in civilians: all talk and no action unless I'm in charge, let's reason with crazies, guns are always bad and soldiers are worse. I felt my back hair rising as I opened my mouth.

Cyntoj touched my shoulder and stopped me. His voice was as calm and patient as before. "You are correct, Mr. Thomsen. You deserve some answers and explanations. First, about myself. I am a respected Tyrellian citizen. These people are not. I know, because I was instrumental in their exile from the kingdom. If need be—if we had time—I could place proof of their atrocities before you. But we do not have the time. And, unfortunately, in a court of Tyrellian law, the words of Kyren Sedek would be given precedence over mine."

"Because you're no better than him!" Thomsen snapped.

"No. Because I am dead, and he is not," Cyntoj replied calmly.

We all stared.

"In revenge for foiling their crimes, the Sedek clan took steps against me. It is rather like, in your cultures, being taboo, or legally dead. In the Tyrel empire, I am a nonperson. I have no rights. No Tyrellian may speak to me or notice me." He smiled that strange little smile I was beginning to hate. "I am— the *late* Captain Cyntoj Smantek of the Confederation Fleet, dead with honor."

"The Dead Man," I muttered.

Brief nod. "The Dead Man. I am dead—ruined—useless to anyone for over two years now, and it shows. I'm sure you've noticed. It is naturally expected that I will die of the ostracism. Second, the women are not in mortal danger. The Tyrellian Empire is a matriarchy. Whether or not they become someone's wives, the women serve as a focus point for the men. They are safe."

Eduardo had enough of talking. He was cleaning the blade of his big knife. He never wasted time making decisions. "Okay, I'm with you."

I cut short any more debate by turning away from the group. "Let's go."

"Macho man," I heard Thomsen mutter.

"Merely impolitic," said Cyntoj. I shot a quick, suspicious glance at him. I swear his eyes twinkled. "Brannon is more at home with the Fleet, and it shows." I glared at him.

I was crawling through the grass with a knife in my hand,

concentrating on avoiding fire-ant piles and critters dropping off leaves, before it occurred to me that Cyntoj was perfectly right.

When it comes to demoralizing the enemy, Tyrellians wrote the book. Nonetheless, I thought that Cyntoj was exaggerating how much his mere presence would disrupt the camp. I knew he had a grudge, and I knew he was taboo. But I also knew that Tyrellians were fierce and vicious fighters. We were also moving in daylight, because it would be easier for us humans to maneuver. If Cyntoj had some kind of edge, it couldn't be much.

From my vantage point at the edge of the compound, I bided my time, waiting for my cue.

Cyntoj appeared at the main square and came down on the whole bunch like a ton of rough ore. From there on, he had exactly the same effect as a porcupine in a nudist camp. He knocked two sentries unconscious immediately. Someone else nearby saw him, aimed a gun, realized he'd screw himself for taking notice of a dead man if he shot, and lowered the gun. By then he'd gotten a rock alongside the head that put out his lights. Cyntoj was a hallucination with one helluva mean sling.

That scene was repeated at least eight times. From my end I could hear the sound of panic in the streets. It was mighty obvious even though I didn't know the lingo.

Cyntoj strode toward the central firepit, where items had been heated to toast Tyler not so long ago. Tyler's eyes flickered when he saw Cyntoj, but he didn't speak. Cyntoj shot one of his newly-adjusted walnuts toward Kyren Sedek's cabin.

I swear the wooden cabin didn't go up in flames, and I'll still swear it. The entire front wall simply seared away in a flash, like a singed hair. The stone archway was still in place. Light flowed into the darkened cabin. Kyren Sedek had his arms tightly around Polly Gonderjhee.

Sedek moved slowly, as if drugged. He could only have said, "No. It can't be."

"So. How desperate Kyren Sedek has become!" Maybe those weren't the words, but that was the tone. Sedek's eyes flashed, and he dragged Mrs. G. into the light.

"Yes, Kyren Sedek will survive!" Of course, *he* did not refer to the nonexistent person before him.

"And I have something Kyren Sedek does not have," Cyntoj said mockingly. "I have the freedom to do—this!" He turned and ran, straight toward one of the outbuildings.

"No!" Sedek tore after him. Perfect.

Cyntoj pulled out another of the walnuts and threw it. It hit the building.

A column of blue flame rose skyward. If we were on Earth, we could have signaled Mars with it.

Sedek's own lash-belt snapped out. Cyntoj dodged it as though it wasn't there. His reflexes were superb, and he had had plenty of practice in the past few weeks.

Secure in the knowledge that Sedek was fighting the Dead Man and was screwed in any case, I sidled around to the spot where the interphase rifle was propped against a wall. Someone saw me, just a movement from another corner, and I shot. I saw blue blood as I dived into the trees. No one followed me. The rest were all down watching Sedek and the Dead Man, horrified.

I got back to the porch. I noticed that the front of the cabin didn't look too burnt, though I was focusing on Mrs. G. "Polly!" I hissed. "Mrs. Gonderjhee!" She stood numbly on the porch, staring in the Tyrellians' direction. She must be drugged, I thought in discouragement.

Suddenly there were two people beside me: Araee and Eduardo. Araee took in the situation at a glance, and said, "This I can handle." Her hand dived into her pocket and came out with a small vial. She mashed the vial into Mrs. Gonderjhee's hand.

I watched Polly Gonderjhee come back to life. She looked down at Araee, then at me. I breathed a sigh of relief as she reached for the rifle. We scrambled out of sight.

"All okay," said Eduardo. They had rescued Tyler.

I nodded. "Cyntoj told us to clear out and lie low after this." I didn't fool Mrs. Gonderjhee. "Why?"

"My guess would be, so he could blow up the compound and take them all with him. He's reached his limit." I met her eyes. "After all, he's the Dead Man, you know."

"I know. I'm rather dead myself." *Snick* went the rifle. "Where are you planning to be?"

"East side. Want the west?"

"You and Araee take the west. East will give me better cover."

"Yes, *ma'am*," I said. Eduardo grinned, and put away his knife—blue with blood, he'd actually killed a real Tyrellian—and got out his pistol to join us. "What a bloodthirsty bunch we've become," he commented.

"We'll outgrow it," said Mrs. Gonderjhee.

The munitions shed still lit up the sky in a manner that must have been appalling to a bunch of Tyrellians who wanted to stay under cover. I wondered how he'd done that with nothing but a walnut. I'd bet ConFed Ordnance would like to know, too.

Right now, though, he had the belt-sling and no walnuts. He was doing pretty well for himself; Kyren Sedek looked to be in much worse shape, and there was one Tyrellian laid out on the ground. He must have decided to damn himself and go after the Dead Man anyway, for the honor of the clan, and Cyntoj dispatched him in his spare time.

They were fast and vicious, like two Ninja fighters on speed. The rest were circling. They looked like wolves. They were closing in. If Sedek didn't get him, they would.

I had just realized that this location was well-protected from sniper attacks on both the east and west sides. So, apparently, had Mrs. Gonderjhee. Eduardo, Araee, and I were sneaking closer, clinging to buildings, when I heard the sound of the interphase rifle. Sneaking was pointless. I stepped around the corner of the building. Most of the remaining Tyrellians had turned their backs on Sedek and Cyntoj, and were drawing pistols for a new threat—the woman with the rifle, in the middle of the street.

Mrs. Gonderjhee wasn't being coy. She had the rifle on wide range and mowed four of them down, while Araee, Eduardo, and I worked on the rest. She had control, to shoot down the nearer Tyrellians while not touching Sedek and Cyntoj. I saw Sedek falter, and I saw Cyntoj's belt wrap around his throat. Cyntoj choked him dead. Unlike all the other Tyrellians Cyntoj had attacked, he made sure that Kyren Sedek would not live. When Sedek was unconscious, Cyntoj slit his throat.

Then he stood, and looked at me accusingly. "I don't recall telling you to do this."

I never got a chance to speak. Mrs. Gonderjhee interrupted, "Cyntoj, come here, please." She said please, but with Mrs. G., you knew an order when you heard one. When he obeyed, she looked up into his face. "As long as you work for me, you will never put yourself in a suicidal position again."

He was silent.

"Have I made myself clear?"

"Perfectly clear, ma'am," he muttered.

"We can discuss this later." She turned on her heel. "I don't want any more casualties. And that pillar of flame should be visible for miles. We must leave the area. Come. We have a long way to go."

I heard a chuckle. It occurred to me I'd heard that voice before. Now it was above my head. "I don't think so, my lady."

"What—?" She stared at Korgorite Captain Garkin as he slid down from the tree. I never realized that happy Korgorites showed quite so many teeth.

"I think it's high time I put you all out of Heland, back east to wherever you came from. I owe you my apologies, Captain Smantek. I thought you knew the Sedek clan was somewhere in this region. I knew that, although I didn't know exactly where. I do keep informed on *some* Tyrellian clan politics."

"You knew they were here," Mrs. Gonderjhee said sharply.

"Madam," said the captain quietly, "did you see what one Tyrellian did to eight of my soldiers? Of course you did. You were the sharpshooter in the brush. Better to face a pack of maddened boars than to take on a desperate Tyrellian clan."

"And you chose to fight fire with fire," I said.

He continued to speak to Cyntoj. "I keep informed, I admit, in the hope of learning that someday, someone will eradicate the Shimtek clan, and possibly all of Tyrel Fleet Base 3."

"Considering Tyrellian politics," Cyntoj replied, "it is not such a vain hope."

The grin got wider. "You have your friends and supporters, as the Sedek clan does." He amended, "Or did."

"My friends," said Cyntoj, "are not Tyrellian, as you may have noticed."

Garkin waved a foreclaw. The bushes responded, producing the rest of our group, under guard, not looking happy.

"I have standing orders to shoot all non-Korgorite intruders. I am bending an important rule, but you have done the Korgorite Nation a great service. Have you all your equipment? And your records? Good. No, you may not travel another day west, if you wish to live. Well, madam, Captain, and company, I certainly enjoyed your visit. But I think you must go. No, not another word; eastward ho, or I shall become very severe! Guards will check you along the way."

We were sunk. The contract said we had to get within sight of the city. It had to be at least three or four more days, walking, before we even got near enough to see people. I looked at the Korgorites all around us. We couldn't shoot our way out of this.

Mrs. Gonderjhee swallowed. "So close. So close!"

Cyntoj blinked, and looked at her in surprise. Apparently it took him a moment to recollect why we were here. Then he turned to Garkin.

"We want one look at the city, Captain. I will never return. My friend has never seen my home."

"I cannot allow you to travel farther westward."

"We need travel no farther—" He glanced upward. "—than the top of that waterfall."

Garkin and I both tilted our heads back to look at the jungle-covered, nearly-sheer rocky stretch. "Are you kidding me?" I said. "I can't climb that."

"I can," said Cyntoj.

Garkin's teeth showed. "My orders were to prevent you from going west, not up. But not your entire group. Your friends will stay with me."

"It's more than fair," Cyntoj said. He turned to Mrs. G. "Do you trust me?"

Mrs. G. didn't think twice. She spoke only one word: "Yes."

I watched them climb the rocky, scrub-covered waterfall, my heart in my teeth. Cyntoj never really let go of her, but he never really held on. He just coached her, to the top of a wall that I wouldn't have taken on a bet. I saw them reach the top and disappear from sight. I was sure she was looking at the city with her scope, which was also a recorder. She had the first official outside view of the walls of Tyrel City. Then they came back down again. The trip totaled four hours. My neck ached and I was drenched in sweat by the time they reached bottom. It hadn't helped that Araee had stayed right beside me, watching, making little noises occasionally. Garkin was still showing all his teeth.

For the first time since I'd met her, I saw real peace on Polly Gonderjhee's face. Cyntoj's face showed something more than peace. There was also another emotion I couldn't identify.

We started east.

We made much better time going out. Eighteen days in, but only fourteen days out. This doesn't mean we got out unscathed. The first day on our way, Tyler died of his wounds. He had a last whispered conversation with Mrs. Gonderjhee before he died. Apparently she forgave him everything. Mrs. Gonderjhee placed his body in a wolf-spider cave, and cleaned the cave with the interphase rifle.

The trip back, along another route, was faster, shorter, and somehow worse. We had the records, and we'd done ninety-five percent of the job. We were successful. But more than half of our party had died, and we didn't have anything to keep our minds off our troubles.

Once I realized that, I told Mrs. G. that we needed to plant walnuts, Korgorites or not. Bless her, she only smiled and said, "Yes, let's." So we planted walnuts, surreptitiously, in between surprise drop-in visits from Korgorite scout parties. It kept our minds doubly occupied—even Cyntoj, who was as silent as a statue most of the time.

I saw that thoughtful look of Mrs. Gonderjhee's every once in a while. Sooner or later, she'd tackle him.

It happened one night, inside a cave, after a meal. Eduardo and Thomsen were on guard duty; for a rare change Cyntoj and

I were eating and sleeping at the same time. Mrs. G. crumpled her food wrapper thoughtfully and tossed it into the hot rocks, where it flamed and fizzled. The flare must have reminded her of the munitions shack. Quietly, she said, "He was a vampire."

"All Tyrellians are." Cyntoj understood. "Some more than others. Kyren was one of the worst."

She shook her head. "I don't mean that just because he was Tyrellian."

"I understood what you meant. I have learned to deal with many races. Treat them as equals, Tyrellian to Tyrellian, and they will respond equally, with dignity. Treat them as slaves, Tyrellian to Korgorite—and you get what you deserve, rebellion and anger."

"So you treat all the universe as your equals—except your own people," Mrs. Gonderjhee said thoughtfully. "You treat them the way they treated their slaves—and they respond like those poor Korgorites once did, in the days of their enslavement."

Cyntoj chose his words carefully. "Even in our legends— Tyrellians are not native to this planet. Did you realize that?"

"No."

"Our blood has a different color, and a different base, from all other life on Tyrel 3. Our reflexes and thought patterns are different. Even our neural systems run backward. Unlike every other civilized nation, we have a pantheon of demons rather than gods, and choose our pets for their violence. No. Someday, Tyrel shall cleanse itself of the so-called Tyrellian race. I do not think it shall be such a great loss."

Mrs. Gonderjhee asked, "What of you, Cyntoj? What of your parents? Your family? What do you claim, in all of this?"

Cyntoj stared for a long time at nothing. When he spoke, there was a strange tone in his voice—almost ironic. "I was raised by the empire, so to speak. My parents were murdered when I was quite young. My clan did not need me, and so they turned me over to the government. I became a Tyrellian soldier when I was seven years old. Tyrel is required to send a minimum number of residents to the ConFed for education, as a measure of good faith. So, at age fourteen, I was sent to Fleet Academy—not because of the honor. Because I was expendable." He shrugged. I had never seen him shrug. "I have always been expendable."

The words were out of my mouth before I thought. "You still had the Fleet! Why didn't you go back?"

"Murdered, you said." Mrs. Gonderjhee spoke as if I had never asked a question.

"Yes. Kachira Sedek never forgot an injury done to her by my mother."

"What was the injury?"

"Marrying my father. I proved to the empress that the Smantek clan was eliminated only to satisfy Sedek's grudge. She lost many faithful supporters during that purge. The empress responded in kind. Kyren Sedek responded to that. It never ends. Eventually, they will eat themselves alive."

"Mmph." Mrs. Gonderjhee leaned back, nowhere near as shocked as I was. "If I looked at Fleet personnel records, I would find a gap where some respectable long-time officer took a sudden, unexpected leave of absence recently. Who might that farsighted officer be?"

I'm sure Cyntoj didn't even realize he smiled. "Harry Jackson," he admitted, "after I blew three civilian jobs and gave it up to go home. He came to Tyrel 3 and told me not to be such a damned fool. If I wasn't going to teach, the way I ought, then for Christ's sake stop feeling sorry for myself and go help some people who needed it, while he set me straight with the Admiralty." His imitation of his friend and superior officer, whom I had seen, was perfect.

Mrs. Gonderjhee did not smile. "That's who you love. That's where your life is. I wondered."

"Then why does it matter to you," I asked him across the coals, "if all the Tyrellians in the galaxy call you a dead man? Why should that affect your abilities, or your career?" Araee, sitting next to me, rapped me with her foot warningly. I chose to ignore her.

"Wherever I am, I am still Tyrellian. That is all I have."

Mrs. Gonderjhee added her response. "You might as well

ask, Mr. Brannon, why it matters to me to have a proper annulment, to go through—as the yogi phrased it—'years of faultless virtue.' Because it does matter, that's all—to *me*—and nothing else will ever be right."

"It's only psychological," I argued, "not physical. Anyone taking a damn good look at Cyntoj could see there's nothing wrong with him."

Araee looked very thoughtful.

"I wonder," Mrs. Gonderjhee murmured, "what Captain Garkin gains from this. Aside from the Tyrel blight removed from his landscape without raising his hand."

Cyntoj admitted, "A perfectly good ammo dump, for another. I only damaged one of the three buildings with the walnuts."

"—Using techniques which you cannot remember how to do," said Araee.

He confirmed this. "I marshaled all my strength to deceive Sedek, and only Sedek. I felt the lethargy fall away in my concentration. Now, I feel as though my memory and strength are greater than ever before. I do not understand it."

I looked at him, then at Polly Gonderjhee, and suddenly *I* understood it, quite well. I glanced down at Araee, still intent on Cyntoj, and realized I was the only one who did. I remembered what Polly Gonderjhee told Sam. The four Earthly virtues could be found in places other than Earth. She got mercy from K-Law, pity from the Kikkens, peace from Orion. That left one virtue to go. Someday she'd get it, from Tyrel 3.

I wiped away a smile. "Well, whatever happened, your power is up to speed now, Cyntoj. No more ducking into corners." I slid down into my sleeping bag and closed my eyes.

"You have my promise, Brannon."

Cyntoj ducked away from the village again when we reached the shore. At least now I understood why. If he could panic twenty Tyrellians, a village of three hundred would be bedlam.

Sam had drifted north of town, and no one had cared. The *Rustbucket*—I mean the *Ridstock*—was wonderful to see.

So was Sam. He'd held his own against the Tyrellian government. There was a glint in his eye that promised a few stories of his own. I was never so happy to see anybody as when he popped out of the top hatch, and the ship drifted in to shore.

"Welcome back," Sam said in relief, pulling Mrs. Gonderjhee aboard. "It's been a time. Where are the others?"

Mrs. Gonderjhee looked back at us: Four, and herself. Six less than when we started. "This is it, Sam. Now, let's get out of here."

"God in Heaven," said Sam Byner.

The office of Gonderjhee and Company now sported a bright sign on the outer door, painted in red and gold bonding paint. Just like the ship. Sam stood up when we entered the office.

He paid us both. My God, did that look good! One thousand credits apiece, half a year's salary at my last job. In scrip. He watched us each tuck the cash in our bags.

"Where's Mrs. Gonderjhee?" I asked. Sam pointed to an inner office. (Oh, did I mention it was a four-room office *suite* now?)

"She's making calls. She just chatted with Internal Revenue. We're clear."

"We are?"

Sam nodded. "Tyler gave her some passwords that did the trick." He sighed. "I am sorry about him. I liked him." Then he smiled. "She's also lining up some new jobs."

"Jobs? Plural?"

He nodded. "And easier. Oh, we'll still get dirty jobs, I suppose, but we've proven our reliability. I'm almost afraid to say, we're an established company now."

"I'll hang around long enough to say good-bye, then," I said.

There was a quizzical look on Sam's face. Cyntoj looked at me strangely, too. "Going somewhere?" Sam asked.

"Yes."

Sam shook his head. "Cyntoj I expected to move on, since he got that peculiar message about the tree that still bloomed. I knew that meant he was still persona grata in the Tyrellian Empire. But you, Brannon—I always figured you'd stay. We can still use the help."

I understood what he didn't say. "Mrs. G. will always find supporters, Sam. I don't think you have to worry."

We turned when she stepped out of the back office. "Sam," she said, "talk to Annie from Contracts, will you, please? She and Araee have a misunderstanding. Use the line in my office." Sam nodded, and tactfully slipped out of the room.

She looked up into Cyntoj's face. "You're leaving."

"I am." His voice sounded gentle. "As Sam pointed out, I am free now. I may come and go as I please."

"I am grateful." She lifted a hand, and clasped his. "Very grateful for the time and effort you gave us."

"Now you have your work, as I have mine."

"True. In a way, I'm glad you both showed up together." She included me in her gaze. "Somewhere about the sixth Heland Ridge, I decided to offer all survivors a partnership in the company. Now that it looks like we're going to survive, of course. I mean to offer both of you, even though I know you're both free now."

I was surprised. "What did Thomsen and Eduardo say?"

"Eduardo said this place would bring back bad memories," she admitted, "and Thomsen said we made him itch."

I took a breath. "I can't stay, either. I'm sorry, but I'm going to be busy. I'm going back to Orion 4." I was embarrassed. "Where you know damned well I jumped on a ship one step ahead of a theft rap."

I saw a real Polly Gonderjhee smile. "Mr. Brannon, are you developing morals and scruples, at your age?"

"If you can face this—" I waved in the general direction of Gonderjhee and Company. "—Then I can stand that. If I could stay, I would, but—it wouldn't feel right."

Very gently, she said, "I'll hold your job open for you."

"Then I'll be back as soon as I can." After all, Rez Kikken was a friend of hers. She could pull strings.

"Fair enough. Good-bye, gentlemen." She turned and left for her office.

Cyntoj looked puzzled. "I thought you were staying. Why are you doing this?"

I was rude. "Time to put my money where my mouth is. If you had any brains, I wouldn't have to explain it to you."

Cyntoj wasn't insulted. He did have brains. He looked at me, then at the corridor to the space lock. He picked up his gripsack—and headed back toward Polly's office. The last words I heard as I left for the departure lounge were Cyntoj's: "What is the value of a partnership, in round figures?"

About the Jacket Artist

KEVIN MURPHY has been an illustrator for six years. He is the winner of the 1995 World Fantasy Award for best Epic Fantasy Painting for his cover painting to Terry Goodkind's *Blood of the Fold*. He was nominated for the Chesley Award in 1995 for Best Non-Published Work for his painting *Void Engineers*. Past projects include the *Paratwa Series* from Tor and the *Technocracy Series* from White Wolf. He is currently working on a CD-ROM game for MTV, several ongoing projects with Milton Bradley in conjunction with Lucas Films for *Star Wars*, and with *National Geographic*.

About the Editors

WARREN LAPINE was born in West Palm Beach, Florida, and raised in Greenfield, Massachusetts. He began writing at the age of ten and decided to become a professional writer at the age of fourteen after reading Roger Zelazny's *Nine Princes in Amber*. He attended the University of Massachusetts at Amherst, where his professors managed to take the magic out of writing. He grew his hair and began playing in a heavy-metal band. After seven years of this he realized that all he had to show for his time in rock and roll was permanent hearing damage and a few unsavory friends. He decided to take three months off to get some perspective. During that time he stumbled upon a copy of L. Sprague De Camp's *Guidebook to Writing Science Fiction* and the magic was back. He sold his first story within three months and has never turned back. Three years later he has sold more than thirty short stories, nearly completed his first novel, and he still has his hair.

STEPHEN PAGEL (who shortens his name to Stephe—after all, why should he spell his name with a *V* just because everyone else does?) is a book lover who has done a bit of everything: taught high school math, managed a pizza place, and designed and programmed ATM machines for New York banks. While he was doing all that, he fed his habit by working part-time in a bookstore. In 1985 he realized that books were more fun and went into the book industry full time, managing a store first, then becoming a national buyer for the Barnes & Noble/B. Dalton chains. Ten years later he moved to Atlanta and became White Wolf's director of sales. He is also the coeditor with Nicola Griffith of *Bending the Landscape*, a series of gay-oriented genre fiction anthologies.